"This book is a work of fiction
contain perhaps more truth than t
the mag

DS1PB1:
ISBN: 978-0-9567700-6-6
1st Edition
Published by BenGalley.com
Cover Design by Mikael Westman
Original Illustration by Ben Galley
Professional Dreaming by Ben Galley
Printing by Lightning Source

Want an eBook instead? Dead Stars Part One is available on Kindle, Kobo, and Nook. Scan the QR code below to find out more:

about the author

Ben Galley is a young indie author and purveyor of lies. Harbouring a near-fanatical love of writing and fantasy, Ben has been scribbling tall tales ever since he was first trusted with a pencil. When he's not busy day-dreaming on park benches or hunting down dragons, he runs the self-publishing advice site Shelf Help, zealously aiding other authors achieve their dream of publishing.

For more about Ben, Shelf Help, or more about Emaneska, visit:
www.bengalley.com

Simply say hello at:
hello@bengalley.com

Or follow on Twitter:
@bengalley

After four long years I think it's only fitting. After all the darkness and shadow, the fire and flames, the blood, the guts, and the ever-evasive glory. After all the snow and sand and steel. After all the countless wounds of both mind and body, I think he deserves it.

Farden, Emaneska's favourite mage. This book is dedicated to you.

Chin up.

Dead Stars

Part One

By Ben Galley

A crude map of Tayn, torn from Farden's notebook.

Prime Map of Emaneska, created by Arka scholars of Arfell in the year 819.

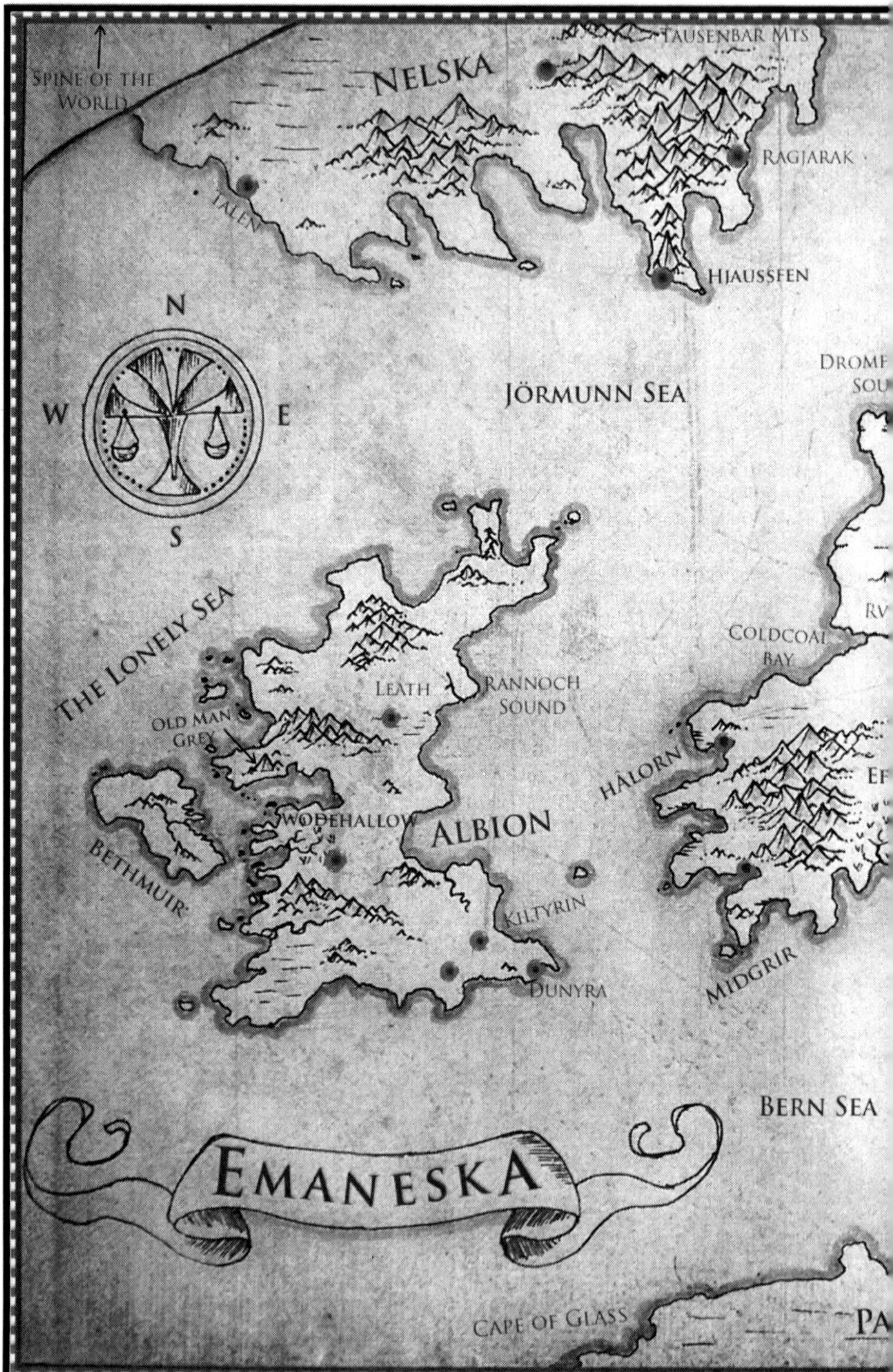

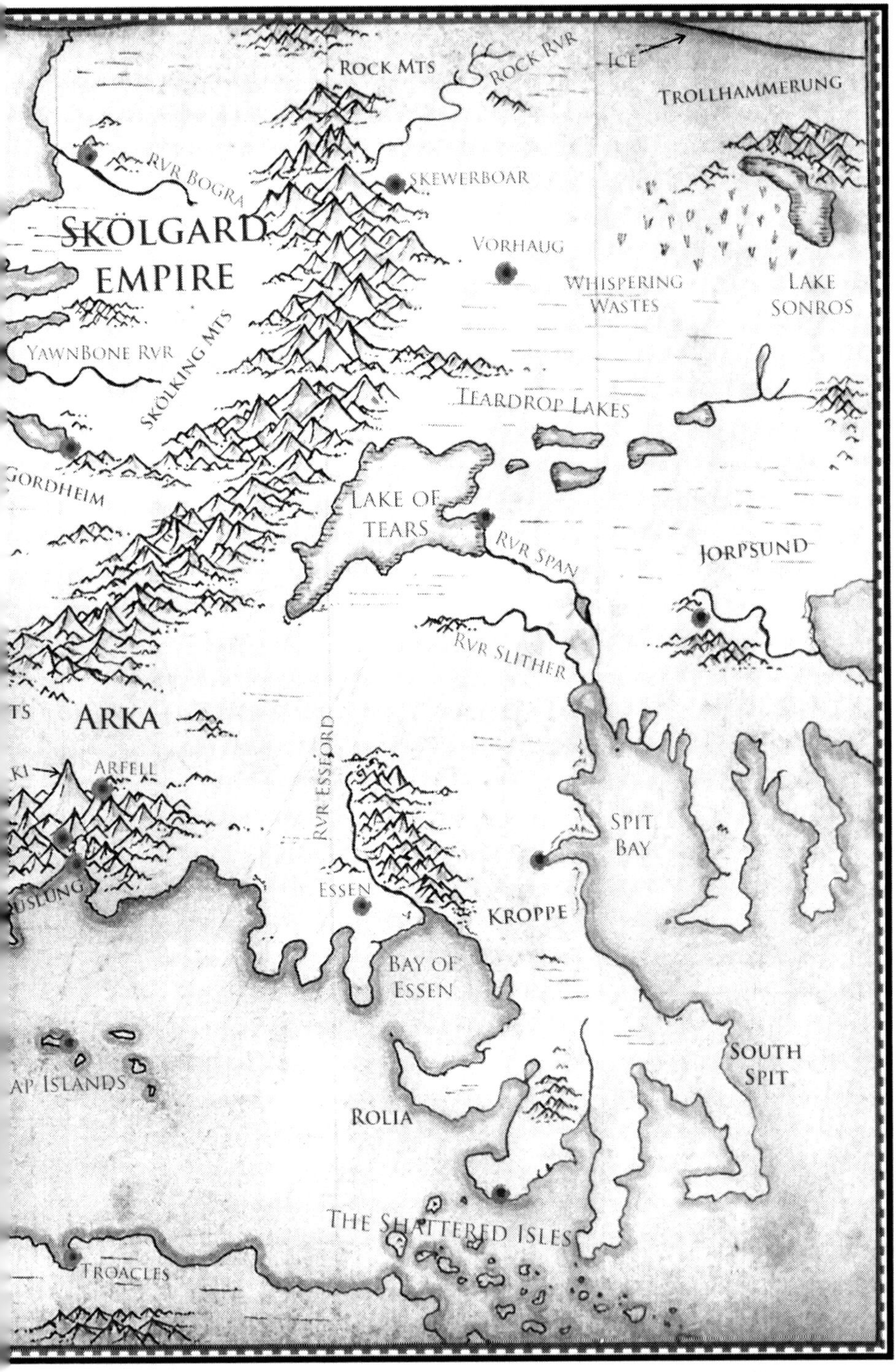

ROCK MTS
ROCK RVR
ICE
TROLLHAMMERUNG
RVR BOGRA
SKEWERBOAR
SKÖLGARD EMPIRE
VORHAUG
WHISPERING WASTES
LAKE SONROS
YAWNBONE RVR
SKÖLKING MTS
TEARDROP LAKES
GORDHEIM
LAKE OF TEARS
RVR SPAN
JORPSUND
RVR SLITHER
ARKA
ARFELL
RVR ESSFORD
SPIT BAY
ESSEN
KROPPE
BAY OF ESSEN
SOUTH SPIT
ROLIA
THE SHATTERED ISLES
TROACLES

prelude

In another age, at the most northern tip of the Scattered Kingdoms, where the ice wrestled the black rock of jagged mountains...

One.

Two.

Three.

Names were ripped from the scroll and tossed into the air. Names were strange things in large quantities. So many could slide by, unremarkable and foreign. Meaningless, until suddenly one would jolt the monotonous roll-call into life and pluck at a particular ear in a particular way. A head would snap forward. A hand would shoot up. Suddenly the name grew flesh and clothes, colours, eyes, and the package was assembled by the beckoning of a silk-gloved finger. These names, hoarsely barked in the sweet cold of the morning mists, assumed the form of a muscular man, or a tall man, even a woman. Yes, he had spied a few women amongst the crowds. Names were funny things indeed, when you're waiting for yours to be called amongst thousands. Especially when there are only nine to be called.

Korrin was his, and it was a name he wasn't particularly proud of. Who would be? It was a farmer's name. The very pronunciation of it sounded like the coughing of his father's mudpigs. Korrin. The legacy of some uncle or brother, worm-food before his time. A guilty nudge from old toothless grandmother to father, a suggestion with a forked tail of duty, and there it was. Korrin. How could that ever be a soldier's name? A lord's name? His father had doomed him with a wobble of tongue and lip.

'Estina Flar?' came another bark.

Four.

There, another hand flew up into the air. A woman again. Korrin tried to sneak a glance through the packed and sweaty ranks. All he caught was a flash of scarlet hair.

'Fogrindle, son of Dalinast?'

Five.

Now there was a name. A man nearby shook his head. Positively rural. Korrin let out a little of the breath he'd been holding. Maybe his name wasn't to be the worst after all. He saw the man and sagged a little. A beast of a man, all beard and tiny head.

'Fogrindle! Son of Dalinast!'

No hand yet. Another coward. At least Korrin had stayed.

The black silk glove reached for a quill and scraped a name from existence with a stroke of scratchy ink. The fingertip moved to the next.

'Rosiff Ro-Harg Thold?'

This one answered. Five. Korrin counted with the crowd. Each number mouthed in silence by a thousand cracked, tired, mud-painted lips.

'Lopia...' Trouble with this one. A southern man probably. Korrin had been told in whispered mumbles that a dozen or so of the dark-skinned had come all the way from the deserts for this.

'Lopia K'Bephrin?'

Six.

Southerner indeed. A Parash by the looks of his intricate beard. And still no name to tickle his own ear. The crowd was getting tense now; not a soul moved.

Korrin's father had always said that no matter how the kings tried to bind a man beneath them, nothing could shackle his name. The man could be broken with the tooth of a whip, the blood-slick curve of a club, but his name was a gemlike thing, worn around the neck on a chain too thin and strong for any blade to find and slice.

'Gaspid, son of Furssimion!'

Seven.

But names were weapons too, in their own ghostly right. Korrin knew this. A name could be a flag-wrapped halberd drenched in ichor, a warlord's name to be whispered in fear among waiting ranks. A name could be sullied and dipped in shame by deeds. A fallen hero perhaps, whose name could never be forgotten thanks to song and tune, could be driven into the ground like a stake at dusk by whispers. Others, like Korrin's, were thorns worming their way slowly in.

'Balimuel, son of Gorvid!

Eight.

Another hand shot up, a giant hand, with huge sausage-like fingers waggling in relief. The man that held them was a veritable giant, almost twice as tall as any other in that endless crowd.

One left. Korrin shrugged and began to look for a gap to escape into. His father had been right; even though it stung to admit. A waste of time Korrin! You're a farmer's son, a farmer's boy, not a warrior. You've got your own life to live. Stop dreaming! His father's words echoed in his ears. They had flown from the doorway and pelted him in the back as he had left.

His name had picked him up as a child and placed him on the back foot. It had turned him around and pointed him at the farm rather than his grandfather's swords. Korrin looked up at the sky, imagining the last name falling to earth as a pebble, striking some lucky person in the forehead. Korrin lifted his dusty hand up to search the sky. A pale saucer of sun, curious behind the mists, looked back at him. A lone rabbithawk hovered by a nearby flagpole. The flag hung limp in the still air. It dangled from its hook like a thief from a noose, waiting to be resurrected by a fortuitous breeze. A storm maybe. It would soon have its chance. Summer was slowly sinking into the earth.

Korrin reached for the handle of his haversack, feeling his tired, strained muscles ache. Wasted. Farm-bred. He knew his name had not been a soldier's name. It was a farmer's name, like all the other children in his village. It was time to leave, he told himself. Go home. His father would be pleased. His old grandfather not so much. Strange, how men can differ in just one generation.

'Korrin, son of Ust!'

Nine.

part one

to the lost (rumours)

1563 years later

9 years after the Battle of Krauslung

chapter 1

"What wants to stay hidden, oft gets found, and what wants to stay found, oft finds itself lost, and forgotten."

Albion proverb

'Wine,' grunted a cracked voice, a tired voice, hoarse with the scars of copious late nights and alcohols of questionable purity. A rough hand ventured out across the wooden bar-top and then slowly retreated, leaving a silver coin in its wake, its edges notched like an old sword blade that had seen too many wars. It glistened in the dim light of the smoky tavern's torches, where the sweat of the hand lingered on its metal face.

'You sure, friend?' replied the landlord, standing at the end of the bar. The glass in his hand squeaked against the cloth he rubbed it with. His face was lopsided but kindly. He had kind eyes too, of a soft, glazed green like the rows of bottles that lined the greasy bar behind him. A little beard sprouted from his chin, which made up for the lack of hair on his bald, freckled head. His skin was the darker hue of his country and its men, and his forehead was adorned with the creases of frequent frowning. Not surprising, given the calibre of the tavern's usual patrons. Patrons like the man sitting alone at the centre of the bar, the owner of the cracked and tired voice.

The man in question lifted up his head, groggily, and fixed the landlord with a narrow, impatient gaze. 'I'm not your friend, I'm your customer, barkeep, and I say I want more wine,' he slurred.

The landlord sighed and reached for the half-empty bottle of purple wine that sat waiting behind him. He sauntered over to the foreigner slumped over the edge of his bar. He looked like a man clinging to the edge of a precipice, trying to decide whether he should just let go. The landlord held the bottle with both hands and topped up the stranger's glass. When he pulled away, the man irritably tapped the bar-top with the butt of his finger. The landlord sighed and filled the glass to the very brim, so that the purple liquid teetered at the lip of the glass.

'You can leave the bottle,' grunted the stranger, as the landlord reached for the coin.

'And you'll be lucky, for a silver,' replied the landlord, quietly. The others in the tavern, maybe four men at most, all sitting alone and separate, watched from the corners of their curious, wary eyes. Locals all. Strangers were common in that dusty corner of Jorpsund, where the Fool Roads led east, but not usually tolerated for long. This man had been in town for a day, and already his welcome was wearing thin. A few of them eyed the box sat at the stranger's feet, the box wrapped in thick grey cloth that occasionally rattled, as if all by itself.

The man sighed, rubbing tired eyes with his grime-thick fingers, almost black with dirt and char. He had the look of a man perhaps too young for his skin, as if his body had seen a few decades more than his dull eyes. What skin was not covered in clothing was weathered and tough, almost leather in itself, and there were more than a few scars to be counted. Most of his head and face was covered by a wide-brimmed cloth hat, dyed black to match his cloak. In terms of build, he was a stocky man, with a beer belly larger than his belt would have preferred. A foreigner by the paleness of his skin. Arka skin. Maybe Albion at a push. His winter clothes seemed too small for his ample build; his wool shirt and tunic were stretched to the point of unravelling, and his cloak barely cleared his shoulders. There were leather bracers around his forearms. The tavern owner sniffed. He had encountered enough mages in his life to recognise one sitting at his bar. He also knew well enough not to trifle with them. He waited patiently while the mage rubbed his tired eyes, careful to keep the wine well out of arm's reach.

His eyes suitably chafed, the mage reached into the inside pocket of his cloak and dug out a battered coin-purse. After a musical rummaging, he produced a shiny gold coin and flicked it at the landlord, smiling. 'Here,' he said. 'Now leave the bottle.'

The landlord didn't argue. He held the coin to his lips and pinched it between two yellow teeth. It was real. 'Right you are,' he said, and set the half-empty bottle and the silver down with a thud.

There was a creak and a bang and a sudden gust of crisp, cold evening air as the door to the tavern opened and shut again. The mage didn't bother turning around; he had no enemies in those parts that he was aware of. Nobody else would be stupid enough to try him, even as dog-drunk as he was. He just sipped his poison, and watched out of the corner of his wine-glazed eyes as a woman and her child approached the bar.

The landlord greeted them with a smile that was missing one tooth. He bowed slightly, stiffly. 'Ladies,' he said. 'The finest of evenings to you.'

'And to you, sir,' whispered the woman, lips numb with cold, her accent a hint of southern. At the sound of it the mage turned his head ever so slightly.

The woman tossed back her hood and ran a hand through a tangled fringe of jet-black hair. The landlord couldn't help but smile at her. She was stunning, though not in the traditional sense. Striking would have described her better. Her features were sharp, angular even; every bone, feature, and measurement seemed to be accentuated in an odd, yet strangely attractive way, as though she had been sculpted rather too vigourously. Even her obsidian hair was extreme; had it not been apprehended and clasped in a tight knot behind her head, it would have reached to her hips. She was a foreigner as well, by the looks of her pale skin. Her cheekbones and the cheeks that hid beneath them had been pinched red by the cold evening air, and her smoky blue eyes twitched back and forth between the landlord, his wines, and the man sitting to her right, slumped over the bar.

The landlord leant forward and peered over the edge of the bar at the child by the woman's side. They were quite obviously mother and daughter. She too had long black hair, and had huge, unblinking eyes like blue-green marbles. She couldn't have been older than eight, nine maybe.

'I am sorry,' began the landlord, smile fading, 'but there's no children allowed in here. 'specially not little girls like that 'un.'

The woman frowned and pulled the little girl tight to her side with her left arm. She held the other close to her side. She looked worried. 'Oh, she won't be any trouble.'

'Sorry, miss. Rules is rules.'

The woman bit her lip, concerned. She looked around at the others in the inn, the handful of men reclining in corners, mumbling to themselves and sipping ale, pretending not to watch and listen.

'Well, who makes the rules here?' asked the woman.

The landlord flicked his cloth over his shoulder and stood a little straighter. Another smile sneaked onto his face. 'That would be me.'

At this news, the woman smiled right back, flashing two rows of very white teeth. 'And what is your name, sir?'

'My name?' blinked the landlord. Strangers didn't usually ask his name. 'It's Darnums, lady, and, er, what might yours be?'

The woman leant forward a fraction, almost imperceptibly, and put her hand on the bar. 'You see, Darnums, sir, we've been travelling along the road all day. We had intended to travel on all night you see, but we heard rumours of bandits in the woods to the north, and so we've had to stop here in your most lovely town. The man at the stables didn't have enough space for our bears and so we've had to tie them up outside, and as we've just found out that the inn across the road has no rooms left, we thought we might come in here, save ourselves from the wind and the cold for an hour at least, before we go back to camping with our bears in the street.' Here the woman paused to wipe a strand of hair from her eye, sniffing. 'We were just hoping to get a mug of warm brandy or ale you see, just to rid the cold from our bones for a short while,' said the woman, shivering. 'But I understand, Darnums, sir. Rules are indeed rules. I'm sorry to have bothered you. Come, Samara, let's leave. Back to the bears.' The woman took the child by her hand and pulled her gently towards the door. The child looked up at her mother and then back at Darnums, and her eyes glistened in the torchlight. The mage was smirking surreptitiously around the rim of his wine glass. He almost wanted to clap, the performance was so good.

Darnums winced as they opened the door. The influx of air was cold and sharp like little knives. He could feel it even at that distance. The woman and her child hovered at the door, tucking their sleeves into their gloves and pulling their hoods up. Just before they closed it behind them, Darnums shook his head and rapped his knuckles on the bar. 'Wait!' he called. The woman turned, door half-closed, cold air rushing in. 'Yes?' she asked, in a small voice.

Darnums beckoned them in. 'Come back! And close the door!'

The woman hurried back indoors, the subtlest of satisfied smirks hiding at the corner of her wind-bitten lips. She ushered her child back towards the bar, both shivering violently. 'Yes?' she asked, hope glinting masterfully in her eyes.

Darnums smiled. 'You can stay here a while, if you'd like. I'd be a lesser man if I sent two ladies like you out into the dark and the cold.'

'What with those bandits about,' muttered one of the locals, from his grimy corner. The others grunted and sipped their ales in agreement.

The woman beamed. 'Thank you sir! Thank you. You're too kind.'

Darnums held up his hands. 'It's the least I can do. Please, have a seat by the fire,' he said, pointing to his "fire," which in all honesty was more of a cast-iron soup pot tipped on its side and welded to a makeshift chimney that wandered up the wall and into the ceiling like an escaping snake. A handful of embers glowed in its sooty bowels.

'I'm afraid I can't offer any warm ale, but I can offer some brandy for you, and some milk for the little one, if you'd like?'

The woman smiled again and curtseyed as she moved towards the fireplace. 'That would be most kind.'

'It's not a trouble,' replied Darnums, watching as the woman led her daughter to a pair of threadbare stools by the so-called fire. They rubbed their gloved hands in front of the glowing embers, smiling at each other. Darnums fetched two chipped porcelain mugs from a cupboard, put them on the bar, and then took his second-best brandy from the shelf on the wall. While he poured with one hand, he smoothed out the creases in his apron with his other.

'Don't get many women in here then, I take it, barkeep?' mumbled the mage, the lip of his glass still firmly glued to his smiling lips.

'What?' Darnums flinched, realising he had been caught staring.

The mage chuckled hoarsely. 'I said…'

Darnums shook his head, popping the cork back into the brandy bottle with a little squeak. 'I heard what you said, friend, and no, we don't,' he replied.

‘Figures.’

Darnums set the brandy back on the shelf and rummaged in a cold chest for some milk. He found an open bottle, sniffed it, and then topped up the brandies with a few glugs of milk.

‘No warm milk?’ chuckled the mage. Darnums paused, a hand wrapped around each mug. He flicked the mage a sour glare, but then he paused, and while he glared, Darnums absently pondered whether the mage was one of the fire and flame sort, and whether he should ask, or whether it would be rude. He opened his mouth, but before he could speak, there came a rattling sound from the other side of the bar, at the mage’s feet. The mage kicked at something with the toe of his boot and the rattling stopped immediately. He grunted, satisfied.

‘Wouldn’t keep them waiting. Their drinks might get even colder,’ the mage snidely advised, smiling at his own joke. Darnums shook his head. Holding the two mugs tightly in each hand, as if the short walk and a tight grip might warm them just a little, he made his way over to the quiet females leaning close to the fire-pot, smiling his very best of smiles. The mother turned at the sound of his footsteps. She saw the drinks in his hand and put a palm to her chest. ‘Oh, bless you, sir, we are in your debt.’ She reached inside her fur coat with one hand. ‘How much do we owe you?’

Under the pitiful wash of the woman’s gaze, Darnums bent down to place the mugs on an empty little table and smiled even wider. ‘I think, on this one occasion, I can allow some charity. They’re on the house.’

The woman’s pronounced features melted into such a picture of gratitude that, for a moment, Darnums thought she might shed a tear. She put her hand to her chest again and simply mouthed her thanks. Darnums stood up and nodded courteously, trying not to swell with pride. He strode back to the bar, picked up his cloth and a dirty glass, making it squeak loudly. The mage rolled his eyes at the man. ‘Watch my wine,’ he muttered, putting his hands on the bar.

Darnums was about to inquire why he would need to do such a thing when the mage grunted and pushed himself off his stool. He rubbed his eyes a little more, cleared his throat, and then walked, a little unsteadily, toward the mother and child. Darnums stopped polishing and watched with concerned eyes.

Much to the landlord's horror, and the surprise of both females, the mage didn't even bother to introduce himself. He simply sat down on the nearest stool and stamped his boots on the floor. The woman and her child looked at their new companion with a mixture of worry and intrigue. There were purple smears of wine on his lips and chin, and he had dirty, grubby hands. He tipped back a wide, cloth hat and leant forward, grinning, taking in the woman's striking features and long, dark hair. She seemed to favour her right arm. The left lay on her lap as if she had recently injured it. Its fingers were of a hue so pale they bordered on white. 'If you'd like?' he offered to the mother, holding out a grimy hand.

The woman couldn't help but recoil. She held her mug close to her chest and stared down at the proffered hand. 'Like to what?' she asked, in a whisper.

'The drink, lady, give it me.'

The woman looked to Darnums, who was hovering at the edge of his bar, to the man, and then to the hand. She spied a key-shaped tattoo on his wrist, hiding under a dirty bracer. It was black like the wing of a crow. A mage then. Not just any ordinary one at that. 'Alright,' she replied, and held out her mug of brandy. The mage smiled and gestured to the little girl perched on the edge of the other stool, eyes wide and more than a little scared.

'And yours, little madam?' he asked. The mother nodded and the little girl gave up her mug too. 'No use stopping for a drink on an evening like this if it don't warm your innards, eh? Cold brandy and cold milk can only do so much,' he said. He tapped the two mugs together with a clink, and then pressed them together, one in each hand. 'Do you like magick, little girl?' he asked, and the little girl nodded eagerly, a tiny white tooth biting her bottom lip, still pale from the cold, in earnest. 'You do? Well, you'll like this then,' he replied, winking at both of them.

It began slowly at first. The mage fixed the mugs with an intense stare. For a moment, nothing, and then, very gradually, his palms started to glow with a warm, ruby light. Then the air around his hands began to waver and shimmer. Before the mother and her child could lean closer, little flames sprang up from his fingers and began to lick at the bases of the two porcelain mugs. Tendrils of steam rose from their contents to sketch patterns in the air. The little girl clapped her hands with delight, drawing stares from the others in the tavern. With a grunt from the mage, the flames in his hands died away, and he leant forward so that the woman could take back her drinks. 'Take them by the handles, m'lady,' advised the mage, and she did, passing one to her daughter and then taking hers. The two of them were soon enjoying the feel of the warm steam on their cold faces, sipping tentatively at the hot liquid.

The mage rubbed his knees and watched the two cradling their mugs. He smiled and reached inside his pocket for his tobacco and pipe. 'Do you mind?' he asked. The woman shook her head. She found herself watching the mage closely as he packed the bowl of his briar-root pipe with the tobacco. It was the cheap sort. More like bark shavings than the shredded moss. He didn't seem to care. He had the look of a man several weeks of wine past caring. He put the pipe to his lips and pressed his little finger into the bowl, a lick of flame hovering around its tip. A few moments later and he was sucking happily on the pipe, blowing smoke rings at the ceiling, much to the little girl's pleasure.

'So,' grunted the mage. 'You're not from the Crumbled Empire, I can't hear any of that in your accent. Definitely south, but not too south, by your skin. I'd say Arka, if I had to guess. Essen, to be exact.'

The woman raised her mug. 'And you would guess correctly, stranger.'

The man held up his hands and exhaled smoke. 'I'm at an advantage. It's hard not to recognise your own accent,' he said, clapping his chest, 'Arka myself, as you've probably guessed.'

'Well, mage, I fear that your keen ear is wasted in your current employ.'

The mage laughed heartily then, until a cough caught him, and he thumped his chest with his fist to get it out.

The woman smiled, confused. 'I wasn't aware I made a joke.'

'You didn't, lady. I've just never heard being a mage like me described so light-heartedly.'

'Well, isn't it your job?'

The mage held the pipe in his mouth, testing it against his teeth, eyes half-closed, thinking long and hard. 'Curse, more like it.'

The woman looked shocked. 'A curse?'

The mage shuffled in his seat and blew another smoke ring towards the girl. He was rewarded with a giggle. 'Any path that leads a man to, to *this*,' he gestured at the tarred pine walls and ceiling of the tavern, 'is bloody cursed.'

The woman smiled politely. 'But is it the path, or the way the man treads it?' she asked.

The mage shrugged, brushing off the question. 'So,' he said. 'What brings you through Jorpsund? Trading? Rich husband send for you and the girl? Not much of a country for sight-seeing, is it?'

The woman shook her head and took a careful sip of her drink. 'We are in search of an education,' she said, nodding towards her little girl.

'For your daughter?'

The woman nodded.

'So you're heading to a school?'

'You could say that.'

'I see.'

'And you? What business brings you out this far along the Fool Roads?'

The mage waved the stem of his pipe in the air, shaking his head. 'Aptly named, those roads.'

'I've never understood them. Is it foolish to want to explore? Foolish to seek strange lands and new peoples?'

'They call them that because of the people that tread them, lady, as far as I've seen. You could say that's what brings me out here. On a fool's errand.'

'And what is that, good sir?'

The mage turned around to check on the cloth-wrapped box sat nestled against the foot of the bar. Darnums was still staring at him, furiously polishing glasses. The mage rested his elbows on his knees and his chin on his pipe. 'Secret,' he whispered, winking at the little girl.

'I like secrets,' said the girl, in a voice as clear and musical as a bell made of glass, bright as her eyes. The mage held her inquisitive gaze for a moment and then turned to the girl's mother, who was combing her tangled fringe with her fingers. She sensed a trade was coming.

'I'll tell you my secret if you tell me your names,' offered the mage.

'Our names?' she asked. She gave him a shy smile. A secret in exchange for a brace of names. 'And what would you want with those?'

A moment passed as a smoke ring drifted to the ceiling. 'What any man would want; to use them. Would you prefer me to call you "woman" and "girl" all evening?'

The woman looked at the little girl, who had already caught on to the game. 'I see. And what gave you the idea you would be spending the evening with us?'

The mage shrugged. 'Your choice.'

'Tell you what. My daughter's name for the secret, and my name for a glimpse of what you're hiding in that box of yours,' said the woman. She uncurled a finger from the warm handle of the mug and pointed towards the bar, towards the mage's empty stool and the box between its legs. She had a sly glint in her smoky eyes. 'And your name, as well. Unless you'd like me to call you "sir" or "mage" all night?'

The mage bit the mouthpiece of his pipe and drummed his grimy fingernails against its wooden bowl. He shook his head, closed his eyes, and stuck out a hand, which the woman shook daintily. 'Thialf,' whispered the man. 'Manesmark, born and bred.'

'A pleasure to meet you, Thialf. The little one is Samara, and my name is Lilith.'

'Lilith eh?' mused the man. 'A pretty name for a pretty woman.'

The hollows beneath Lilith's cheekbones turned a soft crimson. Thialf wondered if it was still all an act. He was starting to hope it wasn't.

'And Samara. What an interesting name.' The little girl smiled at this. 'Did you choose it?' Thialf turned back to her mother.

'I did indeed.'

'I've never heard it before. What is it, Paraian?'

Lilith shrugged, looking down at the little girl, who was now perched on the very edge of her stool, an inch from falling off. She was busy cradling her warm mug and swinging her legs back and forth as quickly as she could. 'It just came to me one day,' she said.

'Fair enough,' grunted Thialf. He stood up and adjusted his belt. He sauntered over to the bar to fetch his cloth-covered box and wine. He gave Darnums a wink before he returned to Lilith. He could feel the heat of the landlord's eyes on the back of his neck as he returned to the little fire and the enraptured females. There might have even been a little swagger in the way he walked, and this time it was not because of his wine.

With a thud he set his half-empty glass and almost-empty bottle on the little table and placed his box very gently on his lap. There was a handle at the top of the box, under the thick, grey cloth, and Thialf held onto it while he topped up his glass with the remainder of the pungent, purple wine. Lilith tried hard not to wrinkle her nose at its vinegary smell. He looked around the little tavern, trying to see if the other patrons were watching, which, of course, they were trying *very* hard not to do. They had watched the mage and the box for hours. They murmured between themselves, feigning conversation and sipping their ales while they waited for the reveal, stealthily leaning into better viewpoints and shuffling in their moth-bitten armchairs. Even Darnums was intrigued. For the moment, his glass and cloth lay dormant in his hands.

Thialf lowered his voice to a hoarse whisper. 'You might have heard the rumours in your travels, you might not, but it's common knowledge in Krauslung that something's happening to the magick in Emaneska. Something wrong they say. Something in the water.' The mage took a sip of his wine. 'I'll be damned if I can feel it, like the Arkmages and the others claim, but I can see it, I'll tell you that. I see it on every street corner of every town and city I've wandered through. They're all the same now. Magick markets. Spell pedlars. Charm merchants. Meddlers the lot of them. Amateurs. I even see it in the wilds too, and if I don't see it then I hear it. Rumours of strange beasts and creatures emerging from the forests at night to hunt magick and meat. Magick bending trees to the ground. Magick tainting the waters of a well. It's like a disease that everybody seems to welcome. Even Albion, superstitious Albion, whose Dukes had their spell books and spell-libraries burnt out of fear, usher these magick markets through their gates. I remember when magick used to be a privilege, a skill, not something to be worn on a finger to bring good luck and light your mansion at night.'

'You sound bitter about it.'

'That I am.'

'But why? From what I hear the magick markets are booming. Trade has never been better.'

'And what of us mages? What of us Written?'

Lilith held a hand to her mouth, almost dropping her mug. 'You're a Written?' she whispered. At her side, Samara leant forward a fraction more.

'One of the last I am. Look at what's become of us now. Sent on errands like common mages. Fools' errands like this.' Thialf venomously flicked his box with a finger, a bitter sneer on his purple lips. Something fluttered beneath the cloth. 'Now there are farmhands being recruited into the army. Farm boys and peasants with stirrings of real magick in them, casting spells like they think they deserve to. I've never heard of such a thing. Whatever's happening to the magick in this world, it's pushing the real magick users into the shadows.'

Lilith pointed to the box. 'And what is your errand?'

Thialf frowned. 'The reason I'm out here in this backside of nowhere is simple. With so much magick around these days, and so many magick markets travelling to and fro, it's getting dangerous. More often than not, the merchants end up eaten or beaten. Creatures or bandits, that's their fate. And the Arkmages can't have that, can they? Not when they are so insistent on controlling the traffic of such things. No. Such a trade is too insistent to ignore, and too profitable to ban, so instead they act as its enforcers, like the good old days of the Arkabbeys, except that this time, the glory is confined to shepherding trade caravans, frisking merchants, and hunting down whatever nuisances rear their head.' Thialf quaffed the rest of his wine and let the glass drop on the table, making little Samara jump. 'M'sorry. Frustrating, is all,' he grunted.

Lilith nodded sympathetically, and then reached out her left hand to pat Thialf's. 'I understand,' she sighed.

Thialf looked down at her slender hand resting on his grubby knuckles. 'So you want to know what I'm doing out here then?' he asked. His little audience nodded. There was a round of creaking as the other patrons quietly shuffled forward, coughing and mumbling.

'Faeries.'

'Faeries?' gasped Samara.

'That's right. A whole swarm of them. They've been terrorising some of the Rolian caravans moving up from the Shattered Isles. Causing quite the ruckus, until I was sent to solve the problem. Three weeks, I've been hunting them down. Three weeks I've been alone, scouring the wilds for the little bastards, 'scuse my language. You see, they can turn invisible at whim, which makes catching them all the more bloody difficult. Yesterday I finally caught the last one.' A proud look came over Thialf's face then, a look that momentarily replaced his bitter mask. His finger tapped the handle of his cage as he slowly gathered the corners of the cloth in a tight fist. With a gentle tug, the cloth unravelled and fell onto the mage's lap, revealing a strange and vicious-looking creature.

Samara finally came off the edge of her stool and inched forward, her face the very picture of fascination. Lilith held her back ever so gently. Thialf was too busy testing the bars of the cage to notice that she was not staring at the creature, not in the slightest. She was staring at the mage instead.

Thialf prodded each of the bars, careful to keep his fingertips away from the little beast's maw. Though the base and roof of the cage were thick oak, the bars were iron, and were covered in tiny notches and scratches, where the teeth of the faerie had been busy gnawing. Samara knelt down so she could meet the thing at eye level. It was too busy watching Thialf's tasty-looking fingers to notice her.

Insect-winged, with skin mottled like old, forgotten bone, the faerie stood as tall as a man's hand, no more, and no less. It was the shape of a man too, for the most part, though disproportionately elongated and hunched. In the weak, fluttering glow of the soup-pot fireplace, its skin took on an almost translucent quality. Samara could almost see tiny veins, no wider than the thinnest thread, pumping blue and purple under its pale hide. Sprouting from its back were two pairs of wings, crystallised like that of a dragonfly. These too were throbbing with nervous, purple veins. Its head was an ugly, twisted stump, barely more than an ambitious neck, with scarcely enough room for a cluster of blue eyes and a savage, salivating mouth filled with rows and rows of needle teeth. There was a smear of dried crimson on its milky chest, where a cage of spiny ribs protruded so prominently from its shape that they looked as though they would break through the papery skin at any moment. The strangest thing about it was the noise it made. Aside from the snap and hum of its twitching, crystalline wings, it made a constant chattering sound with its jaws, as though its very teeth rattled in their sockets. It sounded as though it was on the verge of speaking, when suddenly it spat a guttural word that sounded almost like *Clatterfoot! Thunderboot!* Whatever it was, it wasn't any language anybody in the tavern had heard before. The beast was an ugly, vicious thing, from the serrated claws of its feet and hands to its tree-stump of a head. Samara found herself loathing it on sight alone. She crossed her arms and gazed at it, calmly.

As Thialf's fingers wandered around the bars, the faerie followed them. It gnashed and bit, making a terrible noise that had most of the tavern's patrons on their feet. Darnums was now hovering nearby, brandishing a gnarled bat that he had produced from somewhere. As the creature followed the fingers it suddenly met the serene gaze of the little girl kneeling barely two foot away. It was as if the beast had suddenly been jolted by a lightning spell. It threw itself at the metal bars, straining and stretching to claw at the face of the girl. Its wings fluttered so fast they became a blur. Little sparks flew from the metal as its teeth ground against them.

Thialf shook the cage and flicked a tiny flame at the creature to calm it down. But it refused to snap out of its little frenzy. It chattered and spat words in its vicious little language. The mage quickly wrapped the cage in the thick cloth and put it by the wall, near to the fire. He kicked it once, and the creature fell still.

There was an awkward silence in the tavern.

'Nasty little creature,' mumbled Thialf, shaking the last drops of wine into his glass. He waved it at Darnums, who was still standing nearby with his bat. His wide eyes hadn't left the little cage. 'Another, landlord,' ordered the mage.

'I think you'd better leave,' whispered Darnums.

Thialf turned around so he could gauge whether the man was serious or not. His ashen face and pursed lips suggested that yes, indeed he was.

Darnums pointed to the door. 'I don't want that *thing*, or you, in my tavern a moment longer.' The locals rustled in agreement.

'It's perfectly safe in the cage.'

'I don't care.'

'All I want is another bottle and some quiet conversation.'

'Please take it away, and yourself with it.'

Thialf got to his feet, bottle still in hand, and stood uncomfortably close to the landlord, so close that their noses almost touched. The brim of the mage's hat tickled Darnums' forehead. There was a nervous silence, prickly like a bramble, filled only by the muffled beating of anxious hearts.

Darnums, to his credit, stared straight back at the mage, unblinking and unflinching. Lilith, Samara, and the other men in the tavern didn't move a muscle. 'Please go,' said Darnums, pointing once again to the tavern door.

Thialf spun the bottle in his hand and rocked backwards on

the heel of his boot. He curled his lip. ‘Fine. I’ll do as you ask,’ he replied. He placed the bottle down on the little table and picked up his cage. It rattled once, then stayed silent. Thialf looked down at Lilith and flicked the brim of his hat. ‘Looks as though I won’t be spending the evening with you after all.’

Lilith said nothing. Samara shuffled on her knees, looking sad and a little confused.

‘Well, thanks for your hospitality,’ Thialf grunted, and made for the door with his cage hanging by his side. As he wrenched open the door, a flurry of snow blew inwards and danced around his knees. ‘Figures,’ he mumbled to himself, and closed the door behind him.

Inside the tavern, Lilith jumped slightly as the door shut with a wind-chased bang. Darnums knelt by her side and shook his head. ‘My apologies madam, I should never have allowed him in in the first place. Dangerous sorts, these mages, especially one with that much wine in him. Never mind that creature in the cage.’ Lilith didn’t reply. Instead she turned around and looked at him with a cold stare. Darnums’ smile wavered. ‘May I get you another drink? On the house again, of course.’

‘No, thank you, landlord,’ Lilith replied as she got to her feet. She passed her empty mug to Samara. ‘Stay here,’ she instructed. Samara nodded.

As she walked towards the door, Darnums quickly jumped after her. ‘Where are you going?’

Once again, the woman did not respond. Darnums put a hand on her arm and she froze, fingers hovering on the door handle. She turned and looked at the landlord’s hand as if it were a parasite gnawing its way through her fur coat. Darnums quickly withdrew it and hid it under his cloth. ‘He’s dangerous, lady, the kind of man that I expect would have no qualms about harming you and the little one. And that beast he’s got with him… I wouldn’t feel proper letting you chase after him,’ he implored.

'He's a fire mage. They don't feel the cold,' whispered one of the nearby men.

'Wouldn't trust a drunkard like that if I were you, miss,' said another.

Lilith scowled at them all in turn, saving Darnums for last. 'Where's your charity now?' she snapped. With a turn of her wrist and a leap she was out the door and into the gusty night, slamming the door behind her.

The cold night was murky like curdled milk, washed white and grey by the frenzied haze of snow, dyed yellow by the brave lanterns that hung from tall poles dotted along the dirty street. A row of dark, faceless buildings sat hunched in the darkness, their edges blurred by the snow. Windows glowed with the light of candles, like eyes peering. For all a stranger knew, they were giant beasts waiting to pounce. The sign of the tavern rocked back and forth in the wind. Its hinges squealed in unison with the moaning of the wind. High above the little town, a forgotten moon hung in a gap between the thick clouds, the colour of old chalk. Lonely.

Lilith held her hand up to her face and shielded her eyes from the stinging sleet. The cold was biting. It found the gaps in her clothing, the weaknesses in its defences, and crept inside. Not a soul stood in the street. Not a shadow in the murkiness. Lilith cursed under her breath.

'I thought you might follow,' grunted a voice, a voice mumbling around the end of a pipe pinched between lips. Lilith turned around to see Thialf sitting atop his vicious cargo by the corner of the tavern. He was attempting to light his pipe, and somehow succeeding. She walked over to him and stood close.

'Where will you go?' she asked.

Thialf shrugged. 'Wherever they sell wine. And somewhere with a fire. Cold doesn't bother me, but this little creature,' he tapped the cage with his heel. 'has to arrive in Krauslung safe and sound.

Orders is orders,' he grimaced.

'I have some wine,' Lilith smiled, looking to the other side of the street, where a smaller road peeled away into the snowy darkness. A cluster of dim lights sat somewhere at the end of it. 'In my pack. A little bottle for emergencies.' Thialf looked up. She could see the thirst in his eyes hiding behind the veneer of half-drunkenness.

'Why do you drink, Thialf?' she asked.

The mage laughed at this. He pinched the bridge of his nose between thumb and forefinger and winced. Another headache was brewing. 'Keeps the memories at bay,' he whispered. Lilith held out a slender hand, keeping the other close to her chest. Thialf took it and got to his feet. 'What happened to your arm?'

Lilith smiled again and held on to the mage's hand. His hands were warm. 'Maybe I'll tell you over some wine,' she whispered.

The offer took a brief moment to sink in. Thialf grinned. 'Sounds a good idea to me. But where's your daughter?'

'Inside, safe.'

'Then lead the way, Lilith,' the mage waved his pipe.

The woman, the mage, and the caged faerie made their way across the street and down the little road. It wandered side to side like the mage's sense of balance. Lilith held tightly to his arm as he rambled on about nothing in particular. She smiled and nodded, giving him the occasional lingering glance, the subtle bite of the lip. Thialf's wobbling walk became infected with a slight hint of a swagger once again. His grin became permanent.

Eventually, the stables appeared out of the snow. Their lights were brighter now. The scent of animals, of bears, cows, and sheep, flew with the wind. A few stableboys wandered to and fro, tending their furry guests and yawning.

Thialf tucked his pipe inside his cloak and rubbed his hands together. He gestured towards a little shed that clung to the side of the stables. Lilith raised her eyebrows and made an attempt to stifle a rather girlish giggle. Thialf's hands snaked around her back and reached for the hem of her coat, but she patted his chest and shook her head. 'Why don't you go first, and I'll bring the wine,' she hissed in his ear, letting her wet tongue brush his cold neck.

'If only I could see the look on that landlord's face,' chuckled the mage. He released her, winking, and sauntered to the shed. After jiggling the lock, he went inside and shut the door quickly behind him.

Lilith's coquettish smile faded like an icicle in a fire. She marched into the stables, ignoring the curious stares of the stableboys, and made for the back of the building where her bears slumbered in their tiny pens. Waking up at the sound of purposeful footsteps, the larger of the two, an old flea-bitten sow with a notch in her ear, raised her big head and growled.

'Silence, you,' spat Lilith, stepping inside the pen. The bear did as it was told, letting the woman rummage around in the pack that was still strapped to its saddle. No sense entrusting an opportunistic stableboy with valuables when a bear can guard them just fine. Lilith delved deep into the bag and brought forth a slim object wrapped in a thin blue cloth.

'Where is he?' asked a small voice, tiny and musical.

Lilith didn't even turn around. She unwrapped the cloth and bared the sharp blade to the light of the stable lanterns. 'In the shed, outside.'

Samara crossed her arms and frowned. 'How'd you manage to get him in there?'

'Another trick for another day, child,' answered Lilith. She turned around, keeping an eye on the stableboys, and held out the knife. Samara walked forward to take it, a blank look on her innocent little face. 'Time for your education. Now, you remember what I told you, hmm? He's a Written. This ain't some bandit or slave. Quick and true, like we've practised.'

'Yes, Lilith,' replied the girl, without a heartbeat of hesitation.

She held the knife low at her side, half-covered by the edge of her fur coat. Her face was expressionless. There was no fear there, nor was there excitement. Her skin was pale with the cold rather than trepidation, or worry. Her long black hair seemed to flow from her scalp like black liquid. Her eyes were as bright and twinkling as ever, though now they had something else at their core, something cold, and bitter, like the weather outside.

'Good. I'll be right behind you.'

The two of them used the back door of the stables. They trod quickly and silently through the mud and half-settled snow. When they reached the shed, Lilith halted a few steps behind the girl. Samara stood facing the door, knife glinting at her side. She took a breath, reached up for the door handle, and went inside.

'Lilith?' grunted a shape in the darkness. It seemed to be sprawling across a pile of hay. Samara shut the door quickly and melted into the gloom, waiting for her eyes to adjust. The blade felt so light in her hand. She could smell the man, his sweat, smell the wine on him. Something rattled in the corner.

'You took your time,' said the mage. 'Where are you?' Samara could see him now; her eyes had adjusted quickly. He was lying on his back. A pair of trousers lay discarded on the hay bale next to him. He groped at thin air and empty shadows. Samara circled to the side, moving as softly as a mouse.

'I'm not one for games, Lilith,' coughed the mage. He sat up groggily and rubbed his hands together, and a little flame blossomed in his palm like the petals of a blood-stained flower. The blade swinging through the air caught its light for the briefest of moments.

In the end, it was the wine that killed him. Thialf might have reacted in that last moment, flinched maybe, dodged, ducked, anything, and perchance saved his own life. But in his numbed state, in the darkness of the shed, expecting nothing but the taste and touch of a willing woman, he had no chance, even a mage like him. The little red flame still burnt in his right hand, and in the dying light of it he looked down in amazement at the sharp knife that had somehow punctured his cloak and slid between his ribs to stab at his heart. There was a hand at the end of the blade, and small white knuckles wrapped around a handle. His expression a mask of confusion, Thialf's gaze followed the hand to a wrist, and then to a slender arm, up to a fur-wrapped neck, and finally to an expressionless face, a face that had barely seen nine years pass by.

'S...Samara?' whispered Thialf. Blood was already filling his lungs. Her blade tickled his heart and he twitched. He groped dazedly for her arm and she let him grab her wrist. But he twitched again at the feel of her skin, as though a jolt had passed through him. The tattoo on his wrist flashed with a bright white light.

'You can't...' he managed, as Lilith walked into the little shed. Thialf swayed. Samara left the blade in him and stepped back into the shadows.

'Good,' said Lilith. She crouched beside the mage and watched as he slumped into the hay. He reached out to her with fingers bent like claws, sparks crackling at his fingers, and she smiled. 'Your spells won't work,' she tapped the handle of the knife. 'Belladonna and nevermar paste. The first you might have survived, given your Book, but the second has numbed your magick.'

Thialf bared his wine-stained teeth and let his head fall in the hay. 'So this is how it all ends, is it?' he coughed hoarsely.

'What did you expect, fool?'

'Something... glorious. Out with a flash of fire and a thunderclap... the Written way.'

'Sorry to disappoint,' Lilith murmured.

The mage's eyes burnt into hers with a hatred softened only by futility. His arms and legs were numb. Something itched on his back and shoulders. It, like him, was slowly fading. Thialf shook his head and stared up at the ceiling. The flame died in his palm. 'Stabbed by some brat and her whore mother in a stable,' he coughed. 'Cursed, indeed.'

It only took a few seconds for his heart to surrender the will to pump, for the poison to freeze it solid. When his lips stopped twitching and his final breath left him, Lilith curled a finger at Samara. The girl stepped forward. 'Help me roll him over,' Lilith ordered.

With the whisper of wet steel, Samara withdrew the knife from the dead mage's side and used it to cut the cords of his cloak. Lilith lifted his limp arm and dragged him onto his side. She slid the keen blade up the middle of the cloak and sliced it in two. Together with the help of Lilith's eager fingers, they peeled back the damp, blood-soaked cloth and exposed the incarnadined tunic beneath. Something flickered underneath the stained cloth, something written in white light. Lilith tapped the corpse's back. 'Get to it, girl.'

Samara nodded. She slid the knife under a fold of cloth and shoved it up and forwards. With a rip, the mage's back was bared to the cold air. Light spilled out. Words written in light illuminated the walls of the shed, casting strange shapes and shadows across their faces. Lilith quickly hid her face and covered her eyes. Samara leant forward. She stared at the tattoo, the Book, with wide eyes. It was the first time she had ever seen one. It covered the man's entire back, from the base of his spine to the root of his neck and across his shoulder blades, intricate and foreign-tongued. Its ink was jet-black when not alive and glowing. Every now and again a pulse of light would surge through a particular line or word or rune, and it would paint itself in light on the wall or the ceiling, a spasm of dying life. Samara let her fingernails wander over the words, trying and failing to mouth them. They felt hot and sticky to the touch. Her eyes tingled in their fading light. The Book was dying too.

Samara held the knife up and hesitated, unsure of where to start.

‘Quickly, girl!’ hissed Lilith.

Samara frowned. ‘Do we have to?’

‘Yes, now get to it.’

Samara shook her head, squeezed the knife-handle tightly in her hand, and touched the sharp tip to the lifeless skin. Taking a breath, she began to cut.

In the corner of the shed, stuck behind its metal bars, the faerie twitched and snarled at the scent of the bloody magick in the cold winter air.

chapter 2

"In times of hardship, prayers are either answered, or they are not. The latter, unfortunately, is infinitely more likely. You could be forgiven for thinking this is to say that the gods ignore us. Quite the opposite, for gods have their own hardships to face. No, every prayer is heard, for the simple reason that the gods survive because of them. Just as every leaf or grain of sand cannot be counted, not every prayer can be duly answered.

Our prayers, thrown so readily into the sky, have the effect of splitting a populace in two. Those who have their prayers seemingly answered become ambassadors for their faith, crying for piety and repentance and belief, while those who go "ignored" become dissenting whisperers, unbelievers, and stokers of the fires of conflict. Such is the sad way of humanity, to be so fickle with belief and the rumours of gods, to be ever searching for answers, as though to fill a hole we have not yet discovered. We are forever doomed to be torn in such ways, and I believe that we have only just begun to uncover the shallowest roots of our violently discordant nature. This new fetish of opinion, religion I hear them call it, will split Emaneska in twain."

Excerpt from a letter sent to the Arkmages Durnus and Tyrfing in the year 899, penned by an anonymous writer

6 years later

There was a faint, yet tantalising, whisper in the brittle air. Trees shivered with it. Grass passed it back and forth, scribbled notes between lovers. Beasts pricked their ears and flicked their tongues at it. Birds felt it between their pinions and between their claws. The earth, shackled and bound so cruelly for so long by the frosts, trembled at the feel of it.

Spring, that most welcome emancipator of seasons, had finally arrived.

It was as though the wind had been sugar-coated. As though the keen winter winds had been unexpectedly and suddenly usurped by a sweeter, warmer cousin from a faraway land, returning to claim its rightful throne. Like a tyrant cast to the rocks, the Long Winter had been broken. The feeling was infectious.

Not that Emaneska could remember, but seasons had never come gradually. There was no real ebb and flow like the tides. No subtle waxing and waning like the bony moon. Mark it down to human perception, but seasons don't come and go like the slamming of a door. They creep in under the cover of darkness, like thieves, so that one morning curtains and windows can be cracked open and there they would be, a sun dripping with warmth. Snow shrinking, soon to be forgotten. Nervous buds and blossoms grinning at dawn. The bitter blade of winter's breezes dulled and ground to sand.

Today was one of these mornings.

Standing on a Krauslung boardwalk, feeling the warm fingers of an unfamiliar sun on their skin, the small huddle found it hard to resist closing their eyes and turning their faces to drink it in. They could feel the change in the air like everybody else; the winter sagging and capitulating, a fallen king sliding from a throne. Thank the gods for it, too.

Even the Bern Sea had given up its wintry siege on the rocky coastlines. The rolling blue-green carpet that stretched from the Port of Rós to the distant islands of Skap was calmer than it had been in decades. The little waves that managed to sneak through the harbour walls slapped playfully against the hulls of the moored ships and boats. Seagulls and little rimelings rode them, chattering amongst themselves as they preened their greasy wings. Sailors and workers saw to their busy chores as usual, but that morning, in the light of a new season's sun, they somehow seemed less arduous.

Arkmage Tyrfing stood with his arms crossed. His eyes were not closed, but they were halfway to it. A single bead of sweat perched on his forehead; he could feel it slowly venturing toward his nose, a wanderer. An Arkmage's robe was a heavy thing, made for winter and cold halls instead of an unexpected spring. He shuffled around, trying to coax some cool sea air into his clothes.

'Uncomfortable?' asked a voice beside him, hoarse, old. Durnus stood as straight as a rod. His eyes were wide open, though they might as well have been closed. Durnus had never regained his sight after his battle with his brother. His eyes were now permanently glazed, frosted over, like portholes trapped in ice.

Tyrfing peered at the blinding orb hovering in the clear, cloudless sky. 'Looks like we'll have to commission the maids and seamstresses for new clothes, old friend.'

'Indeed we shall,' he replied. Durnus turned his head slightly then, like a hooded hawk regarding the rustling of a nearby rabbit. 'They're rounding the bay now,' he said, waving to the four port workers he knew were standing behind him. They scurried off down the boardwalk towards an empty jetty.

Tyrfing shook his head. He knew better than to doubt or to ask. Blind Durnus was, but blind means different things to different folk. 'My fascination with how you do that will never wear off.'

Durnus smiled. 'That makes two of us.'

He was right, of course. A small blotch soon appeared on the western side of the bay and tacked northwards towards the mouth of the port. Tyrfing ran his finger across his eyelids for a moment and then squinted at the little carrack. Even though it was a smear of white and brown in the distance, the spell let him see it as clearly and as close as though it were already docked. 'All three are aboard. I can see them standing at the forecastle.'

'And do they look well?' asked Durnus, keeping his voice low. It was a question wrapped in code. The little group that surrounded them was comprised of a handful of magick council members, a few esteemed traders and merchants, and the usual smattering of Arkathedral and Evernia guard. Not a single one knew the true reason why they were meeting this ship. Trade dignitaries from Hâlorn, they had been told. The rest was up to their greedy imaginations.

'A little seasick, maybe, but well enough,' replied Tyrfing. More code from the old mage. Durnus nodded and said no more. Tyrfing rubbed his spell out of his eyes and turned to the rest of their group. A cough momentarily lodged itself in his throat. He covered his mouth quickly with his hand. 'Shall we?' he asked, after recovering his breath. The council members nodded and smiled.

'Lead the way, Arkmage,' replied one of them gruffly, a short man with a shock of red hair.

With Durnus' hand resting on his shoulder, Tyrfing led their little party down a set of salt-encrusted steps and onto the main thoroughfare of the boardwalk. Even though it was still early in the morning, the port was dauntingly busy, buzzing like a half-drowned beehive.

Krauslung had never been so busy. Trade had never flourished as it did now. Every possible type of ship and boat crowded the oily waters of the port, occupying every available inch of dock that the eye could see. Masts, booms, and spars swayed back and forth, like a forest with a mind of its own. Men infested their rigging. They shouted and called to one another as they worked. Ship hammers thudded. Axes chopped. Ropes squeaked. It was an orchestra of hustle and bustle. And they had magick to thank for it all. Magick, and the glittering coin it brought with it.

As the Arkmages and their party walked across the boardwalk towards their empty jetty, passers-by bowed and curtseyed and fawned. Tyrfing nodded courteously in return, giving the occasional wave or two to faces he recognised. Mages, maybe, soldiers, a few council members perhaps, or well-known traders, all seeing to their thirsts. Ale, coin, and women, thirsts well-known, and there was plenty to slake them down on the docks.

Tyrfing couldn't help but notice the few citizens that stood still and did nothing as the Arkmages passed, arms-crossed and narrow-eyed. He made sure to catch their gazes, and match their sour looks with his own. Authority is never without its opposition, its dissenters. The only true measure of leadership is how many and how vocal those disputers were. Krauslung's were getting louder every day.

Tyrfing and Durnus descended a flight of worn, salt-washed wooden steps and walked to the edge of the jetty. Beneath the boards at their feet the water danced and frolicked as if to please them. A strong smell of fish hung in the air. The few women of the group held handkerchiefs to their sensitive noses.

'Fishing boat must have docked here last,' explained one of the nearby workers, a length of rope coiled in one calloused hand. 'My apologies, ladies and sires.'

'What would a port be without the smell of fish?' asked Durnus, trying to hide his own disgust. His lack of sight had made his other senses many times more powerful. The odour of dead fish almost knocked him into the water. Tyrfing saw the flicker of disgust in his friend's face and smiled.

Thankfully, the group did not have to wait long for the carrack's arrival. The morning breezes were blowing in a strong northerly direction. The white sails of the carrack bulged with them.

Her bow cut through the rolling waves like a plough through a field of blue-green grass. She was soon drifting gracefully between the gap in the thick harbour walls.

They waited patiently for the small ship to traverse the busy harbour and creep alongside them. When it came near enough, ropes were swapped with deft hands, and within moments the carrack was tightly lashed to the iron rings set deep into the wood at their feet. The leather-bound fenders that dangled in the water squeaked as the barnacled hull pressed up against them.

Three tall, narrow figures, swathed in warm clothing despite the unexpected weather, stood at the railings of the ship. One, a man, was very tall, with eyes of a deep tawny gold and flaxen hair. Another man was shorter, slim of frame, with a young face, burning with intrigue. He wore a long leather coat, and had brown hair with a hint of orange. The last was a skinny woman who swayed with the ship's movements like a sapling in a breeze. Her hair was the hue of discoloured copper, greenish, with flecks of metallic red. Each one of them had skin as pale as alabaster. Patiently they waited for the deckhands to wrestle the gangplank into position, and then slowly disembarked, treading lightly across the slimy ridges of the plank, almost walking on the tips of their toes.

The Arkmages bowed to the three visitors, and then to the carrack's captain, a short fellow with a patchy beard. He blinked furtively. He had already received his pouch of coin. His business was finished. Strangely, the visitors did not bow in return. They stood as still and as blank as three marble pillars. Tyrfing moved forward to shake the tall man's hand. He did so with his back to the rest of the group. 'Thank you for coming,' he announced loudly, so all could hear over the bustle of the port and the chopping of the waves below the jetty's planks. 'It is an honour to have you here in our city. I hope this visit will be very profitable, for both our countries.'

The tall man played his part perfectly, albeit a little gruffly.

'And to you, Arkmage Tyrfing, for inviting us to your great and prosperous city. I am sure by the end of this visit, we'll have made some mutually lucrative arrangements.'

'I hope so,' echoed Durnus. Behind him, the council members and traders murmured in agreement and smiled their most winning smiles at the three new arrivals. Deep in cloak pockets, fingers rubbed together. Tongues probed gaps between teeth, and teeth bit at eager lips. They could almost taste the profits hovering in the spring air.

'Shall we?' Tyrfing gestured towards the city proper. 'You're probably very tired and hungry after your trip. Let us show you to the Arkathedral.'

The visitors nodded, and the group began to climb the steps back to the boardwalk. As they moved off, the woman tilted her head and sniffed the wind then, an odd movement, if anyone had been watching her. They were too busy swapping furtive, greedy glances to notice.

The Arkmages led their entourage and the visitors along the busy, people-infested boardwalk and onto a winding cobbled street that snaked north and further into the city. The three visitors stepped as though they walked across glass, or nails. They gazed about, frowning, squinting, devouring every inch of their surroundings.

They would have been forgiven for thinking that the further away from the port they walked, the quieter, the calmer, the city would become. Sadly, they were mistaken.

Krauslung proper was already clasped in the frantic grip of a busy morning by the time they reached it. With the arrival of this strange and exciting warmth in the air, everybody had dragged themselves onto the street to gossip and gawp, to huddle and squabble, to barter and shop. Never ones to miss a trick, the myriad merchants and shopkeepers were also out in force, bellowing about spring bargains and special summer offers. Shops had their innards quickly turfed into the street in an effort to entice; bars and taverns bought or pilfered chairs and tables so the minglers could sit outside and bask; merchants procured carts so their stalls might wander and follow the groups of rich folk out to enjoy the air. It was as though the sun had brought madness along with it.

The city itself sparkled with the sun and with the frosts not yet burnt away. Krauslung, like the earth and its people, had felt the chains of winter slacken. Windows leant into the sunlight and felt the light on their panes. Doors were wedged wide. Chimneys poked at the blue sky, leaking the last of their smoke. Long-frozen drainpipes and gutters began to trickle.

It was hard not to notice the cranes balancing atop the lofty roofs, or the occasional pile of stones and bricks, or the dusty workers taking a moment to smoke a pipe and stare at the hubbub below. For the three visitors, it was easy to see that Krauslung was still, and slowly, being rebuilt. For every building stretching into the sky, there was one that slumped like a drunkard, gutted and dusty, burnt and broken. Under their feet, where the road had once been gouged by dragon feet or spell, sleek-eyed cobbles shared their space with fresh grey bricks. Pinned here and there on door-frames, they could spy little wreaths of flowers in varying stages of freshness. Here and there were little plaques, or stones leant up against the walls. The wounds of war were only just healing.

The strangest wounds of all, it seemed, were the people themselves. As with every war, it's the aftermath that can be the most damaging. It is not the visceral, pounding moments of its fire, but the dull, wounding glow of its embers that will maim. And it may not maim a limb nor a face, but it will dig its blade deep into the minds of its survivors. The loss, the questions, the outrage, it all manifests in different ways. For Krauslung, it had manifested in the strangest of ways indeed.

As the group was led north and west by the Arkmages, the three visitors began to spot little huddles of people standing in street-corners. Some were simply little groups wearing strangely similar colours. Other wore home-made robes with little insignias on the breast. Some, ensconced in back-alleys and off-road squares, stood on flights of steps and waved their arms about wildly, preaching to little groups at a time. The visitors could see their lips moving animatedly, see their faces in the grip of angst and passion, but their distant words were lost in the clamour of the streets, to all but one of the visitors. The tall man frowned at the sound of them.

Tyrfing noticed the skinny woman staring at one of these little groups, a sorry-looking half-dozen wearing white tunics and holding cloth bags by their sides. Their whole party looked a little on the glum side. A few of them yawned, head bowed and eyes fixed on the ground, as if they were not worthy of using their necks. If one had looked a little closer, they might have spied bruises under their eyes, or little spatters and flecks of red on their white tunics.

Tyrfing leant close to the three strangers. 'The Company of Repugnant Souls.'

The woman said nothing. She simply curled her lip with disdain. It was the tall man by her side that answered instead. 'And what exactly are they?'

One of the council members butted in. 'Absolutely crazy, if you ask me. But pay them no heed, sir. They're obsessed with the gods. Goddess Evernia if I remember correctly. Don't half scare you, when they start strutting about, whipping themse…'

'Of course,' interrupted Durnus. 'What Council Harrigin means to say is that in the recent years, we've seen a number of sects spring up in the city.'

'*Sects*?' asked the man with the youthful, clean-shaven face.

'Nothing to worry about, young sir… I'm sorry, I didn't catch your name?' Harrigin piped up again, but quickly fell silent as Tyrfing coughed loudly.

Durnus quickly continued. 'Societies, movements, sects, cults, guilds, factions, call them as you may. Opinionated, I call them. They all seem to have some sort of idea, or belief, that they incessantly preach. Their existence is due to the newest fashion, or rather obsession, of trying to define oneself with belief, or creed. People are asking questions now, and everybody thinks they have the answer. We're living in a time of deep thought and passionate soul-searching, a time that we should be welcoming, had it not spawned these strangely radical cults. Some of them seem to be passionately defensive of certain gods or practices, some of them are sadly the opposite, and some seem to be political in nature. A few we've had to watch very closely indeed.'

'Why?' asked the tall man.

'Competition. One thing they do share in common is their desire to rally others to their cause. The other cults don't take kindly to this. The streets have become a battle for believers. There is coin in it for some of them. Subscription. Collections. Membership, that sort of thing. Some have started taking matters into their own hands. We can't have that,' explained Tyrfing. The council members and traders behind them were beginning to look uncomfortable. This conversation didn't bode well for first impressions.

The skinny woman spoke up. Her voice was airy, faint. 'And when you say *matters*?'

Durnus could feel the tension of the others behind him. He quickly decided to alleviate it. The ruse had to be maintained, after all. 'We can discuss this further over a lunch, if you'd like, madam?' he asked. The woman nodded and the others surreptitiously blew little sighs of relief. They quickly moved on.

With the streets as busy as they were, and under a constant hail of questions and proud comments from the council members, it took them just under an hour to reach the monolithic doors of the Arkathedral. The three visitors seemed very impressed as they took a moment to stand at the base of the fortress and gaze up at its sheer, pale marble walls and the parapets that coiled around them, like the layers of an enormous cake. At its top, near where the great hall had once stood, the walls bristled with spindly wooden cranes. They swung lazily back and forth, docile from that distance, but no doubt hard at work.

As they passed under the thick archway of the main entrance and into the atrium beyond it, they marvelled at the thickness of the stone, now reinforced and rebuilt after the battle. The doors themselves seemed to be both stone and wood, bricks pinched between thick panels of stout oak. On the inside and outside, they were plated in ornately-engraved sheets of steel, as thick as a man's thumb at their widest. They were a great feat of engineering, and once again the visitors seemed impressed. The council members, seeing their raised eyebrows and hearing the murmurs, nudged each other and winked. There was nothing like a bit of mind-boggling construction to show off the wealth of a nation.

The visitors were led across the marble-tiled atrium and after a brief apology from Durnus regarding the amount of stairs and the state of weary travellers, they pressed on towards the peak of the Arkathedral. It took them almost half an hour to walk to the top. Strangely, once they arrived, the visitors were not the slightest bit out of breath. Tyrfing took a moment to clear his throat again, receiving a grimace from Durnus, before he clapped his hands and bowed to their entourage. 'If you will excuse us, Councils, gentlemen, ladies, I think it's time that we served our guests some lunch.' He turned to the three. 'You must be hungry after your travels?' The three nodded in unison.

One of the others held up a hand, a grey-haired crow of a woman. 'I assumed we would be joining you?'

Durnus shook his head. 'Let our visitors rest for now, Council Fessila. There will be plenty of time for that tonight, after this afternoon's council meeting.'

'As you wish, Arkmages,' sighed Harrigin.

Ignoring the frowns and pursed lips they imagined were now firmly fixed on the faces of those they left behind, the Arkmages turned to lead their guests further down the corridor, towards their private rooms and towards peace and quiet. They were almost safe and sound when a jovial shout caught them mid-stride.

'Your Mages! Guests!'

They turned to find a well-built man wrapped in fine attire jogging down the corridor towards them. His face was one giant, welcoming smile. He slowed to a walk and then bowed as low as his spine could possibly allow.

Malvus Barkhart was a snake. He had slithered into the magick council and made his home beneath its marble trees. Unfortunately, a great many of its members seemed content, and even pleased, with his presence. The man was charming to say the least. Sickeningly so. He had the ear of almost every member the council had to offer, which might not have been a problem had his vision aligned with the Arkmages'. But it didn't. In fact, he opposed them on every single matter, however trivial. How he had been elected, they would never know. They had long suspected it was his deep, silken pockets, or his connections in the dark alleyways of the city and the velveteen offices of the traders, or his forked tongue perhaps, equally silken and yet as poisonous, and sharp as a dagger too. He had used them all to worm his way in.

Malvus folded his hands behind his back. His waxed hair, slicked back and plaited into a tail behind his neck, glistened in the sun that was sneaking through the windows of the long, curving hallway. There was a narrow goatee on his pointy chin. He was a tall, narrow man, almost as tall as Tyrfing, and dressed in the finest clothes Krauslung's markets had to offer. His shirt was blue silk and buttoned to the collar. His trousers were of a light grey and baggy around the knees, an eastern trend. The short boots he wore were polished to obsidian mirrors. There was a small necklace hanging around his neck, a thin silver chain with a ruby pendant. The jewel glowed softly even in the daylight; a trick of whichever spell its maker had written in the silver beneath it. 'Sirs, madam, allow me to say on behalf of the entire council that it is a pleasure to have you here in Krauslung. It has been too long since we have seen visitors from Hâlorn. Far too long indeed.'

Once again, the three visitors chose not to bow, but instead nodded deeply. It didn't faze Malvus in the slightest. 'We are eager to discuss how our two countries can further benefit each other. Gods know the Arka need every alliance we can get these days.'

'You speak as if we were at war, Council Barkhart,' muttered Durnus.

'Aren't we, Arkmage? Our soldiers may fight with spears and spells, but our war will be won with politics and coin.'

The woman spoke up. Even inside, away from the breeze and the city noise, her voice was still distant, zephyrous. 'And who might your enemies be, sir? I see none.'

Malvus bowed again, eyes fixed on the slender woman's pale eyes. 'The enemies of progress, madam. The same enemies that would see Krauslung's expansion and well-being damaged beyond repair.'

Durnus sighed. 'As always, Council Barkhart, you distract us with your outlandish opinions. Our guests are hungry and tired. You will have a chance to speak to them later, over dinner, if you wish.'

Malvus' eyes narrowed. 'I wholeheartedly look forward to it. I bid you a good day, sirs, and madam,' he replied, and with that, he walked away, hands still folded firmly behind his back, polished boots squeaking on the marble.

Tyrfing and Durnus quickly led the others into their rooms and locked the door firmly behind them. 'Finally,' Tyrfing sighed, spreading his hands over the door. The door seemed to hiss and quiver for a moment. When he rapped his knuckle on its gilded wood, it sounded as though he were knocking on stone. 'We're safe from eager ears.'

The three visitors stood in a little triangle in the middle of the room. They were staring at a red velvet armchair in front of them, an armchair which held a blonde man dressed in steel armour, wrapped in a black and green cape, his head back, limbs limp, and snoring contentedly. Tyrfing shrugged off his heavy robe and hung it on a hook. He looked over at their guests and followed their confused gazes to the man in the armchair. With a sigh, he wandered over and flicked the ear of the man, eliciting a grunt and a surprised snort. The man came awake with a start and sat bolt upright in the chair. Rubbing his ear, he looked up and saw three strangers staring back at him. 'Well, isn't this embarrassing?' he muttered. 'I was on the night shift again.'

Tyrfing gestured to the three. 'Modren, might I introduce our three guests. The goddess Verix, and the gods Heimdall and Loki. My lords and lady, this is Undermage Modren.'

Modren jumped from the chair and instantly dropped to his knees. 'It is an honour,' he whispered. Durnus and Tyrfing also dropped to their knees, now that they could show the proper amount of respect.

'Please, rise,' said Heimdall. 'We have not come here for that.' The god shrugged off his warm, woollen coat and let it fall to the thick green rug that covered most of the floor. He looked around at the swollen bookcases and drowned desks, the trunks stuffed with trinkets and artefacts and scrolls. He took it all in with slow movements of his tawny eyes, as he had in the streets, absorbing every minute detail like a hawk examining rabbits. A moment of weakness washed across his face, and he rubbed his eyes. The prayers had been strong enough to wrap his ethereal form in bone and skin, but his powers had been left behind. Summoning them was difficult. He sighed and went to one of the six chairs that sat in a circle in the middle of the room. He tested it with his hands, feeling its soft velvet and its plump cushions, before settling awkwardly into it, almost as though he had never sat in a chair before, or if he had, he couldn't remember how to. Modren and Tyrfing watched with blank expressions, while Durnus felt his way to an oak cabinet.

'Please, sit,' he asked, feeling for the cabinet's handles. Tyrfing didn't move to assist him. He knew better than to offer help. The blind Arkmage's hands soon found a trio of glasses. 'Would you like a drink? Some wine? Food perhaps?'

Loki opened his mouth to speak, but was interrupted by Heimdall. 'We will not require any, thank you,' he answered. 'Our bodies are merely shells.'

Tyrfing and Modren took their seats. 'Well, you might have to pretend they aren't. Gods might not eat, but trade delegates from Hâlorn definitely do. We don't want to arouse any suspicion.'

'Very well,' said Heimdall, smiling politely. While Verix found her own armchair beside Heimdall, Loki wandered to the windows that spanned the entire length of the far wall. He stared out at the city far below, hands still firmly in his coat pockets. Modren watched him intently. He didn't look like a god. Like the mage, he was fair-haired. He had deep brown eyes, flecked with yellow, and his skin was pale and clean-shaven, youthful. Modren tried to assess his age, but found himself getting confused the more he watched him. He looked younger than Heimdall, that was for sure, but it was hard to tell. He was neither tall nor short, somewhere in the middle, neither muscular, nor skinny. He just *was*. The Undermage frowned. It was an odd sort of description, but it was the best he could summon. Maybe he was still sleepy.

Durnus soon joined them, bearing three glasses of amber-coloured wine. Modren and Tyrfing took theirs, and Durnus felt his way to his chair. Verix was staring at him intently. Somehow, Durnus knew it. He smiled in her direction. 'What is it?' he asked.

'You look nothing like your brother, Ruin,' she whispered.

'Then I will take that as a compliment,' replied Durnus, with a tight smile. 'And please, call me Durnus, or Arkmage, if you prefer. Anything but Ruin.'

'Though your blood reeks of daemon.'

Durnus' smile faded. 'That it probably does.'

'Verix,' chided Heimdall, and the goddess looked confused. She ran a hand through her strange, sea-green hair.

'I'm sorry. I'm used to speaking my mind,' she said.

'As goddess of truth, I'm sure you are,' chuckled Durnus, and the moment was forgotten.

Heimdall clapped his hands. Modren was trying to assess him now, staring as intently as he dared. The god was pale-faced, like his comrades, and his hair was golden, like dried wheat. The god was as tall as the Siren Eyrum, but once again, impossible to fathom. It was the same with Verix. Their faces, aside from the colour of their eyes and hair, seemed to evade scrutiny like the very stars themselves. Modren found that the harder he looked, the stranger they became. Their chests did not rise and fall with their breathing. They did not blink. Not a single mole nor blemish marred their skin. The closer he leant to them, the larger they grew. Modren moved forward to take his drink from the little table in the centre of the circle, and found himself confused at how much Heimdall had suddenly grown. The god towered above him, in ways the Undermage's brain couldn't comprehend. He felt bludgeoned by his mere presence, breathless in the man's shadow.

'Modren?' said a voice, shattering the mage's thoughts. Modren blinked, and realised Heimdall was staring down at him, a bemused look on his face.

'Sorry, sir,' he muttered. 'It's not every day you meet a god.'

At this, Heimdall laughed. It was a deep booming sound, like thunder. For a moment, it shocked the others in the room, and then somehow some of the tension seemed to bubble off, and the mages and Durnus found themselves relaxing.

'I imagine not, Undermage. I imagine not.' Heimdall shook his head. 'What strange times these are, that gods sit in armchairs and watch men drink wine. For the first time in my existence, I have trouble trusting my eyes and ears.'

Durnus smiled and sipped his wine. 'To business, then?'

'Indeed. Loki, come sit,' ordered Heimdall. The younger god did as he was told. He tore himself away from the window, and, ignoring the last spare chair, he perched instead on the edge of a stool.

'Where do we possibly start?' Verix asked.

'First things first,' sighed Tyrfing, running his hand across his jet black beard. 'Has there been any sign of her?'

Heimdall shook his head sadly, a hint of frustration in his flaxen eyes. 'Wherever the spawn is, I cannot see her, not here, nor from our fortress. She is too strong.'

'What of the woman that travels with her?'

'She too is hidden.'

Tyrfing and Durnus sighed as one. They had secretly been hoping for some good news from Heimdall. If anyone could find Farden's child, it would be a god who could watch a blade of grass growing from a hundred miles away, a god who could see the shadows slinking back to their holes at dawn. If he couldn't see her, then nobody could. This was dire news indeed. They sipped their wine.

'What of the other gods?' asked Durnus. 'Can they be of any help?'

Loki sniffed. 'Are we no use to you?'

'Loki,' growled Heimdall.

Durnus looked in the direction of the younger god's voice. 'That is not what I meant. I know the prayer is strong at the moment, and therefore so are the gods. What I meant was are any of you capable of helping physically, in battle?'

Verix shook her head. 'If we were, we would not have come

here on a ship.'

Loki looked out the window again. 'No, we would have fallen from the sky as brimstone and fire instead of slipping down a shaft of moonlight.'

'That's a shame,' said Modren, eyeing the younger god.

Heimdall leant back in his chair and spread his hands over the velvet. It felt so foreign to him. 'What Loki and Verix mean is that if we could have, we would have. We would not waste time with ruses such as these.' He rubbed his eyes. 'What have you done to find her? I have seen some of your efforts already.'

'Everything in our power,' replied Tyrfing. 'We've sent countless messengers, trackers, ships, hawks, and mages into the wilds, chasing every lead we've ever had. Every time, she disappears like smoke.'

'And we've lost plenty of good mages because of it too,' said Modren. The gods and goddess looked questioningly at the Undermage. He elaborated, narrowing his eyes. 'The only clues we ever get are the dead she leaves behind. The maimed, skinned dead that they are. She and that old crone seem to make a point of actively hunting down our best mages, and then taking their Books. I hope they go mad, and save us the bloody trouble.'

'She is hunting Written?'

Modren nodded. There was bitterness in his eyes. He rubbed his knuckles together. 'Almost always. But she isn't picky, either. If a normal mage gets close enough, she'll kill them all the same. I've lost more mages to that little bitch than I care to count. That's why I've recalled every single Written to the city. I intend to keep them here too, sirs,' he said.

'Why Written?' asked Loki.

'Because we've become stronger,' Tyrfing answered. By his side, Modren nodded. 'We're more dangerous than we've ever been. I think she must be worried.'

'Picking us off on our own, rather than facing us as a group.'

Loki looked confused. He frowned. 'And how is that possible?'

Heimdall hummed. 'The magick in this world is getting stronger by the day. Like a storm brewing or a season shifting. Even Evernia is puzzled by it.'

Loki's frown got even deeper. 'Why haven't I felt it?'

Verix closed her eyes and sniffed the air again. 'Because you, like I, have never travelled here before,' she told him. 'Do you think it is her?'

'Are you serious?' asked Modren. 'One little girl, affecting the whole of Emaneska's magick? That's ridiculous. I spent the all of last night watching ten year-old farmhands flick through beginner's spell books and cast spell after spell. Half of them had never even seen a spell book before last night. Yet here they are, a mere handful amongst the thousands of people that flood into Manesmark every day, all showing signs of magick in their blood, keen as daggers to be a mage. Young, old, rich, poor. One man set fire to his wife's dress just by singing a song that he swore he'd never heard before. Just the other day, another turned a chicken inside out. I, for one, find it very disturbing. The magick is simply tumbling out of these people. And don't even get me started on the things I see in the magick markets these days… Something's wrong with the magick in this world.'

Tyrfing stood up to circle his chair. 'I agree with Modren. It's not just the magick or the markets. Stranger and stranger things keep appearing in the wilds. Faeries, huldras, ghosts, talk of other gryphons even. There is talk of creatures even we have never heard of, creatures that seem to have emerged almost from nowhere.'

Durnus tapped his fingernail on his wine glass. 'Almost as if they're drawn to something.'

Tyrfing shook his head. 'It *can't* be her. If she's that powerful, why would she be hunting us Written down, sneaking about like an assassin? Why would she fear us in number?'

'Then maybe she's just hunting *one* Written...?' ventured Loki. The room fell silent. Tyrfing and Modren both sipped their wine, while Durnus just stared sightlessly into space. His pale eyes said nothing. His lips however, said it all. They were drawn tight, almost as white as his eyes, as if the blood had been sucked straight out of them. Durnus didn't trust himself to speak. If Loki felt the tension, he didn't show it. He just waited for his answer. It never came.

Verix sighed. 'If that is the case, and what Loki suggests is true, then it is either because Farden is a danger to her, or she and the old woman want vengeance. Both can be useful to us.'

Modren glowered at his wine. 'And what of my dead mages?'

'Collateral.'

'I don't think I've ever cursed at a lady before, never mind a goddess, and I don't intend to start today. I would appreciate it if you could inject a little tact into that truthful tongue of yours. With all due respect,' Modren said, slowly and carefully. Verix simply closed her eyes and said nothing in return.

Heimdall held up his hands. 'We digress.'

'Indeed we do,' Durnus sighed. 'I think we have time on our hands. We'll discuss what our defences are later, after dinner. For now, you three need to change. Elessi has supplied clothes for you in the adjacent rooms. She will get you anything else you need.'

'Thank you, Durnus,' said Heimdall, getting to his feet. Loki went to stare out of the window again. Verix stayed in her chair, eyes closed and concentrating on something. As he moved to leave, Heimdall put his hand on Tyrfing's shoulder. 'I should like to see Ilios, when there is a chance.'

'Tonight,' muttered the Arkmage. It was impossible to miss the flicker of angst in his face. He caught the god by the arm as he moved away. His ocean-blue eyes met Heimdall's tawny ones. There, under the weight of them, it felt as though the god was looking through him, as if he were as faceless as glass. 'Do you know where he is?' he asked. 'Farden?'

Heimdall shook his head. 'I do not.'

Tyrfing took a breath and nodded, and slowly but surely, released the god's arm. 'Fine,' he replied. With a squeak of his boot, he grabbed his glass and the bottle of wine, and then went to an ornate pine door at the far end of the room, by the window. Durnus listened to his footsteps and made a face.

'Where are you going?' he asked.

Tyrfing's reply was almost sliced in half by the slam of the door. 'To my forge.'

Modren and Durnus looked at each other. Heimdall look confused. The Undermage stretched and yawned. 'Be glad you're not a chunk of hot metal, sir,' he said.

❦

Drowned, like the cracked hull of a stricken ship, was the city in its night-time noise. The sun had vanished over the peak of Hardja no more than an hour ago. The western sky glowed like dying coals. Krauslung seemed intent on making up for the failing light with its own manmade glimmering. Candles, torches, fires, lanterns, they all came alive. That, and the interminable sound of evening in the city. The ruckus seemed louder tonight. Call it a funeral for the winter. Call it an average night in a city full of coin, sailors, and people who knew how short life could be. Call it an excuse. It was all of those things.

Heimdall, the god who could hear the shadow of a cat sliding across a floor tile, stood alone on the Arkmages' balcony, letting himself melt in the noise. For the moment his tawny eyes remained closed and squeezed tight. He would occasionally wince at the smash of glass, a window, or a carafe of wine maybe. He could hear the dripping of the taps in a tavern below the fortress. He could hear the feet stamping along to the lively tune of a skald and her ljot, somewhere by the boardwalks. He even knew which floorboards needed repairing. He could hear those who used the night to meet in alleys and cellars, to conspire and to rile. He could hear them whispering. Every single one of them.

Heimdall dragged himself from the ocean of noise for a moment, feeling a wave of nausea. It was hard, being so close to it all. So loud and so bright, here in the midst of it all. If he let himself open his eyes and ears to their fullest, he would be blind and deaf in seconds. Heimdall made sure to keep himself distant, as he was accustomed to.

Ignoring the dull beginnings of a headache to slake his curiosity, the god moved forward to the battlements and put his elbows on the stone. It felt warm to his skin, perhaps from the day's sun, perhaps from always knowing nothing but ice-cold stone. The god smiled for a moment, and opened his eyes.

Heimdall leant forward to watch the glittering city below him. His eyes flicked about, hopping from street to street in an effort to keep them distracted. A cat was stealing some milk from a kitchen pot. On a balcony a man knelt down in front of a woman and lifted up a jewel, a ruby, if the god was not mistaken. It was a fake. In the north, between the walls and the city, a small girl sat on a stone with her head in her hands, whimpering. A few streets away, a man hammered at the door of a house with an iron bar. The man behind him was holding a knife. His hand was shaking. Heimdall drank it in. Tiny sips.

Behind him, he heard the padding of feet in soft cloth shoes. He heard fingers sliding across stone and feeling around door-frames. He waited patiently for the Arkmage to join him at the battlements before speaking. 'I see you finally escaped the feast,' Heimdall said, in a whisper that still managed to rumble.

Durnus chuckled in his own hoarse way. 'Duty calls. You and the others are lucky; you can rely on the tired guest routine. I cannot.'

Heimdall smiled and sighed. He seemed to have relaxed since the morning. It would take them a while to acclimatise, he thought. It had been so long. He and Verix had definitely softened somewhat during dinner. Even Loki had been polite, and had managed a smile or two, even a laugh at one point. The Arkmage had been worried about exposing them to the hordes of greedy, curious councillors, but he had to give his compliments to the three gods; they were fine actors.

Durnus was feeling the effects of his favourite amber wine. He let his blind eyes droop until they were half-closed. Even in the darkness of his blindness, he could pick out a faint glow of the city lights. That was all he ever tasted. His ears did him proud. He too let himself melt into the noises of Krauslung. Although the beast had been stripped from him, his old vampyre senses had remained in place of his sight, and he too could hear and smell things no ordinary man could. He rubbed his tired face, feeling the creases under his fingertips, and sniffed the salty air. 'So blissfully unaware,' he said of the city.

'It is the best way to keep them. I have watched a thousand cities over a thousand years, and they could not be more different, every single one of them. But their people? The same. As soon as they get the scent that their lives may come crumbling down, they tear themselves apart in panic. It is better for them to think they are safe,' rumbled Heimdall.

'Even if they are not,' Durnus replied, more of a statement than a question. For Durnus, leadership meant spending a lot of time being a bare-faced liar. Even after a decade and a half, he was still finding the concept of Arkmage foreign and difficult. For a man who had spent most of his life in isolation, commanding nothing except a tiny outpost and a stubborn Written, it had been a back-breaking transition to Arkmage. Not to mention battling the rumours and suspicions of his origins the magick council regularly entertained, or of his great power. It had been worse for Tyrfing, of course, but somehow, together, they had managed. At least they could rely on their magickal authority. A five-runed Written and a pale king on the twin thrones. Nobody would have ever guessed it, and nobody knew the half of it, but one thing was for sure: their prowess was undisputed. It occasionally crept to the edge of terrifying.

A loud roar suddenly erupted from one of the taverns at the foot of the Arkathedral, and Durnus thought he heard Heimdall wincing. The god leant a little further back from the edge of the battlements. Durnus didn't remark on it. Instead he enjoyed the cold breeze on his warm skin. It smelled of the sea, spices from the markets, and brick-dust.

The god soon asked a question. 'And what of Tyrfing?'

'Surely you can hear him?' Durnus asked, and then cocked his head to the side so he could listen to the breeze. There it was: a faint and rhythmic thudding, coming from somewhere below them. Repetitive, angry, the sound of steel being punished.

'I have listened to him all night. A blacksmith in his spare time. An Arkmage and a forge-stoker, how strange.'

Durnus shrugged. 'Perhaps. But Tyrfing has been instrumental in our defence plans. He has been working day and night with the army blacksmiths to lend our soldiers and mages every edge, pardon the pun. His armour designs have been refined and put into mass production. He spends hours poring over forge-spell manuals and sketching plans with the city architects. The Arfell scholars are tired of being summoned by him. Did you know the new Arkathedral gates were his design? Of course you did. He's even commissioned specialised armour for the Written, based on the Scalussen pieces he's been collecting. I do not think this city has ever seen a more proactive Arkmage in all its years.'

'He's been collecting Scalussen armour?'

'Drained half the coffers in the process, much to the anger of Malvus and his council cronies,' muttered Durnus. He sighed and shook his head. 'It's for Farden.'

'Farden?'

'Tyrfing thinks that it will entice Farden back to Krauslung. The mage has always been obsessed with that armour, as you probably know. He's searching for the Nine.'

'Is he now?' mused the god.

'Foolish, I know. The last we ever heard of him, he was in Skewerboar, in the Crumbled Empire.' Heimdall said nothing. Durnus continued. 'He waylaid an old Skölgard general's hunting party in the middle of the mountains. Killed half his honour guard, so we heard, incapacitated the rest, and then, without even a word, he stripped the general of his Scalussen helmet and put it on. Apparently it was not to his taste, whatever that might be. He beat the general half to death with it and then left them both in a puddle. That helmet was most likely worth the weight of a dragon in gold, and yet he left it right there, and disappeared into the mountains. That was the last we heard of him, and that was ten years ago. Every messenger we send comes back empty-handed. The mage is a ghost. I just hope not in the literal sense,' Durnus explained. He turned his blind eyes on the god. 'But you already knew all of this, did you not?'

Heimdall looked out across the city. He scratched at his chin, not because of an itch, but because it was something to occupy him while he thought. 'I have watched Farden in the past.'

'I didn't think a god could lie.'

'We are more than capable of it.'

'This partnership between gods and men is supposed to be an honest and beneficial one. How is that going to work if you are already lying to us?' demanded Durnus.

'It is for your own good.'

'I have heard that before.' Durnus looked angry. 'You know where Farden is, don't you?'

Heimdall took a moment to answer. 'I do.'

Durnus slapped his hands on the stone. 'Then where? We need him.'

'And that is exactly why he will not return.'

'Excuse me?'

There was a quiet click as the balcony door shut behind them. Durnus and Heimdall fell silent. Tyrfing stood beside the door. He was still wearing his blacksmith's apron, a smoky-white affair, made entirely from salamander wool. 'Farden doesn't want to be needed, he wants to be left alone. Trust me, I know the feeling. He doesn't want to be found, any more than I wanted to be,' he said, his voice tinged with sadness.

Heimdall nodded. Durnus sighed. The god turned to face Tyrfing. 'Although I do not regret lying, I believe an explanation should be offered.'

'Please, offer away,' Tyrfing grunted. He folded his arms.

'It is as you say. If I tell you where he is, you will go there and you will root him out. You will tell him that the fate of the world rests on him aiding us in our fight. He will be dragged back, kicking and screaming, and will not be of use to any of us.'

Tyrfing scowled. 'Verix said that *she* may be hunting him.'

Heimdall nodded. 'She probably is. And if he isn't dead already, then we need him here with us, to draw her to the city, and then to fight against her.'

'You want to use him as bait? Are we and a city of mages not enough?'

'Do you think this woman that journeys with her has been truthful? Do you think she told this girl that Farden was her father? Verix believes, as I do, that she has told her that Vice was her father. She seeks revenge. We all know how powerful a vehicle that can be.'

Tyrfing threw his hands in the air. 'Bait. My nephew is bait.'

Heimdall half-closed his eyes. 'If you say so. He, and all of us. We are all bait to her, in the end. But Farden is a fighter too, if he is willing. And that is the crux of it. He needs to make this journey *willingly.*'

Tyrfing opened his mouth to speak but Durnus beat him to it. 'What then? We wait for him to change his mind? It has been fifteen years since he disappeared, Heimdall, what makes you think he will change it now?' he asked.

'One of us needs to go,' added Tyrfing.

Heimdall nodded. 'Indeed, one must, but not you, nor you, Durnus.'

'Who then?'

'Loki,' replied Heimdall, simply and quickly.

Durnus pulled a face, confused. 'Loki?'

Tyrfing looked equally bewildered. 'Why him?'

'Because Farden has never met him before. And despite him being a young god, and a petulant one at that, Loki has a certain, *way*, if you will,' said Heimdall. 'It is why I brought him.' That, and the god's insistent pleas, but he chose not to mention that.

Tyrfing remained unconvinced. While they stood in silence, deep in dark thought, a woman bustled into view behind the windows of the balcony; a woman with curly brown hair that reached all the way to her hips, a woman in a simple maid's outfit, a woman who was busy cleaning up the empty wine glasses and tutting to herself. A woman called Elessi. As she cleaned, the door behind her opened, and in walked Modren, fresh from duty and more than a little tired, dark rings circling his eyes. He quietly closed the door behind him and walked over to the maid. She smiled at him. There was a muffled mumble as the Undermage said something incoherent to all but Heimdall, something that made her laugh. The Arkmages and Heimdall watched them through the dusty glass, a pleasant and momentary distraction from their conversation. Modren and Elessi were unaware they were being observed; inside the room, the glare from the bright candles had turned the balcony windows opaque. The three on the balcony were invisible for now.

Just as Modren turned to leave again, he leant forward and gave Elessi a long kiss on the cheek. She laughed and pushed him away, and he left. As Elessi went back to her cleaning, a wide smile on her face, Tyrfing turned back to Heimdall. He sighed. 'And what magick words is Loki going to use to get my nephew back?'

Heimdall was still watching the maid. 'That, I believe, is up to *her*.'

Tyrfing couldn't help but sneer. 'Elessi?'

The god turned back to the city. 'Elessi, and her husband-to-be, of course.'

chapter 3

"Father, Father, why do the stars shimmer and shake?"
"Son, Son, because everybody shakes when they know they are soon to die. Even a god."
Excerpt from the book 'The Righteous are the Foolish,' author not known

A day later, and half a world away, Albion could only dream of Spring. Spring may have sprung in mainland Emaneska, but in Albion, it was running late. Here winter was still playing the last few bars of its dreary tune, a little ditty of drizzling rain and cold, careless, sleet. Like a talentless skald down on his luck, it knew its time on the earth was short. A storm was gathering over the sea in the east. That night there would be a thunderous finale to winter's song.

The man crouching on a slimy branch, halfway up the old, cracked oak tree didn't care for the rain. Nor did he mind it. He had seen more than his fair share of dark and dreary afternoons in his time. One more wasn't going to kill him. Besides, it made his job easier. A grey blanket of clouds had stolen away the sun. The afternoon was dark and gloomy, wrapped in premature shadow. The perfect sort of afternoon for killing.

The man reached up and flicked a bothersome drip from the lip of his black hood, and then reached down to massage his right leg. It had gone to sleep about an hour ago and was now stubbornly refusing to wake up. The man reached up to the gnarled, twisted finger of a tree branch that hung above his head and lifted himself up so he could move around without falling. With a grunt, he kicked his sleepy leg aside with the other and then settled back into a seated position on the slimy bough that was his perch. The fingers of sleep were slowly beginning to paw at him, like misty hands reaching up from the sodden bracken below him. He scrunched up his eyes and rolled his tired shoulders in a circle, hearing the wet leather of his cloak squeak.

There was a muted rumble in the distance as the storm tested its voice. The man looked up through the tangled, leafless, branches of the half-dead oak and spied the faint flicker amongst a cluster of dark, faraway clouds.

Gripping the branch above his head again, he wiggled his sleepy leg until it had thoroughly woken from its numb slumbers, and then side-stepped along the thicker branch until he could hold himself against the rough trunk of the oak. He looked down at the ground beneath him, covered and obscured as it was by the sea of dark green brackens and brighter ferns that seemed to infest this side of the forest. It was quite the fall, for an ordinary man.

Farden had never been an ordinary man.

With a scrape, his boots slid from the branch and he plummeted into the bracken below. There was a snap, a crack, and then a resounding thud as Farden collided with solid ground. With no more than a wince, he stood, grunted, and simply flicked a bracken frond out of his face with a grimy finger. He pushed his way into the undergrowth, heading for the dirt road he knew was only a stone's throw away from the foot of the oak.

Farden crouched at the edge of it, watching the rain do battle with its broken cobbles. It was an old road, old and tired; the well-worn wheel ruts were testament to its age, as were the patches of churned mud and puddles where greedy peasants had dug free and liberated entire barrowloads of cobblestones, for use in their cottages and walls. Some of these ruts had been thoughtfully filled with sand or gravel, while the rest had been left as gaping, wheel-jarring holes. Farden assessed his section of road once again, as he had earlier that afternoon. None of the holes were severe enough to stop a coach, and even if they had been, the driver would see them in time and steer clear of them. Cow-drawn coaches were not known for their breakneck speeds.

Thunder vibrated the sky again, louder and bolder this time, and Farden stood up. In the booming echoes, he cupped his ears, hearing an unmistakable rattling coming from somewhere in the rain. Somewhere further down the road. The sound of rusty axles and loose bolts. Of iron-shod wheels kissing old cobbles, getting closer all the time.

It was time. Farden rubbed his hands.

On the far side of the road was a pine tree. Wrapped in lichen and drowned in ivy, the tree was rotten to the core. Its bark had flaked away, exposing the flaky splinters beneath, dyed green and yellow by the rot. It looked as though it would topple at any moment. And that was exactly why Farden had spent the afternoon hacking at it with his axe.

Farden quickly crossed the road, hopping over the puddles and potholes until he had been swallowed by the bracken once more. Farden cast around, rubbing the rain from his face and pushing aside the intrusive bracken. 'Where is it now?!' he hissed to himself, cursing. Something clanked against his foot and he reached for it. It was his axe, slimy with the wet. Farden hefted it, ignoring its blunt, notched edge, and instead turned his attention to the gaping notches he had already gouged out of the tree, one on each side. He prodded them with the toe of his boot and was rewarded with a wet squelch. The tree creaked in the wind. There was barely any wood holding the tree up at all. It was perfect.

Farden gripped the axe and held it against his shoulder, waiting. The clattering wheels were rolling ever nearer, he could hear them as clear as day. The sky shook with thunder once more, and Farden raised his axe to the sky as the lightning flashed again, and let it bite deep into the rotten wood with a wet thud.

A moment passed, filled with nothing, nothing but the rain and the storm. Farden stepped back, leaving the axe embedded in the tree. He pulled a grim face. *Shit.* The coach would be on him any moment. Farden pushed on the tree. Nothing. Not even a creak. He tugged on the axe, but the blade had bitten deep, and refused to budge. *Shit again*, he told himself. There was nothing else for it. Farden took a step back, grit his teeth, and aimed a wild kick at the handle of the axe. There was a resounding crack as his boot collided with the axe, forcing it deeper. Farden had to keep from clapping as the tree whined a slow, sad whine and slowly but surely, began to topple. It was just in time.

A team of four tired-looking brown cows emerged out of the rainy haze, a faded purple coach close behind them. The cows pulled in pairs; each wearing a thick collar with curved hames around their thick necks, to which the traces of the coach were harnessed. The patchwork beasts were soaked to the bone. Steam billowed from their grimy noses. They plodded along sullenly, paying almost no attention to the impatient coachman and skinny footman that sat behind them on the narrow box at the front of the coach. They were dressed in the bright yellow and purple livery of the Maudlow Duchy, or to be exact, the livery of Maudlow's rather extravagant and flamboyant son. The coat of arms emblazoned on their chest was a tree wrapped in a ribbon, a large, stylised *H* held in its branches.

The two men on the box looked half asleep, heads and eyes drooped, hands limply hanging onto the reins. They probably would have been asleep, had it not been for the rain. They soon came awake when they spied the toppling tree in their path. Their sleepy expressions turned to ones of exasperated horror. The coachman leapt to his feet, thrashing the cows with his coach-whip, yelling for them to stop. The footman was shouting too, nervously tugging at the coachman's tunic. For a brief moment, Farden thought the cows would refuse to stop, and plod straight into the shadow of the falling tree. Thankfully, they were only tired, not stupid. The docile animals saw the tree just in time and instantly dug their hooves into the road. They lowed fearfully as the rotten pine crashed to the ground barely a foot from their steaming noses, showering them in moss, mud, and splinters. The two men hopped down from the coach, noticeably relieved. Farden wondered blithely if the skinny footman had soiled himself. He had that look of nervous guilt about him, clinging to one of the wheels, wringing his hands. The coachman was in no such mood to dawdle. He marched across the wet cobbles to confront the tree blocking their path. In a moment of utter fury, he began to flay it with his coach-whip.

Farden quickly ducked back into the thick bracken and reached for the longbow that was strapped alongside the quiver on his shoulder. He pulled it loose and unravelled the waxed catgut bowstring from his pocket. It took him three grunting attempts, but he finally managed to string the stiff bow. He plucked at it to test its tautness, making it hum, like a one-stringed harp. Satisfied, the mage snatched two arrows from the quiver and ran his fingers through their bright green feathers to remove the beads of rain. Farden notched one on the bowstring and the other he pinched between his teeth, tasting the beeswax and the aromatic tang of the cedar arrowshaft on the tip of his tongue. He knelt to the wet earth and rested the bow sideways on his lap, ready, waiting. The mage watched, a cold smile on his cold lips, as the infuriated coachman continued to thrash the pine tree with his whip, berating it. Then, for some reason known only to himself, in a moment of pure and senseless desperation, he tossed the whip aside and began to grapple with the wet and muddy bark like a fumbling wrestler, trying to shove the pine tree out of the way. Needless to say, the old tree didn't move an inch, and the man ended up slipping and falling to his face in the wet mud. He got to his feet and brushed the filth from his livery, his breathing a little on the heavy side. He thumped his fist against the tree. 'Bah! By Jötun's balls!' he could be heard yelling. 'Just when you thought nothing else can go wrong!' he shouted over the pitter-patter of the rain, a pitter-patter that was growing heavier and louder by the minute.

'I better go talk to his lordship,' ventured the jittery footman, still a little bewildered by the spectacle of desperation he had just witnessed. He was hopping nervously from one foot to the other. Perhaps he had soiled himself.

'That you'd better, before he has us both flogged right here on this very road! We're already an hour late,' hissed his comrade.

The skinny footman shuddered. He went to the door and tapped timidly on its faded paint. There was a moment before anybody answered. The footman's knuckles hovered in the air, debating whether to knock again. Deep in the bracken at the side of the road, wet fingers curled eagerly around a bowstring.

The door cracked open, no more than an inch, and the footman bowed, narrowly missing banging his head on the door handle in the process. A shrill voice, slippery and slurred with wine could be heard now. 'What's the problem now? Why have we stopped?' it demanded.

'M'lord,' burbled the footman, a nervous babble. 'A tree has fallen across the road. An old rotten thing. We…'

A velvet-gloved hand shooed the man away from the door. Barely fifty yards away, an arrowhead, blackened with soot, touched its barbs to the neck of a longbow. 'Well, fetch the axe and get cutting, servant, before I am made any later than I already am! Lady Gavitt will have my guts for her stockings if I miss her banquet!'

The door slammed, and the arrow relaxed. Farden cursed below his breath. He needed a clear shot. He couldn't give his prey the slimmest chance of escape. The gloomy afternoon and drizzling rain was perfect for hiding and sneaking, but that also went both ways, should prey manage to bolt. Farden didn't fancy spending the night prowling through the damp and dreary forest, looking for a Duke's son to skin. He squinted at the door of the coach, hoping to spy a target, but the glass was fogged and speckled with rain and mud, and the lace curtain behind it obscured everything else. Farden began to edge sideways through the bracken.

The footman hopped up onto the box of the coach and rummaged through the chest that was hiding beneath their narrow seat. He quickly produced an axe and waved to the coachman, who was now sat on the tree, arms crossed and face as gloomy as the sky. The front two cows were now lying down, sneaking a moment or two of rest. He was currently engaged in a staring contest with one of them.

'Hoy!' called the footman as he splashed through the puddles towards his colleague.

The coachman looked up. 'What's that for?'

'It's an axe. What do you suppose it's for?'

The coachman snatched it from the skinny man's hands and tested its blade. He rolled his eyes. 'Well, you make a start, and I'll finish it off. I need to feed these lazy creatures, or we'll never get to Gavitt's shindig. I, for one, have a young and willing kitchen maid waiting for me at Gavitt's mansion, and I don't intend to let her spend the night alone, or with another coachman, for that matter. Now, get chopping,' he said, handing the axe back to the footman. He got up, stretched, and sauntered back to the coach, muttering something dark and dangerous to himself.

Farden waited for the wet thump of a dull axe biting into wood, and then let his arrow fly on the second. He timed it near perfect; the green-fletched arrow leapt from the bowstring and buried itself in the coachman's head just as the axe fell for the second time, masking the sharp crack of an arrow punching through skull. The man slumped to the ground like a sack of rocks, quietly enough not to alert the attention of the footman, who had barely made a dent in the tough bark of the fallen pine. Farden put him out of his misery with an arrow to the neck. The cows lowed, confused, as the footman folded limply over the tree, gargling blood. The puddles around their hooves began to turn a shade of muddy crimson.

Farden held his breath, waiting for a slam of doors or a shout or a scream, but nothing came. The mage slunk forward, sliding gently through the mud and moss until he was slightly behind the purple coach, still hidden by the bracken. There was a window on the back of it. It too was smeared with road-mud and rain. The white lace curtain behind it was still.

The mage slipped another arrow from his quiver and onto the longbow. With a sniff and a crack of his knuckles, he sidled onto the road, hoping the people inside were too busy quaffing wine and chortling amongst themselves to notice a hooded figure in the rain. There was a flash of sheet lightning, so quick it made the eyes wonder if they had blinked, and then thunder followed, making the air and the wet forest tremble. Rain drummed on the mage's clothes and splashed in the puddles around his furtive boots. He crouched to the cobbles, just beneath the back window. He could hear a thudding from inside, and the cackles of laughter. Tobacco smoke, fragrant with cloves and thick like the prying fingers of sea-fog, leaked from the seam of the coach's door, to be harangued and perforated by the heavy rain. Holding his bow with one hand, Farden loosened the long knife at his belt, shuffled forward, and then pounced.

Farden wrenched the coach door open with his free hand and then fired at the first thing that he clapped eyes on. The woman screamed as the arrow pinned her to the velvet cushion she lay against, making the others crammed into the hot, sweaty coach freeze, horror on their faces. Two men with long hair and wine on their lips, half-naked from the waist down and fully in the midst of groping each other, began to yell and scream. They fought each other to the other door and away from the steel-eyed attacker standing in the rain. They didn't get far.

Farden let two more arrows fly from his bow. More blood painted the cushions. The remaining occupants, a woman and an extravagantly-dressed man with a sizeable paunch tried to hide themselves under their coats. The man pushed the woman in front of him, desperately trying to find the dagger he had hidden in his boot. A pair of strong hands seized them by their flailing limbs and dragged them out, dumping them on the muddy cobbles. The woman was screaming and sobbing uncontrollably. Farden winced at the piercing sound. He pushed her against the wheel of the coach and waved the knife in her face.

'Quiet!' he yelled, and her screams died into a muted whimpering. She clutched her dress around her and rocked back and forth.

'Thank you,' Farden grunted, turning his attention to the pot-bellied man lying wheezing on the cobbles. A trickle of blood came from a cut on his forehead. The mage pressed the heel of his boot on the man's throat and he squeaked, turning a shade of white. 'That goes for you as well.'

'What do you want?' hissed the man. There was so much venom in his voice, Farden could almost taste it.

'What is your name?'

'And what should you want with my name?'

'Wouldn't want to kill the wrong person now, would I?'

The man turned even whiter. 'My name is Truspin. If you're after the Maudlow's son, Havanth, then you've already killed him, murderer.' The man raised a shaky hand and pointed at one of the half-naked men. 'He was that one, there.'

Farden rubbed his chin, looking at the dead draped about the coach's cabin. 'Is that so?' he asked. The man nodded as much as the mage's boot would allow. Farden smiled down at him and waved his knife in a circle, assessing his velvet coat and its lace trimmings, the man's wine and meat-fuelled paunch, the soft, manicured hands that had only ever seen hard work through a spyglass or a coach window, the embroidered *H* and *M* on his breast. The man blinked as the rain mercilessly pelted his face. Farden turned to the shaking woman. 'Is it true?'

She shook her head once, a little twitch to save her skin. Farden smiled again. He pressed down with his boot and Havanth Maudlow, the Duke Maudlow's one and only son, gasped. 'You know, I've killed so many of you in the last few years I can barely count them all. Some were mere land owners, some were minor lords or ladies, maybe ambitious husbands or mad wives causing trouble. Some might have been the nephew or a cousin of a lord, leverage maybe, or revenge. Some were even the daughter, the sister, the brother, or son of a duke, just like you, Havanth.' Farden pointed the knife at the man's neck. 'And you know what I've learnt about you? You're all the same. From the land owner to the duke-to-be, you will all lie your tongues off at the end. Not a scrap of honesty and pride. You'll say anything to squirm your way out from under my boot. I suppose it's what makes you so easy to manipulate, so I'm told. Certainly makes me feel better about killing you.'

Havanth glared daggers at the mage. 'Is that what your master tells you?'

Farden slammed the blade into the man's chest, feeling the metal bite through the ribs and into the soft organs beneath. 'I have no master,' he lied.

Havanth's mouth sagged open, his narrow eyes now very wide. He died quickly, silently. Farden left the knife in his chest. He would need it again in a moment. Behind him, the woman yelped and scrambled to her feet. Shoes kicked aside, she sprinted across the cobbles with tears and rain running down her face, whimpering still.

Farden sighed and turned to watch her clamber over the fallen tree. *Leave none alive. I don't care who they are*, said the voice in his head, the very same voice that had delivered those orders a week ago. Farden bent down, retrieved his longbow, and took an arrow from his quiver. He took aim at the fleeing woman, shut his eyes and released the string. A few seconds later there was a wet slap and a scrape as a body hit the cobbles. The mage rubbed his eyes and took a breath. *He had killed so many he could barely count them all.* So many, and yet he could still remember every twang of every bowstring, every thud of an arrow in the spine, every swish of a blade, every crack of a spell, every yelp and every scream. That was how he remembered them. No names, just deaths. *What a cold way to count them*, thought the mage. He shrugged, and strapped his bow to his back again.

Make it look like a bandit raid, demanded the voice. Farden knelt to the cobbles, and began the most honourable task of stripping the dead bodies of their coin and jewellery. He shrugged. At least he got to keep what he took.

Farden made quick work of emptying the pockets of the dead. He stood up and stretched, looking up to the sky so the rain could wash his face and bloody hands. He looked down at the body of the Duke's son. His face was slowly turning grey. The mage sighed, and reached for the knife still embedded in the man's chest. There was but one task left to do.

Bring me his head.

chapter 4

"Kiltyrin, Kiltyrin. Who knew the grass of Albion could breed such a snake. And what a slippery snake he is. Trace the path of a hundred murders and I reckon you'll find him sitting pretty at the end of every one of them, hands clean and asking for proof. I don't know why more of us don't suspect him. Why don't I try to beat him, you ask? Well, to beat him, you don't just need to be a better player, you need better pieces too, and I mean one in particular. Nobody's got a better killer than that Duke, but I'll be blasted if anyone knows who or what he is. Nobody is safe from him. I like my family as they are. Alive and whole. Nobody has nothing to lose when they're sitting at the top of a castle."

A letter written by the Duke of Dunyra to his cousin Lunfris Dunyra in 905. Lunfris was found floating face-down in a well a few months later. Dunyra himself publicly proclaimed it as 'an unfortunate accident brought about by too much ale and not enough sense'

A week passed, and with it the storm. Winter finally withdrew itself from Albion. Had Jeasin the sight to see it, she would have perhaps remarked on the way the sun hovered on the strips of feathered cloud lashed across the sky, how the warm air felt strange on her breeze-pricked skin, how the canals, which had always been described as dull, slate-coloured slugs of things to her, sparkled in the sun. Or she might have just shrugged, and called it another day. It wasn't just her eyes that were blind.

There were only two things that mattered to Jeasin, and one of them was coin. Didn't matter who it came from, or why, as long as it came regularly and in reasonable amounts. Coin was more than currency to a woman like her. Coin was food. Coin was a roof. Coin was locks on the doors and blankets for her girls. Guards for the door, if she was lucky.

Jeasin stood at the corner of a house, slouching, letting the wood hold her up. She filtered out the sounds of the riverboats and the gurgling canal and the river birds squawking and listened to the people instead. It was funny how people assumed being blind meant you were deaf as well, as if the two were related somehow. It was also a wonder how many titbits of news a single person could pick up whilst standing on a street corner and simply listening. They ignored the young woman lounging at the corner of the large house, gossiping and chatting about everything under the sun as they walked along the bank of the canal. Jeasin knew their voices all too well. She could hear specific shoes striding across the gravel. Borrol, with his limp. Hunst, the market guard, with his giant boots. She could hear the shrill cackle of Persina and her flock of daughters.

It was the thud, thud, thud of the well-made shoes pacing hesitantly across the bridge that held her attention, the type of hesitant pace that someone exhibits when they see an unfamiliar woman standing next to their door. Jeasin combed her long hair behind her ears and folded her hands in front of her. Ready.

When the shoes stopped a few paces in front of her, she cracked a smile, a smile that many a man had paid heavy pouches of coin for. She could smell the oil of the man's hair, the musty silk of his coat. 'Hello, sir,' she said, waving.

'Hello,' replied a deep voice. She could hear the little scratch of a fingernail on a stubbled chin. 'Can I help you?' the man asked. Straight to the point.

'Why yes, I believe you can,' Jeasin smiled again, making sure to pronounce her words as best she could, as she had been told.

She held her hand out to the man, palm down.

A few seconds passed before the shoes took a few more steps forward, and Jeasin found her hand in the surprisingly gentle grip of a rough hand. A pair of lips brushed her skin. Jeasin beamed. She flicked her long hair and bobbed a little courtesy. 'Jeasin,' she said.

'A pleasure, I'm sure. Now what was it I can help you with? I'm in a rush you s…'

'I understand you're a man of means and pleasures, or so they say.'

Another pause. The voice spoke again, lower this time. 'I don't know what you mean…?'

'Well, sir, they say you like your pleasures, and that you have no shortage of means to pay for them,' she replied. She made sure to comb her fingers through her hair again, making sure it was all in place and tidy. He liked his girls tidy, she had been told, expensive-looking. Expensive sounding.

'And who are *they*, might I ask?'

Jeasin looked to the left, towards the canals. 'The girls from the other side of town. On Gossamer Street. I believe you know the place. They tell many a tale of you, sir.'

A brusque cough. 'Maybe I do. Maybe I don't know what you're talking about. Look, what is this about?'

'Well, I'm not one of those girls. I'm from this side of town. There are girls here too you know, at a certain house not a dozen streets from here,' she said. She took a step forward. 'And we're just as good.'

'I think you've got the wrong pers…'

Jeasin chuckled, almost letting her accent slip. 'Serfesson, if I heard right? All the girls in Kiltyrin know about you.' She smoothed her dress. 'I am here to show you that the girls on this side of the canal are just as good as the girls,' she waved a hand at the water, 'on *that* side.'

Serfesson cleared his throat. 'Look,' he said. 'I'm sure they are, but I don't have the time. Maybe next time I'll come to see you instead, alright? Now, it was nice meeting you…' the voice moved past her, the sound of footsteps moving from gravel to the hollow wood of the doorstep. Jeasin turned around to follow.

'But this offer expires,' she whispered to Serfesson, pulling what she could imagine was her most coy look.

A key hovered in the mouth of a lock. 'What offer?'

'No charge. A teaser, you might say. Of what me and my lot can offer.'

'Your lot?' Serfesson queried. 'As in…'

Jeasin inwardly chided herself for letting her act slip. *Expensive*, she reminded herself. 'My girls, I mean. My girls and I.'

'I see.'

'I do hope so.'

'And this offer expires?'

'The moment you close that door with me on this side of it.'

Another pause. She could hear him looking around, hear his stubble moving against the collar of his tunic. Jeasin took another step forward. 'I can tell you're interested. I don't need my sight to see that.' She heard Serfesson's mouth break into a guilty smile; a tiny click of saliva and lips moving across teeth. She smiled back. She held out her hand again, this time palm up.

'I take it you and your girls are discreet? If you know me and my business then you know about my wife.'

'I do.'

'So I can take your word?'

'We are most discreet, sir.'

The rough hand grabbed hers, not so gentle any more. 'Then come inside. I have a little while.'

Just before she was ushered inside, Jeasin turned her head slightly and looked to the city, knowing she was hiding somewhere, in the buildings on the other side of the canal, watching the whole thing. Jeasin walked inside, and heard the door lock behind her. Serfesson rubbed his hands together. Jeasin turned, and smiled, and waited.

'Lead the way,' she said, when Serfesson didn't move. The air in the house was cold. She could smell the smoke of a log fire, and the sweet aroma of dried lavidern, hanging somewhere above her head.

'Upstairs,' said a deep voice, and Serfesson grabbed her firmly by the wrist and lead her quickly down a corridor and around a corner. 'Mind the steps,' he said, waiting for her to find them with her feet. Jeasin did her best to keep up with him.

They reached the top of the stairs and he pulled her along another corridor and then another, until they came to a door. A handle rattled and hinges creaked, and she was led inside a room that seemed to be slightly warmer than the rest. Jeasin was manoeuvred to a bed and told to sit, which she did. Her smile was now a permanent fixture of her face. It took years of practice to hold a smile like that. She heard a rustling as Serfesson undid the buttons of his coat. She heard it fall in a heap on the floor nearby.

'Lie down.'

She did.

The jangling of a belt buckle now.

A quiet, muffled thud as the door downstairs quietly slid shut. A sound that only a person that lived half the world through her ears could have possibly heard. Serfesson was not one of these people. Jeasin kept smiling.

The sound of shoes being kicked off and tossed under the bed.

Footsteps creeping along the corridor and around a corner.

More clothes landing in a heap on the floor.

Serfesson approaching the bed, his hands resting on her knees.

Jeasin pulled up the edges of her dress, feeling how soft the borrowed fabric felt.

The creak of an old floorboard down the hall.

The creak of the slats under the bed as Serfesson leant over her. She could feel his cold, rough hands on her hips.

The rhythmic stamp of footsteps coming down the corridor, confident now they knew they had their target trapped.

Now this, Serfesson did hear. Sadly, it was just a moment or two too late.

The door swung open and the doorhandle bounced off the wall with a bang. Serfesson, an unbuttoned shirt away from stark-naked, looked up in alarm to find a buxom woman and a muscular man in a formal-looking black tunic standing in the doorway. The woman was pointing and jabbing her finger at Serfesson. Her face was beetroot red. 'See! In the very act! I told you!'

Serfesson jumped off of Jeasin and grabbed his clothes. 'Karleah!'

'Husband,' replied the plump woman. She turned to the man in the black tunic, who was staring at the whole debacle with the most disapproving expression on his face. Karleah put her shaking hands on her rather buxom hips. 'And do you believe me now?'

'I do,' said the man, in a dry and monotone voice. Jeasin could feel his eyes on her. She shuffled into a sitting position and smoothed her dress. A calm smile still sat on her face.

'Well?' demanded Karleah, 'what are you and the Reever going to do about it?'

The man in black tore himself away from Jeasin and looked Serfesson up and down. 'Well, m'lady, you're absolutely right. An unfaithful husband 'e truly is. Law dictates a compensation, as you pointed out. I doubt the Reever will 'ave any objection to it, not after *this*,' he said.

Serfesson turned a shade of red that rivalled his wife's, crimson thunder. 'You scheming harlot!' he shouted. Jeasin was pretty sure he had aimed that at her. She didn't move. 'You set me up, didn't you?!'

The man in the tunic gingerly tried to grab the half-naked Serfesson and usher him out of the room. 'Come along you!' he ordered.

'You won't get a single coin, Karleah!' bellowed Serfesson, but it was all useless. After much pushing and yelling and threatening, Serfesson was finally manhandled out of the room and was escorted down the corridor. Karleah hovered in the doorway until she heard the bang of the door below and the faint sound of laughter drifting up from the people in the street. Karleah reached inside her coat and tugged a fat purse from a pocket. She weighed it in her palm, looking at Jeasin out of the corner of her eyes. The purse jangled.

'As we agreed?'

'As we agreed. Fifty. Gold.'

Jeasin stood up and smoothed out her rumpled clothes. 'An' I can keep the dress?'

There was a snort. 'Fine.'

Jeasin walked over to where she knew the woman was standing and held out her hand. A heavy purse dropped into it and she quickly tucked it between her breasts.

'I don't want to see you again, hear me? Otherwise this won't work.'

Jeasin shrugged and tapped the corner of her right eye with her long, painted fingernail. 'Can't promise that. But at least only one of us 'as to worry 'bout it.' She didn't need her sight to know that Karleah was scowling.

'Time to throw you out, then,' she said.

Jeasin was marched out of the room, down the stairs, and to the front door, where Karleah made a great show of pushing the harlot down the steps and into the street. She stumbled, but stayed upright, and listened to the whispering of the crowd that had gathered. They already knew who she was. What she was. It was no secret. Just another little slice of gossip for the streets. Jeasin smirked as she heard her name shiver through the crowd like autumn leaves, skittering across the flagstones.

Karleah played her part well. She sauntered onto the doorstep with her hands on her big hips and waved her fist at the young woman. 'And *stay* out, whore!' she yelled, slamming the door. Jeasin combed her hair behind her ears and shrugged, leaving the crowd to mutter as she walked away.

Jeasin felt for the wall of the house, the touch of the sanded oak beneath her sensitive fingers, and followed it to the street. Somebody brushed past her and hissed, 'Harlot,' in her ear, but she barely even flinched. Insults fade after years of use, becoming blunt like battle-weary blades. Insults rely on probing the open wounds of shame and guilt. She had neither. Their opinions affected her as much as the passing of night and day. What was another insult thrown about by strangers in the darkness? After all, what is an insult, when it is true?

Jeasin traced the face of the wall to the next building, and then to the next, her arms out in front of her like the waving branches of a tree in the wind. Her fingers read the wall like the features of a map. A drainpipe here, a boarded window there. She knew them all.

She paused at a crack in a wall to flick an offending shard of gravel from her sandal, and when she reached up to balance herself, she put her hand on leather and firm flesh rather than wall, and she jumped.

'You ought to be 'shamed, sneakin' up on a blind girl,' she challenged.

'There was no sneaking involved,' said the stranger, a man with a deep, yet quiet voice, the fringes of which were frayed with tiredness and travel.

'Farden,' she breathed.

'The very same.'

'An' what could you want, I wonder?' said Jeasin, with a dry smile. She crossed her arms. His ability to sneak up on her, *her* of all people, was infuriating. She could never sense him until he was right under her nose. And now there he was, and suddenly Jeasin was wishing he was anywhere but under her nose. She could smell him now, taste him almost; the copper smell of blood still under his fingernails; the scent of mud and leather fighting for air. Metal. Week-old sweat.

'You tell me, Jeasin,' mumbled the mage. Leather shoulders creaked.

'Bath, by the smell of you.'

A shrug. 'That too.'

'Same old Farden. You'd better be careful. The Duke's dog is becomin' predictable.'

The mage grunted. 'Watch your mouth, and keep your voice low.'

Jeasin lifted her chin. 'Would you 'ave me dumb, as well as blind?'

There was a silence. Farden smirked. The sun was hot on his stubbled face. He examined a muddy stain on the back of his hand. 'I'd call you many things. Dumb isn't one of them.'

'I meant…'

'I know what you meant. That was quite the little scam you just pulled. Almost had me fooled. Especially the wife. We should find her a stage,' said the mage. He reached out and flicked the bulging coin purse hiding under the embroidered neckline of her borrowed dress. It clinked. 'Quite a bit of coin for a day's work,' he said, his voice low, quiet, dangerous if she didn't know him any better. Luckily, she did. She slapped his hand away.

'Nothin' wrong with a bit of work on the side. Anyways, women have to keep together.' She waited for the nearby footsteps to recede. 'I was doin' Karleah a favour. Serfesson's been tourin' the brothels like they're goin' out of business. Now she can finally be free of him and get what's 'ers as well. Reevers don't pay no heed to us girls or to the city gossip. Those law men need to see proper proof,' she asserted in a hushed voice. 'So we gave 'em some.'

The mage leant forward. 'Jeasin,' he said. 'It's not a favour if you charge for it.'

The woman shrugged, wondering why she was trying to justify her actions. The mage was right; she couldn't have cared less about Karleah or her husband. There was no use trying to paint her life with a varnish of virtue and morality; it would have flaked off in an hour. Most of the people in her town were just purses with legs, open hands holding gold, waiting to be taken. That's how she saw them in the murky darkness, and she didn't care to be proven wrong.

Farden though, now here was one of the precious few with qualities other than his coin, although Jeasin grumbled to admit it. She poked the coin purse deeper into her dress and reached for Farden's hand. He let her find it. 'If anyone's the authority on morals 'round here, Farden, it ain't you. Not by a bloody long shot,' she said to him, gesturing towards the street. 'Come on then.'

❦

A few hours later, a bathed Farden stood in front of a grimy window, drying his tangled black hair in the sun. In a mixture of apathy and forgetfulness, he had let it grow down to his shoulders, and now it spent most of its day trying to annoy him, trying to escape. Farden gave up trying to unravel it with his fingers. He turned around, casting about for some sort of brush or comb. Jeasin was dozing on the bed, wrapped loosely in a blanket. A nearby window was propped ajar. Sounds of the canals and waterways floated up and rested on the windowsill like the grey pigeons that roosted there. They burbled and cooed sleepily, mumbling to themselves. A cold breeze ruffled their feathers, prickled the mage's skin. Farden walked to the window, hands ready to shut it. He lingered there for a moment, looking out over the confused little city.

Tayn was the sister city of Kiltyrin's capital, imaginatively named Kiltyrin, and what a strange little place it was. Built straight in the path of a river, the city had bent it to its will, dissecting it into a hundred little waterways and canals, wrapping them up in brick and stone. It made the city looked like a bursting capillary. It was a jumbled place, full of dark stone and slate roofs, gravel and spindly bridges.

The breeze was turning colder now that afternoon was dying, making way for evening. He stared out of the window, half at his grizzled reflection, half at the city, with its veins of dubiously-coloured water. A lone and brave star hovered in the eastern sky, just to the left of a chimney-pot across the street. Farden scowled at it, and shut the window with a thud.

The mage walked to the other side of the room, where a thin sliver of polished bronze had been propped up in the corner. Farden confronted his metallic reflection. It had been so long since he had seen it. Now he curled his lip at it, like an unwelcome guest.

His hair was even longer than his fingers had suggested. It was a tangled, black mop, the ends of which had clumped together in places to form long knots. Even the bath hadn't helped them. Farden pulled at one and frowned.

Next he looked to his shoulders and chest, probing them with his rough fingers and feeling knots of a different sort, hiding under his dry skin and in between his tired muscles. Every few inches of so, his fingers would come across a gnarled lump, or a puckered indent, or a twisted line. Scars, young and old. Some were camouflaged by the black hair on his chest, others were in plain sight, like the missing finger on his left hand, Vice's parting gift. He ran his palm across his chest and felt them all, bloody memories, every single one. Farden reached down and lifted his towel up over his shins and knees to look at the scars there too, a tapestry of bloody blades and daggers and sharp, evil things.

Farden turned to the side, slowly, and looked at the tendrils of black script that curved around his ribs. He turned some more, craning his stiff neck so he could see his whole Book, splayed across his back. He noticed that not a single scar dared interrupt the lines of black script. *Selfish magick*, he thought. There was a patchwork of scars across his shoulders and spine, silvery, wandering trails like snail-grease, but wherever they met the obsidian ink of his tattoo, they faded and gave way, reappearing in between the lines and runes for brief moments until they died completely. The same could be said of the key-shaped tattoos on his forearms. Farden looked down at them and scowled.

On the bed, Jeasin rolled over in her sleep. Two coin purses sat on the side of her bed; one large and stuffed, the other smaller and lighter, with a few flecks of clay-coloured mud on it for good measure. Farden tiptoed over to the end of the bed, where his clothes lay folded over the curved spine of a chest. His pack and haversack lay on the floor to the side of it, crumpled and tired. New equipment was needed, he thought. That meant the market. Farden had grown to hate them with a passion that bordered on violence. Markets meant magick, and Farden had already had enough of that in his life.

With a snort, he rubbed his forehead. The dull headache had returned to pester him. Farden lifted up his clothes and reached for something gold and red and shiny underneath. He sat on the bed, garnering a sleepy groan from Jeasin in the process, and put the two vambraces on his lap. They clinked as they rolled together.

'What's that?' muttered Jeasin, head entrenched in a pillow. Farden turned to look at her. Her hair covered most of her neck and her chest. Gold, curly hair. Even though her eyes were blind, they looked as perfect as could be. They were not misted, nor scarred, and had her eyelids been opened, she would have stared out of eyes the colour of an empty winter sky. Blue and cold. Farden reached out to move the hair from her face, thought better of it, and cleared his throat with a deep cough instead.

'Nothing,' said Farden, sliding one of his vambraces onto his arm. The metal was cold, and at the touch of the mage's skin, the overlapping scales of steel shivered and rattled. They contracted around his arm until they fit perfectly. Farden savoured the coldness against his skin, cooling his veins, numbing his head. He reached for the second one.

'What's that noise?' asked Jeasin again, lifting her head out of her pillow.

'Nothing, I said.'

With a groan, the woman sat up. She was stark naked. She reached out and found the mage's muscled, scarred shoulder, and traced it down to his arm. The mage watched her nimble fingers prod and probe the metal of his vambrace.

'Don't you ever leave these off?'

'They're safer on than off.'

Jeasin looked offended. 'Sayin' you don't trust me, Farden?'

He put a hand on the back of hers. 'Habit. And no, I don't trust anyone.'

'What are they then? What makes 'em so precious?'

'Old family heirlooms. They're nothing,' he told her. An easy lie.

Jeasin sniffed, shrugged, stretched. She ran her hand back up the mage's arm and down his back. The mage naturally shied away from the feel of her hand across his Book. 'I wish I could see it,' she said.

'Count yourself lucky that you can't. Why do you think I come to you, instead of the other girls?' A half-lie, this time. Somehow it was harder.

Jeasin ran her hand through her golden locks and smirked.

'Sure. You come to me 'cause I'm blind. That's the reason.' She lay back on the bed. 'So I take it I owe this little visit to the Duke, then? You off to see 'im?'

Farden hummed a "yes." He looked down at his vambrace and shook his head. He had forgotten about the Duke. He pinched the metal between finger and thumb and it slithered apart. It soon found itself firmly back in his haversack, hidden in a nest of dirty clothes.

'Why don't you stay 'ere, tonight? Keep us company.'

'Trying to squeeze more coin out of me?'

'Usually, but no. Either way, I can make it worth your while.'

Farden hesitated, and then shook his head. 'It's not safe.'

'Be safer for us girls havin' a mage like you in the house.'

'I was talking about me.'

'As if'n anybody in Kiltyrin would dare challenge you. Need to protect my girls.'

'You've got more than enough coin to hire some men. Do that.'

'And why do that when I can 'ave an Arka Written instead?'

Farden thumped his fist on the end of the bed. Jeasin jumped. 'I told you to keep your mouth shut about that. I am *not* a Written,' Farden growled. 'Not any more.'

Jeasin folded her hands behind her head and tutted. 'Funny. Thought that tattoo thing on your back said different. Told you, I'll make it worth your while. No charges.'

Farden hoisted his pack over his tired shoulders and pulled his hood over his head, checking his belt. He had only the dagger; he had burnt the longbow and its arrows in a campfire two days before. Evidence, there would not be. He knelt and picked up a sack, a sack he had been carting around for a week, and slung it onto his back. 'I'll see you soon, Jeasin,' he said, moving to the door.

Jeasin scrambled to her knees. She pulled the blanket around her body, anger flickering across her face. Her eyes searched about wildly. 'What kind of man are you, to turn down an offer like that?' she spat.

Farden paused for a moment. 'A man that can't be relied on,' he grunted.

The door shut behind him.

Jeasin threw her hands up in the air and tossed herself back into her pillows. She listened to the clomping of the mage's boots as they hurriedly receded down the wooden hallway. Damn that mage, she cursed. Pinning him down was like trying to hammer a nail into a wriggling river eel. Jeasin lifted her head and let the sounds of her cat-house fill her sensitive ears. The whooping, the moaning, the dull thudding. Normality, for now. More and more girls came to her every day, looking for a shiny coin and a way off the streets. Jeasin thumbed her nose. Coin, and her girls. Her two little cares in her dark little world. Jeasin closed her eyes and let herself drift into it.

She didn't get long. There came a timid knock at the door and a little voice called her name.

'Jeasin?' it ventured. It was little Osha.

'What?' she yelled.

The door inched open and a little face to match the little voice poked into the room. Osha had a pointy little face like a mouse's. She was still young; only just ten, if Jeasin remembered right. She was a housegirl, born and raised, literally speaking.

'There's a man here for you,' she whispered, pointing to somebody behind the door.

There was always a man somewhere in this house, sighed Jeasin. 'Tell him I ain't available. Give 'im to Latissia.'

Osha bit her lip. 'He says he wants you.'

'Well, I'm busy. Go 'way.'

Osha ducked her head behind the door and Jeasin heard some hushed mumbling, too quiet for even her to pick out. The little girl quickly returned, flapping her paw-like hands. Her nails were painted a bright, gaudy blue. The product of the boredom of one of the other girls, stuck between appointments. 'He says not for, er, *that*… He says it's business. A proper…' More mumbling from behind the door. 'A properstition.'

'*Proposition*, Osha.'

'That's it.'

'Ugh. Hold on.'

Jeasin grabbed the coin purses sitting on the side table and tucked them under the straw mattress of her bed. She stood up and wrapped the blanket tightly around her, feeling her way to the window and a little wooden box on the window-ledge. She lifted its carved lid and reached inside, feeling the cold kiss and scrape of a little blade. She tucked it under the fold of her blanket and shut the box.

'Show 'im in then.'

Osha pushed the door wider and gestured to the man. Had Jeasin been able to see him, she would have seen a tall, thin gentleman, almost treelike with his spindly arms and skinny legs, like a winter-bitten willow escaped from a riverbank. His face was gaunt, his eyes a dark shade of brown, and his nose wide and crooked, a sign it had been broken some time in the past. It hadn't been set well. His hair was shaved within a fraction of its life, so that the landscape of his skull could be seen, and already the years were beginning to pull its borders back. He wore a tight-fitting tunic and a long, heavy-looking jacket made of bear-leather.

As Osha opened the door, he took three long strides into the room and stood patiently at the corner of her bed, a round cap clutched in his hands. He stared at the woman by the window, and waited for Osha to shut the door behind him. Osha waited for Jeasin's word.

'It's alright, Osha. You can go now,' she said, trying to sense the manner of man standing in her room. The door shut and Jeasin smiled a tight, impatient smile. 'What can I do for you then?'

'Straight to the point then, miss. Right you are,' replied the man, in a clipped and formal tone. His accent was from the Leath, maybe Clannor, duchy. 'I have a proposal for you, from the Duke himself.'

At this, her ears pricked. 'Which one?'

'Why, Kiltyrin, of course. Your very duke. Kiltyrin himself.'

She wanted to ask why Farden couldn't have delivered it, but decided that was a dangerous question. The mage was right about keeping her mouth shut. Farden was supposed to be a shadow, the smoke to Kiltyrin's fire; faceless, deadly, and impossible to grasp. The Duke might get nervous should he learn that his favourite killer, and his employment, was known in a city cathouse. She had worked miracles to keep it quiet the last few years. Nobody gossiped like the girls of her house. Jeasin had often cursed the mage for telling her who and what he was; no doubt he did the same. 'And what is it?' she asked.

The man looked around at the little room, at its peeling wallpaper and well-trodden floor boards. Its rickety bed. 'A man just left this room, a man in a hood and cloak.'

Jeasin shrugged, trying not to show that her nerves had just been plucked. This line of questioning had a sharp, sour edge to it. Was this man even from the Duke? 'If you 'adn't noticed,' she pointed to her eyes. 'I don't see what people are wearin'.'

The man smiled. 'My apologies, miss. But do you know the man to which I refer?'

'I know *a* man. Don't know 'is name. Never had 'im before, sorry.'

'I already know his name. That's not what I'm after.'

'Then what d'you want from me?'

There were two thuds as the man took a step forward. Under the blanket, Jeasin throttled the handle of her little dagger. 'I noticed that you've got a lot of girls here, and not a lot of men to protect them.'

Jeasin could tell the blood was draining from her face, betraying her. Her confidence was cracking. 'It's somethin' we've been meanin' to fix,' she said.

'Guards cost a lot of coin, especially in this part of Tayn. The Duke could help you. Keep your girls safe here. Remove the competition, so to speak. Give you his seal of approval.'

'And why would 'is lordship do such a thing for me?' asked Jeasin, suspicious. Nothing like this ever came for free. Not to a woman like her.

The man spread his hands wide. 'Because you're going to do something for him.'

'Am I now?'

'When that man returns tonight, which we both know he will, I want to be in the next room, watching.'

Jeasin pulled an acidic face. 'I'm sure the Duke's business ain't whatever strange fantasies happen to light your candle, sir.'

The man laughed then, a loud braying laugh that made Jeasin jump. 'That's where you're wrong, miss, on both accounts. I just want to make sure of something, that's all. Check we've got the right man, understand? We wouldn't want our lordship making any uninformed decisions, now would we?'

Jeasin shook her head. Was this a trick? Was Farden in trouble?

'Of course not. So then, miss, will you do something for your Duke?'

'An' who's to say this man'll come back?'

The man smiled. 'I think we both know he will.'

Jeasin was torn. Torn, confused, and filled with the dull burn of unease. There was something decidedly suspicious about all of this. Why would the Duke send a man to check up on Farden? Was this man even from the Duke? In the silence after his question, she heard a bang and a crash downstairs, the man shouting something incoherent, and the unmistakable yells of women. She winced. 'I need somethin',' she blurted. 'Up front. Token o' good will.'

The man chuckled. 'The Duke and I guessed as much.' The man reached inside his coat and withdrew an envelope made of yellow parchment. He tapped the front of it, where a circular design was stamped in blood-red wax. 'Consider this a fraction of what's to come, should you play your cards right, miss. And if you have any doubt, there is a seal on the front of this envelope, made by the Duke's own ring. Have your girls take a look at it,' the man instructed. He tossed the envelope on the rumpled bed, placed his flat cap on his balding brow, and turned to leave. 'I will return in a few hours.'

Jeasin found herself asking a question. A sly hope maybe. 'An' what if he don't come back?'

The door creaked as the man opened it. There was a scuffle as Osha leapt away from the door, innocently scratching her ear. The man gave the little girl a dark look and she scuttled off down the hallway. 'He will,' he replied, and with that he shut the door, and left.

Jeasin took a big breath. Her thoughts all spoke at once, each demanding an audience. She laid her dagger on the windowsill and felt her way to the bed. She patted the sheets until she found the rough parchment envelope, ran her finger over the rubbery seal, and quickly delved inside. She froze. Very rarely did she curse her blindness and long to witness certain things, but in that moment, she did.

It wasn't every day that one gets to see their hands full to the brim with tiny, cold gemstones.

Chapter 5

"If a man is defined by his actions, then call a man who quaffs ale a drinker, call a man who plies the waves a sailor, and call a murderer a murderer."
Old Arka proverb

If there was one aspect of Tayn that annoyed Farden the most, besides the lingering odour of the canals, the infuriating and constant use of gravel as a road surface, and the dullards that inhabited its walls, it was the insects that ruled the hours of twilight.

Not content with the usual sort of flying pests, like mosquitos, gnats, moths, and the other routine offenders, Tayn's dirty canals had bred a few of its very own species in the last few years, as the winter had weakened. One of these pests in particular was something the citizens of the city had fondly dubbed "firefangs".

Farden slapped his chest for the tenth time, wondering how the creatures kept infiltrating his clothes. He winced as he felt the sting of the insect's teeth spreading across his skin. Firefangs had earned their name from the size of their vicious jaws, their burning venom, and the way they intermittently flashed with a sickly, green-yellow glow. They were like fireflies, crossed with a sabre-cat. Vicious little buggers. Nature wasn't completely merciless, however. The firefangs of Tayn came with a little advance warning. A man could see them coming for him, at least.

Farden pulled his cloak tight around his chest and folded his arms as he strode up the gentle hill towards the Duke's castle. Night had begun its descent upon Albion. The shadows had grown long and enveloped the narrower streets. Around him people were hurrying home, shops were shutting, and lamps were being lit. Farden kept his head down and kept walking, ignoring all. The air around him hummed with the wings of countless hungry insects. He could feel them on his ears. He ducked every time he saw a bright flash of sickly glow. The slight breeze did nothing to deter the bastards; the sunny afternoon had made them thirsty and bold, and now they were out in force. Farden hurried on, watching the growing darkness pulsate and flash. A cluster of them pulsated in the mouth of a nearby alleyway, circling around a mottled wolfhound sleeping in a shop doorway. Farden gave them a wide berth, breaking into a stiff jog. A pained yelping chased him.

Farden looked up at the hulking blotch of rock that leant against the darkening sky, Castle Tayn itself. From high above, he imagined that Tayn looked a little like a pointy hat, half-drowned by a brown ribbon of river. Tayn was a relatively new city compared to the others of the duchy, barely a hundred years old. During its construction, the builders of the city had used the rocks and mud from the nearby hills to ford the river it sat on, and they had centred their efforts around a natural spike of limestone that rose vertically out of the water like a spear out of a corpse. It was on that spike of rock that Kiltyrin had built Tayn's castle. Why the builders hadn't been content with building the city *next* to the river, Farden would never know. He doubted even the Duke knew, and if he did, he probably didn't care. Besides, intentional or not, what better display of resources and power was there than successfully building a city in the middle of a river?

Like the jumbled buildings that surrounded it, Castle Tayn was a mound of grey parapets, walkways, angles, towers, and walls, all of which clung onto the huge limestone shard for dear life. It was actually quite an impressive structure, considering its foundations. During the long ascent to its gates, to numb the dull boredom of the climb, Farden always found himself counting the castle's myriad windows. He had never finished.

The gravel road curved gently to the right and took a steep turn as it reached up to meet the castle's gates. Farden strode up the hill, breathing heavily. He was tired. He had already walked several hundred miles; his legs didn't need the extra exercise. With a grimace, the mage ignored them and kept walking.

As he reached the gates, he wasn't surprised to find them wide open, and himself thoroughly ignored. As always, the guards, standing like bored statues, tried their best not to look at him. They had seen him coming. They had their orders. Unchallenged, Farden sauntered through the gates and into the narrow corridor betwixt the first set of walls. The same thing happened at the second gate, and at the third, until he was walking through the bowels of the castle, padding softly across the limestone and granite floors, followed by glances and hushed whispers. Everybody, save a privileged few, knew better than to speak to him. Such things were forbidden in Castle Tayn.

Farden found a flight of stairs and barged past a group of women. One tutted loudly, and was about to add some venomous words when one of her friends, nervously eyeing the brown stained sack hanging from Farden's shoulder, grabbed her wrist and shook her head. The mage walked on. His head was pounding now. He tried his best to ignore it.

At the top of the stairs was a man with a halberd, clad in an ill-fitting suit of mail. He stepped into Farden's path and lowered his weapon. Farden halted several steps down, crossed his arms, and stared at the sharp steel point hovering in his face. His eyes wandered up the weapon to its owner. The man was bald, with a scar across his forehead. The rest of his face was like an avalanche. He had quite obviously suffered some sort of awful injury in the past. His nose and cheekbones were squashed and broken inwards, his top row of teeth seemed to be missing, and one eye was now considerably lower than the other. It was quite a dreadful sight. Farden took a good hard look at him. There was something about him that the mage couldn't quite put his finger on. Something he recognised. 'Do I know you?' he asked, squinting.

The man waved his halberd. 'No, an' I don't know yer. So turn around,' he said, whistling oddly through the gaps in his teeth.

Farden shook his head. 'Let me guess. You're new here, aren't you?'

The man nodded.

Farden pushed the point of the halberd out of his face. It quickly returned. 'The Duke wants to see me. So either you move out of my way, or you can be thrown out of it.' The man opened his mouth to speak, but nothing came out. A strange look came over his landslide face then, and he slowly but surely stepped aside. 'Good man,' muttered the mage, as he passed him. It was then that a voice echoed around through the hallways, a voice with a shrill edge to it, like a dagger scraping across glass. It stopped Farden in his tracks. It made his insides groan.

'Better remember that face, Wartan. He ain't one for patience!' it hollered.

It was quickly joined by another, a deeper, booming voice, equally as exasperating.

'Especially when he's late!'

Farden closed his eyes and begged for patience. Before he could escape down the corridor, two sets of hands clapped him heavily on his back. Farden reluctantly turned around to face their aggravating owners.

To say the thought of drowning these two men in a shallow puddle had occasionally crossed Farden's mind would have been a severe understatement. He longed for the day the Duke ordered their quiet removal. Longed for it, dreamt about it. For the last ten years they had made it their mission to irritate the mage to the point of violence. That was their goal of course; they wanted to see what the mage was made of, mainly so they could try to fight whatever it was. So far, Farden had not given them the satisfaction.

Farden raised his eyes to look at their grinning, oafish faces. If ever two men were to be chosen to be the definition of thug, these were the two for the job.

Kint was a thin slice of a man with a narrow face. He was wiry, taller than Farden, and apparently handsome, according to the tittering castle maids. They must have been short-sighted, or desperate, or both. Kint was the smarter of the two, if that were possible, a merchant of sarcasm and the proud owner of a furious temper. Word had it that he had killed over thirty men, and had tattooed every single one of their names on his upper arms. Nobody knew for sure. He never let anybody get close enough to see. Kint and his shrill tongue had a sinister reputation in the city taverns. Worse still, nobody had ever plucked up the testicular fortitude to challenge him, on account of him being one of the Duke's right-hand men, of course. That, and his irrefutable skill with a blade. So it was that Kint was now the bearer of an ego so big, Farden marvelled that his neck didn't snap. He turned to his counterpart.

Fat Forluss was exactly that. The most redeeming part of the man was his skill as the castle's torturer, if that could be called redeeming. It was a skill anyway, though there are some skills the world can do without. Rumour had it Fat Forluss could show a man his own heart before he died. He was a huge man, constantly sweating and dabbing his damp forehead with his grotty sleeve. He sported a giant brown beard that rested over his protuberant belly and a mop of brown hair tied back in a tail behind his head. Farden tried to remember a time when he had ever seen him without his favourite toy, a nasty-looking club, the one currently hanging from his belt. The thing was a knotted limb of oak that bristled with shards of glass, bent nails, barbed wire, and a variety of other sharp and ugly things. Forlass had even given the gruesome-looking thing a name: he called it "The Fiend."

'I've patience enough to stomach you two,' spat Farden.

They stared at Farden with sneering looks, marvelling at the mud on his clothes. The mage could almost hear the cogs of their small minds whirring.

Kint sniffed. 'Patience that the Duke don't share, Farden Four-Hand,' he jibed, ogling his missing finger. It was an insult that Farden hated with a passion.

Fat Forluss let out a low, ponderous chuckle. His belly wobbled with it. He pointed at the cloth sack that was slung over the mage's shoulder. 'Yeah. He ain't happy with you. You're two days late.'

'Says who?' Farden spat.

'Says me,' Kint butted in. He put his hands on his belt buckle. Farden could see his cocky smile fading into something much nastier.

'Did you give me the job?' countered the mage.

Kint sniffed. 'Duke relies on me to make sure his orders is carried out, whatever they be. That means making sure you do your job properly,' he said. At his side, Forluss sniggered.

Farden flung back his hood. 'And who's watching you, Kint? This fat lump?' he challenged, pointing at Forluss.

If Forluss hated anything, it was being called fat. Unfortunate, really, for a man of his size. He laid his fingers on the hilt of The Fiend. 'Say that again, I dares you.'

Farden's headache was pounding now. His own fingers itched for his knife. Itched to let it loose and finally put an end to the two detestable bastards that stood glaring at him. The mage clenched his fists, eyes burning. No, he told himself. It was more trouble than it was worth. It hurt to do it, but the mage shook his head and turned around. 'You're not worth the time of day,' he mumbled.

Kint laughed again as Farden stomped down the corridor. 'We never are.'

'Coward,' chuckled Forluss.

It took everything Farden had to keep walking.

Thankfully he did not have far to go. He ascended several more flights of curving stairs until he reached the main tower and the Duke's own door. Kiltyrin's crest had been painted on the door: a crimson three-pointed shield, a pair of crossed daggers, and a black cat. Whoever had painted the door had embedded two shards of jet into the wood to fashion the cat's eyes. The mage looked up at the feline as he reached out to bang on its chest. Farden could have sworn the eyes moved.

He barely had a chance to touch the wood before it was swiftly wrenched open by a sobbing man clutching a hand to his ear. Blood was leaking from the gaps between his shaking fingers. Farden moved aside to let him leave, which he did, and very quickly too. Farden shrugged, and entered the room. The Duke was standing next to a huge fireplace. He was wiping something with a white handkerchief and muttering to himself. 'Shut that behind you,' he said.

'Another eavesdropper?' asked the mage, pushing the door shut with the toe of his boot. He looked down. Like tiny crimson stepping stones across a sea of limestone tiles, little droplets of blood led an unswerving path towards the Duke. Farden found himself deliberately stepping on them, making little smears across the tiles as he scuffed them. At least there was less blood than last time. Kiltyrin made it his personal duty to slice an ear off anybody he or his men caught eavesdropping or gossiping. The first time, they lost the right ear. The second time, they lost the left. If they were stupid enough to be caught a third time, then they lost their balance, usually whilst standing on the ramparts of Castle Tayn's highest tower. Farden had to admit, the servants were slow learners.

'They're like rats in a cheese-cupboard,' hissed Kiltyrin. He tossed whatever he was wiping onto a nearby desk. The blade landed with a heavy thud and the handkerchief quickly followed. He turned and assessed the mage. 'No matter how many traps you set, the bastards keep coming back.'

'Apparently so,' mumbled Farden.

Kiltyrin walked over to a large window and spread his hands across the windowsill. His face glowed orange in the city lights. The years were starting to turn on the Duke; his once fire-red hair was greying at the edges, as was his trademark goatee. The stresses of long days of politics and longer nights of scheming were beginning to show in the form of creases at the corners of his eyes and lips. His once-muscular build had sagged in certain places. Simply, he was growing old. Now, for a Duke, that also meant growing desperate.

There comes a time in every man's life when he begins to sift through his life, sort through the countless sea of moments and nuances and try to condense it into the crash and pound of the shores of the current, to take stock of what he is. Memories, they say, make a man, but a lifetime of them, like a handful of dry sand gripped hard, sneaking through fingers, is hard to hold, fragile and finite. And, like his bones and skin, memories also die with him. So he turns to what he has in front of him, to the scars, to the weight of his purse, or the fields he still toils in, or the view from his castle window, to see what he has made of himself. A man's final handful of years hinge on whether he is content with what he finds there, or whether he is disappointed. Kiltyrin was beginning to look from his castle window, and look hard. 'You're two days later than I expected,' he began.

'So Kint told me.' Kiltyrin turned and raised an eyebrow. Farden swallowed something bitter in his throat. 'I'm sorry,' replied the mage.

'Was it done as I stipulated?'

Farden rolled the sack off his shoulder and walked over to the window. He dropped it onto the floor beside the Duke's left shoe. 'Every last little bit.'

Kiltyrin looked down at the sack. 'Show me.'

Farden knelt and gingerly prized it open. After a week on the road wrapped in a sack, the disembodied head was starting to rot. Fortunately, he had wrapped it in another bit of cloth so as to keep the smell from arousing suspicion.

Using the tips of his fingers, Farden picked apart the cloth, grimacing as he did so. He held it open long enough so that Kiltyrin could peer inside and see the dead face staring back at him. Its eyes were milky, and its face was beginning to turn the colour of winter lichen, but he recognised it well enough. 'And there you are, Havanth. I bet your father is reconsidering now, hmm? How I wish I could mount your face on my wall for when he next visits,' muttered Kiltyrin, more to himself than to the mage. He looked up at the wall to the left of the window, where a herd of disembodied animals hung on plaques and hooks. They grinned at the two men standing below them, lips shrunken and stiff with resin, peeled back to show their sharp teeth. Deer, boars, sabre-cats, ice bears, even the enormous tusked face of a bastion clung to the wall. Farden had seen the Duke's grisly collection many times before, and he wasn't surprised to see a few new additions.

Kiltyrin waved his hand at the sack. Wrinkling his nose, he turned back to his view. 'Toss it in the fire before it fills my room with its stink.'

Farden nodded and quietly obeyed. The fire in the huge brick fireplace was already roaring. Farden tossed the head, sack and all, into the fire. It landed in a fountain of sparks and a burst of flame, and the mage leant forward to hold his hands near the flames, cleansing them of the smell of the rotting head. A flame caught his finger, and he flinched away, hissing through his teeth at the unexpected pain. He heard the soft scuffing of Kiltyrin's shoes behind him.

'Something wrong, Farden?'

Farden swiftly stood up and clenched his fist. He tried his best to ignore the pain in his finger. 'Not at all,' he quickly replied.

Kiltyrin had a sly look on his face. 'You haven't burnt yourself, have you? Farden the old mage? Surely not. Too much of that nevermar, that's your problem,' he mused, sardonically.

Farden glowered and sat down on a neighbouring chair. He turned to stare at the fire, which was now sizzling and spitting as it attempted to devour the sack and its putrescent contents. 'Good riddance, I say.'

'You look uncomfortable, Farden, why don't you take off your cloak and your pack?'

'I'm fine.'

'Suit yourself,' Kiltyrin shook his head. 'Wine?' he offered.

Farden shook his head, even though his mouth was dust-dry. His brain was pummelling him from the inside. The tips of his fingers ached. Something about Kiltyrin's mood had put him on edge. He had borne the brunt of these moods before. Suddenly he couldn't wait to leave.

'No of course not.' Kiltyrin got up and went to a table, where a carafe of ruby red wine sat lingering in the light of the fire. The Duke poured himself a large glass with one hand while opening a drawer with his other. Out of the drawer came a leather bag tied tightly with a string. The coins inside it clinked as he set it on the tabletop. Farden gazed at the pouch, already dividing its contents up in his head. *A quarter for the jester, some for supplies, clothes, food... Food I can do without...* Kiltyrin left the pouch on the table, sipped his wine, and began to pace up and down in front of the fireplace. 'I have another job for you,' he said.

Something inside Farden sank while simultaneously another part of him perked up, sending a little whisper to scuttle through his mind, a whisper of coin and something else. He tore his eyes from the leather bag. 'Who is it this time?'

Kiltyrin smiled contentedly. Farden might have pretended to be different, but like every other thug under his thumb, he still had his weaknesses. Kiltyrin prided himself on being able to weasel out the weaknesses of a man. It was the only thing that never changed between a peasant and a Duke, and it was the secret of how far he had come in the last ten years. Sometimes it was a wife. A son. Or daughter. Sometimes it was a field, others a house. Sometimes it was as simple as a pat on the back. But more often than not it was coin. Cold, dull, coin.

Farden was no different.

Kiltyrin came right out and said it. 'Duke Wodehallow,' he hissed quietly.

The mage was shocked to say the least. 'You want me to kill a *Duke*?'

'Are you deaf, man?'

'No,' replied Farden. 'It's just you've never made a move this bold before.'

'And why should that be any of your business, Farden? Tell me that. I don't keep you around for your opinion. I keep you around because you're good at killing things. Damn good. Don't think that because you once had the ears of the Arkmages means you can comment on my orders.' Farden simmered quietly in his chair. Kiltyrin sipped his wine. 'Ah yes, you forget that I know everything about you,' he chuckled.

Farden shrugged. Kiltyrin liked to remind him every now and again. It was rather like reminding the man who had just fallen from a cliff how high the cliff was. 'It doesn't matter to me,' he grunted.

'Yes, I know all about you,' chuckled Kiltyrin. 'You and your story. I have eyes and ears all over Emaneska these days. Farden the outcast, the dangerous one, hiding in a Written's skin. Arkmage Vice's prodigy with a princess beneath the sheets. A lowly soldier who thought he saved the world... Now look at you. Farden Four-Hand. You're a fairytale tragedy if you ask me.'

The words grated against the mage's ears, grit against raw skin. A decade and a half ago he would have beaten the Duke to a pulp just for daring to utter them. Now, he bit the inside of his lip, tasting his own blood. This wasn't the first time Kiltyrin had berated him like this. It was his way of keeping the mage in place and, sadly, it worked. The years had been long under Kiltyrin's shadow. The darkness had eroded him more than Farden was prepared to admit. 'And as I keep telling you, that Farden died a long time ago,' mumbled the mage.

'And yet they still look for him. Yes. I thought that might surprise you. An Arka man came to me a few months ago, asking if I had ever had dealings with a Written mage. He didn't mention your name, but you fitted his description almost perfectly, the same as when I first found you, the year of the Battle. Fancy that.'

Farden scrunched up his face. 'And what did you say?'

Kiltyrin rolled his eyes. 'Relax. Do you think you'd be here today if I had said yes?'

The mage shook his head.

'Of course you wouldn't. Why would I give up my best assassin? My favourite killer?'

Farden sat very still whilst Kiltyrin paced back and forth some more. He stared at the fire for a moment. 'What was his name, the man they sent?' he finally asked.

'I didn't catch it. I doubt he was anyone important,' Kiltyrin smirked behind the lip of his wine glass.

'Oh.' Farden picked dirt from his nails. He didn't care anyway. It changed nothing.

'To business then,' announced the Duke.

Kiltyrin walked over to the table and snatched up the leather bag. Farden quickly stood up. The Duke couldn't help but sneer. He flicked the bag as if to throw it, but then changed his mind at the very last second. The mage flinched, and then glared. 'Look at you,' chuckled the Duke. 'I've had you figured out since we first met at the Bartering. Part of me hoped that under my wing you might have shone, grown, blossomed even, set yourself apart from the rest of the brainless thugs outside that door. I hoped a man like you might actually be different from the drunkards and the brawlers. You could have become my right-hand man. A lord in your own right. But instead all I see in the man slouching before me is just another blade for hire, a drug addict, a beggar on a street with his hand out for charity, just like the rest. Look at you, eyeing this,' he jiggled the leather bag in his hand. 'It's all you want, isn't it?'

Farden took a step forward and for the tiniest of moments the Duke's contemptuous expression cracked just a little. Only for a moment. Farden pulled his black hood over his throbbing head. 'What I'd like to know is, why does everybody think it's their right to tell me what's wrong with me?'

'Because there's barely any right in you to mention,' he spat. 'Now, are you going to kill the Duke, or have you had enough? Hmm?' The Duke waggled the pouch of coins.

'Do I have a choice?'

'You've always had a choice, Farden. Keep doing what I say or go back to living in a hovel in the hills like a leper, with no coin and no nevermar. Who knows, maybe you could take up holding passersby at knifepoint? I imagine that would be easy to turn your hand to.'

'Unlike you, I still have morals to which I abide.' *Did he though, really?*

That made Kiltyrin grin. 'Do you now? An assassin, with morals. Tell me, which of us in this room is the murderer?'

Who's more of a murderer, the one who holds the knife, or the one who pays him to hold it? The mage thought, but he said nothing. 'I want four times the coin,' he spat.

'Two times.'

'Three.'

'Twice. One now. One when you return. That should keep you in your beloved nevermar for at least a few months.'

Farden bit his lip again, and stiffly held out a hand. He soon found a heavy pouch of coin occupying it. 'Give me your orders then,' he muttered.

Kiltyrin waved his hand. 'On the table, near the door.'

Farden looked confused.

The Duke turned his back on the mage and walked to his window, waving his hand at the door, the paintings, and the grisly trophies. 'Rats have ears, Farden. Rats have very, very good ears. Now get out of my sight.'

Farden turned around and sauntered over to the little table by the door. He spied a lonely slip of parchment sitting on top of it. But as he reached out for it, it was the shining object sitting just to the right of the little table, the object perching on top of a flat-topped oak chest, the object that gleamed and shone in the light, forcing the flames to play in its facets and polished curves, that caught his attention.

Farden almost tripped when he saw it.

'Something wrong?' asked Kiltyrin, watching intently from the windowsill.

Farden could feel his eyes on the back of his head, and his thoughts turned to the vambraces nestled deep and safe in his pack. Farden cleared his throat, and stamped his boot on the floor, as if punishing it for tripping him. He kept his back to Kiltyrin. 'No,' he coughed.

Farden approached the table and picked up the folded parchment that held the particulars of his next murder. He pretended to fold it and fiddle with it while his eyes eagerly took in every glistening inch of the armour, barely a foot from him. Forged from the trademark gold and red metal, it was a Scalussen breastplate, and a fine one at that. Its scales were etched with circles and spirals and filigreed runes. No straps could be spied at its edges, no fastenings. No strings. No hinges reared their greased heads, and no rivets dared to show their flat and beaten faces. There was a depiction of an insect on its central plate; a shallow carving of a beetle in flight, with two tiny rubies for eyes. Like every piece of Scalussen work, magick or ordinary, it was a work of art. Farden's finger itched to touch it, to feel it. To test it.

'Caught your eye, has it?' asked the Duke, smiling proudly. He strolled towards the mage.

Farden played innocent. His pack suddenly felt very heavy on his shoulders. 'What?'

'That, there, by your elbow. That *exquisite* piece of armour.'

'Oh, that,' replied Farden, trying to sound nonchalant.

'Yes, that. A present from a friend in the Crumbled Empire. I did a deal with him a few months ago, and seeing as most of the old Skölgard nobles are considerably short of coin these days, he paid me with this. I think I came off the richer of the two, don't you?'

Farden nodded. He stared at the breastplate, trying to find a fault in it, a scratch, something that screamed *fake*. If only he could run a finger across it to feel if it had any power, he strained. See if it shivered like his other pieces did.

'I suppose you've seen a few like it, in your time?' asked Kiltyrin. Farden shook his head and the Duke laughed. Of course he had. 'Now I doubt that very much. You must have seen Scalussen armour before today?'

Farden tapped his shoulders. 'Never bothered much with armour. Used to slow the magick.' It was true. Some metals like lead and bronze slowed the flow of magick, while others, like the Arka blacksmiths made for the Arkathedral and Evernia guard, could deflect it. Steel was usually fine. Iron tended to melt. It depended on whatever spells the blacksmith uttered or carved into the metal during the making. But Scalussen was different. It allowed magick to flow as freely as it did through skin and bone. It had been one of the first reasons for his falling in love with it.

Kiltyrin kept pressing. 'Well, surely you must have heard of it? Heard the fables of its Smiths? The eddas?' he asked.

The mage shook his head and shrugged again. 'A few. Impenetrable stuff.'

Kiltyrin walked forward to admire his prize. Even he didn't touch it, as if it were deathly fragile. They both knew that was far, far from the truth. 'All Scalussen armour is extraordinary, but only a precious few, if they even exist at all, are legendary. The eddas say that in the troubled times of the old Scattered Kingdoms, the Scalussen smiths created nine suits of flawless armour, perfect in every way. Impenetrable, as you said. In fact, they even protected their wearers in ways the smiths didn't originally intend. Not just against swords and spears, but *time* itself, Farden. *Age*. This armour protected its wearer from the weapons and wounds of time itself. So it was that the smiths decided that in such war-torn times there should be a set of knights that could wear the Nine, and protect their makers and Emaneska. Of course, like all noble ideals, they failed.

'The Nine filled every king, queen, duke, and lord with either greed or fear. Army after army marched on Scalussen, and war was declared on the smiths and their Scalussen Knights. In time, they were wiped from the earth, all their secrets and skill lost.' Kiltyrin paused to smirk. 'According to the skalds the Knights threw themselves into a volcano to stop the war, to rid the world of the armour, once and for all. But I know better. You don't just throw away something like that. Stolen and scattered, I think. Like in some of your Arka songs. Pieces of the Nine out there somewhere, I believe it. Not that I think this is one of the Nine, mind you, but even ordinary Scalussen armour is said to have some strange properties to it. Magick or not, it's mine now. I'd like to see an assassin's dagger get through that.'

Farden snorted. He felt like braying with laughter. So the Duke's latest scheme was hunting the Nine. Of course it was. It made perfect sense. There wasn't a single thread in Emaneska that Kiltyrin wasn't trying to tug at with his greedy, conniving fingers. Farden knew that better than anyone. If the thread couldn't be tugged, wrapped around Kiltyrin's finger, Farden was sent to cut it. That was how it had worked, for fifteen years.

A fear dawned on him then. Was the Duke aware of his vambraces, his gauntlets, or his greaves? Did he know? He had eyes everywhere, after all. But Farden had been more than meticulous. Before, he would have worn them brazenly and smirked in the face of anyone who challenged him for it. These days, anybody who was lucky enough to glimpse his armour found their throat slit soon after. Farden had realised very early on that now, in this life, in this current company, it was far wiser to avoid greedy eyes, his current company especially. Farden would never have admitted it, but hiding under his skin was the fear that he could no longer protect it if he was challenged.

'What?' the Duke was eyeing him intensely.

Farden tucked his orders into the pocket of his grey trousers. He felt the urge to leave. 'There's always something, Kiltyrin. There's always a piece of armour that stops you ageing, or a sword that shoots fireballs, or some sort of cheese that makes you bloody invisible. The eddas wouldn't be eddas without them. When are people going to learn they're just songs?' he said with a sigh, trying his best to appear as though he didn't care If Kiltyrin was hunting the Nine, then Farden would have to redouble his efforts to keep his armour out of sight.

Kiltyrin narrowed his eyes. 'Probably when they stop being true,' he said. 'Didn't I tell you to get out of my sight? Get out. And remember, I want Wodehallow's head. I don't care how. Slink back to whatever hole you hide in, but make sure the job gets done. You have two weeks.'

Farden walked to the door. 'Clear a space on your wall. And have the coin ready.'

Kiltyrin watched him leave. The door clicked shut behind him and the Duke shook his head. He grabbed the Scalussen breastplate with one hand and lifted it up to shake it viciously back and forth. It wobbled and moaned until something inside it twanged, like the sound of a tense ljot string giving up on life. The Duke threw the flimsy fake onto his bed and went back to his window. It had done its job.

He heard the man let himself in and lock the door behind him, but he ignored him for a moment, waiting for him to announce himself.

'It's all arranged,' said the man.

Kiltyrin nodded.

'Did it work?' the man asked.

'Exactly as we hoped. Couldn't take his eyes off it. Make sure you congratulate your man in the forge.'

A silence. 'Do you think he still has them?'

'You've seen his face. He hasn't aged a day. You were right.'

'Well, we'll know for sure tonight.'

'Make sure he doesn't spot you.'

'Nobody ever does.'

'You'd better hope not. If he doesn't rip your throat out, I will.'

There was a polite chuckle. 'Without me, Duke, you'd be none the wiser. Just remember our deal.'

❦

Farden left the Duke's room and scuffed his boots along the limestone floor. A man walked towards him, a tall man in a bear-leather jacket with a shaven head and a broken nose. He had a flat cap in his hands. He nodded to the mage and smiled. Farden just scowled and walked past him. He had no friends in Tayn. He didn't need to pretend.

A lesser man might have emerged from such a meeting with a tremble on his lip and a down-trodden heart. A better man wouldn't have entertained the thought of such a meeting at all. Farden thought himself somewhere in the middle. Coin was coin. All his life, he had been trained to kill, so why should he not charge for it now? As a drunk man had once whispered to him in a lonely tavern, if you are good at something, never do it for free. Besides, he had spent a long time learning to ignore, and to justify, the sour taste of his contemptible profession. He was now somewhat of an expert at it. What did he care about the people of Albion?

But it was not his murderous job that was tugging at his mind, it was the Duke himself. Kiltyrin's vindictive words had stung the mage. The mention of the Nine had prickled him, and the meeting had dug at some old wounds and sore spots that Farden had thought he had buried. A life he had left behind. Mistakes he had made. Fortunately, Farden had learnt exactly how to deal with these sorts of thoughts too. Like little corpses that refused to stay dead, the answer was to bury them once again. Only deeper.

The mage retraced his steps back to the lower levels of the castle, avoiding Kint and Fat Forluss in the process. He traipsed through the corridors and hallways and found his way to one of the smaller banquet halls, near to the north wing of Castle Tayn, where the windows tentatively peered out over the precipitous edge of the limestone spire. The hall was empty for the most part. A few of the castle's kitchen boys lounged in a corner, laughing and tossing a pair of dice against the wall, betting meals and days off. They stiffened at the sound of boots, but Farden ignored them, and so they went back to their huddled gambling.

Farden wasn't interested in them. He was interested in the colourful little character that was crouched on a stool in the far corner of the room, squinting at an upside-down book and humming to himself. Farden walked towards him, quickly, eagerly, hand already molesting the warm coins in his pocket.

Bastio was the very definition of a sore thumb. He was an eye-offending splash of colour in the middle of Castle Tayn's palette of greyscale stone and tired wood. He had the look of a skinny rat that had been doused in paints and left to dry. His attire wasn't out of choice, no, of course not; a castle's jester always wore what he was told. Or else. In this case, he had been given a headache-inducing one-piece outfit of lemon yellow, spattered with a sky blue and moss-green diamond pattern. His pointy hat was a dark red, and his shoes the same, only muddier. It was almost as if a rainbow had vomited upon him.

Farden grabbed a stool in passing and sat down next to the man. Bastio was the type of fellow that always moved in quick, jerky increments, like a rodent, always snatching, twitching. It wouldn't have been a problem had it not been for the fact that his hat and clothing were festooned with tiny bells. Every time he moved they tittered and chimed with him, making every little movement annoyingly musical. To make it worse, the jester also had a habit of humming. No wonder Bastio spent most of his days alone, thought Farden. More than an hour in the man's company could have driven anybody to a level of madness.

Farden looked at the book, and then back to Bastio. His mouth moved as if trying on the words for size. The mage leant forward. 'You know it's upside down, don't you?'

Bastio stopped humming for a moment. He gave the mage a suspicious glance, and then turned the book around so he could assess the truth of that statement. On seeing that the title of his book was lingering near the bottom of the cover, he huffed and flipped the book the right way up. 'What d'you want, Four-Hand?' he asked. 'Cannae a man read in peace?'

'That usually depends on whether he can read or not.'

'I can read.'

Farden reached out and snatched the book out of his hands 'What's the book about?'

Bastio crossed his arms with a jingle. 'What'll it be then, Farden?'

'Double what I had last time.'

Bastio winced and rubbed his hands together. 'Double? Might wanna have a think 'bout that, Four-Hand. Prices 'ave gone up.'

Farden scowled. 'What?'

The jester tried to look as innocent as possible. 'Taxes, see.'

'Taxes? What taxes?'

'My taxes, Four-Hand. For reading lessons.'

'Don't test me, clown. I'm not in the mood. I'd hate to see you try to play the lute with a pair of broken hands.'

If Bastio was worried by that threat, he didn't show it. 'My prices are what they are. 'Less of course, if'n you want to try findin' another like me in this town, one that'll do business with the likes o' you.'

Farden stared hard at the skinny man. Bastio stared right back with his beady little eyes. This game was loaded in the jester's favour and they both knew it. Farden hadn't ever been clever enough to hide the intensity of his habit. Bastio knew this very well.

Farden stood up. 'Maybe I'll do just that.'

Bastio simply chuckled, jingling.

The mage clenched a fist, briefly contemplated beating it out of the man, and then sat down again. 'How much are we talking?'

'Two bags. Fifty.'

'Silver?'

'Gold.'

'Gold?! If you think this is funny...' growled Farden. *What else had he expected from a jester?* He dug deep into his pocket and let his hand hover there, finger and thumb pinching the coins to count them. Fifty was half what the Duke had paid him. 'Thirty. I should get a discount. Nobody else buys as much as I do.'

'You say it like it's a good thing, Four-Hand. I ain't ever seen a man like it as much as you. Rot your brain one day, you will.'

'And that would be my business, not yours.'

Bastio rubbed his chin. 'Forty-five.'

'Thirty-five.'

'Forty.'

'Fine,' Farden consented, eager to leave. He could almost smell the scent of the nevermar escaping the jester's pocket, taunting him. Farden licked his lips.

Bastio reached inside his multicoloured collar. Farden looked around warily. He needn't have bothered, but old habits died the hardest. Nevermar wasn't forbidden in Albion like it was to the Arka. In Krauslung, Manesmark, or Essen, the rules had always been that anybody found with it had the nevermar confiscated and burnt, and a black eye or worse to show for it. Mages were lucky if they spent a few months in the Arkathedral cells. Written faced a hanging from the gates. No exceptions. It was a wise approach from the magick council: a completely intolerant approach meant nevermar and its ilk were very hard to come by in Arka lands. Temptation was a foreign thing. It was a fine idea if a mage never left Arka lands, but as Farden had discovered very early on, the rest of Emaneska had never been so strict.

Bastio produced a cloth bag from his pocket. Farden snatched it quickly. He teased apart the neck of the bag and peered inside to assess his spoils. He let the bitter-sweet, oleaginous tentacles of its scent fill his nose and his forehead.

'Hâlorn's finest that is,' said Bastio, proudly. Farden wasn't listening. His mind was already halfway out the castle and filled with smoke.

'Mhm,' the mage hummed. He got to his feet and tucked the cloth bag deep into the inner pocket of his cloak. 'It better be. Now if you'll excuse me…'

'I wager that I'll be seeing you soon enough, Four-Hand,' Bastio sniggered.

'Any time would be too soon.'

The little man smiled. 'Enjoy.'

Farden didn't reply. Feeling slightly cheated and yet strangely satisfied at the same time, he left Bastio to his book and made for whatever door could lead him out of Castle Tayn. The mage wasn't in the mood for any more of today. Farden had often contemplated buying a hawk to relay his orders and bags of gold to and from the Duke. That way he wouldn't have to see anyone at all besides the people he killed, and they wouldn't bother him. Not for long anyway. Farden could be what he wanted to be, a ghost. Farden shook his head. Gold via a hawk. He hadn't even touched the nevermar yet.

The mage strode down the halls, barging some of the slower people aside. Their yelps and cries of surprise were music to his ears. Once he had descended to the lowest level of the Castle, he spotted a purple square of torchlit sky sitting in the gap between two open doors, and set a course for it, like a ship escaping a storm.

He was almost free when he heard a high-pitched shout from behind him.

'Farden!'

Farden stopped inches from the doorway. The guards stared dully at him. Farden knew exactly who was calling him, and that knowledge made him smile just a little.

The mage turned around to find a woman, slightly grey of hair, slim, and somewhat attractive, walking towards him down the corridor. She had a small smile on her lips. There was a small rusty-haired boy by her side, his expression as vile as the little trickle of snot that was slowly making good its escape from his left nostril. It was Kiltyrin's son, Timeon, and already every inch his father and growing more every day. He had his hands firmly clasped behind his back. He couldn't have been more than eleven years old, yet he was glaring at the mage as if he held an ancient grudge against him.

'Farden Four-Hand. Here at my father's bidding, are you?' he piped out, voice squeaky in its youth. Farden made a point of snorting at him, and looked to his mother, the Duke's lonely wife, Moirin.

'Leaving already?' she asked him.

Farden let his shoulders rise up, helpless. 'Orders are orders.'

'Only if you follow them,' she smiled, a vacant sort of smile, sad, resigned, yet one that still curled in a way that was reminiscent of brighter days of wit and charm. Farden found himself smiling back, but it was then that he noticed a slight smudge of yellow on the angle of her jaw. Half a week old maybe. He reached out a hand to examine it, but she flinched away. The brat by her side coughed noisily.

'I thought he had stopped coming to see you?' Farden asked, ignoring Timeon. The boy was one big scowl. He spared a quick glance at him, and spied the faint shadow of a bruise on his pale wrist too.

Moirin made her excuses. 'A banquet for one of his Fidlarig friends. He was drunk.'

Farden clenched his fist so hard that one of his knuckles clicked. Moirin moved her dark hair forward to hide the bruise. Farden had first met her a long time ago, a year or so before Timeon had been born. She had been a striking, sharp-tongued lady of Kiltyrin's court, well-known for her activities during banquets, and after them too. In the first few years, when Farden had been invited to accompany the Duke to banquets with more than a dubious guestlist, he had often found her outside, roaming the gardens. They had spent the nights talking. Only talking. It had been all Farden could manage at the time. The thoughts of Cheska were still rawer than a battlefield. He had long suspected that his past inaction nettled her, but they had never spoken of it.

Now, however, Moirin was more like a rusty trophy than a wife, one that had been assumed gold, but found to be brass, and thus locked in an attic. Kiltyrin usually ordered her confined to the sanctuary in the eastern corner of the castle, kept out of sight, just as he liked her to be. That way she could be ignored, summoned when needed, and in the meantime keep Timeon out of the way until he was old enough to be interesting. The little brat might have been a boil on the cheek of Castle Tayn, but giving birth to him had been Moirin's saving grace.

Farden looked at the stairs he had come down, as if contemplating going back up them, but instead he just grunted, and shrugged. 'Drunk,' was all he could say. Moirin pursed her lips, almost as if disappointed.

'Gods, Farden, it's not the first time in this world that a husband's taken his hand to his wife,' she said. *And not the last*, Farden inwardly hissed.

Timeon piped up again. 'So, Four-Hand, what's my father making you do now, hmm?'

'None of your bloody business, Dukeling.'

Timeon went as red as his hair. 'You can't speak to me like that.'

Farden contemplated flicking him in the face, hard, just on the bridge of his nose where it would make his eyes water. The idea of the wailing wretch fleeing down the corridor almost made him smile. But he didn't. He restrained himself, out of respect for Moirin. He prodded the boy in the chest instead. 'You aren't Duke yet, Timeon. 'Til you are, I'll speak to you how I please.'

'One day…' Timeon burbled. 'One day you'll… you'll…' but he lacked the cerebral wherewithal to finish his threat. This time, Farden did smile.

Moirin pointed her son up the corridor. 'Timeon, go wait for me on the stairs.'

'But…!'

'Go!'

Timeon sullenly did as he was told and stalked off, stumbling for a moment over his own laces. Farden heard the faint hiss of a snigger from the guards behind him.

Moirin watched her son stamp across the floor. 'He will be Duke one day.'

'Now there's a scary thought.'

There was a moment. Moirin leant a little closer. 'So what has my husband got you doing this time?'

'You know he'd beat you for asking me that. Better if I don't say. Better if…'

'…If I don't know.' Moirin nodded. 'I understand. Just make sure you don't get yourself killed doing my husband's dirty work. Somebody might miss you,' she sighed, and slowly turned to walk away. Her long velvet skirts made it look as if she were floating across the stone. Farden's eyes followed her to the stairs. She didn't turn back to look at him. Only Timeon looked back. He had the gall to flash a pair of fingers at the mage before his mother slapped him across the cheek. Farden grinned at that. *Make hay while the sun shines, why not.*

He heard more sniggering from behind him. The guards again, up to something. Farden turned around to find one of them busy humping the shaft of his spear, making his armour rattle, while the other was trying, and failing, not to laugh.

The sight of Farden marching towards them soon put a halt to their little joke. They tried their hardest to ignore the stony-faced mage as he walked up to them, lips tight, holding back the laughter. Farden brought his face within a hairsbreadth of the nearest guard's face, so close their noses almost touched. Farden's eyes flicked to the man's spear. 'How about we shove that thing up your arse, and see how funny you feel then?' he growled. 'Fancy that?' The guard quickly shook his head, his laughter dead as a stone. 'I thought not,' Farden said, jerking his hand up to brush a stray bit of hair from his face. It made the guard flinch, and Farden walked away, chuckling.

Farden walked out into the twilight of the town and the timid stars. As his boots hammered the endless, knee-jarring steps that led down into Tayn, he found a little calm in the buzzing of the fattened insects and clatter of the town. Music spilled from the open windows of taverns. Alleys and streets murmured with hushed conversation. He passed a house, and heard somebody screaming, in the throes of passion by the sounds of it. Alittle idea blossomed in Farden's mind then. He gnawed his lip at the thought of the nevermar in his pocket. *No. It can wait for now.* Perhaps he would make one quick stop before he left town.

When he took the next turning, so did the silent shadow lingering behind him.

1569 years ago

a dagger.

Fast and blunt yet bright as sunlight, it slipped behind the tendons of his knee and deftly pulled the earth out from under him.

Korrin hit the sand with a crunch and a wheeze. He wasn't surprised to find the same dull blade tickling his windpipe when he lifted his head to breathe. The scarlet-headed woman squeezing its handle threw him a contemptuous look and stood up. Exasperation glinted in the russet shards that were her eyes. She gazed down, lip curled, at the wan figure sprawled at her feet.

Korrin had rolled onto his stomach. He lay there like a beached whale, tasting sand. It tasted of disappointment. It tasted the same as the last time.

'Again?' brayed a nearby man, a giant of a figure, and even more so looking up from the sand. 'Estina, I owe you a mug of valtik after all!'

'Peasant,' snorted Estina, from a little distance away. She had gone to fetch a white towel from a barrel by a door.

'Hope for him yet,' advised another voice, finding time to speak in between the sharp clack and clatter of spear shafts repeatedly colliding with a pole. 'He was chosen, after all.'

'Well, maybe the Smiths and the Pens made a mistake,' asserted the woman, Estina, a thin switch of a warrior, topped by a shock of bright red hair.

'Easy now,' warned the huge man who had spoken first.

'I'll make the same wager I made with Balimuel, Gaspid. One more time.'

Gaspid shook his bald head. 'I do not wager on the futures of other men.'

While the others debated his apparent uselessness, Korrin pushed himself wearily to his feet and sauntered to the edge of the tabletop of stone atop which the circular training grounds perched.

Barely a knuckle of brick sat between his feet and the shingled precipice. Even the ivy that embroidered its grouted edges seemed to cling on for dear and hallowed life. Korrin had often taunted that edge, late at night when he was given an hour, two at best, to sleep and to watch the wolves caper across the ice below. What was an hour of sleep in those days, when all it did was make the aching more obvious? The others didn't sleep, so why should he?

Korrin put a bare, blistered foot on a brick he knew to be trustworthy and looked down at the vista spread like a knobbled carpet below him; a carpet of white and brown, bronze and blue.

Scalussen was a dismembered town. Many who lived in the Frostsoar, its towering heart, claimed it was a city, but those clinging to its skirts snorted and said otherwise. It was more a collection of towns, villages, and the occasional fort, spread out roughly and randomly as if they had been thrown there in the wake of an ice-flood. But despite its jumbled nature, Scalussen was a jewel in the ice. The top of every building glinted with the morning frosts, as though the roofs had been scattered with diamonds. Blue, red, and yellow flags shivered atop poles. Seagulls, rimelings, and berghoppers flew in swarms of hundreds, all dancing and wheeling around the taller towers, skimming low over the river that snaked through the settlements. In the day it was a curving band of the deepest blue. Broken chunks of ice, flowing west, joined flotillas of sea-birds to speckle the smooth sapphire waters with spots of white and grey and black. On the pure white ice, lingering just a fraction to the north of Scalussen's edge, tiny black dots covered the ice. Penguins, or waddlefoots as the locals called them, gathered in ranks of thousands.

Korrin had yet to see them up close. He had heard stories that they were as tall as a man, with a beak so sharp they could punch through a foot of ice in one peck. Behind them, in the distance, where the ice rolled and cracked like foothills, mountains rose from its clutches. Black mountains forged of dark, jagged rock. Here and there, Korrin could see plumes of yellow and black smoke leaking from the earth. The Spine.

Korrin had never been this far north, where the blankets of permanent ice jostled shoulders with the rocky earth, and this wild, cold land fascinated the young lad. The animals of his father's farm seemed drab in comparison to the strange creatures that called the ice fields home; patchwork whales with spears stuck in their noses; seals with horns and others with teeth like those of sabre-cats; white bears that vanished into thin air like mist on a sunny morn, rainbow-beaked birds; foxes as white as the snow they hid in; hares and rabbits the size of baby deer; and huge furry monsters that walked in never-ending lines, with curving tusks and trunks like snakes, beasts that the Scalussen called mammoths. And wolves. Always wolves. Korrin could hear them calling to each other at night, under the ethereal light of the Wake. Perched on the edge of his precipice, he would listen to their faraway songs and wonder at their meaning.

The beauty of it all was swiftly interrupted by a sharp slap on the cheek. Korrin whirled around, face stinging, to find Balimuel standing behind him, one knee forward and leaning on it, peering over the edge of the precipice. 'What was that for?' Korrin snapped.

'To wake you up, lad.'

'I was already awake…'

'Really now? Doesn't look like it. Staring off into space, getting turned on your arse every other second by Estina and the others. Piss-poor job, if you ask me.'

Korrin opened his mouth for a retort, but both his brain and his tongue failed to come up with anything.

Balimuel must have had giant blood in him. No man got that big by chance or training, and food made a man grow out, not up. Balimuel nudged ten foot on a bad day. His arms and legs were as thick as young oak trees, and his hands were so large he could have wrapped his fingers around a man's thigh and still touched his fingertips. His head seemed to be one part face and two parts beard. A very dark brown, almost obsidian black, the big bushy thing rested lightly on his chest, the odd bit of sand and droplet of sweat hiding in it after the morning's training. His eyes were a rain-cloud grey, like the hue of his fingernails, and that alone hinted at his unusual bloodline. He had fixed Korrin with those overcast eyes.

Korrin looked over to the seven others. Each of them was a whirling blur of blade or pole, and each of them frightened him intensely. He was nothing compared to them, these seasoned, trained, and deadly fighters from across the Scattered Kingdoms and beyond. Each of them had seen a war or two in their time, for war was easy to find in those years, and each of them had come out grinning and shining with blood. The only blood Korrin had ever spilt had been from the throats of his father's mudpigs.

Ain't no difference between a soldier and a fool, Korrin, and there ain't no pride in either, said the voice that had plagued his thoughts since he had first set foot in Frostsoar tower. Korrin wiped the sand from his lip. 'Estina's right. They made a mistake with me, didn't they?'

'Did they now?' mused Balimuel, in a voice as deep as a bear's. He combed his beard with his hand, eyes still fixed on the young man slouched before him. 'I saw you, you know, in training? Yes. Caught you in the corner of my eye. Hard to miss if you ask me. You were clenching your teeth so hard I thought they might crack. Beat me through most of the tests, did you know that? No, I don't suppose you did. Never seen a boy nor man with so much grit in their face, and I'm not talking about this.' Balimuel reached out and cuffed

Korrin on the cheek again, where a streak of sand clung to the man's skin. The blow was softer this time but still painful. Korrin flinched away.

'Hey,' he cried. 'Stop it.'

'Never seen a man with so much anger hiding under his skin. So much to prove.' Another swipe, and this time it caught Korrin on the back of his head, waking up a number of old bruises. Korrin jumped out of Balimuel's reach, but the giant stood up and stretched to his full height. His shadow enveloped Korrin as he took a step forward, hand raised to strike again.

'Enough!' yelled Korrin, but Balimuel did not halt. He swung again and Korrin ducked. The young man reached for a pole that had been left propped up against a wall, but Balimuel batted his hand away.

Korrin winced. 'Leave off! What's wrong with you?'

'What's wrong with me? What about you? Where's that fire I saw in the tests, eh? Where's the fire that brought you here, farmboy?' Balimuel kicked out and caught Korrin in the shins. He was fast for a ten-foot tall man. Korrin hopped backwards. The others were watching now. Gaspid frowned, while Estina looked on with a mixture of sneer and grin pasted on her scarlet lips.

'Where is it, lad? Show me!' Balimuel grabbed the spare pole and began slapping Korrin on the thighs and forearms with it, sharp, stinging blows that went straight to the core of his tired muscles. Korrin managed to fend some of them off, his training doing some good, but he was running out of room. Balimuel was slowly trapping him in the corner of the training yard.

'Have they made a mistake then?'

'Leave me alone, Balimuel!'

'Got the wrong farmboy, did we?'

Whack! The pole connected with his knee and Korrin half-fell to the ground. 'Stop it!'

The pole poked him hard in the chest. Gaspid moved forward to interrupt the two men, but Balimuel waved him back. He knew what he was doing; he could see the first tinges of rage blossoming in Korrin's cheeks and in the corners of his eyes.

'Stop wasting our time, lad!' he shouted.

Whack! This time to the side of the head. And this time Korrin snapped.

He bellowed something drowned in unexpected rage, a raw scream that made all eight of the others jump. Korrin snatched the pole from Balimuel's giant paw and lunged at the man. Balimuel managed to fend him off for a few moments, strike after vicious strike glancing off his arms and ribs and thighs, until, very unexpectedly, the end of the pole snaked under his heel and Korrin yanked, hard. The giant toppled like an ancient oak and landed in a cloud of sand. There was a whisper of shock from the others. Not in ten weeks had any of them managed to fell the man. And here was Korrin, the farmboy, the supposed clerical error, beetroot-red and breathing heavy, brandishing a dusty pole inches from Balimuel's left eye.

For some reason, the man was smiling. Korrin was shaking. 'What is your problem, Balimuel?' he gasped.

The man lifted up a hand, gently moving the pole to the side, and then lightly prodded Korrin in the centre of his chest. 'There's our number nine,' he said.

A faint smile might have appeared on Korrin's lips then, but it disappeared as quickly as it had ventured out. Instead, he threw the pole to the sand and tottered over to the edge of the training grounds, where he sat down and stared out at the ice and smoking mountains in the distance.

Gaspid stood beside Balimuel as the man got to his feet. He was still smiling. 'I say, what was that about?' he asked.

Balimuel wiped the dust from his rolled-up sleeves. He was sweating ever so slightly. 'That boy's got a fire in him. Just needed to let it out.'

'So what? A lucky shot,' said a woman. Her hair was short and cropped.

Balimuel sighed. 'Did anyone see him during the testing? Gaspid? Estina? Rosiff? No? Well I did. Barely a scrap of muscle nor a season of battle in that lad and he beat most of us in half the tests. Beat us with his mind, he did. Roll your eyes all you want, Estina; I saw it. I'm glad the Pens did too.'

'Doesn't mean he can fight. He's useless,' muttered a tall man standing nearby, a wiry fellow from the east, with a beard like a dagger.

'And how many times have you toppled me, Chast?' challenged Balimuel, crossing his huge arms. The tall man didn't reply. 'Thought so. Ten weeks he's kept at it, ten weeks he's been thrown on his arse and had dust kicked in his face, and today's the first day I've seen him waver. There's a passion in him that you can't train or buy. If it were up to me, I'd get rid of all of you and pick another eight just like him. He wants this more than any of us. Longs for it. Like a prisoner longs for the kiss of freedom.'

'We don't even know what this is yet,' said Gaspid.

'We'll know soon enough,' hummed the giant. 'We all will.'

How wrong he was.

chapter 6

"To say that the Grimsayer is a rather special book is as to say that the sea is somewhat wet. The eddas tell us that the book was once a ledger of names; names of dead dragons that had passed to the other side, recorded in way of remembrance. Started by the very first Siren, millennia ago, it held the names of dragons like a tearbook holds memories. But, as those few who have ever laid eyes on it will know, the Grimsayer doesn't just hold the names of dragons, but of all sentient creatures since the dawn of time, and their faces too. Ask their names and the Grimsayer will show them to you. How? Legend suggests a few explanations. One, that it was a mistake. A miscalculation of a spell. The Grimsayer is a spell book, after all. Its keys are the names that are uttered to it. Another speaks of a goddess, her name and purpose forgotten, spilling her own blood on the book, infusing it with her power. Yet another suggests the book simply sprang into being. This last suggestion, of course, I hold to be utter rubbish."

Excerpt from a book on Siren legend, by a little-known author Lastu Resst, salvaged from Farden's collection

In the southeast of Albion, the rolling land and pasture faded into foothills, and then to moorland, and what an endless moorland it was. Fleahurst the locals called it, a stretching lowland of gorse and tor, and today it was caught, pinched and trapped, between two enormous banks of cloud. A storm in the west, a storm in the east, each reticent to pounce. They both postured and frothed at the mouth, gesturing with their frosty tendrils, while the land beneath looked up anxiously, wondering which one of its attackers would be the kinder. If a traveller had looked long and hard enough, they might have even spied a few storm giants lingering at the bases of the clouds, stretching and flexing and getting ready to fight.

Farden, on the other hand, couldn't have cared less. It had been two days since leaving Tayn, sneaking off in the middle of the morning while Jeasin had been asleep. His brief visit to the loathsome Duke was still playing on his troubled mind. He had chewed some of his precious nevermar on the first day, but it had slowed his pace too much. For now, he simply let the sound of his boots striding across broken flint calm his churning thoughts.

Farden looked up from his feet and towards his destination. A snake of flint road, empty save for nervous deer and the occasional curious rat or vole, led east towards the sea and the larger of the storms. The sky was a sculpture of chaos. There was a narrow band of bright sky stuck fast between the faraway waves and the roots of the impenetrable clouds. He was heading straight towards it. The wind ruffled his clothes, unsure in which direction to blow.

Any mind wandered when encouraged by long walks and lack of company, but for Farden, it was incessant. In all his years, the mage had never quite discovered why his mind insisted on wandering into dark corners and tiptoeing along the precipices of deep, gloomy wells of memory. It simply did what it did. Farden counted out his steps. The numbers would keep his head distracted for the time being. *One, two, three, four... Crunch, crunch...*

Soon a white cottage came into view, hidden in a dip between two low hills. It had a driftwood barn, a little flint wall across its front, and a half-moon of misshapen fields hugging its back. A little trail of grey smoke leaked from its chimney. Farden hadn't realised he had come so far already, and the sight of it made his stomach roar, a sound a sabre-cat might have been proud of. Farden quickened his tired pace at its behest.

Just as the eastern storm was reaching out to throw its first colossal punch, Farden reached the cottage and the corner of its flint and drystone wall. A sliver of lightning scampered across the sky above him. Its thunder came a little afterwards, lazy and slow. The mage followed the wall to a gate with a canewood arch. He gently pushed the gate open and then stood at the edge of the flint path that led to the cottage door. A man was leaning against its driftwood door-frame. Any other man would have grimaced or flinched at the sight of the travel-muddy, bitter-faced mage, but instead this man smiled, and even went as far as to tip the brim of his farmer's hat.

'Rabbit's in the pot,' he said, jovially. He had a face like a weathered oak. Wisps of grey hair were sneaking out from under his hat.

Farden smiled a rare smile. One that he rarely used these days. 'I was hoping it would be.'

The man tapped the door with a finger that looked more like a dirty parsnip than a human appendage. 'Seria's finishing it up now. You hungry?'

Farden reached for the handle of the gate. His eyes turned towards the east and the sea, and his hand reached to his cloak pocket for his nevermar. 'I can't stay long though,' he mumbled.

'No bother to me, lad. I know you never do. One day, mayhaps, and then Seria can stop worryin' 'bout you.'

Farden closed the gate behind him. 'One day.'

Old Traffyd held out his arms and Farden embraced him stiffly. He and his wife Seria used kindness like a gang of thugs used their clubs. They bludgeoned their rare visitors with it until they either gave in or ran away. Farden was a runner, but he also kept coming back. They were masterful cooks, and the only scrap of humanity for miles. Nothing lived out in the east wilds of Fleahurst save for the creatures that could scrape a living from the thistles and the gorse or those that nibbled them: deer, rabbits, voles, hawks, perhaps the occasional wandering wolf. The human population was just as sparse, a handful of wide-flung, isolated farms, an old watchtower, one or two cottages, and, unbeknownst to everyone apart from Traffyd and his dear wife, one wandering mage. It seemed that mages and wolves had something in common.

Ducking his head under the driftwood frame, Traffyd pushed open the door and led Farden inside. The air inside the cottage was smoky and thick, but it smelled delicious. The scents of smouldering driftwood and gorse bush, peppered rabbit, boiled carrots, crushed potatoes, and rockthyme all assaulted his senses. He could even smell the sweet tang of nettle tea in the air.

A rather large woman stood with her back to the door, busy stirring the contents of a huge iron pot. She was singing snatches of some unknown tune in a high-pitched voice, the half-hearted, uncaring sort of singing somebody does when alone and preoccupied. Farden stood by the door and waited for Old Traffyd to tap his wife on the shoulder.

'Visitor,' he said. Seria looked up quickly. Her eyes lit up, just for a second, and then immediately narrowed at the sight of Farden's muddy boots and dusty skin.

'You'd better take those boots off in my 'ouse, young man. I don't serve supper outside.'

'Yes Seria,' Farden nodded. He found himself a stool and set about untangling the fraying laces of his boots. He could feel his bones sighing at the taste of sitting down. It felt as though his legs were gluing themselves to the stool. Farden kicked off the boots and stayed where he was, content with watching the husband and wife bustle about.

'Fetch 'im some tea, Traffyd, afore he dies of thirst. Look at him.'

Traffyd did as he was told, as he always did. Farden had never heard even the faintest mutter of complaint from the man, not in the eight years he had known them. He dutifully fetched a waxed skin cup and poured the tea from a small kettle that hung on a pole over the flames. He gave it to Farden with a grunt and a wink, and went back to his wife.

The cottage was small but homely, in the way that small places often are when care and attention is poured into them. Despite the sooty fire, the flint-dust, and the rickety thatched roof, it was also spotless. Seria was the queen of her own home, just as Traffyd was the king of his garden and his fields. She saw to it that dirt stayed at the front door and never ventured in. She was always in one of two states, cooking, or cleaning, and on rare occasions she even did both at the same time. Farden couldn't remember a time when she had actually sat down to eat dinner with the two men.

Traffyd found some bowls in a cupboard and beckoned to the mage to put them out, which he did, bones and weary muscles complaining. He was then given a pair of spoons to arrange beside the bowls.

'Sit down, Farden, afore you fall down,' ordered Seria. Farden smiled politely; he knew better than to argue. 'Traffyd, you're like a slow worm. Get 'im some stew, you rude old man.' Traffyd laughed and rolled his eyes. He took Farden's bowl and returned it full and steaming and overflowing with thick, chunky rabbit stew. He tucked in eagerly.

By the pot, Traffyd nudged Seria and they both shook their heads at the sight of the mage fervently slurping at his spoonfuls. She filled her husband's bowl and shooed him away to the table. Then, instead of fetching herself some stew, she immediately began to clean the fireplace, sparing random moments to sip at the stew ladle and hum to herself about the apparent invasion of spiders.

The stew was delicious, as Seria's cooking always was. It was a marvel how they made the moorland fare taste so good. Out here in the eastern wilds, a simple cabbage would have looked exotic. Farden and Traffyd ate it in relative silence, mumbling about the weather and rabbits and the sea and other things that were simply said to fill the gaps between the chewing. Seria bustled around them, occasionally butting in with a reprimand for Traffyd or a comment on Farden's muddy attire. Farden didn't mind it in small doses. Seria wasn't Kiltyrin; her comments, although wrapped in severity and muttered from pursed lips, actually stemmed from a genuine care for the mage. Hers were never insults nor compliments, just her way.

Both men finished their bowls, and Seria swiftly whisked them away to be cleaned. Old Traffyd went to the back door of the cottage and out onto a rickety porch he had made from thatch and driftwood. Farden followed. It had begun to rain, and heavily too. The world had suddenly turned noisy indeed: the clattering patter of the raindrops on the stone path, the muted hiss of it on the thatch above, the dull thud of single, heavy drips here and there.

Traffyd reached inside his woollen coat and brought out a short pipe and a tin box of tobacco. He slowly and gently packed the bowl of the pipe, taking his time over every single scrap of dried leaf. Farden joined him, fishing out his own pipe. It was an old, scratched and battered thing he had bought in a market a decade ago. It had served him well. His fingers brushed the cloth bag inside his coat and he licked his lips. *Not long now*, he told himself.

Traffyd and Farden sat on a pair of stools that flanked a little round table with a square box on it. Farden sat hunched over, while Traffyd leant against the flint of the wall behind him. He stared at his garden, mentally listing the things that needed doing. Farden pointed at a row of vines snaking around a gorsewood frame. 'You making wine now?'

'Traders are scarce these days. Got to trade what I can,'

Traffyd mumbled, still deep in thought.

Farden nodded. He sucked on his pipe, eyeing the little box on the table. With a little sigh, he reached down to his belt, and plucked at the strings of a little pouch with his dirty fingers. Half of him, the darker half, the half thinking of the cloth bag inside his cloak, yelled at him to stop. The other half, the half that had grown used to living in the shadow of the first, shouted too, and for once it turned out to be the loudest. He fumbled one-handed with the pouch, worming his way inside and grabbing a handful of its contents. They were cold and sharp to the touch. Then, without a word, he lifted the lid of the square box on the table, and dropped his handful into it. The box closed with a thud and Farden went back to his pipe. 'I've been meaning to do that for a while,' he said.

Traffyd scowled. 'And what's that?'

'Something for a rainy day.'

Traffyd pointed at his dripping garden and the sodden view before them. 'Plenty of those about.'

'Something for your kindness then.'

Old Traffyd didn't reply. He didn't even move. Then he reached out and lifted the lid of the box with his work-tough fingertip. He lifted it an inch, no more, peered inside, and then shut it again. 'I weren't hinting when I said… That is…'

'I know.'

'I shan't tell Seria where those came from.'

'Probably best.'

'There would have been a time where I would have thrown that back in your face, lad. Never needed no dead man's trinkets before. But, as they say, hard times change hearts.'

'I know that more than anyone. Take it. You need it and they didn't.'

'That we do, though it pains to think what it came from, and how.'

'Then don't think about it. Leave that to me.'

'Right you are,' Traffyd sniffed, and fell silent for a while. When he finished his pipe, he stood up and lifted the box from the table. 'My offer still stands, you know.'

Farden scratched his head and tapped the burnt tobacco out of his pipe, leaning forward so the rain could lick its bowl clean. His mind was so full of thoughts that he had to shrug. 'Which one was that?'

'Never had no children, Seria and I, and a man of my age can't work the fields as much as he'd like to. There's always a need for strong hands around here, Farden. It's not just trinkets and baubles we are in need of.'

Farden nodded. He mumbled something and shook his head, and Traffyd sighed. 'Right you are,' he said. 'I'll see Seria puts some of that rabbit in a pot for you. You can give some of it to Whiskers.'

Farden sat alone and watched the rain for a while before going back indoors. When he did, he found Seria busy scrubbing the table. She stopped when she heard the door click shut, and looked up at the mage. She said nothing, but rather came around to the other side of the table and gave Farden a short and simple hug. 'Always nice to see you,' she whispered, and then in a louder voice, 'but I don't know anybody in their right mind who would want to go traipsing about in weather like this!'

Farden smiled and hoisted his trusty hood over his head, buttoning his cloak tightly around him. 'Never did mind the rain.'

'You'll catch your death of cold out there, if the Ghoul-king don't catch you first,' Seria replied, and Farden rolled his eyes. Albion's latest superstition. The Ghoul-king and his Shrieks. An old fairytale that had leapt from a child's fable to common lore. If there truly was a Ghoul-king that stalked the stormy nights, dragging travellers and children to their cold, clammy deaths, then let him come. Farden would see to him, too.

Old Traffyd was waiting by the door. He put a hand on the mage's shoulder as he tied the laces of his tired boots. 'Don't go getting yourself killed, is what the wife means, lad.' He leant an inch closer. 'We'd rather have you than baubles.'

'Then you're a strange pair,' Farden shook his head. That rare smile hovered on his face again. He turned around so Seria could push a pot, covered by a waxy cloth and sealed by twine, into his hands.

'Go see to that Whiskers of yours. He's sure to be starving,' she ordered, hands on hips. Her cheeks were blossoming into a deep red, and Farden didn't know if that was due to him leaving or her constant bustling.

'Or he's found another hermit to pester,' added Traffyd.

Farden snorted. 'I doubt that.' The mage pushed open the door and stepped out into the rain. Without so much as a goodbye, he jogged down the steps, through the gate, and back onto the flint road. He was soon lost in the haze of the downpour, leaving an old couple to stand in the shelter of a driftwood door-frame, arm in arm and shaking their heads.

❦

Every ghost needed a place to haunt, and if Farden was to be a ghost, then this lonely little shack was his.

Moss-licked and brave, the little shack stood in a dip between two hills, square on to the boisterous eastern sea and teetering on the edge of the land. Rocks and stranded seaweed were its garden. Boulders and valiant, flint-crushed soil its foundations. A little curving dagger of sand fell out of its back door, wandering through the rocks and down into the roiling slate-grey waters of the eastern sea. The sand did its best to hold back the waves. Some days it triumphed, other days it failed. Today it was failing.

The shack itself was a makeshift house of brick, gathered

driftwood, stolen doors, and pilfered iron sheets. It had four windows, two on the front, and two on the back, and a door that swung open at a drunken angle. The windows had been filled with borrowed glass, and behind them, thick blue curtains had been drawn. Moss gave the place a slightly greenish hue. Rust painted whatever metal had bared its face. Seagull droppings and sand coated the roof and the stubby chimney. Between the gaps in its three stone steps, patches of curious molluscs shone bright red and yellow, adding a little vibrancy to the jumbled-up shack and the overcast sky.

The storms had almost abated by the time Farden reached his little house. The flint road had died a few miles back, fading into the earth, but even in the remote wilds Farden had never failed to find his abode. He'd had a decade to practise, after all, and besides, he always had the tree to rely on.

He looked up through its branches as he passed underneath it, as he always did. An ash tree, so he had been told by Traffyd. A spindly, skeletal thing, he was sure he had never seen it blossom, not in all the years he had lived beside it. The tree itself was unremarkable. It was just an average tree, but what was strange about it was why such a thing had decided to grow here, on the edge of a barren moorland, without so much as an explanation nor a hint of how. There were no other trees for miles around. There weren't even any gorse bushes nearby, just sharp-tongued grass. Farden had often puzzled over this on long walks and lonely days, and the answer had always eluded him.

The mage left the tree behind and walked down the hill to the shore and his shack. Two seagulls were perching on its roof. They looked half-asleep. Their long yellow and red beaks were gently resting on each other's backs. Farden clapped loudly to shoo them away, and then went inside his little house.

The smell of mould was the first thing to hit him. He always noticed it after spending a long period away. He sniffed and grimaced;

he would soon come to ignore it. He set his pot of rabbit stew on a nearby, and rather wonky, table, and then threw his haversack onto the cot of straw and cloth he called a bed. The haversack clanked as it landed.

The shack was barely big enough to swing a cat in. It couldn't have measured more than twelve foot by eight in total, and the roof was low enough that if Farden jumped in the right place he could have made himself a new skylight. There was a half-stove, half-fireplace on one side of the room. Farden sat down in front of it. Even after all these years, his first habit was to reach out and spread his hands over the dry wood he had left inside it, but he caught himself, and swore as a shiver of pain ran across his forehead and down his back. Instead, he dug flint and tinder out of his pocket, drew his knife, and after a few moments, he had a crackling fire.

Before he could get comfy, Farden went to the bed to open up his haversack. He fished around in between clothes and supplies until he found his vambraces. Rolling up his sleeves, he swiftly put his hands into both of them and felt the cold metal contract around his skin, pinching it ever so lightly until it adjusted to him. Farden stood there for a moment, letting the cold seep across his forearms.

When he was done, he knelt down and used his fingernails to pry one of the rickety floorboards from its rusty nails. The floorboard came up easily, and he rolled it aside to reveal four pieces of red and gold armour: a pair of greaves and a pair of gauntlets, all covered in a thin film of dust. Farden grabbed them greedily. He clapped the greaves to his legs and then slid the gauntlets over his hands. They were cold too, and the mage drank it in.

He lingered there for a few moments, eyes closed and savouring the metallic kiss of his armour against his rain-battered skin, before getting up and sitting himself in front of the fire.

About nine years before he had somehow managed to salvage an armchair from a ship that had wrecked itself several miles down the coast. If one had looked very closely at the shack and its innards, they probably would have spotted several more things that had been pilfered from the stricken ship, such as the ropes tying the roof together, the glass from an iron porthole, a lobster trap serving as a basket. Farden had liberated them all. The armchair had been in the captain's cabin, with a dead captain in it. It had taken several months to get the smell out of the threadbare cloth.

Farden sat down with a groan and kicked off his boots so he could warm his toes on the growing fire. He was teetering on the edge of exhaustion. Even the cold, sweet feeling seeping into his veins from the Scalussen armour could not stop his eyelids from drooping. He let his fingernail wander between the folds and scales of his left vambrace. He closed his eyes and tried to picture the breastplate Kiltyrin had somehow got his claws on, but all he could see in his tumultuous mind was the Duke's smug face, and the etching of a beetle.

Farden clenched his fist and listened to the cold metal whisper. Was it all a dream? A psychosomatic effect from his intense desire for them to be something special? Farden had asked that question countless times. From what he remembered, his uncle had been oblivious to the feeling of the gauntlets and the greaves. Farden pinched the bridge of his nose between his finger and thumb and tried to clear his busy mind. Exhausted he might have been, but he needed to write this down before he forgot. With a sigh, he reached down the side of the armchair and felt around for his notebook and his stick of charcoal. But instead of a notebook, he found something hairy instead. He tested it with a squeeze and was rewarded with a squeak.

Whiskers.

The rat scuttled up the side of Farden's armchair and onto his rain-wet lap. It sat back on its haunches and tail and sniffed the air in the way that rats do: head back, snout out, bobbing up and down. Farden reached out and cupped his hand and the big rat jumped in. He was getting fat in his old age. And old he was.

Whiskers had come with the armchair. It had shocked Farden no end to find a rat perched on his shoulder one afternoon. The beast had seemed perfectly tame, and industrious too. It had fashioned itself quite a warren in the bowels of the chair. He had often wondered if the captain of the ship had known about him, trained him even. Now he was Farden's tailed nuisance. The animal had refused to leave, no matter how many times the mage had shooed him off or tried to scare him away. He had even carried him back to the ship and left him there, but lo and behold, three days later, the rat turned up again, sitting comfortably inside one of Farden's Scalussen gauntlets. And that was how Farden had been given his idea.

Farden put the black rat on his shoulder and reached down to the side of the armchair where he kept his notebook. He lifted it up with a heave and laid it out on the nearby lobster pot. The notebook was more of a tome than a book. It bulged with scraps of parchment and snippets snatched from scrolls. Places, names, histories, all here, and every single word pointing in one direction of thought and one direction only: Scalussen. Durnus would have been proud.

Farden lifted its fraying cover and pried a small scrap of charcoal from a pouch glued onto its underside. He thumbed through the bedraggled and mouldy pages until he finally got to where he had left off, only a month before. With Whiskers watching intently, the mage began to scribble:

WHISKERS STILL AS FIT AS EVER. NO MORE GREY IN HIS COAT. HIS NEST INSIDE ONE OF MY GAUNTLETS SEEMS TO HAVE STOPPED HIM AGEING FOR GOOD. IT MUST BE AT LEAST NINE YEARS NOW. FOR ALL I KNOW, HE'S THE OLDEST RAT IN HISTORY.

THE BASTARD DUKE HAS FOUND HIMSELF SOME ARMOUR. BREASTPLATE NO LESS. SAYS IT WAS A PRESENT FROM

SOMEBODY IN THE CRUMBLED EMPIRE. LIES. I DON'T TRUST IT FOR A SECOND. I'LL HAVE TO ADD HIM TO THE LIST OF OWNERS AND POSSIBLES.

IS IT REAL? ONE OF THE NINE? I CAN TELL IF I CAN TOUCH IT, BUT HE WATCHES ME LIKE A HAWK. HE KNOWS SOMETHING.

BE CAREFUL.

HE KNOWS THE PIECES OF THE NINE ARE SOMEWHERE, AND THEY EXIST. DON'T KNOW WHO HE'S BEEN LISTENING TO, BUT HE'S RIGHT. DANGEROUS.

NEED TO EXAMINE THE SKETCHES FOR ANY SIGN OF BEETLES ON ARMOUR. NEVER SEEN THAT BEFORE. USUALLY BASTIONS, SABRE-CATS, WOLVES. ONLY HAVE FOUR PICTURES SO NOT IMPOSSIBLE.

MUST KEEP MINE AS HIDDEN AS POSSIBLE.

IF ONLY I HAD THE GRIMSAYER... I COULD SEE IF HIS BODY HAD THE ARMOUR... WHERE HE MIGHT BE...

That last sentence surprised him. He had thought of that strange book many times in the past, but it hadn't crossed his mind in years. He could barely remember what it looked like. It was a silly notion, anyway. The book was locked up in Nelska. Even if he did have it, he didn't know the name of the Knight whose armour he wore. Useless.

Farden shook his head and reached down to the other side of the armchair to retrieve a broken, jagged slice of mirror. He grimaced, but forced himself to check his temples, hair, and face before putting the mirror aside and scribbling some more notes:

FEW MORE GREYS. SKIN FINE. SCARS STILL THERE. TIME RUNNING OUT. NO MAGICK STILL. GOOD. WILL SCRIBE MORE TONIGHT.

Farden tossed the charcoal into the centre of the page and slammed the book shut. Whiskers squeaked in his ear. The mage sighed and stared out of the window at the wind-blown sea. His mind was still churning. Usually the note taking, like his counting of his steps, kept him distracted for a while. The sad truth of it was this: that if a man was bound by his actions, then Farden was tethered and chained by his thoughts.

Three things cleared his mind those days: the cold, quiet purpose of a kill; Jeasin, his blind favourite who looked like his lost Cheska; and lastly, the bitter acridity of a mouthful of nevermar smoke. His old favourite. The first two, aside from mental distraction, were means to his ends.

His work for the Duke gave him an iota of purpose at least. Even as questionable as it was, the mage had become used to it. It kept him busy. He had lied to Kiltyrin in Tayn. Whatever morals and sense of higher calling he'd had before had all but been numbed. Numbed as a blizzard numbs a lost traveller. It simply put coin in his hand. Coin that made the other two possible.

Jeasin satisfied the cravings that any lonely man felt and more besides. Somehow, his times with her managed to patch the gaping, dusty hole in his heart, if only for a little while. None of the other girls over the years had quite managed it. Maybe it was because of her appearance, maybe her brusque coldness, but somehow, she did.

But it was the third of these things that formed his true crutch, his true bolt-hole and sanctuary, as it always had been through the years. Nothing decimated thoughts and dark minds like the intoxicating, smoky tendrils of nevermar. Most of all, it kept his magick away, and that alone was precious. Farden had realised a long time ago that magick had been the root of all his problems. The wheels of the cart of sorrow. Without magick, he would never have been in this position. He wouldn't have been sat there, hunched over a lobster pot, staring out at the waves rolling back and forth like windblown shale.

Farden growled bitterly at himself, and stood up. Placing Whiskers gently on the arm of his chair, he briefly stoked the fire and then wandered to the opposite end of the shack, where a large cabinet had been nailed to the wall. Farden took his knife from its sheath and then opened the cabinet doors. Inside, fifty candles had been crammed onto four shelves, and almost all of them had a face.

Some were long faces with bulging eyes, earlier attempts by the looks of them, while later ones exhibited freckles, wrinkles, even hair. Some stern looking ones had been half-melted, so that their faces were caught in the midst of their ghastly death-throes. Their eyes sagged, their features twisted, globules of wax residue clamping their mouths shut.

Farden used his knife to pry a chubby, half-melted one from the shelf. Squinting, he examined its unfinished features and then closed the cabinet. He walked to the back door and undid its latch. The mage kicked it open with his heel, and then, ignoring his lack of boots and the wild weather, he sauntered out onto the rocks and down onto the sea-battered spit of sand that arced into the frothing sea. The wind tugged at him, but he ignored it too. He paced across the gritty yellow sand, making sure to stamp on every single discarded seashell he could find, and then stood at the water's edge, where the olive seaweed desperately tried to escape the pounding of the waves. Farden stood there for a moment to eye the receding storm, and then began to whittle the unfinished face of his fat little candle.

When his feet had gone numb, and the stump of the finger on his left hand throbbed with the cold, he wandered back indoors. He shut the door firmly behind him and slumped into his armchair. Whiskers had nibbled the twine from the pot of stew and was currently fishing around inside it, using his tail to hook himself to the side of the pot lest he fall in. Farden snorted. *Clever rat.*

It was growing dark outside now, and the fire was going out.

Farden examined the face he had carved into his candle. It was a chubby face, with jowls that hung beside its pursed mouth like curtains. A bulbous nose hovered above them, and squinting eyes above that. It stared at the mage with a mixture of distaste and judgement. Farden returned its haughty gaze and set it on the upturned lobster pot while he stoked the fire and removed his cloak. He returned to the armchair with a pipe, a length of smouldering twig, and a cloth bag.

Farden had made himself wait long enough.

He lit the candle with the twig and tossed it back in the fire. The little face began to sweat. It was the work of a moment to fill the bowl of his pipe with the precious nevermar. He made each little movement of his fingers meticulous and careful, in case he accidentally lost even the tiniest scrap. The smell of it, even now, made his mouth water. Farden took the candle, its face already sagging, and held it over the bowl.

Farden took a deep breath, and after setting the dying candle back onto the lobster pot, he melted into the armchair. Fingers of warm smoke clutched his brain, and he felt his face go numb as the feeling of the nevermar spread outwards from his lips, to his cheeks, to his neck, and down. Down. Down into his chest, until he was staring at the molten face of the candle through blurry eyes. It curled its lip at him until the very last moment.

chapter 7

"Today a council member asked me an intriguing question. Are the Written getting more powerful? I had to say yes.
If Modren and Tyrfing's observations are accurate, the Written, like the rest of Emaneska, are experiencing a surge of magick like never before. I must say it is an exciting time, if not one that is a little worrying. Even I can feel it in my bones, my blood. I can feel it humming in the air on certain nights. Spell books are coming alive by themselves, whispering to scholars. The magick markets and caravans and trade ships bring stranger and stranger things every week. Quickdoors spontaneously open. Ordinary soldiers are using magick like the mages. Written are suddenly wielding spells that would challenge the skills of Tyrfing or I. It seems that the Written are only now reaching their full potential. How painful it is then that we are losing so many of them to the murderer in the wilds.
Emaneska's magick has truly been set aflame. The question is why? I dearly hope it is not something to do with Farden's murderous spawn. The search for her continues."
Taken from Arkmage Durnus' diary, Firstdew 904

Hide! Screamed the voice inside his head.

The hand of fear ran its razor around his heart once again. His breath came in ragged slurps. Knees ached. Feet blistered. Owls and other night things screeched and laughed at him. Spirals of mist rose from the spiny loam, early wreaths to a grave not yet dug.

Hide where?! Vossum shouted at his own useless thoughts. He blinked. More blood. The cut must have been deep indeed. Vossum quickly clamped a hand over his forehead and rushed on. Trees groped at him and scratched his neck and bare arms with their long fingers. Pine cones splintered under his pounding boots.

Hide!

Vossum peered through blood and darkness for a place, any place that could offer him sanctuary. The night was thick, the forest too, and the trees were thin and arrow-straight. No gnarled fallen trunk for him. No void in the earth to curl up in. The ground was flat and its only foliage needles and cones. He crouched, tempting the mists to swallow him, but they were still too thin and timid.

And then he saw it.

A fist of rock half-sunk in the earth, surrounded by trees. Narrowly missing a tree trunk, he veered violently towards it, grazing his shoulder in the process. He barely felt it. The mage hurtled on towards the rock, his sanctuary, his hiding spot. Breathless prayers fell from his lips and wafted into the cold night air.

Skin met dirt as he skidded and crumpled into a foetal position underneath a jutting lip in the rock. Vossum held his lips tight and forced himself to breathe through his nose, slowly, gently, as quiet as he could. His lungs were on fire. Darkness clutched him close.

Who was she?

What was she?

Somewhere in the screeching darkness a twig snapped, and Vossum held his breath tight in his throat. Behind closed lips, he slowly began to weave together another spell with his tongue. Something with light and noise, a distraction maybe, something to give himself time to escape. *Curse his lack of meld magick,* he thought, fingers probing the stone around him, trying to dig into it, become it.

Another twig split in twain, closer too. A foot scuffed a pile of leaves while the trees whispered above, as if telling the hunter where her prey hid. Vossum peered into the shadows, lit only by the curious, bony fingers of a half-moon delving into the pine woods. Tonight the sky was picked clean of stars. Ambitious fog graced the sky like ghostly entrails. Sunken clouds and spiny trees obscured all but the aloof, phantom moon. Vossum glanced up, moving his head slightly to see if he could catch a glimpse of her. He couldn't, and it made him shiver.

Something was watching him, in the misty folds of night.

Two pinpricks of sheer darkness, even blacker than the night around them, hovered by a tree a painfully short distance away. They tugged and pulled at the night around them, as if sucking it in and feeding off it. Grey smoke leaked from their corners.

Vossum's breath caught in his throat. He stared at them, desperately trying to decide if they were human or beast, or both, or whether his mind had finally snapped. When they inched closer, accompanied by the sound of crunching pine cones, he felt his veins fill with ice. By the hands of the gods, they were eyes! Black, terrible eyes, swallowing what paltry light the moon offered.

Vossum felt naked. He wilted into the loam as the ghastly black eyes marched forward. A shape emerged behind them, with a waterfall of black hair and a pale face as hard as the steel in its hand. He lashed out wildly, but the girl was too quick. His spell sprang half-formed from his mouth, and as light and magick sputtered, Vossum saw the blade plunge into his stomach. He crumpled to the ground again, moaning a brief prayer as a slender hand wrenched his head backwards by the roots of his hair, and a blade slipped into his throat.

The girl stood upright and wiped the wet blade on her leather sleeve. She closed her pitch-black eyes, squeezing them as tightly as she could. When she opened them again, the hungry darkness in them had died, and the trails of grey smoke had evaporated. She didn't need her eyes now; she cast a spell that burnt away the shadows with a bright white light.

The girl stretched, making her back click in several places, and then knelt to the needle-strewn ground so she could begin to cut the man's sweat-drenched leather jerkin from his back. The seasoned blade took a few moments to bite through the tough leather, but with a swift yank it came free, and was tossed aside. The strange girl paused then, hand hovering, knife wavering, as she stared at the dead man's back. He wore a thin yellow shirt under his thick jerkin, again soaked with fear and sweat. But something was missing.

Knife forgotten, the girl seized the shirt and ripped it off his still-warm skin. No light, no runes, no Book, nothing. She grabbed the man's nearest arm to examine it again. There it was: a tattoo in the shape of a long, skeletal key. This man was a fake.

Fuming, the girl got to her feet again and stared down at the corpse. She spat on it, and then kicked it in its lying face; once, twice, three times, pounding it viciously with the toe of her thick boot. She stopped only when she heard the sick crunch of a skull cracking. Sheathing her knife, the girl marched north into the misty darkness lurking between the pine trees, eyes black and smoking once again.

The frail half-moon looked on, confused.

❦

A crimson stone landed in the dust, rosy with the dawn glow. Then a black stone, chipped and scarred with age and use, landed next to it, rolling in a circle before it waddled to a stop. The last stone was a milk-white, like an eyeball that had misplaced its pupil. It fell between the other two and shoved them both aside with a sharp crack.

Lilith frowned, and took a sip of the brackish tea she was clutching between her cold knees. She looked up from her befuddled stones and stared at the day. The mist still clung fervently to the daylight, like a ghost clutching at the unravelling threads of life. The sun had just woken from its slumbers and was sitting nonchalantly on the hazy horizon. It would be a hot day, as far as Emaneska was concerned. Sleepy insects were already beginning to buzz. In the distance, somewhere in the stubborn fog, near to the outskirts of the foreign little town, cows lowed.

Lilith shuffled around to look at her seerstones from a different direction, but that only deepened her frown. She muttered something and pushed the stones away with the back of her hand. The fire beside her had burnt out in the early hours. It was now a ring of charcoal and smoking twigs. The green-wood spit that hung over it sported the carcass of a huge water rat. It was mostly bones and emptiness now, something for the crows to pick at. She could hear them in the edges of the pine forest, a little way to the south. Bored, Lilith sipped her tea and waited.

Fortunately, she didn't have to wait long. Barely half an hour later, Samara trudged out of the fog and crouched by the dead fire. She didn't speak. She simply dug two fingers into the cold innards of the water rat and prized out some meat that had been missed. She stuffed the greasy strands into her mouth and chewed silently. Her face was a frown.

Lilith looked at her hands, her pockets, and all around her. There was barely a speck of blood on her hands. 'Where is it then?'

Samara ignored the question. She stared at the weak, yellow morning sun and frowned some more.

In the years that had passed, Samara had grown into a wiry, lithe little figure. A frame of bones and skin on tall legs. Those foolish enough to judge her by her skinny form, those who had even tried to take advantage of it, had quickly found themselves the new owner of a broken something, or worse. For her age and size, Samara was unnaturally strong and painfully quick. Not that she was anywhere close to *natural*. Her whole being seemed to vibrate on a different level from those around her, even Lilith. That was the magick at play.

Samara's obsidian hair was now braided in places, knotted in others. Her eyes, those dangerous little orbs, could never decide on which colour was their favourite. Like her moods, they were unpredictable and ever-changing, morphing from a piercing ice-blue to a deep sapling-green with a flick of her eyelashes. Those young eyes hid an animal behind them; stained glass windows through which a brave person could glimpse a monster drenched in magick, and when coupled with her seemingly-innocent tongue they could weave lies alongside the best of them, just like Lilith had shown her. And Lilith had shown her very well.

Lilith crossed her legs and entwined her fingers. She narrowed her eyes at her young charge. 'I'm talking to you, girl. Where is his Book?'

Samara rolled her eyes. 'He was a fake, Lilith. His key tattoos were cheap imitations.'

Lilith scowled. She had been wrong again. 'Well, didn't you follow him beforehand? Didn't you watch him?'

'Of course I did,' asserted Samara, growing angry. 'You're the one who showed me him.'

'Well it's your responsibility to make sure of it! You obviously didn't look close enough.'

'I don't see why it matters. Another mage is dead. So what if he wasn't a Written?'

Lilith held up her hand for silence. Samara reluctantly bit her tongue. The seer rubbed her eyes with her good hand and sighed. Samara watched her mentor closely. The more she looked, the more she could see the years eating away at her, like a mould slowly seeping into her skin. Her cheeks and brows were beginning to sag. Grey was beginning to infiltrate her once-dark hair. Her left arm was wilting again. Samara knew what this meant. 'Where next then?' she asked.

Lilith cracked open an eye to stare at the three seerstones that were still lying in the dirt. It was a while before she answered. 'I don't know,' she hissed, pained.

'You're losing it.'

'I 'aven't lost *anything*!' Lilith snapped, whirling around to face Samara. The young girl didn't flinch. It had been a month since they had killed their last Written. Last night's had been a fake and the other two hadn't even existed. 'The questions are… *difficult*. Ambiguous. Just as your magick clouds your future, the world's magick clouds my stones. They're confused,' she muttered. Samara rolled her eyes. Either Lilith's seerstones were failing, or she was. Samara offered an explanation to calm the seer down. Not that she cared, but she couldn't stand her when she was in one of her foul moods. It wasted her time.

'Then maybe we've killed them all,' she shrugged.

Lilith's mouth curled. 'Don't be foolish, girl. I don't recall killin' an Arkmage, or that bastard Farden. Do you? Please inform me if I missed those wondrous occasions.'

Samara stood up. Lilith might have flinched then, but she hid it well by shuffling closer to her seerstones. She looked away from the girl and prodded the red stone by her sandal. 'Where are you goin'?'

'Why don't you ask your stones?'

'Don't give me that lip, girl,' Lilith warned. Samara was becoming more and more recalcitrant with every week that passed. The seer couldn't tell if it was boredom, or sheer petulance, or maybe her father's streak rearing its ugly head. Whatever it was, Lilith didn't like it. She wouldn't have ever voiced it aloud, but she also feared it. 'Where you off to?'

A reluctant answer floated out of the mist. 'For a walk.'

Lilith cupped her hand around her mouth and shouted after it. 'Well, be quick about it. I want t' move on before the day is wasted!' There was no reply. Lilith put her chin on her hand and took a deep breath.

Samara followed a thin trail of scuffs and hoof-prints through the brown dust. A collage of tracks wove in and out of her feet. Some were the cloven horn shapes of cows. Others sported the faint pinpricks of claws. Foxes probably. Samara tilted her head, and the soft clucking of chickens and geese reached her ears. Her stomach rumbled at the noise, but she swiftly slapped it into silence.

Through the misty haze and low cloud, the early sun could be stared at without squinting. Still lingering just above the horizon, it was a humble yellow ball, yet to bring any heat to the earth or pain to the eyes. Samara could simply watch it, daring it to do its worst.

The air was deathly still. Not a single breeze nor zephyr disturbed the morning air. It would have been stifling, had it been any warmer.

Samara wandered on towards the animal sounds of the farm and the town hiding in the mist, somewhere up ahead. While she walked, she scanned the dusty, grassless ground, looking for something in particular. Whatever it was, it wasn't to be found.

Samara soon came across a dry-stone wall that had seen better and more attentive times. Slumped and spilled in places, the wall was clogged with moss and mouse-droppings. Behind it lay a dust field dotted with tough grass and the odd woven basket of pale hay. Large shadows lumbered about in the fog. They mooed and dug at the dust with their hoofs. Samara dug her toe into the wall and swiftly vaulted it, landing with a light thud.

The cows quickly sensed the presence of something in their field, something very strange indeed. As a thin shape emerged from the mist, striding nonchalantly towards them, the patchwork beasts began to low fearfully. She oozed danger, and they could smell it. Luckily for them, cows were not what she was after. The girl paid them nothing but a sideways glance as they bowed their heads and quickly cantered to another corner of the field.

The chickens, on the other hand, were not so lucky.

Samara followed the sound of the muted clucking and burbling to a tumbledown hen-house that stood by a wooden gate. She crouched beside it and scraped a handful of dirt from the ground. A few sleepy hens stood on the little ramp that sloped from their raised door down to the earth. A few feathers sat like a rune at the foot of it. A smattering of blood lay in the dirt, an accidental blotch of scarlet ink, the signature of a fox. But chickens were not known for their lengthy memories. They had already forgotten their lost comrade and the red-haired predator, and were now staring at the unfamiliar girl crouching by their house with a mixture of curious intrigue and hunger.

Samara held out her hand, cupped as though full of grain, and offered it to the stupid birds. The docile creatures were used to humans handing them food, and quickly came down the ramp to investigate. It was the last mistake they ever made. In a flash, Samara seized two of them by their necks and spun them around in a circle until their necks snapped with a loud squawk. She was back at the drystone wall before their feathers had fallen to the dust.

Crouching behind the wall, Samara found a length of twine in her pocket and used it to tie the two chickens together. She slung them over her shoulder and followed the wall to its crumbled corner. Pausing there, she flicked a feather from her leather sleeve and looked around. There was a dirt road a few yards away that no doubt led into the town. Samara looked right, towards the town, and then left, where the road sloped gently up a small hill, and where a dark shape hovered high in the mist. She gazed at it, trying to make it out, but it was just a shapeless blotch in the morning haze. Curiosity piqued, Samara went to investigate.

It took a moment for its features and edges to loom into clarity, but once it did, Samara stood underneath it, and let her eyes rove over its greasy hinges, its rusty bolts and locks, its spikes and its bars.

It was a gibbet, suspended high over the road by a sturdy pole and a moss-covered beam choked by iron chain. It looked as though it had seen ten thousand dawns in its time; its iron cage was half-rusted away and tired, while the wood it hung from was grey with age. Cracks ran up and down the pole like thin veins of coal in a granite face.

There was a skeleton inside the gibbet, a crow-picked and weather-bitten frame of bones. It was easy to see the man had been dead for a decade. Whatever flesh its cracked armour had once protected was now long gone. Even the maggots had moved on. The armour itself, bent and buckled, a memory of polished steel now washed moon-grey by rain and time, was that of an old Skölgard soldier. Samara recognised its style. Even though the empire had fallen, some men and women still clung to their old life, in the way that the lost do. Here, in the remnants of old Skölgard lands, now dubbed the Crumbled Empire, some still wore their old armour and their memories on their chests. Depending on which way the empire had crumbled, some towns and lands didn't mind the relics, while others despised them. This man, now staring hollow-eyed at the sleepy sun, had obviously stumbled across the wrong town.

Samara reached up to rock the gibbet. Its chains and bars squealed like a strangled cat. The dawn was creeping into day, and a blunt glow was beginning to caress the wooden beams. Something glinted at the girl's feet and she looked down to find a muddy puddle. It held the reflection of the gibbet in it, making it wobble and waver slightly. Samara smiled. Tossing her dead chickens to one side, she quickly knelt down in the dirt.

She put her finger in the puddle and swirled it around curiously, watching the mud dance underneath the rippled surface. The water was cold, despite the dawn sun. Samara put her elbows on her knees and waited for the water to calm again, for the reflection to grow still and mirror-like once more, and when it had, something rather disturbing happened.

The girl watched intently, not a sign of fear or surprise on her face as the reflection of the gibbet began to move. There was a squeak of rusty chains as something twitched above her. Bones clicked. The skeleton reached up to push its jawbone back into place and then wriggled it about, testing, trying. Had it a tongue, it would have licked its jagged line of broken teeth to wet them. With a rattle and a whine of metal, the skeleton looked down, and slowly sank to its knees. It stared, still empty-eyed and very much dead, through the gaps in its cage at the young girl in the puddle's reflection. Samara leant forward to greet it.

'Where are you?' said the dead thing, in a breathy voice that slithered over its weathered bones and climbed the bars of the gibbet, dripping, seeping.

'North, near the border of what used to be Vorhaug,' replied Samara, calm as could be.

The skeleton waved its bony hand. Its teeth chattered as it tested and prodded its jaw again. 'What of the seer? She prays to us no longer,' it hissed.

Samara frowned. 'She's… distracted.'

'By what, indeed?'

'By her problems.'

The skeleton squinted. Its eye-sockets cracked and splintered. 'The stones again?' it said. The tone of its voice was growing angry.

Samara nodded. 'She says her questions are too… am… ambiguous. The stones are confused, she says.'

The skeleton grumbled to itself. 'How many have you shown your knife to now?'

'Twenty-four Written. A dozen other mages.'

'And how many remain?'

Samara shrugged.

The skeleton reached down and jabbed its finger at the girl. 'Dare to shrug at me? Give me numbers, girl!'

Samara bowed her head. 'A score, perhaps thirty. Three that we know of for sure. The Undermage and captain of the Written, the Arkmage, and of course, *him.*'

The skeleton sniffed. The bones around its dead nostrils shivered. 'Powerful as we are growing, we still cannot see Farden, just as the seer cannot. Something hides his magick. But something tells me he will be unwilling to stand in your way. Do not worry about him.'

'I wasn't, though Lilith says I should fear the Arkmages, especially my father's brother, Ruin.'

'You have the blood of both, and therefore are stronger than both, child. Ignore the seer. We continue with the plan.'

'And once you fall...?'

The skeleton waved its hand. 'You will not be alone.'

The girl nodded to the puddle.

'How do you feel?'

Samara looked up at the mist for a while. The skeleton above her creaked and sighed, impatiently waiting for her answer. She finally gave it. 'Ready.'

'Then you have wasted enough time stalking mages in the shadows. It is time. Don't let the seer delay you any more.' The skeleton sagged slightly, as whatever magick that was animating its lifeless bones began to drain away. 'And child?'

'Yes?'

The skeleton slumped into a heap at the bottom of the gibbet. The voice wafted into the misty air, echoing in her mind. 'If the seer continues to prove herself useless, or stands in your way, you may remove her.'

Samara pulled a face, not quite a wince, but not quite anything else. 'Of course,' she replied. After a while, she got to her feet and stood in the puddle, looking up at the slumped, broken skeleton hanging above her head. One of its feet had slipped through the gaps in the bars and dangled in the air. Samara reached up and flicked it with her finger. One of the toes broke off and flew into the mist. With an amused hum, the girl grabbed the foot by its ankle and wrenched it downwards. As the skeleton's foot came loose, the gibbet and its frame exploded into countless splinters, spraying the dirt road with molten iron and charred wood. The skeleton and its armour were vaporised in a cloud of fire and smoke. As the chaos cleared, Samara, completely untouched, walked calmly away, two smoking chickens slung over her shoulder.

When she returned to the little camp, Lilith was still sitting cross-legged in the dust. She was nudging her stones back and forth with her knuckle. At the sound of footsteps she looked up. 'Finally,' she hissed.

Two chickens landed on her lap in reply. Lilith lifted them up. She squinted at where their feathers were slightly charred. 'So that's what that bloody noise was. You want to watch yourself, girl. You'll draw attention to us.'

'So what?'

'What do you mean?' snapped Lilith, swivelling around to face the girl. 'You know…'

Samara remained standing 'We've wasted enough time hunting Written in the dark. It's time.'

'*I* decide when it's time.'

'No, Lilith, you don't. We're leaving tonight. Krauslung's time is up.'

Lilith slapped the dirt, making her stones wobble. 'There are more Written left, not to mention Ruin, Modren, and Tyrfing. And Farden. And not just them either, there are other mages in that city, Written, and Siren wizards no doubt!'

'I'm ready for them.'

'Are you? You might be able to take down a single mage, but what about ten at a time, twenty, fifty? They'll swarm you. They've grown stronger now too, you know that.'

'As have I.'

'There's only one of you.'

Samara lifted her chin. 'Well, it won't just be me, will it?'

Lilith spat. 'You think you're ready for that? You've barely seen fifteen years pass by, and you think you're ready? Fool of a girl! We're going north, so pack your things.'

Samara stepped forward and grabbed the old seer by her hair. Lilith yelped and screamed, lashing out with a handful of sharp fingernails. Samara lifted her from the dust and held her in mid-air. She ignored the fingers clawing at her long hair. 'We're going south,' she said. 'It's time I did what I'm supposed to do. You've had your fun.'

With a snarl, Lilith wrenched herself free and stood, fuming and fearful, beside the burnt-out fire. 'Fine,' she relented. 'Fine.'

In the pocket of her tunic, Samara relaxed her grip on the little knife.

Moodily, Lilith sat back down and picked up her three stones. Samara sat opposite her and put a hand in the dead coals of the fire. They quickly came back to life, and after adding a few more scraps of wood and removing the carcass of the water rat, the spit was soon rotating over a crackling fire, sporting a freshly-plucked chicken.

Lilith had said nothing since their brief argument. She was still staring at her seerstones and silently begging them to make sense. Samara watched her as she fiddled with the spit. The girl pitied her in a way. Sometimes, in the dark depths of a wine-sodden evening, Lilith would occasionally let stories slip from her drink-stained lips. Samara would listen to the seer rant about her life and about its brief peaks and the more consistent troughs, about how she had lost her arm, about her stones and what they had whispered to her on stormy nights.

A seer was never supposed to look at her own future, so she had said, but Lilith had been stupid enough to look. She had evaded that future ever since, living off wine and daemon blood, becoming twisted and bitter from both. Fate could be evaded, but not for long.

Samara sighed as she watched the old seer draw circles around her stones with a long fingernail. Lilith had raised her, after all. For whatever reason, be it her selfish, thirsty ways, or a promise to her dead father, Vice, or maybe even something resembling fondness, Lilith had taken Samara under her dusty wing, and taught her everything.

The girl reached for her knife and a flask of water. The glint of the steel in the morning sunlight caught Lilith's eye and she looked up, wary. Samara held the knife with its blade pointing down and dug it into the soft flesh of her palm. She barely winced. Blood sprang into the sunlight, eager to escape, and began to pool in her hand. Samara put the knife down and reached for the flask. Holding the mouth of it between her fingers, she tilted her hand so that the blood dribbled down its throat. She held her hand there for several minutes, until the cut began to close up of its own accord. The blood dried a purplish-brown on her skin.

Lilith could already feel the saliva flooding her mouth. When Samara silently handed the flask to her, she couldn't help but snatch it from her young hands. The girl went back to her cooking, and said nothing. Lilith turned away from her and began to sip, and then gulp, and then slurp at the bloody water. The pain came as it always did, and Lilith curled up into a convulsing, sweating ball for the rest of the afternoon.

When she awoke, night had fallen, and there was a shred of blanket covering her shoulders. The fire was still burning and the second chicken was now rotating above it. Samara sat on the opposite side of it. She was hunched over but wide-awake. Her face was expressionless.

Lilith, on the other hand, was not herself. The grey had disappeared from her hair and face, and now pinpricks of crimson dotted her cheeks. Her skin had pulled itself together. Her eyes had lost some of the dull mistiness they had been clutching. Lilith looked down and attempted to wiggle the fingers of her withered arm. Rewarded by a faint twitching, she cackled quietly to herself. Then, remembering her seerstones, she cast about frantically for them. 'Where are they?' she hissed. Samara pointed to the side of the fire and Lilith scrambled to grab them. She clutched them in her hands for a moment, warming them, whispering to them, before throwing them to the charcoal-speckled dirt. Samara looked on.

Lilith moved her head from side to side, as an owl would look at a blind mouse. She looked up at Samara. 'So, you want to go south, do you?' she asked, quietly.

'I do.'

'Want to do what you were made for?'

'Yes.'

'Fine.' Lilith nodded and sniffed. Her fingernail caressed the red seerstone. Visions sprang before her eyes. She saw a mage walking out of the fog. She scowled at him, shuddering. *Him.* That face had invaded her dreams many a night, haunted her for years now. He was in a city. Krauslung called to her like a shout caught on a breeze. Another face appeared as the city faded, one she had never seen before. Strong, proud, scheming. Her stones whispered frantically. Years flashed by before her, unveiling futures she had never grasped at before. It must have been the magick. Lilith began to smirk, then smile, then grin, as decades flew before her eyes. They all came crashing to a glorious, bloody end.

Lilith leant back, and sighed contentedly. 'Then I think I've just found the perfect opportunity,' she said.

chapter 8

"Take two hens and the finest goat, and make of them small chunks. Wit' the innards, set aside for a-later. Their bones and skins make the most mouth-pleasing of broths. Boil them so wit' a fistful of hewn onion, a basketweight of peelt soil potato, and half that again of carrot. Be sure to remember the herbs: cragleaf, rosemary, rockthyme, and most of all, garlick. Seethe for a two-hour, perhaps three. Once thickent, take the bones and skin away, and add yon meats, the goat, the hens. Boil them 'gain for an hour, and whilst it boil, grin'd the innards to a dust, and add a-halfway. Stir one last time. Crack one hen's egg atop the dish, and serve wit' fresh bread."

Translated from a very old cookery manual found in a cellar in Krauslung

If cities were people, then Wodehallow would be a corpulent, bloated slob, slumped and half-sunk in a marsh, still waving its goblet at the world with a sneer. It was a pit painted gold. A gash covered with a silver plate. Farden had half a mind to burn the whole place to the ground and put Albion out of its misery.

In the last ten years, Wodehallow had grown fat off the spoils of the magick trade. No wonder then that its walls had been moved twice to accommodate its swift and greedy expansion. But it was not just magick that flooded the purses of Wodehallow's finest. Slavery had come galloping to the marshes, poisoning its waters. Albion's unofficial capital now had another dark feather in its ill-fitting cap.

Slave labour: hired to the highest bidder, and all for a gross profit. Farden loathed many things. Slavery lingered near the top of his list.

Well, at least it would make killing the man responsible all the easier.

He might even enjoy this one.

The mage sat on a rock near the north wall of the city, munching on an apple and watching a gang of poor souls working on Wodehallow's latest venture. It was a huge canal, being dug one mile at a time, like a festering scar ripping south through the marshes and down to the mountains. No doubt Kiltyrin had been eager to congratulate this latest plan. *Shake with the right, stab with the left*, thought the mage. And he was the left.

Beneath his muddy rock and a stone's throw away, the clang of hammers and picks and chains was painfully constant. Farden remembered seeing the children digging for clay the day he, Durnus, and Lakkin had come to ask the Dukes for help. He remembered the man in the top-hat standing on the bridge, with his callous laughter. If he had known that this would be the result of those poor children, he would have drowned that man there and then. Hindsight was a wonderful thing, after all. Everybody is an expert at it. Farden didn't dare look too closely. There was enough disappointment in this city.

Above it all, night was falling. In the west, behind the walls and spindly cranes, the sky was still alight with the dying glow of the sun. In the east, stars had ventured out, warming up for their nightly dance, looking west for their tardy partners. Streaks of cloud stretched out between them like rafters to the sky, the colour of a bruise. Farden looked up from the busy slaves and tried to see the beauty in it all. It wasn't easy when his eyes throbbed with the pounding of the headache behind them. Nevermar wasn't without its consequences.

It had been three days since he had last touched his drug. His body now felt weak and tired. The long trek from Fleahurst hadn't helped matters. At least the weather had been kind to him; there had only been a little drizzle to contend with. Now, he had a headache which would have embarrassed even the mightiest of hangovers. It threatened to hammer Farden into the ground. All he wanted to do was sleep, but he had a Duke to kill.

Ignoring the pain in his jaw that sparked every time he chewed, Farden bit through the core of his apple and put the two halves in his pocket for later. He didn't want to add insult to the slaves' injury. He had already caught the eye of a few, glimpsed their pronounced ribs, hips, and every other bone they had to offer him.

Farden picked his way down the sloping side of the granite lump and hopped onto the wooden walkway that provided the digging pit with access. It was covered in muddy footprints from the slaves.

The mage set his sights on the glittering structure dominating the centre of the city. Wodehallow's keep, like the walls surrounding it, had also bulged and swelled like the pockets of its more ruthless inhabitants. It had almost doubled in width and girth since the last time Farden had seen it. Fresh stone jostled with old masonry, making its walls a patchwork of construction.

Farden tucked the corners of his hood into his collar and stuck his hands in his pockets. In the twilight and amongst milling throngs of people, the mage was almost invisible. Just another weary visitor on his way to gawp at the keep and the rich folk. Just the way he liked it. He closed one eye to keep the headache at bay and walked on.

To peel back his cloak, however, would have told a different story indeed. Underneath it, Farden was carting around a veritable armoury. Knives, daggers, vicious spikes, poisons, a shortsword in the small of his back; he could have supplied a small army with what he had brought. It was his way of preparing for every eventuality. Without his magick, he had only his hands and whatever they could hold.

When Farden reached the sloping road up to the keep, he was a little surprised, and a little gladdened, by the lack of guards standing at the narrow gates. Albion was obsessed by class. It wasn't unusual for cities to have concentric sets of walls to divide the echelons, to keep the peasants and the beggars from offending the eyes of the rich. That night, however, the guards were nowhere to be seen. There was even a group of beggars hovering at the empty, open gate that led up the hill. They were muttering agitatedly to themselves and peeking around its corner, as if afraid to set foot across its threshold. As the crowd around him thinned out, some disappearing down side roads, others in their finery continuing up the hill, Farden quickly fell in with the beggars, hunching over and rubbing some dirt on his cheeks so he would blend in. He listened to their eager whispers.

'I'm telling you, there ain't a soul in sight. None of the spears tonight, lads and ladies,' hissed the apparent ringleader.

'Tonight we get to see what the rich scraps taste like,' said another, a leper by the looks of his scarf and gloves, and the way he stood to one side.

'I heard that if just one thing in their cupboards spoil, they throw out the entire cupboard.'

'Full bellies tonight then.'

One of them, a woman wrapped in a blanket turned to grin at Farden, and was immediately crestfallen to find a grim and dangerous-looking man lurking behind her. His grimy face was hidden from the evening's torches by a hood. 'Ere, who's this?' she said, backing away.

One of the younger ones piped up. 'You a guard, sir?' he asked.

Farden opened his dry mouth, feeling his head pound with every fraction his jaw moved. 'I look like one?' he rasped.

The ringleader, a man with a shock of bright red hair and a face that had seen the underside of a boot a few too many times, moved forward. 'No, but you ain't one of us either.'

Farden produced a handful of silver coins. He winced as he held them out; his coffers were already dwindling. 'Let's just say I don't want to venture up the hill alone. Pretend I'm not here.'

The beggars didn't argue with that. In wide-eyed silence, each of them took a coin. Some bit them to test their worth, others bowed or curtseyed, and then, as if some lever had suddenly been pulled, they turned their backs on the mage and pretended he was invisible. Farden smiled. At least beggars knew the value of inconspicuousness, he thought.

The ragged little group finally moved forward through the gate, wary and careful, as if they had suddenly been shown into a poisoned larder and left to their own devices. The guards of inner Wodehallow were paid well to keep riffraff out of sight and mind. Were these poor souls, little better than slaves, caught lingering in this part of the city it would be boots and clubs for them, and a swift trip back the way they had come. Farden didn't care. He wasn't there to beg. He wasn't one of them.

However, discretion was his top priority, and to clash with a pack of guards was the last thing he wanted to do. He might have been searched, or worse, forced to fight, and that would raise an alarm quicker than a dragon could light a campfire. Farden kept his head down and his eyes peeled for quick exits and alleyways.

But much to his surprise, they saw not a whisker of a single guard. Farden began to wonder whether there had been some sort of trouble in another part of the city. He had been prepared for a night of sneaking about, flitting from shadow to shadow. *How fortuitous*, thought the mage. The only thing they had to deal with was the wrinkled grimaces from passers-by, curled lips and shivers. The beggars and the mage kept their faces down and their hands out for alms. Farden did the same, muttering with the best of them.

The group of beggars shuffled on, deeper and deeper. With every passing street, one or two of them would peel off, licking their lips at the sights of bins and buckets nestled beside back doors. Farden soon found himself alone with the leper, who, like the mage, seemed to be heading straight towards the keep itself.

Farden hung slightly behind him, staring at the stars emerging from the velvet bruise that was the darkening sky. The sunset was fading away. Wodehallow had begun to glitter and glow with torches. The leper turned around to look at Farden over the lip of his scarf. The mage couldn't help but wince at the scars and open sores on his face. 'You got a name, stranger?' he asked.

Farden shook his head. 'No,' he grunted.

The leper chuckled. 'So be it. I'm Beren. I'd shake your hand, but, well… you know.'

Farden said nothing for a while. Curiosity finally loosened his tongue. 'Where you headed, then?'

Beren pointed up at the building dominating the evening sky with a hand wrapped in dirty bandages. It loomed above them. They were getting closer now. The road had become steeper and cobbled. 'The keep. Same as you, by the looks of it.'

'Why?'

'Could ask you the same question. Something tells me I don't want to know.'

Farden narrowed his eyes at the man. 'Mark my words; you don't.'

Beren held up his bandaged hands with a chuckle. 'No good threatening me, man-with-no-name, I'm one step away from the grave as it is.' He lowered his scarf to taste the night air. It wasn't an inspiring taste. 'Some men in this city think we don't exist. Others'll tell you it's the way of things. But it ain't. Cities need schools, hospitals, places for people like me. We've got none of that. Wodehallow is blinder than a mole in a sack, he is.'

'So?'

'So, I'm going to tell him.'

Farden fought the urge to laugh. 'Good luck.'

'Thank you,' said the man, shrugging off the sarcasm. He

coughed then, a horrible choking cough that shook his body. Farden paused by his side while he recovered, though he wasn't sure why. He could feel the looks of disdain and disgust from passers-by. 'Getting worse by the day.'

'You or the city?'

'Both.'

Farden nodded.

Beren took a few deep breaths before they walked on. He sighed. 'I've asked the gods every day to heal me. Put those marketplace priests to shame, I do, the amount I pray.' *Men with death sentences always do*, thought Farden. He snorted and spat on the cobbles.

'I learnt a long time ago that the gods only care about themselves. They're meddlers and time-wasters.'

'Is that so, stranger?'

'Trust me. I heard it from a good source.'

'You blame the gods for who you are? Whatever that may be?'

Farden shrugged. 'I am what time and circumstance have made me,' he replied, echoing words a certain goddess had hissed to him long ago, in another life.

'As am I, man-with-no-name. The gods didn't do this to me. Way of the world. But what good would light be without shadow to show it, eh? Look at these torches.' Beren flapped his hand. 'They only come alive in the dark. Wouldn't know they were here if the whole world was on fire, would you?'

Farden stumbled over that last sentence, the leper's words tugged on a long-buried memory. His headache suddenly jabbed him, and the moment was forgotten.

Beren continued. 'At first, I blamed myself for catching the rot. Then I blamed the gods. Then I blamed myself for getting others sick, and they blamed me too. I spent years on my own, just wandering about the marshes. I was lost in more ways than one, I was, but then I had one of those things that scholars have. *Epiphanies*, I'm told they're called. Why was I spending the time I had left moping about in bogs when I could be helping others? Hmm? Even a life as cursed as mine is precious, so who am I to squander it? Life deserves better than that. It deserves to be lived, not endured.'

'So that's why you're here,' replied the mage, trying to ignore the wisdom in the man's words. 'To help someone?'

Beren nodded. 'More than just someone. As I said, one step closer to the grave than the rest of us. What have I got to lose?'

'Your life?'

'Overrated, in the face of the cause. There are others in this city that deserve better. If I can make a little difference, then that's all that matters.' Farden resisted the urge to snort again. Morals and causes. *Overrated, in the face of reality*. The leper must have spent his youth inhaling books of philosophy and wise words, he surmised. He'd plenty of it to regurgitate.

Farden looked up and noticed how near they were to the keep. Its main entrance, a huge set of double doors, was only a few hundred yards away. Here there were guards. Throngs of them, and plenty of people too. The babbling brook of fortuity had finally dried up. Farden slowed to a halt. Beren turned around and watched the mage tuck himself into a doorway and begin to plot his entrance. There appeared to be only one way in, and that was out of the question. Unless... Farden's gaze roved over the roots of the keep and the cluster of buildings that had been built around it. A drainpipe. A skewed roof, bristling with wind-torn tiles. Scaffolding. A balcony... There. It clung to the side of the keep walls, only two levels above the street, far enough away from the main entrance. The mage lifted up the back of his cloak and began to feel around in his haversack for his coil of rope and the hook.

Beren sniffed. 'Thief,' he stated.

Farden shook his head. 'No. Much worse.'

'I…' Beren looked as though he was about to back away, but he stayed put. 'And you do this… for a living?'

'Wouldn't call it a living.'

It was hard to tell behind his scarf, but Farden guessed the leper was unimpressed, grimacing. 'You may not be a leper like me, but something's still eating away at you,' he said.

'Mhm,' Farden hummed, unwilling to give that a response. Beren shrugged. He'd tried. With a little sigh, he turned and walked away, heading straight for the main entrance.

Farden lifted an eye to watch him go. 'Good luck, Beren,' he mumbled.

Beren didn't respond, but he had heard. His ears still worked just fine.

Farden followed in the shadows behind. Successful or not, the leper would be a distraction at the very least, and he could use that to his advantage… Farden bit his lip, feeling the little sting of guilt for thinking in such a way. But it was cold, iron fact, he told himself, and he kept moving.

The streets surrounding the keep were narrow, and irritatingly well lit. They were noisy too. As night had only just fallen, there were plenty of people wandering the streets; rich folk in their finery, heading to dinner, or home, or, if they were lucky, to whatever banquet the Duke was holding that eve. Farden worked a jagged path around to the eastern side of the keep, lurking in doorways or alleys. When he couldn't hide, he simply crouched down with his hands out, muttering about alms. It worked a treat. The people hurried past, ignoring him, save for the occasional gob of spit on his cloak, or in his hands. But no shouts. No calls for guards.

Farden could hear shouting coming from the keep entrance now, only a street or so away. A shrill squeal of a woman rang out. He quickened his pace.

Whatever it was, by the time he reached the corner of the keep, between his balcony and the main entrance, the number of guards had doubled, and there was a throng of agitated nobles clustered together, clutching each other. They were all trying to get a glimpse of something inside the keep, but the guards were holding them back.

'Keep back there!'

'Be still, lady!'

'Oi! No pushing!'

'He's a leper! You wanna get sick, do yer?'

Beren had been a distraction after all. Farden quickly stepped into the bright street and put his back to the crowd. A throng of people rushed past him. Even a guard or two. They barely noticed him. Perfect.

A few minutes later, the mage was crouching by a barrel of rainwater. In front of him was the eastern wall of the keep. A sheer construction, slimy with age, with no doors or windows at street level, just one lone balcony hovering about thirty feet above him. A single torch sat on its railing. The door behind it was closed, and its little window dark. Perfect indeed.

Farden leant out into the street and cupped his ear. He could still hear the muted rattle of a commotion, tumbling through the streets. It was quiet here, between the low buildings and dark, grand houses. Distractions were wonderful things. Nobody noticed a double-sided hook, painted black with soot, soar upward into the air. Nobody heard the thud of its padded spikes as it caught the stone railing of the balcony. Nobody saw a cloaked figure run up the wall and haul himself up the skinny rope.

The mage dragged himself over the railing and crouched behind the door. His breathing came in heavy slurps. His head pounded like a blacksmith's forge with the effort of the climb. His arms burnt. Farden grit his teeth. He had never felt this weak before.

When the feeling had passed, he staggered to his feet, coiling up the rope and its hook. He left it on the balcony, just in case, and then went to try the door. Unbelievably, it was open. Farden had to keep from laughing. Whomever owned this room obviously hadn't expected any intruders to be so bold, or so stupid. Farden gently pushed it open, wincing with every little creak and whine the hinges made, and slipped into the dark room.

He let the glow of the city light his path while his eyes adjusted. The room was empty. There was a large bed on his left. A wardrobe on his right. Somebody had laid out an outfit on the bed. Farden frowned at it. A gaudy pair of stockings with matching pointy shoes, a tartan tunic, and a jacket with ripped sleeves to show the silk lining. *Fashion*, he thought, a practice of the vacuous, the time-rich, a notion for the pyre. Farden barely resisted hawking a great glob of spit on the display. That would have made a nice accessory at the banquet.

Farden was reaching for the doorknob when it suddenly began to turn. The door sprang open and the mage was abruptly confronted by a portly man wearing naught but a towel and a very confused expression. Farden's reactions snapped into life. Without hesitation, he grabbed the man by the throat, choking the shout that was about to escape, and dragged him into the room. *Bang!* He kicked the door shut with the toe of his boot. *Thwack*! Farden slammed the man onto the floor with both hands.

'Where is the Duke?' he hissed.

'Gurgh!' choked his victim.

'Come again?' he snapped, releasing his grip on the man's neck ever so slightly.

'B…banquet hall!'

'Thank you,' said the mage. He grabbed the man by his hair, lifted him up by it, and then slammed him back down, cracking his head neatly against the stone of the floor. The man went as limp as a sock. Farden knelt down and held a hand over his chest. His heart fluttered weakly, but it fluttered all the same. Farden shrugged and pushed the fat, naked man under the bed, using his own towel to wipe the little streak of blood from the stone, lest any maid come to check on her master. His head was pounding once again. *All this excitement*, he cursed.

Farden tentatively reached for the doorknob for a second time. He turned it slowly, pulled, and a shaft of yellow light fell in to pierce the darkness. He pressed his eye to the crack and spied a well-lit corridor beyond. Two women in long dresses floated past, nattering softly to each other. There was a guard standing by a window at the far end of the corridor. The mage wrinkled his nose. This wasn't going to be easy.

Farden leant away from the door and rubbed his stubbled chin in thought. Out of the corner of his eye he spied his reflection standing in a thin mirror beside the wardrobe. The mage leant into the shaft of light spilling through the open door. He grimaced at the sight of himself. If he were a guard, he would have speared the mage on the spot, no questions muttered. Everything about him screamed trespasser. Intruder. Deadly. Halt! Farden let his head loll to the side, looking at the outfit splayed across the bed. He took a deep breath. *Very well*, he told himself, trying his very best to think of the large sack of gold waiting for him back in Castle Tayn.

No more than a minute later, Farden was standing in the corridor, dressed from head to toe in his stolen finery, and feeling very uncomfortable indeed. He pulled his tunic down for the tenth time and made sure his knives weren't showing. His tights itched. His shoes bit. The jacket smelled of flowers and scented oils, and his tartan tunic was too small. The man hadn't just been portly, but he was short too, and the mage, being a hint over six foot, barely squeezed into his clothes. The Albion fashion of long, flowing sleeves was his only blessing; they hid his vambraces perfectly. With a sigh, Farden combed his long, sweaty hair to one side, tried on a polite smile, and walked confidently towards the guard at the end of the corridor.

The sound of his shoes on the carpet thudded out a death march. One, two, three, closer and closer he got to the guard. Farden stretched his smile to the very limits of his jaws, fingers tightly clasped behind his back. Shoulders back. Toes pointed. He smiled and he smiled and he…

'Good evening, sir,' said the guard, bowing low and waving him past.

'Evening!' Farden cried, a little over-enthusiastically. He tried to smile even harder, but ended up grimacing, so he nodded and hurried on down the corridor, trying to keep his pace slow and calm. He barely managed.

Silence. He had begun to notice it, hanging in the corridors and doorways like a low, heavy mist. Where was the music? The clattering sounds of banqueting? The whooping and drunken braying of the dancers? Save for the shuffling of his feet, all was quiet in the corridors.

He soon found out why.

Farden turned a corner and came to an archway leading out onto a balcony. The light and smell and warmth of a crowded hall washed over him as he left the corridor to lean over the railings. Spread out below him was a circle of tables holding a feast that would have made a beggar cry. Nobody seemed to be eating, just staring. Farden followed their gazes to a man in rags, lying on his stomach near the entrance. Specks of blood surrounded him. A trio of guards held their spears, at arm's length, to his neck, where a scarf had been tightly wrapped. Beren. The poor leper had his hands and feet bound by rope. His chest heaved slowly. There was a crowd of nobles and guests standing in a crescent around him. Nobody wanted to get too close. A large man in a purple robe was pacing up and down before him. Wodehallow. Farden leant further forward. His voice was a low rumble to the mage's ears.

Wodehallow. He had aged badly. The paintbrush of time had daubed his face with liver spots and burst purple blood vessels. His hands were clasped across his ample belly. His grey hair had been waxed and combed sideways over his head to hide the growing bald spot that was threatening to usurp his hoary tresses. Even from that distance, Farden could see the skin of his hands were like parchment, flaked like pastry. And yet still he wore that guileful, inimical little smirk that the mage could recall from their last meeting, so long ago. His nevermar had stolen most of his memories, burnt them to ash, but that he remembered.

Farden thought of the slaves in the canal. He thought of the children digging for clay. He thought of the beggars rummaging through bins. He thought of the stench of the factories several walls and a window away. He sniffed the air and tasted fat-drenched geese and sweet wine and sugar icing wafting around the hall. He watched the ladies and men in their finery shrug and go back to their dancing. He listened to the bards and skalds as they picked up their instruments as if nothing had interrupted them. He watched Beren as he was dragged away by the rope around his legs. Farden's hand strayed to the knife hiding under his tunic. *This blade might actually do some good tonight*, he thought.

The mage crouched down behind a large emerald flag that had been draped over the railing and loosened his belt so he could quickly snatch at his knives. He had left the sword with his clothes in the room. It was too bulky to hide under anything but a cloak. Farden rubbed his forehead, cursing his headache. It still hammered away at his poor brain. His thoughts were a bruised mess. He clamped his eyes shut, clamped his teeth, and did his best to stifle them.

When he opened his eyes he found an elderly woman with a knot of dark hair standing over him. Her arms were crossed. There was a stern expression pasted across her painted, powdered features. Farden jumped to his feet and adjusted his tight clothes, trying to smile. She pursed her red lips.

'Madam.'

'Tsk. You men are all the same. Why don't you just go to bed if you can't handle your drink, hmm?' she berated.

Farden feigned a sheepish look and shrugged. 'Just a headache, madam.'

The woman rolled her eyes. 'Sure it is,' she tutted, beginning to walk away. 'The feast has barely begun and we're already knee-deep in drunks and lepers.'

Farden cleared his throat and combed his hair back into place. He hoped his dishevelled, scarred face wouldn't attract too much attention. No doubt, in this crowd, he was a new face, and an unsightly one at that. He would have to do this quickly, before anybody became curious enough to challenge him. Farden peeked over the railing and saw the Duke sitting at the apex of the circle of tables, surrounded by his lords and nobles. His fawners. A burly guard with a green cape emblazoned with the crest of Wodehallow, a trio of boars on a harlequin platter, pushed his way between the guests and leant to whisper in the fat Duke's ear. Wodehallow nodded along to the secret words, and then excused himself from the table. High on the balcony, the mage began to move. He could sense an opportunity. It was time.

As Wodehallow rose from his chair and swaggered through the clumps of people swigging wine and chin-wagging, a pair of gaudy shoes padded swiftly down the oak stairs of the balcony and onto the granite flagstones of the hall. The Duke paused briefly to take a goblet of wine from a passing servant. A woman, barely more than a girl, moved past him, a fair hand lingering on his arm. She whispered something in his ear and he chortled, flicking wine on her neck and chest. She giggled and melted back into the crowd. Wodehallow swaggered towards a door at the back of the hall. A door flanked by guards.

Wodehallow reached the door. Farden was barely a few yards behind and swiftly closing in, weaving his way through the minglers and drunkards like a pickpocket. If this kill was to be public, then so be it. He would fight his way out, magick or no magick. He had done it before. Farden's narrowed eyes burnt into the back of the Duke's skull. His head throbbed with the music and the laughter in the hall, but he ignored it all. His sweating fingers throttled the handle of his hidden blade.

The Duke paused momentarily at the door. He laid a chubby hand on its handle while he muttered something to the pair of guards. The mage seized his moment. He surged forward, pushing his way through a gaggle of guests like a river punching through a weak dam. A woman squealed as she was shoved aside, making the guards at the door look up. Wodehallow turned, and saw death staring back at him. Death in the face and hands of a bedraggled, long-haired man in an ill-fitting outfit. His face was like steel, harder than the blade flashing in his hand. Wodehallow's flushed cheeks ran a horrified shade of white.

'Guards!' he managed to gasp, before pushing through the door and hurtling into the dark room beyond. Farden leapt after him, snarling. The guards brought down their spears, but Farden was already too close for comfort. A knife slammed into the eye-socket of the first. A fist ploughed into the groin of the second. Both men crumpled to the floor, one dead, one wheezing. Farden's head exploded with pain after the sudden, jerking movement, but he grit his teeth and ran on, dashing through the doorway and slamming it shut behind him. He was plunged into gloom. He felt for a bolt and found a wooden bar instead. It thudded as he rammed it down into its iron cradle. Farden turned around, and another knife snaked out from under his tunic, hungry for blood like its twin.

The room was musty, low-ceilinged, and dark, lit only by a single candle on the far wall. It was also a dead end. There were no windows, and no doors save for the one at his back. As fists began to pound on it, Farden took a step forward and scoured the shadows for his prey. It didn't take him very long to find it. There, at the far end of the room, lit by the wobbling light of the lone flame, Wodehallow was cowering behind a crate of cabbages.

Farden couldn't help but grin. This was all too easy.

Wait… his pounding brain shouted.

All too late. Something painfully hard and thoroughly heavy struck him square in the back of the skull, sending a shower of sparks surging through his eyes. Farden crumpled to the floor. The pain left him breathless. He gasped against the cold stone of the floor. It pushed against his cheek, urging him to get up. He lifted his hands and began to push, but a blunt object prodded him hard in the back of his neck. He slumped to the stone again. A line of blood began to wander down his forehead.

'The Fiend never misses!' somebody chuckled.

'That it don't, Forluss, that it don't,' a high-pitched voice replied. Kint. It was unmistakeable. Farden groaned with pain and frustration. Somebody crouched beside him. He could feel their breath in his ear, slippery like the blood that was beginning to fill it. The toe of a black boot rocked onto his left hand and pressed down. Farden winced. 'What have you gotten yourself into now, Four-Hand?' Kint again.

The mage didn't reply. His head swam with questions and skull-splitting pain. He twisted his head to watch Wodehallow rise from his hiding spot and waddle closer. 'A fine job, you two,' he gloated. Kint and Fat Forluss quickly bowed. They were wearing chainmail and leather, with surcoats emblazoned with the cat and daggers over the top.

'Thank you, yer Duke.'

'Thank'ee, lord,' they chimed.

Wodehallow folded his arms across his fat belly. 'Roll him over so I can see his treacherous face,' he ordered.

Two pairs of hands grabbed Farden by his collar and turned him over. Farden tried to struggle but he quickly found the sharp edge of The Fiend pressing against his windpipe. Broken glass on rough skin. The mage tried to glare at Forluss but just felt nauseous instead. He wanted to vomit.

The upside-down face of Duke Wodehallow came into view, and an upside-down smirk as well. 'I recognise you,' he mused. 'But why?'

'Never forget a face, yer lordship?' asked Kint, swaggering about behind Forluss, gathering rope and other things.

'Never in a hundred years. It pays for a man of my position to recall every fellow you deal with, especially one as dangerous as this.'

'Dangerous, is he?' Forluss couldn't help but chuckle, that low, burly grunting.

Wodehallow leant closer. He peered into the mage's glazed eyes. 'Indeed. This man isn't just your average assassin. I wonder where young Duke Leath found you then, hmm?' Wodehallow stood straight and kicked Farden viciously in the ribs with the pointy toe of his silk shoe. Farden coughed and spluttered. 'Kiltyrin was right after all, what a vicious card that plucky young bastard Leath has been hiding up his sleeve. And barely off his mother's tit too. Little shite.' Wodehallow had turned an angry beetroot. 'Try to kill me, in my own house? My own city? We will have to teach him a lesson!'

'That you will, sire,' Kint nodded. As Wodehallow stamped towards the door, Kint threw back the thick oak bar and opened the door wide for him. Bright torchlight flooded the room, half-blinding Farden in the process. Outside, two lines of smug-faced guards waited patiently for him, as well as a crowd of curious men and women. The dead guard had already been cleared away. By his side, the Duke leant close to Kint so he could mutter in his notched ear. 'Be sure to thank your Duke for his kind warning. And please inform him I will be travelling to Tayn very soon. He and I need to have a very long discussion about how to deal with Leath's treachery!'

'Of course, yer lordship. I'll tell him.'

Wodehallow plucked one of the gold rings from his chubby fingers and dropped it into Kint's palm. 'Something for your troubles.'

Kint and Forluss bowed low. 'Thank'ee, sire. Thank'ee kindly.'

'Now, remove that bloody tripe from my sight. Do with him as you will. I'm sure you have some ideas,' ordered the Duke.

Fat Forluss grinned and patted the ugly head of The Fiend. 'That we do, sire.'

Still beetroot-angry, Wodehallow stepped out into the hall, arms raised like some sort of victor, basking in the cheering and laughter of his fawning subjects. Kint and Forluss stayed behind.

Farden groaned. His ragged fingernails scraped on the cold stone beneath him, clawing for a way out. The pain thundering inside his skull was unbearable. He grit his teeth and held two hands to his bloody forehead. *If only…* he thought, in between the pounding. An itching at the base of his skull sent a fresh wave of fire through his brain. No. It was far too late for that. Far too late. Even if he could summon it, even if he let himself, the pain of it would kill him now, rather than save him. No. He had banished it a long time ago. He had sworn.

As Kint half-closed the door, Forluss stood over the prostrate mage. He smacked his palm rhythmically with The Fiend. Kint soon joined him, and together they stared down at the gasping, bleeding mage.

'What now then?' Farden coughed. 'This is it? Clubbed to death in a storeroom?'

'Oho, just you wait, Four-Hand. We got a little business to take care of first,' said Kint.

Forluss bent down, not without some difficulty from his ample belly, and began to fold one of the mage's sleeves. Farden wrenched his arm away, wide-eyed and frantic, but Kint kicked him hard in the ribs. He relented with a rasping wheeze. Forluss pulled the mage's sleeve up past his wrist, and a splash of red and gold sparkled in the half-lit room. 'Well, ain't that a pretty sight?' he mumbled, fingers roving the vambrace's folds and joins.

'Look at that. Duke was right after all,' muttered Kint.

Forluss looked up. 'What, you think he was lying?'

Kint had produced a blade. He twirled it around in his left hand while his eyes hungrily tugged at the armour on the mage's forearm. 'No, I just never thought this bastard would be that special. Scaluston armour. Well I never.'

Farden tried his best not to laugh, nor to vomit. '*Scalussen*, you brainless shit.'

Kint's face flashed with rage. He dropped to his knees and seized Farden by his left ear. The tip of the blade nicked his earlobe. 'Listen 'ere, Farden. Right now, you ain't in the place to be insulting anyone. So why don't you just shut it, or I'll see to it that your tongue finds its way to your stomach. Got it?'

Farden didn't answer. His vision was slowly misting over. He could feel the blood seeping into the collar of his tartan tunic. Kint grabbed the mage's other arm. He dug the point of the knife into the sleeve and found metal underneath. 'A matching pair,' he grinned. 'Where's the rest, hmm?' Kint jabbed at Farden's pockets. The mage yelped as the blade punctured his thigh. 'None in there,' said Kint. Next he jabbed at his shins but found nothing but cloth, skin, and bone. Farden grit his teeth. Kint was turning red now. He stared at his fat comrade.

Forluss shrugged. 'Where's the rest of it?'

Kint swore darkly. 'Not here, that's where!' he yelled shrilly as he got to his feet. He kicked Farden again and again, square in the ribs. The mage doubled up with pain. 'Where is it?!'

It took a while for Farden to regain his breath. When he did, a little smile crept across his lips. 'Why don't you ask your mother? She told me she'd keep it safe.'

Kint's face turned purple. He held the dagger high above his head, and would have plunged it into Farden's chest had it not been for Forluss poking him with The Fiend. 'Oi! Remember what the Duke said! No mage, no armour, and no armour…?'

Kint bared his teeth. He made a strangled sound of exasperation in his throat. 'No use coming back,' he hissed. He kicked Farden one last time for good measure and then went to get some nearby rope. 'Looks like we're going on a little journey, Forluss.'

Forluss began to chuckle again, that slow, dumb-sounding *hur-hur-hur* noise he always made when sensing some delicious misfortune ahead. Such a laugh really did nothing to quash the low opinions of the man's intellectual capacity. He poked Farden in the gut with his ugly club. 'South?'

Kint folded the rope into a stout knot and rolled Farden onto his face. The mage could taste his own blood on the floor. 'South indeed. And a little east, if I remember rightly.'

Farden's insides died a little as his heart sank to his stomach. He had been followed back to his shack. Stalked, like common prey. The pain of that realisation duelled with his headache for dominance. He closed his eyes but found himself holding tightly to consciousness. Desperate. The fingers of a man clinging to a cliff. He could not let Kiltyrin get his claws on his armour…

Kint and Forluss were discussing something above him.

'You reckon you can keep him alive?'

'I'm a torturer, I ain't a healer, Kint.'

'I know that, fool, but what I'm saying is does it work both ways? You keep 'em alive for long enough, don't you?'

'Do what I can.'

'Good, now roll that sleeve down. Don't want 'is lordship Wodehallow getting greedy. This armour's meant for a different

Duke.'

'What's so special about it anyway?'

'Who knows. You tie him up and keep him quiet, I'll go see if Wartan is ready with the cart.'

'Right you are.'

The following thwack from The Fiend sent Farden tumbling into a pain-soaked oblivion.

chapter 9

"Greed is a curious monster. It has the eyes of a hawk, the feet of a cat, the poison of an adder, and the smile of a wolf."
Traditional Skölgard proverb

A single tail of cloud split the sky in two. Farden watched it between the gaps in the virescent trees. Above, curious crows hopped from branch to branch, following the rattling, bumbling cart. They peered down at the mage like he stared up at them. They were silent, and watchful. Never what a dead man wants to see.

Only he wasn't dead. Dead men don't feel pain.

The cart hit yet another rut and his head banged on the wood. Farden squeezed his eyes shut as another wave of pain crashed down on him. It almost took his breath away. He had been better off unconscious, he thought.

Even though his neck was numb from the effort, the mage tried once again to rest his head on his shoulder so that it wouldn't collide with the wood. On this flint road, with the cart's iron-clad wheels, Farden's pain-wracked body felt every single bump and stone. Every single one. It felt as if they were being hurled at him. The mage gasped again as the cart hit another. The corners of his eyes throbbed. He hadn't even thought that anatomically possible. There were other tortures too, lying in the grubby cart: the tight ropes around his wrists and ankles were beginning to chafe, his shoulders and hips ached from where he was splayed out and tied down, and his skin was starting to burn in the sun, even weak as it was. Farden closed his eyes and tried to retreat into the quiet semi-conscious darkness inside him, a place where he could cling to life but where the pain subsided. He was almost there when a deep voice dragged him back.

'You still alive, Four-Hand?' it yelled. Forluss was squinting at him. Farden moved his head so he could glare at him. A man, the guard from Tayn with the broken face, Wartan, if Farden recalled, sat beside him. He was staring intently at the mage. Kint was on Forluss' other side. He was busy driving the two cows that pulled their cart. There was a fourth man somewhere nearby. He could hear him whistling a lively tune from somewhere, walking beside the cart. Farden cursed all four of them under his breath.

'I said, are you alive?'

Farden's only reply was to close his eyes and lift his middle finger up. Even that little movement hurt, but it was worth it to hear Fat Forluss grunt with anger. Moments later, he was splashed in the face with ice-cold water. The mage choked, but then quickly tried to lick it from his cracked lips before it slipped away.

'Well, there goes your fucken' water ration for the day. Enjoy. Idiot.'

Another bump in the road, another skull-splitting thud. Farden squeezed his eyes tight, retreating into his darkness. In the gloom of his mind he could see a candle on a little wooden table, beset on all sides by thick shadows. Wind and rain prowled at the edges of the darkness. The candle was weak, but alight, afraid. Farden put his tired head on his shoulders and concentrated on keeping his candle lit. *Always were a stubborn bastard*, said a voice in his head. *Maybe this time it'll keep you alive.*

❦

The cart bumbled on, led by its docile white cows, deep into the east. The forest around them died away, soon replaced by scrub and moorland, miles and miles of it. There wasn't a landmark in sight, only hills, gorse bushes, and the winding flint road.

Kint and Forluss chatted idly between themselves, swapping stories of guts and glory. Wartan occasionally grunted something. All the while, the fourth man, who seemed perfectly content to let the miles trundle by under his feet, kept to his whistling. Farden floated in and out of consciousness as the hot day turned into desperately cold, shivering night, and then into blistering day once again. It was all a matter of moments and brief glimpses of the sky and a bumpy road, all sense of time and distance melted into flashes of pain, and a candle in the dark. Such things are dreams.

It was only when the mage cracked open his swollen and sunburnt eyelids and saw a silvery grey tangle of skeletal branches resting against a grey-blue sky that he truly awoke. A tree. An ash tree if he wasn't mistaken. Just like the one that sat on the hill above his little shack…

Farden tried to sit up but the ropes dragged him back down. He caught a quick glimpse of the countryside over the edge of the cart and groaned. Fleahurst. Against the stench of his sour sweat and sticky blood, of greasy wood and tired cow, he could taste salt in the air. He could hear the hissing of nearby waves. Farden groaned.

'Home sweet home,' laughed Kint, from somewhere nearby. Farden looked up as far as he could, trying to ride the dizziness. His mouth tasted like ash. The four men lingered at the tail of the cart, smoking their pipes. Forluss idly twirled his club around in circles, laughing that doltish laugh of his. The other man, Wartan, was silent and expressionless. The last, the one Farden rightly guessed to be the whistler, simply tipped his flat hat and smiled. It took a moment, but Farden slowly began to recognise him. The man from the corridor outside Kiltyrin's room in Castle Tayn, the tall man with the shaven head and the broken nose.

Farden put his head gently back and looked up at the ash tree, ignoring them all. Maybe this was just a nightmare. Maybe he would wake up. Fat chance. His head still had not stopped pounding. He was awake, and it was very, very real. He cursed it all as four pairs of hands set about untying the ropes that bound him.

Once they were loose, Farden was dragged from the cart and dumped unceremoniously in the dirt. He wasn't even allowed a moment to rub the feeling back into his wrists and hands. After the tall man had bound his hands with some spare rope, Kint and Forluss wrenched him upwards by his long hair and pushed him forward. It was a miracle he actually managed to stand. His legs felt like rotten wood.

'Go,' said Kint, pushing him again. 'Show us where you're hiding the rest of it.' Farden turned around to glare daggers at him, but found a spear-tip pressing against his neck. Wartan was at the end of it, narrow-eyed and broken-faced. He could see it now, in that unflinching stare. The man had murder in his eyes. Farden knew it well. He lowered his head and shuffled along the dirt path towards the sea.

Grudgingly, the mage led the four men down the path and towards his little shack. He desperately wracked his brain for an answer or a plan, but nothing came. Nobody for miles. Not a soul nor saviour, save for one rat. Farden thought of all the things in his shack, mentally assessing each one in turn to see if they could help him.

A crossbow behind the fireplace.

His little candle-carving knife, buried in the top of the lobster pot.

Various pieces of pilfered cutlery.

A pan.

Whiskers' sharp teeth.

The mage winced as the spear nicked the back of his neck. He could feel a trickle of hot blood run down his numb back.

When they came to the shack, Farden was pushed to the side and kicked to his knees. A brave seagull hovered on a thermal above them, mewing plaintively. Kint and Forluss quickly went to the door, while the third man lingered by the step, arms crossed and patient. Wartan stayed behind Farden and kept his spear pressing against his skin.

There was a bang as Kint kicked in the door. Part of the door-frame shattered under the impact. Farden stared at the dirt; there was nothing to help him there either. Hopeless.

Inside the shack, Kint and Forluss wrinkled their noses at the smell of mouldy, rotting food, seaweed, and nevermar. Even for them, it was disgusting, a murderer and a torturer no less. Ignoring it, they began searching in earnest, pushing aside the threadbare furniture and smashing the boxes and chests that had been piled in one corner. Kint found a pan covered with a cloth. He lifted up the corner of it and wrinkled his nose at the foul smell. 'Not in there,' he muttered. Behind him Forluss was busy kicking the stove apart.

'Not in here either.'

Outside, Farden listened to the bangs and crashes, a little part of him dying with each one. A lobster pot flew out of the door, narrowly missing the tall man on the steps. He cleared his throat. 'Kint, Forluss, enough. You're wasting your time.'

Kint and his comrade appeared at the door. There was soot on their faces. 'Well ain't that the truth,' Kint spat. 'What would you suggest then, Loffrey? Any bright ideas?'

The man called Loffrey adjusted his flat cap and turned to face Farden. He stared down at the mage for a moment, and the mage stared right back up at him. All Farden could think of was what he planned on doing to the man's face if he ever had the chance. Farden tried his hardest to look defiant, but deny it as he might, there was a dark hole of fear growing inside him, getting wider with every moment. Farden shivered even in the sunlight.

The man, this Loffrey, tapped his foot on the step. 'What's the strongest part of any house?'

'Roof?' ventured Forluss. He was sweating profusely, as always. He wiped his forehead with the back of his grubby, travel-dusty hand.

Loffrey shook his head. 'The foundations, you dolt. Rip up the floorboards.'

Kint clicked his fingers and the three went inside to start hacking at the floorboards. Farden's head sank into his chest. The dark hole kept growing. There was a grunt from behind him. 'You don't remember me, do yer?' asked Wartan.

The mage didn't answer. He was too busy counting the bangs and crashes, moving his dry husk of a tongue around a sandy mouth.

'Oi. I'm asking you a question.'

Farden looked up at the man and his misshapen face. Whatever had happened to him had been truly brutal. 'No, I don't,' he mumbled.

The spear jabbed again. Wartan moved to stand in front of the mage. He crouched down, spear up, and pointed to his face. 'Remember Biennh?'

Farden couldn't really care less. He had bigger things to worry about. 'I vaguely recall that pitiful hole.'

Wartan beamed. It was not a pretty sight. 'Well that pitiful 'ole was where you broke me face. Remember that? I've been lookin' for you fer many years, I 'ave. Waitin' to get my revenge on the mage who broke me and my gang.'

Farden recalled a stormy night and a band of thugs. He remembered a man with a boot in his face but the rest had been forgotten. Farden shrugged, wishing he had saliva to spit. Hopeless indeed. 'Then get in line. You weren't the first face I broke and you won't be the last.'

'Heh. We'll just see 'bout that now, won't we, mage?'

Farden didn't reply, but the man's words rang true. Wider and wider grew that hole.

There came a shout from inside the shack. 'Rat!' Farden tried to stand up but Wartan kicked him back to his knees.

'Kill it!' shouted Kint. There was a chorus of stamping boots and Farden winced with every single thud. It was over in an instant. The mage strained against his ropes.

'It's gone,' somebody said. Farden sighed with relief.

'And look what we found instead.'

The sigh caught in his throat.

Moments later, Kint and Forluss emerged from the door of the shack. In their hands balanced glittering treasures of red and gold. Loffrey was close behind them, hopping around eagerly. Farden put his head in the dust, straining and straining. 'Ain't they pretty?' Forluss chuckled. *Hur hur hur…*

Loffrey waggled a finger. 'Give one here, and make sure you keep your greasy, sweaty fingers from smudging them, you hear me?'

Forluss nodded, looking to Kint. They obviously didn't like being ordered about by this man. Nevertheless, they did what he said. Forluss handed Loffrey one of the gauntlets, and the man crouched down beside Farden. 'Well these are beautiful, I must say,' Loffrey began, pulling Farden's head up. The mage's dust and blood-smattered face burnt with hatred. Loffrey turned the gauntlet over and over in his hands. 'I do hope they are what I think they are. It would be a shame to waste all this time and coin, wouldn't it? The Duke would be most disappointed. Well, I suppose there's only one way to find out. Do tell me if I'm doing it right.'

Farden growled as Loffrey put his hand inside the gauntlet. The metal contracted around his fingers and he clenched a fist. 'Incredible,' said the man. Farden wondered who the hell this man was and how he had come to know so much about Scalussen armour.

Loffrey closed his eyes and waved his hand in a figure-of-eight in the air.

'What does it feel like?' asked Kint.

'It actually feels like nothing.'

'Must be broken then.' This from Fat Forluss.

'On the contrary, gentlemen. Only very few people can feel the effects of true Scalussen armour. I bet a fair bit of coin that you can, mage, hmm?'

'How do you know it ain't broken then? Or a fake?'

Loffrey shook his head. He tugged at the gauntlet and the metal peeled away all by itself, releasing his hand. 'Do you think that looks broken or fake to you, man?'

Kint had to shake his head. Forluss piped up. 'What's so rare about this lot then?'

Loffrey sighed, a sigh of a man who had explained this a dozen times already. 'All Scalussen armour is rare, you idiot. It was made a thousand years ago by the Scalussen smiths, who to this day managed to make the finest armour and arms known to mankind. That's why you'll only ever see it being worn by those who are rich enough to buy it, brave enough to steal it, or hardy enough to take it.'

'So? I've seen some good armour in my time. The pretty stuff don't always do the job. Why's this lot so special then, aside from doing that shrinking trick and how bloody old it is?'

Loffrey bit his lip. 'Why don't you take your knife and see if you can scratch it, Kint?'

Kint drew his knife with relish. He held one of the greaves he was carrying in one hand and his knife with the other. With a screeching sound, Kint dragged the tip of the knife along one of the greave's steel scales. There wasn't even a hint of a scratch. He tried again, and again, getting angrier every time he tried, until Loffrey snatched it from him. 'See?' he said. 'Scalussen armour is magick armour. Some of it moves on its own. Some of it changes colour.

Some of it even burns you if you touch it.'

'And what does this lot do?' Forluss asked, still sweating.

'*This* lot, gentlemen, is more than rare. So rare, in fact, that everybody thinks it doesn't exist.' Loffrey turned back to the mage and lifted his aching head up and into the sunlight. 'How old do you think he looks, hmm? What would you guess?'

Kint shrugged. 'Not a year older than me.'

'Or me,' added Forluss.

'Or me,' said Wartan.

'And how old is that?'

'Thirty?' Kint looked around and the other two nodded. Forluss didn't actually know. He had lost count a few years back thanks to the perpetual Long Winter and a poorer-than-average skill with a calendar. 'Thirty-ish,' asserted Kint.

'Farden has barely aged a day since I last saw him,' said Loffrey, and at this the mage narrowed his eyes, trying to place the man's face. 'And that was more than fifteen years ago. Who knows how old he was then. Isn't that right, Written?'

Farden glared, confused, defeated. Doomed.

If one looked close enough, it was possible to see the cogs turning in Forluss' head. The man looked down at the armour in his hands. 'So how did *he* manage to get his hands on this? Did yer steal it, Four-Hand? Kill someone for it?' he asked, confused.

Loffrey put his hands on his hips. 'That's what I want to find out. There was a book by that armchair. A diary by the looks of it. Go get it.'

Forluss and Kint traded glances. Kint smacked Forluss on the arm and the fat man went back inside the shack. He reappeared a minute later with a book. He gave it to Loffrey with a grunt and the man quickly flipped through it, noting the names and dates that had been scribbled down. 'Good,' he said. 'Take those back to the cart, and be careful with them. Kiltyrin will have your head if you're not.'

Kint could be heard muttering to Forluss as they walked back up the hill. 'So I can dig a knife into it but I have to be careful putting it in a cart. Who's the idiot now?' he said, quietly.

Loffrey knelt down and grabbed the mage's armoured left wrist. Farden flinched away, but quickly found the tip of the spear digging into the base of his skull again. He clenched his fist as Loffrey probed the metal. 'How did you do it again? Ah yes.' He pinched the bottom of the vambrace but nothing happened. He shifted his grip and tried again, but still nothing happened. 'Let go, Farden,' he warned, pulling at the metal. 'Let it go I say!'

The spear pressed harder, but Farden didn't move. He stared straight ahead at his shack and said nothing. Only when the butt of the spear smacked him hard in the temple did he move, and even then he just slumped to the floor. He didn't want to give Wartan and Loffrey the satisfaction. Loffrey was growing impatient. 'Let go!' he cried, but it was no use; the vambraces refused to part with their mage.

Loffrey was getting aggravated now. 'Kint! Forluss! Bring me some more rope! This bastard is being stubborn!'

Kint and Forluss quickly returned, eager to see what Farden was up to. Somehow one step ahead, Forluss had already made a simple noose with the length of ragged rope, and wasted no time looping it about Farden's bruised neck. 'I'll show you how it's done,' grunted Forluss, as he yanked on the rope. Farden flailed as the noose quickly strangled him. Forluss wrapped the rope around his shoulder and began to drag the thrashing mage up the hill. The man might have been fat, but he was stronger than an ox.

Flints and stones raked at Farden's ill-fitting clothes as if the earth itself had claws. Some cut his flesh. Some bruised. Grass-whipped and dirt-choked, he gasped as the rough rope bit into his neck and made the veins there bulge. Farden's only saving grace was the two or three fingers he had managed to slip in between the rope and his neck. He pushed as hard as he could, gulping a few precious breaths, gasping all the while. The throbbing in his head became a fervent hammering, like that of his tired heart. The cold fear gripped him in a vice. The hole threatened to swallow him. *Was this it?* he found himself asking. He had forgotten how much he feared death. Something told him to pray, but he grit his teeth and refused.

It felt as though it took an hour to be dragged to the top of the hill. But it was not over yet. Forluss left the mage at the base of the ash tree to gasp and wheeze while he looped the rope over a low branch, about a dozen feet from the ground. Kint seized the rope and together they hauled the mage upright by his neck. Farden retched and spat. He had made the mistake of taking his fingers out from under the rope. Farden stood on his tiptoes as the rope pulled him ever-upwards. He thrashed and gurgled and flailed and wheezed, but it was no use. *No, no...* screamed his air-starved brain. His greatest, coldest fear had come to visit.

Loffrey was standing in front of him. Wartan and the spear too. That glint of murder in the man's eye had not gone away. Kint and Forluss stood on the rope and waited. 'Let them go, Farden, or we'll have to see how long you can hold your breath.'

'Do what 'e says, or I'll stick you with this,' hissed Wartan, drawing a look from the others. Loffrey moved to stand in front of the eager guard, lest he do something dramatic. A nod, and the rope pulled him higher. His toes scraped the soil. Farden was turning red. Loffrey pulled on the vambraces but they still refused to budge. The mage clawed for his eyes and he stepped back.

'Farden...' warned the man. With another jerk, Farden's feet left the floor, and he flailed even more. It took a moment for the despair to set in; the exhausted ache of already tired muscles crying out to give in and accept. He slowly stopped thrashing. Flecks of bark landed on his head. A twig rested on his shoulder. Farden stared out at the wandering landscape, eyes bulging and darkness hovering at their corners. The cart cows were staring up at him with blank faces. A crow was a fluttering speck in the distance. He could see a faint smudge of white in the west, a cottage maybe, his vision was blurring. Not a soul or saviour for miles, just the four torturers standing around him.

So this is it, he told himself, as he slipped into the dark hole of his fear. For a man toying with immortality, he had never considered how he'd go. He had stubbornly ignored it. A life of fire and blood and blinding light, only to be finally extinguished by the pinch of a rope on an ash tree. Killed for the very thing that kept him from death and an early grave. His precious treasures stolen. His usefulness exhausted. Farden looked up at the tree, for the briefest of moments hoping that he would see a rat nibbling on the rope that strangled him. But the blurry world before his bulging eyes was not so kind. Just a bare tree, waving in the breeze.

The rope tugged at him and pulled him even higher. Farden writhed for another moment, but then sagged once again. Hanging. He'd never imagined that. Suddenly, the slowness of this death seemed graceful, painfully so, in its inexorable winding down. Strange, he thought, for a man to come into the world screaming, and yet leave it so silently. He had always imagined himself uttering some great proverb at the moment his heart stopped, some great stamp of profundity to linger in the ears of whoever listened. Perhaps a curse, perhaps some iota of defiance against the grave. Even just a guttural cry would suffice, a final lyric for the song of life. Not like this. The fear was numbed somewhat by the hopelessness of it all. The fight died with the air in his lungs. The darkness seeped into his eyes. *So this is it.*

Words floated up to him.

'Cut his arm off,' said Forluss. 'We don't have to bring him back alive.' A momentary flinch from Farden. *Let him be dead before that.*

'We don't have to bring him back at all. Duke's orders.'

'A little barbaric, don't you think?'

'You wanted the armour, Loffrey, time to get your hands dirty.'

A sigh. 'Do it.'

'With pleasure. Might even take one of his fingers for a trophy.'

Hur-hur-hur. Forluss laughing. If there was one sound Farden hoped not to go out to, it was that. The air had left him now. His hands and legs were going numb. He felt the cold kiss of a blade on his arm and a sharp flicker of pain run up it. It was over in a second. Farden closed his eyes and listened to the dwindling of his heart.

'That bloody armour has dulled my blade.'

'Get another then.'

'Oh, fer gods' sake,' cried Wartan. If Farden could have opened his eyes he would have seen the man charge forward, spear up and glinting. The silver blade buried itself neatly between his ribs. Farden momentarily burst into life, gurgling with pain. He kicked his legs, once, twice maybe, and then sagged again. His head lolled to his chest, eyes half-closed but glazed over. Wartan left the spear in the mage's ribs. It dangled oddly like some grotesque, unwanted limb. The man spat on the mage's foot and grinned at the others. 'Been waiting on that fer years,' he said.

Down on the grass, Kint was just about to clout Wartan in the face when there came a thud, closely followed by another. The men turned to see two vambraces lying in the grass. Drops of blood began to drip on them, some from the spear, some from the mage's arm. Loffrey quickly grabbed them and hurried to the cart.

'Job done,' said Kint, sneering at the mage dangling in the wind like a ghoulish fruit.

Forluss wrapped the rope around the tree-trunk and tied it off. 'Goodbye, old Four-Hand. Sleep well,' he chuckled, even having the sadistic audacity to blow Farden a kiss.

The four men climbed into the cart. The wide-eyed cows were whipped into action, and within minutes they were trundling down the flint road and disappearing into the west.

Farden, wrapped in darkness, watched it go through narrow slits. The pain was melting away with every arduous pound of his dying heart. The chasm of death, black like the innards of an elf well, was yawning, and Farden was falling down it.

So this is it, he told himself, as his heart came to a faltering stop. His eyes stayed open just long enough for him to see the sun fade behind a cloud and send shadows flitting across the moorland, the crow swooping to catch something, and the dark blotch of a figure standing in the distance, boots kicking flints from the road.

part two

to the dead (revenge)

1568 years ago

'stonefoot.'

A subtle slide of the leg. Back as straight as a flagpole. A slight bend of the knees. Korrin felt the ground grip him as he felt it with his cold, bare toes.

'To Havestus.'

The blade flicked up over his head. His grip slid down its handle, cupping the pommelstone. He held it as if were the bitter wind itself.

'To Shiverstance.'

Feet slid swiftly back over frozen soil. Elbows dropped like bricks. The long-sword swung in sweeping figure-of-eight arcs. The metal whined as it spun through the morning air.

There was a pause as Gaspid walked around him, ducking the blade to test the tension of the lad's arms and legs. He nodded, to himself more than Korrin, and held up a thick wooden staff. Korrin shifted his weight and his windmilling blade and clove the staff in two with a cracking thud. The splinters had barely landed before he was back in stance.

'Good,' smiled Gaspid. 'Into Dassen.'

Korrin grunted as he wrestled the momentum of the heavy sword into stillness. With a clap of his bare soles on the earth, he jumped and landed with his legs split, one forward, one back, sword jutting upwards into an imaginary throat.

'Who are you aiming for? Balimuel?' chided Gaspid, knocking the tip of the sword down a good foot with what was left of his staff. 'Waterfall, and to salute,' came his last instruction. Korrin

rose to his tiptoes, swung the sword in a low arc, and then slammed his heels together. He flicked the imaginary blood from its edges, held the cold blade to his nose, then sheathed it.

'I say. Very good, lad,' Gaspid remarked. 'Keep on like that and you'll be better than me.'

Korrin nodded and bowed. 'Will you tell me now?' he asked, calming his breathing. Gaspid rubbed his moustache.

'The insistence of the young,' he mused. With an expression that feigned annoyance, he gestured to the edge of the training platform, where the tower fell away to empty space and far-below ice, the place where Korrin spent his spare hours every night and morning, watching the wolves in the distance. 'This way,' Gaspid ordered. Korrin followed and together they stood over the icy countryside, as if they were vultures.

A year had passed since he had toppled Balimuel. A year since the Pens had barked his name into the misty sky. A whole year can mean everything. It had felt like ten.

Did he feel different? Korrin couldn't begin to count the ways. He looked down from the vista to his fists. They were white after the morning's practice. His knuckles were in a constant state of callous. He looked to his bare arms. The scars of sparring and conditioning were like worms under his tanned skin. He couldn't help but smirk. Where once his body had been that of a farmboy: lean, average, scrawny in places, powered only by passion, it was now carved from steel, trained and beaten into a powerful machine, like one of the forge-engines the Smiths kept in their caverns. With every tough new day that passed, he felt more like a visitor in a stranger's body. It could now do things and move in ways that he had thought impossible, things that a year of constant and relentless training had beaten into him. He no longer thought about doing something, he simply did. Training. Korrin shook his head. Torture, more like, but both turned a man as hard as he.

And he had loved almost every moment of it.

His mind had flourished with his body. It too had become a confident and practised machine. Calculating. Silent. Controlled. That fire that had burnt in him through the testing, the fire that long ago had driven him to sneak out the green wooden door of his father's farm that cold, misty morning, still burnt as strong as ever. Balimuel and Gaspid had taught him to nurture it and channel it. What he lacked in experience he made up for with pure yearning. The more he trained, the further away the farm slipped.

On the long nights, watching the slow dance of the moon and the misty blue tendrils of the Wake flutter through the star fields, Korrin sometimes allowed a tired, but contented smile to wander onto his face. He had escaped his peasant name and its muddy, pig-filled destiny. He had defeated his father's ideas and become the man he had always dreamt of being. The man of his grandfather's stories. A warrior like those in the story books he had pilfered from old Grast's library. One of nine elite men and women chosen from thousands.

But one question yet remained. Elites they were. That was unquestionable. Chosen they had been. But for what?

'They're allowing us one month,' said Gaspid, more to the wind than to Korrin.

Korrin almost didn't hear him. 'They're what?'

'Allowing us a month. Sending us home to say our final goodbyes.'

The news was like a hot stone in his throat. 'Why?'

'The Pens and their ways, dear boy. We'll never fathom them. We've barely seen another human besides ourselves and our minders in the last year, and now they're turning us loose for an entire month.'

Korrin frowned. 'What if some of us don't want to come back?'

Gaspid laughed heartily at that. 'Good one, lad. I do not suppose we should fear such a thing from you now, should we?'

'Gäel's been moaning again. Says he's tired of all the mystery. Lop never stops talking of his tribe.'

'We'll have to see then, shall we not?' chuckled Gaspid. He was a man obsessed with his own moustache. He was always either stroking it or combing it. Korrin had always imagined that it made up for his baldness, and that was why Gaspid was intent on keeping it.

'Something tells me that we are almost at the end now, lad. We're close to the reason why we're here. Why else would they give us such a treat?'

'Is that how you see it? A treat?'

'Of course! Did you know I have over twenty brothers, Korrin lad? That I do. I've damn near forgotten all their names. Whatever is to become of us, I should like to see them one last time. Perhaps that is why the Pens are doing this.'

'Well, I don't see it as a treat.'

'No, from what little you have told us of your home, I highly doubt you would,' Gaspid hummed. He turned around and clapped Korrin lightly on the back. 'You're not going back are you?'

Korrin shook his head.

Gaspid made for the indoors. 'Go home, lad, see your father. If you were my son, I would be proud,' he called.

Korrin waited until he heard the thump of the tower door closing before replying. 'If only you were my father, Gaspid. If only.'

chapter 10

"I don't understand all these street-yellers and god-huggers. There're too many to keep count these days. Can't hardly tell the difference between them all."

"I know the main ones. There's the Enlightened Brotherhood, the ones with the shaven heads."

"And who are they?"

"They're the ones who think the gods speak directly to them. And they'll charge you a fistful of coin to hear what they say, too. Snobby gold-makers."

"Figures."

"Then there're the Thunderites, Thron worshippers and Siren-fanciers, those are. Think Thron single-handedly saved us in the Battle. Then you've got the Company of Souls. They think you have to earn the gods' love by repentance and humility and beating yourself with a stick. Then there're the Voices of Jötun. An Albion movement, worshipping their earth god. The Ranks of Starry Vengeance. Word has it they think the gods want battle and death. Think humanity has gotten all soft. Want a war. And of course the Glorified Remnant. Strange crowd. They think magick has caused all Krauslung's problems. From Vice to the old Siren war. They want the mages and the Written disbanded."

"Sound like a clever lot."

"And then you've got the Knights..."

"The Knights? Are those the moon-worshippers?"

"No, the Knights of Fortuitous Balance, so they're called. Evernia-

worshippers, and rightly so. Dangerous, so I hear."

"Dangerous?"

"Let's just say that people who speak out against them and their goddess tend to go... er, missing."

"Dear me. What a mess. What is the point of all this? It gives me a headache."

"It's our human right to ask questions, old chap. The squabble is over who has the answers."

"And what questions are these idiots supposed to be answering? I just don't see it."

"Why, the biggest question of all!"

"And what's that then?"

"What do you believe?"

Conversation overheard between two city guards on the night watch.
Transcribed by a passing Arfell scholar

Krauslung awoke to a morning full of mists and the prospect of sunshine. Between the winding streets, windows were opened and people ventured out into the day. The quiet shuffle of shoes and heels on cobbles, shops being opened, markets being filled, and the murmurs of morning conversations floated into the air and joined the smells of bakers and fish-stalls preparing themselves for the day. It was Krauslung at its most peaceful state, when the drunks from the night before had either fallen into bed or into a gutter, when the city was still yawning, teetering on the precipice of another busy day.

On the western side of the city, where the morning mists still wafted around the roots of the buildings, a man bedecked in sparkling armour emerged from a guardhouse and stretched, relieving his aching muscles. Modren stared up at the glistening, sheer walls of the Arkathedral, several streets away. If he looked hard, he could see the wooden cranes and scaffolding atop its lofty reaches, already in the process of being dismantled. And if he had really looked, he might have been able to see a tiny speck hovering high above them, gliding and swooping with impatience. Ilios, eager for his new nest.

Modren finished his stretching and stepped out into the city, emerald cape swirling around his steel knees. It was a quiet morning, a peaceful one. The best kind. The mists caressed the buildings and turned the streets into veins of ethereal dreams. The sort he liked to start his day with, the kind where he could patrol unhindered, un…

The peaceful morning was abruptly shattered by a hoarse screeching.

'Beware the magick devils in our midst! They seek to pervert the course of human nature!'

With a sigh, the Undermage stopped in his tracks, placing his brow firmly between his finger and thumb. *Not today*, he prayed. *Not this morning*. His pleas went ignored. More shouting split the silence.

'There! That one! Ring-leader of the abominations himself. Undermage Modren is his name!'

Modren turned to face his heckler. A man, a skinny fellow in a violently purple robe, with his hair braided in a long tail, was standing on a wooden box on the corner between two alleyways. Upon seeing the dangerous look in the captain's eyes, he cleared his throat and turned around, wobbling slightly on his rickety pedestal. He raised his arms to his listeners, what few of them there were, and shouted some more.

'Heed my words, friends! We of the Glorified Remnant are campaigning for the banning of magick users in this city. There is an epidemic, friends, an epidemic in the streets of this fine city.' There was a pause as the man took a quick glance at the Undermage. Modren had taken several large steps forward. The man gulped, but continued nonetheless. 'An epidemic that wears armour and g… green cloaks, an epidemic that would see this city fall into ruin again should it be allowed to remain!' The man threw his hands wide to his audience, a little crescent of people that hovered in the middle of the little cobblestone intersection. Some tittered between themselves, shaking their heads at this apparent madman. A few others nodded earnestly and elbowed each other to agree. Others wandered past, a range of intrigue and bemusement on their faces. Modren, on the other hand, had seen quite enough. He took another step forward.

'You mean this sort of green cloak?' he asked loudly, making the man jump. Modren smiled as he brushed a bit of dust from his shoulder and picked at a stray thread. 'It's more of an emerald, really.'

The man took one look at the Written and held his arms across his chest. 'I will not wither in the presence of this dangerous beast! Do you see, friends? We live in the shadow of a marble dictatorship! We are not free, we live at the mercy of the magick-users!'

Modren took hold of the man's robe and gave it a sharp tug. The man swiftly came free of his box. A few people in the crowd sniggered. Others shook their heads and muttered darkly. 'Come on now, I only want to have a little chat,' said Modren, keeping his smile firmly on his face.

'But… but…' the man protested, but it was of no use. Modren's grip was one of steel. The man was trapped. Cloth shoes dragging and stumbling, he tried to keep up with the Undermage's swift pace. His boots thudded in time to his words.

'You know what gets me about you Remnant lot?' Modren was saying. 'Out of all of the preachers and raving lunatics filling our streets, you've got to be the stupidest of them all,' he laughed. The man had gone a sickly shade of white. He tripped momentarily but Modren hauled him straight back up and marched him on.

'I…' he ventured.

'I'm glad you realise it.'

'But…'

Modren shook his head in mock disbelief. 'But of course! Who would imagine that a city like this, a city with a proud past, a past, I might add, that has always been rooted in magick, protected on all sides by brave mages and Written and governed by two of the kindest and most virtuous Arkmages the history books have ever had the pleasure of knowing, could breed such an ungrateful, idiotic band of simpletons such as yourselves!'

The man was sweating now. 'You...'

Modren clapped a hand to his forehead. 'You wouldn't believe it, would you? How can anyone, after all the magick council has done to rebuild Krauslung and keep this city together, believe that its people would then call for its dissolution? Not forgetting all the training my mages go through, and the good job they do protecting this city and its people from bandits, magick pests, and the like. Who in their right mind would try to have them banned and banished, simply for doing what comes naturally to them? *Who*, I ask you?'

Silence.

Modren came to a sudden halt, throwing the man off-balance and then pushing him hard against a wall. He pointed a finger in the man's face, nearly skewering his eye. 'You lot, that's who,' he hissed. 'You got some gall to stand on a street corner and call me and my kind "abominations." I've got half a mind to send you out with the next mountain patrol, and see how long you last with the wolves and bandits.'

The man shook like a jelly.

'Trouble, Undermage, sir?' interjected a passing city guard, intrigued by the man's whimpering. Modren snapped his fingers.

'Absolutely!' he said. 'Take this man and toss him in a cell for a day and a night. See if you can find some of those Repugnant Souls lot to throw him in with.'

The guard, a young man with a shaven head, looked very pleased with that. He looked at the quivering man and then back to Modren. He raised a hand. 'If I might be so bold, sir...?'

Modren nodded. 'Of course.'

'We just arrested some members of the Ranks. They might like to meet this one.'

'The Ranks of Starry Vengeance?'

'Those are the ones.'

'Perfect. They like a good non-believer.'

'*Atheists*, I think they call them, sir.'

'I call them idiots.'

'Right you are, Undermage.'

The man clasped his hands together as the guard seized him by the scruff of his neck. He cried out as he was hauled away. 'P… please, no. I haven't done anything wrong!'

Modren put his hands on his hips. 'Inciting dissent amongst the populace. Spreading fear and false rumours. Slander against the Arkmages, esteemed magick council, the Undermage himself, and my own mages. Anything I've missed, soldier?'

The young guard shook his head. 'Not that I can tell, sir.'

'Good work. Take him away then.'

The guard saluted with his spear, and, with a fistful of the man's violet robe firmly in his grasp, made for the nearest barracks, his quivering wreck in tow.

Modren waited until they had disappeared from view before rubbing his weary forehead. This city was going mad, once again, he thought.

❦

'With all due respect, your Mages, I want to know why we are entertaining these thoughts at all!' yelled Malvus Barkhart, from his bench in the middle of the Arkathedral. He was yelling for two reasons, firstly to make himself heard over the dismantling of the cranes outside the stained-glass windows, and secondly because he was outraged. Livid. It was obvious in his blood-rushed cheeks.

A murmur of agreement came from the council gathered around him. Malvus got to his feet and marched forward, pushing his way through lines of councillors. Most of them clapped him on the back as he passed, whispering and hissing words of encouragement. He shouted as he moved.

‘I have it on good authority that the Schools are now accepting *anybody* who shows the barest inkling of magick in their veins. Not only that, but I’ve heard that the costs we originally agreed on imposing on such admissions are being waived in favour of the sheer number of applicants? I demand to know why this is happening, and moreover, I demand that it stop immediately!’

‘Council Barkhart…’ began Durnus, listening to the impatient squeaks of Malvus’ shoes on the white marble floor. He held up his hand, but the man would not be silenced.

‘Farmboys, milkmaids, goat-herds, sailors… are these the mages we want protecting our borders? It makes me sick, to think of such magickal gifts, gifts that we have spent centuries nurturing in our proud bloodlines, being shared with common rabble! I hear from Essen that the situation has become even worse than here in Manesmark. It’s an epidemic, I tell you!’

Another chorus of agreement from most of the council, louder this time.

‘Enough!’ shouted Tyrfing, nursing his head. He had spent another night in his forge, hammering blades into submission. The pounding of his forge-hammer was now echoing in his tired brain. This blasted meeting was doing nothing to alleviate it.

The council slowly came to a simmering silence. Malvus stood a dozen feet from the twin thrones. Like most of the Arkathedral’s great hall, they had been rebuilt after the battle with Vice, and now they were more ornate than ever before. They rose from the marble tiles like two saplings entwined around a curving set of steps. Their branches curved to form two high-backed seats, gilded and inlaid with the names of every Arkmage and Undermage since the Arka began. At their base, set a few yards to the side, was the Underthrone, a throne similar in shape, yet smaller, and painted with veins of dark green. For the moment, it was empty. Modren was elsewhere, another source of constant comment for Malvus.

'I will not sit here and listen to you moan and rant, Council. Present your views calmly and objectively, or don't present them at all,' ordered Tyrfing.

'Forgive me, but it seems to be the only way to get through to you, Arkmage Tyrfing. You look as if we're sending you to sleep.'

'If only,' muttered Tyrfing. Durnus continued on his behalf.

'I will explain to you and the council once again, Barkhart, that although we are enjoying a period of peace, I refuse to keep our guard down. We are using this time to swell the ranks of the army, and we are using what the gods have given us to increase our number of mages. This burst of magick isn't something to be reviled and feared, Malvus, it is something we can use to our advantage if a foe were to rear its head.'

A young councilwoman stood up and raised her hand. Tyrfing gestured for her to speak. 'What foes, Arkmages?' she said. 'Who exactly have we to fear? The factions of the Crumbled Empire squabble amongst themselves. The Sirens are our allies now. The Albion Dukes are growing stronger, but they fight between themselves for land and coin, so who? Who do we have to fear?'

'I agree!' came a shout.

'Who?'

'What of these Written murders? Should we be worried?'

'Is that what you're afraid of?'

Durnus shook his head. 'The murders are nothing except unfortunate events. Undermage Modren is looking into them. But the possibility of a foe, so far unimagined, unrealised, still remains. Emaneska is changing, and we will see ourselves protected. End of discussion!'

'Soldiers and mages cost more coin than farmhands and milkmaids!'

'Magick is for the elite, not for the peasants!' came another shout, a stance that more and more of the council seemed to share these days. The city's new sentiments were not just confined to the streets; they were creeping into the magick council and infecting the ears here too. Durnus could hear it in their hushed whispers, their corridor murmuring. Some, he suspected, were already part of the new cults, secretly of course, but they grew bolder every day and with every meeting. He heard their names hissed behind hands: the Ranks, the Repugnant Souls, the Glorified Remnant, the Voices of Jötun, the Enlightened Brotherhood, the Knights of Fortuitous Balance, and something called the Marble Copse, a rather secretive faction indeed, deeply embedded in the council itself. Durnus sighed.

'Nobody knows that more than I do,' came a shout. It was Modren, standing at the doors of the great hall, beside the newly restored statue of Evernia. His arms were crossed and his face as stern as a storm front. He, like Tyrfing, was barely in the mood for another cacophonous magick council. He walked forward, sunlight and stained-glass painting rainbows on his armour. The ranks of councillors parted for him, silent. They knew better than to provoke him. Modren had never quite adjusted to the politics like Tyrfing and Durnus had. He was still a soldier at heart, and like one, he strained to confine his arguments to his mouth, rather than let them escape to his fists, or his flames, much to the concern of several council members.

Modren pushed past Malvus and sat upon his throne with a clang, steel striking marble. He rested his elbows on the arm of his throne. 'I'm as worried as you are by this sudden surge of applicants, Council Barkhart. It makes my job harder.'

'Then you'll agree that this needs to be stopped, Undermage Modren.'

The mage shook his head. 'No, I do not. I agree with the Arkmages. If an army marched up to our gates tomorrow, I'd rather have a thousand peasants who know how to wield a spell than a thousand peasants who can only wield a pitchfork. Something strange may be happening to this world, but all it takes to resolve it is the right training. That I can do.'

A man shouted from the back of the hall. 'Better we take them in and teach them, rather than have them causing trouble in the towns, or splintering off altogether.'

Tyrfing clicked his fingers. 'Exactly,' he said, thanking the councillor with a nod. At least they still had a few allies.

'And who pays for all of this?' Malvus challenged.

'They cost too much!'

'We're already stretched too thin as it is with the rebuilding.'

'A war-sized army in peace time is a waste of coin!'

Durnus held up his hands for peace. 'Our coffers can cope.'

Malvus turned around and raised his hands to the council. 'For how long? I would wager that they're already running low. Soon you will be announcing new taxes, and where will we be then? Stunting our trade to feed an army we don't need. Unless, of course, there's something you're not telling us?'

'And thinning your pockets no doubt, Malvus,' challenged Durnus. 'That is what you are truly concerned about, is it not?'

Malvus turned to glare, but quickly remembered his place. He bowed instead, keeping his eyes on the floor. 'I fear you are mistaken, your Mage. My humble coin goes directly to keeping this city on its course; to becoming an empire in its own right. The only true power in Emaneska.'

There were cheers from some in the hall. Others grinned unabashedly. Some even had the audacity to clap, as if it were some piece of theatre. Malvus adjusted his ruffled silk collar. There was the faintest hint of a smile on his face. 'I only wish you could see that, your Mage,' he said, and then suddenly held his hand to his mouth, feigning embarrassment. 'Oh, my apologies, Arkmage,' he said. Close behind him somebody sniggered.

Durnus stood up and folded his hands calmly behind his back. Somehow, he stared directly at the councillor, something which Malvus found incredibly disturbing. 'None required, Council Barkhart. Seeing as you are so charitable with your hard-earned coin, perhaps I can rely on you to help fund a new barracks for our prospective mages? As you are so very concerned with the advancement of our fine country?'

Malvus narrowed his eyes. He was now stuck in a political corner, and a public one at that. He could do nothing but bow once again. 'I will gladly discuss those arrangements with you in private, Arkmage Durnus,' he muttered.

'I am sure you will.'

Tyrfing also stood up. He quickly descended from his throne. 'Until tomorrow then, councillors,' he shouted. The magick council, some two-hundred strong, began to filter out through the gilded doors at the entrance of the hall. Like a lumbering, many-legged beast, it talked to itself and chattered animatedly. Malvus and his little band of loyal followers held the rear. They were deep in hushed conversation. They huddled close as they walked away, like the poisonous spur on the tail of the council beast.

Tyrfing, Modren, and Durnus remained behind. A few councillors came to bow and shake hands, some formal and polite, others overly eager to express their shared views. The Arkmages patiently heard each of them out and then thanked them graciously. They needed all the supporters they could get. It took half an hour for the great hall to empty.

As soon as they were alone, Modren slumped back into the Underthrone. 'Today was particularly trying.'

'And you only had to suffer through a tiny slice of it,' sniffed

Tyrfing. He seemed so distracted at the moment. Modren knew better than to ask why. Durnus didn't have to. Tyrfing coughed then, another one of his choking, rasping coughs that seemed to take him by surprise. He covered his mouth with the hem of his mage's robe and then ran a hand across his mouth.

'Where were you anyway?' he asked, hoarsely.

Modren rolled his eyes. 'We had trouble before dawn, down in the docks.'

'What happened?'

'A group of those Thron nutcases…'

'The Thunderites,' offered Durnus.

'Those are the ones. Campaigning about their beloved god on the western boardwalk. Not very clever to start denouncing all other gods, especially the god of the sea, in that area. A group of Njord-following ship-boys took offence to their preaching. Took a couple of broken bottles to their necks.'

'Gods' sakes.'

'Indeed.'

There was a pause as each man took a moment to collect their battered thoughts after the assault that had been the magick council meeting. Tyrfing ran a charcoal-smudged hand through his hair. Like a drawn-out siege, his mop of black hair was slowly giving way to a silvery grey hue that betrayed his age. His blue eyes, now glued to the floor, were surrounded by deep, dark rings of tiredness, signature of a week of late nights. Still, all things considered, Tyrfing had just crept into his seventies, and although the lines were now showing in his dark, sun-leathered skin, he looked good for his age. And as far as any Written was concerned, he was a marvel. Most mages never lived past their fifties, thanks to a combination of the madness and certain occupational hazards. Fifty-five had been the previous record.

Modren broke the silence with another issue. 'The Written are starting to ask questions.'

'Which ones?' asked Durnus. His face, as always, had the appearance of a crinkled old map, bleached by the winter sun. His immortality had locked his age in time. Cruel irony perhaps, that he hadn't been restored to a younger man, but those who are immortal hardly have cause for complaint.

Modren held his hands up. 'All of them.'

'Then bring them in. I think it is time they knew.'

Tyrfing looked up from this staring spot on the marble floor. 'Are you serious?'

'Very.'

Modren got to his feet and headed for the door. 'Right you are then!'

As the mage departed, Durnus put his hand on Tyrfing's shoulder and let it linger. 'Let us venture up to the Nest. That will cheer you up.'

Tyrfing knuckled his eyes again. 'I don't need cheering up. I just want the magick council to leave us alone, Farden back, and his bitch of a daughter to just kill herself and save us all the trouble.'

'Anything else?'

Tyrfing was about to answer when he abruptly began to cough. He clamped his hand over his mouth as he hawked and barked, deep in his throat. Tears squeezed from his pinched eyes. When he'd recovered, he took a breath and wiped his hand on the hem of his robe. Crimson smeared across the white cloth. Tyrfing quickly clenched a fist. Sometimes, he was glad Durnus was blind. 'I think that's it,' he replied, folding the hem over to hide the blood.

His friend chuckled. 'You don't want much at all then.'

Tyrfing walked Durnus behind the thrones. There was a gap of about twenty feet between them and the back wall, and there, as part of the rebuild, the workers had placed an thick oak door with a silver handle. The design of a splayed hand had been carved into the wood and inlaid with silver. It was quite the piece of craftsmanship.

Tyrfing pointed his friend to the door, and Durnus let his hands wander across it. His wrinkled fingers traced the cold shape of the carving. He sank his hand into it, finger for finger, palm to palm. There was a click and an echoing thud, and Durnus pushed the door open. Tyrfing led him inside.

A set of curving stairs led them into a circular room. There were skinny windows set in the walls, stained-glass panes depicting the Battle of Krauslung. The glass was so new that the dyes looked wet, fresh, like the memories they had been drawn from. Dragons swooped over grey walls. A dozen ships sat in a crescent in the harbour waters. Fire bloomed in one pane, brave soldiers in another. An evil, dead face grimaced in the last.

The Arkmages paced through the room and headed for another door, one that was more like a giant misshapen porthole than a door. It too was made of painted glass. The craftsmen had decorated these panes with feathers. Slate-grey fading to a translucent white, the detail was so incredible it seemed that if the latch were to be loosed, the doors might fly away into the morning sunlight and escape. Tyrfing ran his hand across them. These were new; the final touches to what the workers had come to call the Nest. Tyrfing described them for his friend, and Durnus smiled. He had the smell of the dyes and paints to enjoy, the taste of marble dust on his tongue.

With the gentlest of pushes, the ornate doors swung open and revealed a long balcony with a spiral staircase on either side of it. Above them, the tendrils of marble trees pawed at the sky. Tyrfing and Durnus stepped out onto the balcony and ascended the left-hand set of stairs. The breeze was cold at the pinnacle of the Arkathedral, but gentle. They could hear voices, the hissing of brooms, and the soft tapping of wooden mallets above them.

The Nest was finished.

It had taken one long year to complete, but it was the crown to the Arkathedral's brow. Sitting directly on top of the great hall's marble roof, the Nest was a two-tiered tower built for one purpose and one purpose only: Ilios.

Though the gryphon was nowhere to be seen, Tyrfing could feel his eyes on the back of his neck as they set foot on the top level of the tower. A group of dusty craftsmen bustled nearby, packing their tools into boxes and sweeping marble chips and dust into buckets.

Tyrfing looked around, drinking in the vista. Behind them, the vertical granite walls of Hardja reached up into the sky and pierced the clear blue of the morning with her jagged peak. Directly ahead of them, far on the other side of Krauslung's narrow valley was Hardja's twin sister, Ursufel. She was a black arrowhead in the bright white light of the early sun. In the south, to their right, was the endless sea and a port bristling with masts and sails. Hazy smudges, flocks of gulls and rimelings, parried with each other as they fought for scraps on the boardwalks. In the far distance was a line of black specks, the faraway islands of Skap. Between them and the coast, flecks of white and brown scuttled slowly across the water.

To the north and left sat Manesmark and the jagged range that was the Össfen Mountains. In the distance, dominating all, was Emaneska's loftiest peak, Lokki. Tyrfing momentarily pondered whether there was a reason the mountain's name sounded so similar to the god's. He made a mental note to ask Heimdall.

If the Arkmage squinted, he could just about make out the cranes and the scaffolding around the new Spire on Manesmark hill. It would never be as grand or as tall as the old Spire, but it would do its job of housing all of the new mages. They needed a home. They had to have a home. If the wind blew right, Tyrfing could imagine hearing the thud of the giant granite blocks as they were lowered into place, or the hissing of the fire and water spells as the blocks were melted to join one another, perfectly sealed.

Below the Nest, the great hall pointed directly east. It and its adjacent rooms stretched almost to the precipice of the Arkathedral.

There the thick battlements clung on for dear life as the walls fell away like a waterfall of white marble, plummeting to the cobbles a thousand feet below. Two skinny white towers teetered at the very edge. They were almost as tall as the Nest. They held the twin bells, aptly named Hardja and Ursufel, that rang every dawn and every sunset.

It was the Nest itself that Tyrfing found he couldn't tear his eyes away from.

Open to the sky, it was essentially a varnished oak platform, diamond in shape. But it was what stood around and over it that robbed a man's breath. At each point of its compass, a milk-white marble tree sprouted from the oiled oak and curled into the sky above it. Polished so that they seemed almost liquid in texture, each tree bowed to its opposite and joined together over the centre of the platform, branches forming a knot of carved marble, willows grappling over an oak river. The marble looked pure white at a distance, but up close the tiniest capillaries of grey and blue mica could be seen under their skins. In the early sun, they threw strange shadows on the oak at the Arkmages' feet, shadows that seemed to sway with the breeze despite the stone they were carved from. It was pure mastery. Art, imitating wood.

'I wish you could see this,' whispered Tyrfing, awed, a breath from speechless.

Durnus shrugged and smiled. 'I wish that I could too, old friend.' He was listening to the whispering of the nearby craftsmen. The wooden spars and tangled ropes of the cranes were slowly being ushered below. One of them, a foreman by the look of his spotless blue coat, came to bow.

'All finished, your Mages. I trust you're pleased?' he asked.

'Judging that Arkmage Tyrfing is lost for words, I would say we are, Stonemaster Ret. We finally have an Arkathedral.'

Ret grinned, tipped his cap, and bowed again. He turned to his crew of craftsmen and builders. 'You hear that, boys? You've done a fine job,' he announced, and the dusty men smiled proudly. Ret turned back and a serious, slightly concerned look came over his face. 'There was one thing, your Mages, that I wanted to ask you.'

'And what is that?'

'The, er, *beast*, sir. Now that we've finished, will he be returning soon? The only reason I ask is that last time he nearly frightened several of the younger men into jumping from the roof.'

Tyrfing looked up at the clear morning sky. 'I'll make sure he waits until you've finished.'

Master Ret blew a great sigh of relief. 'Oh, thank you, sir. And again, you've got me and my crew's word that we'll keep quiet about him,' he said.

'Glad to hear it,' Tyrfing said. He beckoned the foreman closer as he reached inside the pocket of his robe. He withdrew a cloth purse, fat with coins. It clinked as he pushed it into Ret's hand. 'For you and your men,' whispered the Arkmage. The craftsmen had already been paid, of course, but it didn't hurt to give them a little something for the taverns. 'Make sure it's used appropriately.'

Ret grinned knowingly. 'Thank you, sirs. I'll make sure it is.' The man bowed one final time and quickly rejoined his dusty and weary band. There was a moment of hushed conferring, and then a chorus of cheers. They turned, swept off their caps, and then bowed to their masters.

'An honour, your Mages!'

'Thank you sirs!'

'Much obliged!' came the shouts.

Ret thrashed about with his cap. 'Alright you lot, back to work! That's enough!'

When they had gone back to their tidying, Durnus sighed. 'Be careful that Malvus and his cronies do not hear of that little expense. That purse was heavier than we had discussed.'

Tyrfing tapped his nose. 'And luckily for us, most of it came from Ilios' own hoard.'

'Well then, all's well,' Durnus replied. He twitched then, and sniffed the breeze. 'Do you feel that?'

Tyrfing slid the sleeve of his robe up his forearm. Even though the fingers of time and age had faded some of his self-inflicted scars, the deeper ones still remained, purple and silvery twine embedded in his leathered skin. But in the middle of them all, as stark as the day the whalebone needle had first kissed him, was the key tattoo of his Book. And it was glowing ever so softly. 'That was quick,' he said.

'Let us not keep them waiting.'

Tyrfing led Durnus back down the marble steps and into the tower. With every step, his tattoos grew brighter. They could feel it growing in the air too, the magick, the thick, hot touch of it, stirring and simmering as though the blood in their veins was coming to the boil. Durnus and Tyrfing let their own magick swirl and mingle with it as they walked, unfurling like wings behind them. Any normal person, unfortunate enough to be walking alongside them, might have felt the pressure of the air drop, maybe even felt their ears pop or their chest tighten, the flash of a headache maybe but they would be clueless as to why. The Arkmages, and the Written gathering in the hall, could taste it, smell it, hear it, wave their hands through it, even imagine it tumbling through the air like an unravelling rainbow, alight with fire. It was intoxicating. Dangerous. Such was how they had grown in the last ten years.

Tyrfing pushed open the door to the great hall and drank it in. His tattoos were now glowing white-hot. Durnus let go of his arm and found his way to his throne without the tiniest moment of hesitation or the slightest hint of a stumble. It was almost as though the magick gave him another kind of sight, one that Tyrfing could only pretend to understand. He took to the steps of his own his throne. Once they were seated, they looked out over the pitifully small group that stood in perfect lines before them. The Written. The last of their kind.

Twenty-six, counted Tyrfing. That number made his heart heavy. The Written had once numbered well over a hundred. Vice's cruel battle had slashed their numbers by half. Nobody was more painfully aware of that than Modren and Tyrfing, for they had been responsible for a good number of Written corpses that day. Corpses of traitors, mind. Farden's spawn had culled the rest. Twenty-four bodies had been counted so far, over the years. Their numbers had been halved again, and mercilessly too. A dying breed, and no Scribe to save them. Such was Vice's legacy.

But the men and women arrayed in formation in front of them didn't look defeated, nor worried by their dwindling numbers. Every single one had their hands folded calmly behind their back, and each one wore a tiny smile on their face. Tyrfing had once worn a smile like it. As had Farden. It was a smile that smacked of confidence and power. A smirk of the elite. The Arkmage looked at each of the mages and recited their names in his head. Modren's earlier words echoed in his head and he found himself smiling back at them. He would rather have twenty-six of those smiles, he thought, and know what caused them, than twenty-thousand men without.

Durnus waved them forward, and one by one the Written fell out of formation and gathered at the foot of the twin thrones. *How did he know?* wondered Tyrfing. He looked down at them as they sauntered forward. Some of them wore gleaming suits of his newly designed armour. Some had been given Scalussen pieces. Some were still waiting patiently for theirs. Some were old, with scars on their faces, while some were young, some of the last to taste the Scribe's needle. All of them were silent and calm. Their magick screamed loudly enough for all of them.

'Modren,' Durnus called to the Undermage, who was standing at the back of the hall. Elessi was there, standing beside him. Tyrfing couldn't help but notice the frown on her face. 'Seal the doors!'

ordered Durnus.

Modren nodded and gently moved Elessi aside. She went to sit on a bench by a window, arms crossed and face ashen, rubbing her head as if in pain. Modren wiped his hand across the gilded doors, first the left, and then the right, and two resounding thuds echoed through the hall.

'Written!' announced Durnus. The Written watched him expectantly. 'It is time for you to hear why you have been training so hard,' he began.

One of the younger mages put her hand up. 'Is this about the murders, your Mage?'

Durnus nodded. His face was grave. 'My dear, the murders are just the beginning…'

❦

There was a cairn at the very peak of Hardja. The little cone of jagged pebbles was a miracle of balance. It had survived a hundred storms, tasted a hundred caps of snow, felt a hundred different faces of the wind, and was now being stared at by a god. A tiny slab of rock sat at its foot. The ice and wind and rain had stolen the words that had once been carved into it, a forgotten time ago.

Heimdall shifted his feet. His boots crunched on the snow that still stubbornly clung to the peak. An inch from his foot, the rock fell away into a sheer, ice-clad cliff, meeting the walls of the Arkathedral far below. If the god was worried by the stomach-churning drop, he didn't show it. His boots were firmly wedged in a snowy nook. One hand firmly grasped the side of the cairn, while the other shaded his tawny eyes against the morning sun, teetering on top of the opposite peak. He was watching two figures standing on top of the Arkathedral, one being led by another, standing under a set of marble trees.

Heimdall turned his face to the distant west. There came a whistling sound from behind him, and the grating of claws on loose rocks and ice. A lion's tail flicked at the brisk morning air.

Heimdall shook his head to the gryphon's question. 'I cannot see him… wait…'

Another whistle, more urgent.

'Wait. Yes, now I can…'

Ilios could hear the dark concern in the god's voice. He crept forward a little more, and put his beak on the god's shoulder. A pair of piercing golden eyes joined Heimdall's tawny pair. 'I see death on him. He is not moving.'

Ilios clacked his beak a few times. His claws clutched at the rocks, concerned.

'Maybe. It is down to Loki now.'

The gryphon sighed, a musical little hiss.

Heimdall shook his head, and stared down at the stubborn snow that was attempting to swallow his boot. 'We will see,' he said. 'And hope.'

Ilios hummed a sad tune through his closed beak. His feathers shivered in the breeze.

'No, we cannot tell Tyrfing. We keep this between ourselves, until we know. Understand?'

The gryphon clacked his beak once, and only once.

chapter 11

"Old Åddren's dying wish cursed us all. Cursed this city. Cursed it with a murdering madman and a blind old fool. How dare such as they sit on the thrones and bear the Weights. A Written? Such a thing has never been allowed, and for good reason. And Durnus, the blind old crone. Where did he come from? Who had heard of him, before the Battle? It is too suspicious. They are unfit to rule, I say. They will see our proud country go to the dogs! Something must be done..."

An entry stolen from the diary of Council member Malvus Barkhart, dated Spring of the year 905

The light was slippery, a nest of eels. Their tails poked through the curtained window, stabbing him every time he cracked an eye. Sound drifted around him like treacle. Time was dust in his mouth. Voices were ancient echoes in his ears, drifting by on a lazy wind from a forgotten land. They were not real. They were not for him any more.

Why isn't he waking up?

Hand me the cloth!

Who did this to him?

Do something!

It's up to time now.

Time, the cruellest of mistresses. Time did nothing but wound. Farden had been in this place before; this cold, dark, and faceless land hemmed by black mountains. He remembered a ship, a half-drowned cat, and a shingled beach that stabbed him like a spear. He remembered a tree and rope. A crow. A shadow. Memories? pondered the mage, dazedly, in a voice that echoed around him in the void, thrown back by the dark mountains that bordered his consciousness. No, not memories. Dreams. Mere dreams to be drowned by a deeper sleep. The mage felt the cold breeze of his void wash around him. He felt sand in between his naked toes, and closed his eyes. He was ready to let go.

Dead men don't dream.

The sand became wet velvet between his toes, icy cold. Farden opened his eyes and found himself by a ribbon of fast flowing river. It was blue. Lanky shadows pushed him forward from behind, bodies half-realised in translucent flesh. They shoved and pressed against him, but the mage stood his ground, and pushed back with his own shadowy arms. Some shouted for him to move. Some jostled past to slosh through by themselves, but the water took them and swallowed them like a leviathan gorging on an overturned ship.

And only the dead belong here.

Farden twitched, feeling the spray as the river swallowed another. This was no dream. This was a thin stab at reality, the precipice before the void. Farden took a step into the icy water, and felt the pebbles grate against the faint skin of his feet.

'Back!' boomed a voice. Farden looked upstream and saw a ship surging towards them. The ship was long and narrow, sporting tall, gaunt masts that scraped at the mists of Farden's dream, sail-less and empty.

As it came nearer, flowing with the strong river, Farden saw it had a figurehead, and what a ghoulish thing it was. Half a vulture, half a grinning man, both spat from some nightmare. From its ribs down, ribs that had been picked garishly clean by its own curved beak, it was an emaciated man wrapped in a blood-red loincloth. His insides were all splinters and rotten flesh. His porcelain feet dangled in the frigid waters and kicked at the shadows that pawed at the ship's sides. From the chest up, the creature was a giant vulture, like the ones Farden had seen in the Paraian deserts, in another life. An old life. In the place of arms it had wings, and they had been nailed to the crusted bow of the ship at many points. Some of the nails appeared to have wormed free and then bent back into place like rusty hook. Its head, that terrible head, was a giant beak framing black eyes. Dead eyes. Dead eyes that flicked back and forth from shadow to shadow. The creature was screeching at him.

'Back! Back I say!' it yelled, with a vulture's pink tongue.

But it was the ship itself that was truly nightmarish. Now that it was close, Farden saw it for what it truly was. Not wood, no, nor metal. Nails. Innumerable finger and toenails, clasped together with some unholy magick. Every inch of the ship was fashioned from them. Farden felt the bile rising in his throat as the ship sidled up to the riverbank, scraping the shingle.

'You!' spat the figurehead, hanging over him. 'You must go back! You do not belong. Straddler!'

Farden turned around, seeing the faces of a countless crowd of shadows queued behind him. An impossible horde, miles and miles in the making. In the distance, Farden's eyes somehow spied a single light burning in the blurry dark. A single candle. Somehow he knew.

Farden winced as a shiver of pain coursed through his insides. *No*. To go back meant pain, in every sense of the word. Farden took another step forward into the river. The grotesque figurehead began to squawk and flap. 'Back! Not today!'

The mage's feet were becoming numb. It was strange to hear himself say the words that followed. 'I don't want to.'

'Straddler! The one who lives in a sea of dead, go away!'

Farden shrugged. He tried to remember why he had come here, but found he could not. How many paths can be blamed for a man's end? There had once been a woman. A child maybe? He thought of a tree, and felt a rope around his neck. 'But I am dead,' he whispered. It seemed so easy now. The incessant thoughts that had plagued him had finally been silenced. How simple and quiet it was by this strange river.

The dead pushed him forward towards the ship. They were flooding aboard now, shadowy feet rasping across the nails of its decks. Something red and gold flashed through his mind. *I planned on living forever*, he remembered.

'Lost!' screamed the vulture. 'Take him away!'

Instead of pushing him, somebody behind him pulled. Hard, for a ghost. Farden was dragged from the river and barged aside. A pain began to burn in his chest, soft at first, and then blinding.

'We will see you again,' winked the creature on the bow of the ship. 'But not today.'

'Then when?' yelled Farden. His shadowy flesh had begun to shiver, to crawl.

The creature shrieked as the ship moved on. 'Take him away!' it screeched.

Farden was lifted up on the arms of the shadows, the countless shadows of the dead, and tossed around like a buoy in a storm. The river and the crowd faded to blackness as he was carried towards the lone candle.

Alive, in a sea of ghosts…

❦

'Hold 'im down, woman! 'Old 'im down!' somebody shouted, their voice muffled and strained with effort. A pair of dark shadows loomed over him menacingly. Smears of light painted the room behind them. Farden tried to open his eyes further but they refused to obey. A pair of strong hands grasped him by the shoulder and Farden thrashed about as wildly as his weakened body would allow. Pain filled every bastard inch of his body. His throat felt as though he had swallowed a fistful of broken glass.

'Get the bottle! An' the cloth, quickly now!'

There was a crash as Farden's foot caught the corner of a table. A cloth was clamped to his mouth. He tasted something foul on his tongue and in his nose. Farden roared out as the blurry world grew dark again.

❦

The next two weeks were a mere snap of the fingers to Farden; a dreamless blur of cold nights and dull aches. It was merciful in a way. While his mind fell into a deep coma, his fever raged like a bonfire through his body. His wounds spent the first week suppurating and festering, and then somehow, with the aid of Seria's needles and the foreigner's strange herbs, they cooled and calmed, and slowly began to heal.

While his body burnt, Farden rambled senselessly for hours on end. Traffyd built a bed for him on the porch so he could heal and breathe in the fresh air, and so they could get some sleep without being woken by his feverish, unconscious raving. Seria had never paced so much in her life. Traffyd barely saw any sleep. The foreigner, Farden's apparent saviour, did nothing but sit in the corner, smoking a pipe and producing strange liquids and herbs from his pockets when needed.

It was on the eighteenth day that Farden finally returned to the world of the living. His fever had broken three days before, but the mage had turned a shade of ghostly white and had fallen deathly silent. Seria sat by his side, her head on his leg, a half-polished fork clenched in her drooping hand. It was the first time she had slept in three days, and she was snoring like a boar. A few yards away, the rain pestered the plants and flowers of the garden. It was a light rain, the tail of a spring storm that had rolled through Fleahurst the day before. The earth was silent save for the pattering and Seria's snoring.

Farden cracked open a crimson-rimmed eye and saw a thatched roof hanging above him. Wherever he was, it was raining, softly but persistently. He could tell by the rattling of the wooden gutter above his head. He opened his other eye, and saw a door-frame, and a wall of dry flint, the colour of dusty bone. There was a rumbling sound coming from somewhere. It sounded like distant thunder. A storm, he decided, after a moment of confusion. His thoughts were like sand trickling through an hourglass. Grain by grain they were coming back to him.

With a great effort and a greater deal of pain, Farden turned his head to look out at the rain. The sight of it softly pelting the leaves and petals of a garden reminded him how dry and cracked his lips were. Farden tried to move his hand and felt a heavy weight on it, a weight that snuffled and croaked as he twitched the lazy, leaden arm. Thunder, it wasn't.

The woman lying on his arm instantly sat bolt upright. It was Seria. She was almost as bleary-eyed as the mage was. 'Farden?' she whispered, half in awe, half in worry. The farmwife quickly rubbed her eyes and then, for some reason known only to herself, she reached forward to slap him lightly on the cheek. Farden flinched, then winced as the pain blossomed inside him, like a thorny rose. The mage was too bewildered to say anything, and his throat was too dry to speak. He just blinked like a newborn, as she got to her feet and rushed inside the cottage.

Traffyd appeared moments later, his old face packed with the same mixture of emotions as his wife. 'Farden,' he said softly. He looked hesitant. The mage moved his raspy tongue around his lips.

'You aren't going to slap me as well, are you?' he croaked, barely words.

'Jötun, no. Did she really? Dear me…' Old Traffyd's face fell solemn when he saw the light red blotch blooming on the mage's wan cheek. 'She's spent every hour with you these past three days. Ain't slept at all, bless her. She don't mean it.'

'Three days,' gasped Farden. Traffyd quickly grabbed a bark cup and dipped it into a nearby rain barrel. He gently lifted the mage's head and held the little cup to his lips. The mage managed a few sips before he choked on the rest. He spluttered and Traffyd fetched a cloth.

'Three days,' said Farden, when he had recovered. 'Is that all?'

'No, my friend, you've been unconscious for three weeks now, by my reckoning.'

Farden let his head droop onto the bed, hearing the gentle crunch of the dried moss and pungent herbs inside the skinny pillow. *Three weeks.* 'What happened?' He squeezed his eyes shut and tried to make sense of the dismembered pictures flashing behind them. A tree. A rope. A ship. Fingernails?

'You died, Farden, several times,' replied Traffyd. Farden turned his head at that. His eyes were wide. 'Stopped breathing on us more than once. You think Seria slappin' you now is bad, you should've seen how she brought you back to life. You gave as good as you got, though. Tried to kill me, you did, when you finally came back around. You were bellowing something about ghosts. Rivers. Traitors. Nonsense mostly.' Traffyd's leathery hand moved to his throat, and Farden, if he looked closely enough, could see little telltale bruises on the old farmer's skin. He turned back to look at the thatch.

'I'm sorry.'

'Psh, you weren't yourself, man. Forget it. Anyways, you had a fever like I ain't ever seen. You burnt for days. It was only when that friend of yours gave me some of his herbs, what did he call them…? Gungfoot? Gritfeer?'

Farden looked even more confused. If he could have lifted his arms he would have grabbed his head and shaken everything back into place. 'Wait,' he said. 'Friend? What friend?' A moment of nonsense capered through his head, an image of a rat gnawing through a rope and dragging him halfway across the moors by it. Farden shook his head.

Traffyd looked confused as well, and more than a little worried. 'Said he's known you a long time. Says he came at just the right time too. He was on his way to visit you, and when he did, he found you swingin' by your neck. He dragged you to this cottage. Gods wonder how he knew we'd take you in, but he did. He's been here ever since, not sleeping, not eating, just waitin' for you to wake up. If you ask me, lad, I don't trust him one bit. But he saved your life, and that counts for something in my book.'

Farden lifted a shaky, heavy hand to rub his crusty eyes. Dried tears and sweat turned to dust under his fingers. His hands felt as if he had stolen them. As did the rest of his body. He tried, very briefly, to sit up, but the weakness forced him back down.

Traffyd put a firm hand on the mage's chest. 'Easy now. A man don't die and then go running around in the same month. Besides, it ain't just the rope you're recovering from. Your friend told me 'bout your habit. Your body's recovering from that too. Still in the woods, if'n you ask me, lad.'

'But I have to… they took my…'

'I know. You were screaming bloody murder for several days. Rest, Farden. You ain't going anywhere just yet,' said the farmer. Farden wasn't sure whether it was the warmth of the heavy hand pressing on his chest, or the calmness in the old man's voice, but he found his eyes closing, and the rain fading to silence.

When Farden next awoke, it was still raining. Even softer this time. The air was cold, blissfully so, and full of mists and swirling curtains of drizzle. The sun was a myth. The day was colourless, save for the paint-blotches of Old Traffyd's garden and the patchwork fields beyond it. Farden blinked at the view, lopsided as his prone position made it.

Somebody came to check on him. A door creaked and the sound of clanking dishes and hushed conversation momentarily spilled onto the patio. Footsteps wandered towards him. Boots, if Farden's ears were not mistaken. There was a tap as a beaker was placed next to his head.

'That bastard gryphon,' said a voice, a man's voice, but not Traffyd's. Farden wondered if his mind was playing tricks on him again. His mind still felt numb, but the pain had gone for now. 'That's what you kept muttering when I was watching you,' said the voice.

Farden turned his head and found a fair-haired man, probably a handful of years above thirty, staring down at him. He seemed tall, but that was probably because the mage was lying down. He had a youthful face. It burnt with a strange measure of intensity he had only witnessed once before. Farden's mind tried desperately to remember where. His clothing was fresh, foreign. He wore an off-white cloth shirt buttoned tightly to his neck and a long leather coat. There was no armour on the man, no jewellery of any kind, no scars. Not even a mole or a birthmark. Every single one of his blonde hairs was in perfect place. He wasn't even blinking. The realisation landed like a brick in a well. It made Farden's heart sink, and made his lip curl. 'And which one are you?' Farden croaked.

The man touched the beaker to his lips. He spoke while Farden sipped. 'For a man who's just been hauled back from the brink of death, you don't seem very grateful.'

Farden lifted his hand to wipe his lips. He felt a little stronger today. 'I'm sure it wasn't out of the kindness of your heart.'

'And why would you say that?'

'It never is with you lot,' replied the mage. He shook his head. 'Which one are you?'

The man ducked his head so he could look out into the garden. He watched the rain for a moment, and then turned a little to point east. 'You can see me, before sunrise. I am the Light-bringer. Aurvandill in our tongue. Loki in yours.'

'Loki. Like the mountain?'

'No, that would be *Lokki*. An unfortunate coincidence.'

'That's a shame.'

'Mmm.'

Farden rubbed his face with his hands. He couldn't help but notice how much his beard had grown, and how dry his face and lips were. He must have looked like a wild man. He could feel the lumps in his neck where his muscles had been bruised and the rope had torn his skin. He dreaded the next mirror he'd see. He sighed through his fingers. 'Why?' he asked, question muffled.

Loki still hadn't blinked. 'Why what?'

'Why are you here?'

'That really doesn't elaborate on your question. Why did I save you, do you mean? Because I arrived just in time. Why was I coming to you? Because I was ordered to.'

'By whom?'

'Heimdall.'

'And who is he?'

'The Guardian. One of the oldest.'

'And where's Evernia in all of this?'

Loki raised a hand and pointed to the thatch roof and the sky above it.

'I see.'

'Why now?'

'Because I have news for you.'

Farden groaned. He felt a tightness in his chest. His betrayal by Kiltyrin was bad enough, but it was his business. He groaned as he imagined his little world crumbling around him, as though it were being invaded and chewed by vermin. Vermin he had left far behind in another world, on the other side of a sea. Now one of them was staring down at him. 'No,' he spat. 'I don't want any news, I don't want any information, I want nothing. Understand?'

'What makes you think I was going to tell you?' Farden pulled a face, confused. Loki looked up and down the mage's tortured body. 'It looks as if you have enough to deal with at the moment as it is,' he said, and without a further word, Loki went back inside the cottage, and shut the door firmly behind him. Farden was left staring at the wood with his eyes-half closed. He was surprised, to say the least.

Farden stared up at the thatch. A god arriving on his mouldy doorstep meant trouble. His past had come to bite him. *Fine*, he thought, *it had saved him, but only so it could bite him later*. Farden squeezed his eyes shut and tried to dig at the pain-sodden blur that had been the last few weeks. The moments flew through his head in flashes of light and colour and noise. He saw the faces of the men who had tried to kill him. He felt the rope tightening around his neck and found himself gasping. He felt the jab of a spear, and the grin of the man, Wartan. Kint was there, beady-eyed. The slow chuckle of Forluss. And the other man, holding his armour, *his* armour in his greedy hands. Loffrey. Farden cursed at them all behind clenched teeth.

Then he saw a ship and a horrifying creature pinned to its bow. The mage felt ice-water between his toes. He felt the dead pushing him, then dragging him. Farden opened his eyes, breathing hard. 'The bastard gryphon, indeed,' he wheezed. Meddlers. They'd found him. He just wanted to be left alone to his own little world. As dark and as murderous and as treacherous as it was, it was his, and his alone.

It took an hour for Farden to summon the strength and the wherewithal to sit up, and when he did, Traffyd appeared at the door with a bowl of watered-down stew and a spoon, right on cue. Farden asked for some bread, but the old farmer shook his head, muttering something about Seria's orders. His stomach wasn't ready for it, and Farden understood why; it took everything he had to keep the simple stew down. He couldn't tell whether it was the nevermar or his dying.

It took yet another hour to make it onto his feet, and even then Traffyd had to carry him to the chair on the edge of the porch. While Traffyd packed himself a pipe, Farden sat with his head on his arm and his hand in the rain, letting the coolness of it calm him. The wound in his left side throbbed and twitched with every little movement, so he thought it best to stay still.

'We saw them, you know. The ones who did this to you.' Farden tried not to look up. Traffyd nodded and tapped his pipe against his teeth. 'We saw them and their cart a few hours before your friend brought you to us. I was in the front garden. Didn't say a word to me. Just sneered and stared, they did.'

'You're lucky. If they had hurt you, I wouldn't have forgiven myself.'

'If they had, then you'd be dead, and have no use for forgiveness, lad,' said the old farmer. 'Bah. Maybe your friend would have saved you anyways. Who knows.'

'He's not my friend.'

'I see,' Traffyd said. 'Then who is he? Seria's beginning to ask questions.'

Farden clenched his fist around the water gathering in his palm. 'He's not my friend,' he repeated.

Traffyd blew a smoke ring. 'But he did save your life.'

'That he did.'

A moment passed, full of dripping and lazy smoke. 'Do you want me to get rid of him for you?' asked the farmer.

Farden thought long and hard. 'No,' he said.

And that was that.

❦

It was another week before Farden could move about freely. The mage was going stir-crazy in the cottage. Old Traffyd took him for short, shuffling walks around the garden to keep him from Seria's concerned fussing. Loki would trail behind them, taking the tips from the herbs he passed and dabbing them to his tongue to taste them. At first, Farden had ignored it, but after a while he couldn't help but remark on it.

'I thought gods didn't eat?' he challenged him one afternoon, while Old Traffyd had gone to fetch some water for the mage and his plants. The spring sun had returned, and his garden had bloomed eagerly.

Loki had shrugged, and nibbled on the base of a tiny carrot. 'We don't,' he said, cryptically.

Oddly enough, the god had also taken to smoking too, and drinking for that matter. He seemed to be intrigued by human occupations and idiosyncrasies, and while he was alone with the three humans, he seemed intent on testing and tasting everything. It was strange behaviour for a god, Farden decided, but after all, Loki was only the second sky-fallen deity he had met. He just kept to ignoring the slippery bastard. It was much easier.

Seria and Traffyd seemed to be tiring of him too. As the days passed, their suspicions were only heightened by Farden's cold attitude to his supposed saviour. The god swapped between streams of constant questions and hours of frozen silence, staring into dusty space. When the old couple challenged him on anything, such as his origins, or why he was visiting the mage, Loki would shrug and change the subject. Gentle and kind as they were, Farden could tell their patience was wearing very thin.

And so it was, that at the end of the week, Traffyd and Seria returned from a walk to find Farden and his odd companion sitting on the front step of the cottage. The clothes that Farden had stolen from Wodehallow's keep were long gone and burnt. He was wearing an ill-fitting tunic and trousers that Traffyd had lent to him. Farden got to his feet, shakily, when they reached the gate.

Traffyd looked the mage up and down and sniffed. Seria's hand hovered on the gate. 'You'd best be going east,' she said. 'Or else.'

Farden nodded. 'I am,' he replied. *For now.*

Seria fixed him with one of her dark looks as she walked up the path to the cottage, husband in tow. 'I ain't joking, Farden. Those men tried to kill you. If they find out they didn't, well, we won't be savin' you a second time,' she said, putting her hands on her hips. 'Too worryin' it is.' Farden might have been wrong, but he thought he saw a tear creep into the corner of Seria's eye. She quickly flicked it away, a trespasser. The mage stood and held out his shaky arms. Seria nearly crushed him to death in the hug that followed. Traffyd stayed behind as she released him, nodded grimly to Loki, and then went inside. Once she had shut the door, the old farmer crossed his arms.

'What are you going to do then?' he asked. Loki looked to the mage, also eager to know the answer.

Farden looked east, where the clouds cavorted like eels and minnows and chased each other across the upper reaches of the distant sky. Their long, spectral fins trailed for miles behind them as they rode the high winds. 'I'm going to kill them all,' he said.

Traffyd looked at the flint in the path under his feet. 'And what about the next time? What about the next batch of thieves and murderers that want you dead?'

'There won't be. Not when I'm finished.'

Traffyd. 'Then what?'

Farden just shrugged. 'Then maybe you'll get that helper you wanted.'

The farmer walked forward and patted the mage on the shoulder. He didn't try to hug him. 'Just you remember that corpses can't plough fields,' he said quietly, and then went into his cottage.

'Thank you,' mumbled Farden, just before the door closed. The words were foreign to his tongue. The closing door paused for a moment, and then shut with a click. A bolt slid into its hole, and all was silent. The mage exhaled.

Loki stood there quietly. There was a blank look on his face. Farden looked at him. 'What of you? Where are you going?'

'With you.'

'I doubt that very much. I told you, I don't want to hear whatever message you have for me. You can go back to whoever sent you and tell them I don't care. That goes for my uncle, that gryphon, Durnus, Lerel, and whoever else. Tell 'em all I'm dead.'

'What about Elessi?'

Farden began to march down the path. 'Her too,' he growled. The sun was hot. He tried to ignore how weak it made him feel. Loki followed in Farden's wake. His hands were deep in his coat pockets.

'Fine. But I can still help you.'

'Help me with what?'

'With your revenge.'

'And for what price?'

He heard the god come to a halt. 'No price. I'm just a messenger. If, after you've slaughtered all the men you need to slaughter, you want to hear my message, you can have it. And if you don't, then I will disappear back to Krauslung, and I will tell them whatever you'd like. No price. You have my word on that.'

Farden stopped and turned around. Loki was holding out a pale hand. His skin almost took on a translucent quality in the light. His eyes, those blue-white eyes that had watched him incessantly for the past week, burrowed into him. Farden felt another shiver of weakness and queasiness run through his body. *Did he trust him?* No. *Could he use him?* Possibly.

'Fine,' he said. He reached out and grabbed the god's hand. He found it cold and hard, just like he'd expected. 'Just stay out of my way,' warned the mage.

'With pleasure,' Loki replied.

chapter 12

"Firstdew, Year 1301 - Last night I dreamt the goddess visited me once again. Her hand was cold as she led me to the deck of the ship. She pointed to the north, where Krauslung lay naked and glittering in the valley. 'There,' she spoke, distantly. 'That is where you will build it. Against the face of Hardja, and facing east.' 'Build what?' asked I, shivering for the cold. 'The crown this city needs. A castle. A fortress. An Arkathedral, *' replied the goddess.*

"I must confess, now that I wake and write this down, I doubt that these are dreams at all. I shall consult Farka, and hear what he says. Arkathedral. *How I could summon such a word from my own imagination..."*

(Diary of the Arkmage Los, one of the first female Arkmages to sit on the twin thrones. A note for the student - you may be confused by Los' use of the year 1301. This is a common theme throughout her diary, as she always refused to use the new count. Los insisted that we should remember how long the humans have been free of the elves and their kin. As you know, at the end of the Scattered Kingdoms period, we began to count the years again, to signify a new age. For instance, I write this in the year 899, but by the old count, I am writing in the year 1899. Why did our ancestors do this? In hindsight, it wasn't the smartest decision. We scholars never have it simple. Prepare for a lifetime of confusion.)

From the notebook of Arfell scholar Yaminas, writing in the year 899 (or

1899)

Whiskers returned that evening. Possibly drawn in by the smell and the light of the fire on the shingly beach, he hovered in the doorway of the shack before entering. He sniffed the evening breeze and squeaked softly to himself. The inside of the shack was still an upturned mess. Farden hadn't bothered to move anything. That afternoon he had simply slumped onto his straw mattress and passed out for a good few hours, leaving Loki to rummage around in his bare cupboards and examine his strange collection of carved candles.

The rat picked his way between the smashed furniture and broken floorboards. He paused at the edge of one particular gaping hole, near where Farden's bed had been. Whiskers sniffed at the straw lying around the edges of the hole, and scuttled on.

Drawn by the muffled sound of a voice, Whiskers wandered to the back door and onto the sand-dusted rocks of the little beach. Two figures huddled around a little cooking fire, sitting under the stars and the fingernail moon. One stoked the flames with an old poker, the other sat a short distance away, running a whetstone along a very long knife. The man with the poker was talking in quiet tones.

As if he were eavesdropping, Whiskers sat for a moment on a nearby rock and listened to their mumblings, trying to make sense of the strange noises.

Farden had been glaring at his unwanted companion for a little while now. 'Where did you get that poker?' he asked, suddenly.

Loki looked up. 'Was that a reply to my question?' he asked. A moment ago he had asked if the mage felt any different after his foray into death. They had been having a one-sided debate ever since Farden had risen a few hours ago.

'No, it wasn't,' he said stiffly. 'Where did you find it? I don't remember ever having a poker.'

'I have a habit of finding things,' Loki replied.

Another cryptic answer to grate on Farden. He ran the stone along his knife again with a metallic whisper. 'Just like you found me?'

Loki raised his poker and his spare hand to the evening sky hanging above them. The stars were pinpricks in its black velvet blanket. 'It's my power. Some of us know the truth in everything; some of us gave birth to the song of magick; some of us usher in the weather and the seasons; some of us wield power like you humans wield a spoon, and what is mine? I lead the dawn.'

'That sounds pretty important to me.'

For the first time since he met him, Farden saw a flash of emotion pass across the god's face. Irritation, anger maybe. 'A servant's task. Ceremonial, rather than an actual duty. A menial chore passed to me when I was born, by an older god.'

At that Farden had to pause his sharpening. '*Born*? Gods are born?'

Loki looked up at the sky and shook his head. 'Of course we are. Why do you think the stars constantly revolve and wander? Our war is still being fought, albeit slowly. I was born in Haven, in your tongue. The sky. This is the first time I've ever set foot on your earth.'

'Well, that explains why you're acting so oddly.'

Loki gazed at the waves and let the susurrations of the calm sea licking the sand fill the silence. 'The others would not condone it.'

Farden smirked. 'You sound bitter, Loki. Almost as bitter as me.'

Loki delved into the inside of his coat and brought out a fork. There was a pan sitting amongst the glowing logs of the crackling fire. Inside it was a fish stew that Farden had thrown together. All fins and heads and mouldy vegetables. Better than nothing. He needed his strength back for all the killing he had planned. Loki lifted its lid and poked at its contents.

Farden ignored him, plucking at the edge of his blade. He hummed satisfactorily and put the knife to one side. He reached for the next and began to sharpen that one. It was at that moment that Whiskers joined them. The rat scurried onto Farden's lap, and the mage couldn't help but yelp with surprise and joy. He hadn't expected to ever seen the little beast again. He dropped his knife and stone and grabbed him. He held the rat up to the starry sky and watched him wriggle and squeak. 'Old boy,' he whispered.

'A rat. It figures,' muttered Loki. Farden didn't hear him.

Farden cradled the rat on his shoulder and he curled up instantly with a contented chatter. Farden picked up his blade and went back to his honing.

The mage and the god sat there in silence for a while. Loki was content to poke the fire with the poker and shepherd the logs and coals into various positions. His line of questioning seemed to have died away. Farden was glad of it. Even if the man had not been an unwanted presence, his choice of conversation disturbed him; deep, invasive questions that Farden would grimace and scowl at. He feigned silence, but inside his tired and numbed mind, Loki's questions rattled around like hot marbles.

After sharpening two more knives, Farden put Whiskers on the sand and got up to check the stew. Loki produced another fork from inside his coat. Farden snatched it away and poked the fish. 'It's ready,' he grunted. 'I hope you have a bowl,' he asked, swiping his from the shingle near the fire. He had only the one. Why need any more, when his only house guest was a rat? Farden dipped the bowl into the stew and walked back to his spot. He tested the watery concoction with his tongue. It was a poor man's stew, but he found himself ravenous, and quickly began to slurp despite the boiling heat.

Loki watched the mage eat. He looked neither dejected, nor angry. He simply reached inside his coat and rummaged for a few moments. Then, like a jester pulling a coin from an infant's ear, he yanked a small wooden bowl from a hidden pocket and dipped it into the pot. Farden caught the movement in the corner of his eye. He scowled. Gods and their tricks.

The two ate in a silence. The sighings of the sea and the breeze were the only sounds. A lost gull squawked somewhere in the darkness. Whiskers nibbled on a spare bit of carrot. Farden grunted as he got to his feet. The broth had made his stomach churn. He collected his knives and headed back indoors. Loki didn't look up. He was too busy examining each individual ingredient swimming in his bowl, nibbling and licking each one in turn. *Idiot*, thought Farden.

The air was cold inside the shack. Farden shivered and clutched himself. His hand grazed his rib wound and he grit his teeth with a growl. There was a shard of broken mirror on the floor. Farden scooped it up so he could grudgingly examine his reflection.

It was worse than he imagined.

Aside from the ugly wounds around his neck, his split lips, and his bedraggled beard, the fever had burnt the fat from his face. He looked horrifyingly gaunt. Farden lifted up his shirt and examined his ribs, which now resembled sharp, jagged fence-posts. The spear-wound was an ugly thing. Puckered like a pair of blood-soaked lips, the spear had pierced him just below his lowest rib, a few inches down from an ancient arrow scar. He prodded it and then almost doubled up with the resulting pain. Seria had done a good job of sewing the wound up. She had been a seamstress in another life, and that had saved Farden's. For the first time in many, many years, Farden wished for his magick. He could have wiped his hand across the ugly wound and have his magick seal it. Farden threw the shard of mirror aside and slumped onto his bed.

What was it about the arrival of Loki that had rattled the mage so much? It was as though someone had picked a scab in his mind, making it ooze. That was how Farden thought of it. Fifteen years he had spent locking away his magick and his memories. It was why he had hidden himself away in a shack by a forgotten beach; why he buried himself in wine and mörd and nevermar and refused to get close to anyone; why he had been content to be a hired blade, so long as he was left alone. A scab for his wounds. Now Loki had come to pick at it.

What wound needed such a scab? Him. Farden himself. The mage was a curse.

Although his world had been shattered by Kiltyrin's betrayal, it was still *his* world. He had let those people, the Duke, Kint, Forluss, Jeasin, this Loffrey bastard, into it and therefore the benefits, or the detriments, he had reaped were his and his alone. They were actors in his morbid little drama. Up until now they had been inconveniences and sources of coin. He had let his guard down and therefore brought this situation upon himself, but it was upon himself, and no other. That was why Farden could handle this world, this melancholy, immoral morass he had willingly sunk himself into.

But the god sitting on his beach was an intruder. An interloper who had come to pick and probe, and laugh like a jester while he did it. Loki was an ambassador for those he had hurt and been forced to leave behind, those he had cared about. Farden had left them behind to save them from further harm. Why in Emaneska were they trying to drag him back? The fools.

Bad decision after bad decision he'd made. Years of them, queuing up like the dead in his dream. Murder, betrayal, death, he had caused them all. He had even… and it hurt Farden to dig the thought out from where he and the nevermar had buried it… even brought a monster into the world.

He had burnt his bridges long ago, and now Loki had been sent to rebuild them. He was sure of it. Messenger or not, lesser god or greater, he loathed him for it. He would use whatever resources Loki had to offer, drown the bastards in their own blood, and then laugh as he sent the god packing back to the east.

Farden, like any disease, needed to be left alone to infect those who deserved it, and no others.

The mage rolled his knives up in a patchwork cloth and left them beside the lopsided door. He rummaged through the contents of an overturned box and found a splintered handle with a length of chain and a spiked metal ball at the end. It was a flail, and an old one at that, speckled with rust. Farden hummed as he felt its points with his sandy thumb. Rusted as it was, it was still sharp. That was what he needed. Sharp, brutal, ugly things to embed into skulls and faces.

Farden folded the flail carefully over his shoulder and rifled through a dishevelled pile of rumpled clothes with his toe. There was a cloak there, a dark red cloth one with a hole in the hood. Better than nothing. He found a spare belt draped over the stove's battered chimney. It would do. His borrowed trousers were good enough, as was the shirt. His boots would barely survive the next few weeks. He only needed one.

As he turned to head back to the beach, Farden instinctively patted his wrists to check his vambraces. He growled darkly when he realised they weren't there. The strange emptiness and lightness of his arms was made stranger by the feeling of the cold, curious air across his naked skin, where normally he would have felt the scales of warm metal, and the rush of their subtle magick.

The mage had forbidden himself from contemplating their permanent loss. He refused to entertain the thought that Kiltyrin could have sold them, or dispatched them to some far-off and secret corner of his duchy. It made his stomach clench every time it crossed his mind. He would have them back. Prise them from as many dead fingers as he had to. And quickly too. He tried not to pay attention to the strange aches that flitted across his joints and bones. Nevermar wasn't the only thing he was withdrawing from.

Blood, there will be, thought the mage, and not a drop of his. He had spilt enough.

Farden clenched his fists and contemplated strangling something. He spied a candle on the floor, one with a smiling, half-drunken face, and he crushed it with a vicious stamp of his sandy heel. Served it right, grinning at a time like this.

The mage donned the dark red cloak and went back to the beach, taking the rusty flail with him. The warm breeze welcomed him. Loki was still playing with his stew. Whiskers had made a bed for himself in the warm sand near the fire. Farden let the flail drop in the sand with a thud, drawing a glance from Loki. 'That looks friendly,' said the god.

'I imagine it looks even better embedded in a Duke's ribcage,' Farden muttered. He sat cross-legged in the sand and began to scrape the rust from the weapon with the whetstone and a scrap of oiled cloth. Whiskers watched and sniffed.

It took him half an hour to make it battle-worthy. Farden tested the points again with his thumb and nodded. 'Good enough,' he mumbled. He swung it around above his head to test it. The weapon rattled and hummed as it spun in its deadly arcs. Farden brought it down on a nearby driftwood log, making Whiskers jump. The metal ball broke the log in two, sending a shower of splinters to float on the breeze. The mage smiled as he pictured what he might do with it.

Loki had finished his stew. 'So what exactly is your plan? I assume you actually have a plan?'

Farden shrugged. 'Go to Castle Tayn, start with Kint and Forluss, and then work my way to that Loffrey man and then the Duke. Kill them all, and make sure the last thing they see is my grinning face. Then I get my armour back and leave,' he said. He suddenly thought of Timeon and Moirin, and Jeasin, and wondered how they would fit into all of this. He rubbed his forehead. 'I'll make the rest up as I go along,' he added.

'Sounds like a fine plan to me,' replied Loki, dissatisfied. He couldn't imagine the dour mage really grinning at anything at all. He wondered, not for the first time, what Evernia saw in him.

Farden clenched his fists once more, almost as if testing his fingers. 'I've been waiting for this for years.'

Loki raised an eyebrow. 'For somebody to try to hang you?'

Farden shook his head. 'For the day when Kiltyrin would give me an excuse.'

'I see. And how exactly do you expect to get into the Duke's castle undetected, and have enough time to kill all four of them without raising the alarm? That's assuming he's still in this Tayn place, and not elsewhere?'

Farden stared at the quiet flames of the fire. 'He's in Tayn. He thinks I'm dead, and therefore has no reason to move. Like I said, the rest I'll figure it out as I go.'

Loki sighed. 'And how do you plan to escape once you've retrieved your precious Scalussen armour? It would be a terrible waste of time for you to make all this effort to get your armour back, only to die again on the castle steps.'

Farden looked up at the god. He was mimicking Farden's exact pose: cross-legged on the sand, knees tucked into his elbows, hands clasped around his bowl. *Why send this one, of all the gods to send?* He didn't seem wise, or ancient, or powerful, or inspiring. He spoke more like a jumped-up stable-boy than an immortal. 'And what do you know about my armour?' asked the mage.

Loki rolled his eyes. 'I'm a god, Farden. Don't insult my intelligence.'

'I wouldn't dare,' Farden sullenly replied. 'I'm sure I'll come up with something.'

But Loki was persistent. 'And what are you going to do after it's over? What are you going to do for coin? It's an expensive habit you seem to have adopted,' he said with a nod towards the shed.

'I'll take what I'm owed from the Duke. I survived before, I can do it again.'

'I can't imagine you really settling down with Traffyd and his wife and living the farmer's life. You might as well keep killing for coin,' said Loki. Farden wondered if he was trying to antagonise the mage, but he seemed serious enough. He was staring at the stars and counting their shapes.

'Served me well so far,' mumbled Farden.

'And I take it you won't be using your magick?'

Farden shook his head very quickly and very firmly. 'No.' If the mage was a curse, a disease, then his magick was the root of it. Even now, when he most likely needed it the most, the stubborn mage refused to even think of it.

'I imagined you wouldn't. It's a shame, to see such skill go to waste, and especially at a time like this, when it could probably come in handy.'

'I said no,' insisted the mage.

'Well then, I suppose you might be needing these,' Loki said. He tapped his bowl on a nearby chunk of driftwood, slipped it back into his coat, and got to his feet. The mage didn't move. He and Whiskers just watched warily. Still with his hand in his coat, Loki crouched down beside Farden. He rummaged for a little while, eyes distant and thoughtful as eyes tend to be when the fingers are doing the looking. Before Farden could ask what on earth he was doing, Loki produced his first item. 'Mistfrond,' he said, dropping a strange object on the sand. It looked like something halfway between a pear and a pinecone, but was a reddish pink in colour, and had furry spines that curled around it. Whiskers moved to sniff at it and quickly retreated. Loki explained while he continued to search his pockets.

'From the shores of the Ghast Sea in the distant east. Grows on a single tree on a single beach each year, and a different beach every time. If you eat it, it will give your skin a fog-like quality, yes *fog*, not frog, for a short while. Makes you very hard to see. It also makes you violently ill, so use carefully.'

Next came a little vial of brackish liquid. Farden wrinkled his lip at it. Loki looked up. 'Beggarbeet sap. I'm surprised you didn't see this stuff in Paraia. It smells worse than anything you can imagine. Might be useful.'

'How?'

'You said you'd make it up as you went along.'

Loki then dug out a length of ship's rope, crusted in salt, a long yet impossibly thin dagger for doors and their locks, a hat with a mop of blonde hair sewn into its hem, and two pages that looked as though they had been ripped from a spell book. Farden nudged these warily. 'I told you. No magick.'

Loki ignored him. 'A few magick markets discovered a little while ago that burning certain spells had the same effect as reading them out loud. It's not a popular trend, seeing as it involves the burning of some very expensive books and paper, but for those who can't manage the feel of magick, it's perfect. These are light spells. Specifically, bursting spells. They'll blind anyone.'

'Where did you get all this stuff?'

'I told you, I've a habit of finding things.'

Farden shook his head. 'And why should I trust you?'

Loki left his things in a pile by the mage's knees and returned to his spot on the other side of the fire. 'Because, mage, you need all the help you can get. You could barely walk twenty miles today. You shake every time you think of your armour.'

Farden resented it, but he was right. He could feel the weakness lurking inside him, as though a leech had wriggled its way to his heart and was gorging itself. It stung to accept the help of the god, but he had to. 'Fine,' he said. He gathered the god's supplies and then got to his feet. As if to prove Loki's point, his legs wobbled unsteadily. 'But don't you get to thinking I'm in debt to you for helping me. Or for saving my life. I didn't ask for either,' he said, as he walked away. Whiskers looked up but stayed by the fire.

'You don't ask for a lot of things, Farden, and yet they come to you nonetheless. Fate, I believe you humans call it. Besides, I'm just protecting my investment. How exactly am I supposed to deliver a message to a dead man?' Loki called after him.

For some reason, and despite the warm breeze, Farden shivered as he walked back to his little shack. 'Don't worry. I died once. I don't intend to do it again any time soon,' he said. *All he needed was his armour back.*

Loki waited until he was almost at the door of the shack before asking his last question. He knew the mage wouldn't answer, but he asked it anyway. 'I understand blaming us gods for your misfortune. I understand blaming your magick too. I even understand seeking out this sort of life, and burying your past in solitude and nevermar. What puzzles me most of all, mage, is why would somebody who lives like you want to live forever?'

Farden hovered at the door. He felt no anger at the question, no shame, just an intense feeling of puzzlement. After a moment of silence, listening to the breeze and the undulating sea, he stepped indoors and slammed the rickety door behind him.

Farden took a moment to stand in the middle of his dark shack and look around. The faint orange glow of the fire outside threw a little light through the windows. The mattress in the corner beckoned to his tired legs and leaden eyes. The corner of a little cloth bag poking out from under the stove beckoned as well. Farden let himself move toward the latter.

Bending down, hearing his knees click, Farden slid the cloth bag from its hiding place and looked inside. The bag was emptier than he remembered. He looked at the mattress, then back at the bag. He would regret it tomorrow, he knew it, but for now… His body and mind itched to feels its numbing claws, its warm glow, to banish his bothersome thoughts. It had been over three weeks, and his body was crying out for it. *Maybe just a little*, he thought. No pipe, just the good old fashioned way…

Farden stuck his fingers into the bag and pinched a grape-sized amount. Rolling it between his fingers he tucked it between his teeth and his lip while he folded the bag away. He shed his cloak and went to his mattress. As he put his head on his pillow, he began to chew, and the room quickly melted into that foggy haze. That glorious numbness. His eyes drooped.

Suddenly he began to panic. His legs twitched uncontrollably and his chest clenched. A cold fist clutched his heart. Farden sat bolt upright and found a dribble of sweat coursing down his face. The nevermar had turned bitter in his mouth, and between erratic and panicked breaths, he began to gather it together with his tongue and spit it on the floor. Farden scrabbled to press himself up against the wall, and sat there, wheezing and coughing.

It took him several minutes to get his breathing back to normal, and even then his heart pounded like a war drum in his chest. No matter how many times he wiped it away with the back of his hand, the sweat kept coming. The dizziness from the drug blurred his vision, and no amount of blinking would make it go away. It was the feeling of dying all over again, Farden suddenly realised, and it terrified him to his very core. The numbness creeping over his body. Ice water washing his veins clean. Breath becoming slow, tumescent, laborious. Darkness lurking in the corners of his eyes. It was all there. It was horrifying. Farden shivered again, and slowly, ever so slowly, slumped into his mattress so he could curl up into a ball. Tentatively, he allowed himself to fall into a fitful, twitching sleep, full of dark mountains, screaming vultures, and a strange whistling sound.

❦

Outside, on the beach, Loki was still staring at the slow-dancing stars. Some he squinted and narrowed his eyes at, others he sighed for. The fire was slowly dying. A faint finger of cold had crept into the breeze. Loki felt it, but he didn't mind. On his right, Farden's rat was crouched in the sand. His beady black eyes were glued to the back door of the shack, as if he were anxiously waiting for Farden to return.

'What is it?' asked the god. Whiskers glanced at him briefly and then looked back at the door. His whiskers twitched with every little breath he took.

Eyes fixed on the rat, Loki reached into one of his many mysterious coat pockets and this time he withdrew a little pipe. The musical sort, not the tobacco kind. He ran his fingers along its tiny holes, testing each one. Once he was happy he put it to his lips and blew a low note, one that seemed to swell and billow with the breeze and the hissing waves. The god let this note wander and waver for a minute before allowing it to fall away into the sand. Its lingering echoes were soon joined by a slow melody that seemed to skip and jump from each note to the next. At points it was slightly discordant and haunting, and then suddenly the notes would tumble over each other and gallop, and then slow again. Whiskers turned to watch the god play the little pipe, and then, as the melody ebbed and flowed, the rat rose up onto his haunches and began to dance. His tail flicked back and forth in the sand, and his tiny paws jabbed the air. Occasionally he would squeak along to the tune, and at other times he would close his eyes. Loki leant closer and played along to the rat's strange little dance.

When he was finished, when the odd tune had faded, the rat settled back down. He watched the god intently. Loki nodded to it, as if thanking him for the dance, and then looked over at the shack, still faintly lit by the orange glow of the dying fire. 'Didn't know gods were born,' he mused thoughtfully. He turned to face the sliver of moon loitering in the south. 'Next he'll be assuming we're immortal.'

chapter 13

"A Written will serve the Arka and the Arka only.
A Written will never reveal his Book to another, nor allow it to be revealed.
A Written is forbidden to breed with Written, mage, or otherwise.
A Written shall not seek to use his powers against his fellow Arka.
A Written will serve the Arkmages, the Undermage, the Council, and the Arka with his life.
A Written, like any mage, is forbidden to consume the poison known as Nevermar.
A Written, if his Book has taken his mind, shall face permanent exile or death.
The penalty for breaking these rules is death by hanging, unless pardoned by the Council."
The Rules of The Written - Updated Charter of the year 799

Far to the east, where the mountains slid into the sea, under the same sliver of white moon, Elessi was staring at the stars. It was a clear night over Krauslung; no clouds had yet been brave enough to come out and bare their nebulous faces.

The maid stood at the edge of the new Nest, one hand resting lightly on a marble branch while the other clutched a shawl about her to stave off the slight but cold wind. At least the oak under her bare feet was still warm from the day's sun and from the rising heat from the Arkathedral below. Her green dress and apron did their best to keep out the wind. It was content to pester her long brunette curls.

Beyond and below her the city was spread out like a long bed of yellow coals. She had stared at the view for what felt like an hour, and now that her eyes had glazed over with deep thought, the scenery had melted into a single blur of black, bespattered with glowing whites and shades of gold.

Ilios slumbered behind her. As a creature of the desert, he was used to sleeping outside. He loved the fresh air. The Nest was perfect for him.

At first, Elessi had been petrified of the beast, but Tyrfing had shown her how gentle and calm he could be, and she had grown to trust him. In fact, she had grown to treat him like a big and clumsy cat, often scolding him for leaving feathers and fur all over the place, or getting claw marks on the marble, or generally getting in the way. Only Elessi could treat a gryphon like that. Only harmless Elessi could get away with it.

Harmless. That word was so closely tied to *pushover*. She pulled a face at that. Elessi had come up to the roof to be alone with her thoughts. She had many of them to keep her company.

Another hour of staring and cold wind passed, and finally Elessi turned to leave. As she left, she patted the big beast on the ridge of his dangerous beak, making his tufted ears twitch. Silently, the maid descended the cold steps to the tower beneath, and then down into the silent, dark, and apparently empty great hall. It was not as empty as she thought.

As she paused by the Underthrone to wipe a patch of dust from its marble arm, a hoarse voice startled her.

'For most maids, I would say it is a little late for cleaning duties, but I know you better than that,' said Durnus. He was slumped in his throne. His head rested sleepily in his hand and his eyes were closed. He was wearing a thin tunic that was unbuttoned to the middle of his chest, and a pair of soft cloth trousers and sandals. Chamber wear, hardly befitting an Arkmage upon his throne. But nobody was around to care. It was his throne, after all.

Elessi would have smiled, had she been in the mood to, had it been anybody else but Durnus. He was one of the reasons behind tonight's staring contest with the city. She hesitated for a moment, unsure of what to say, wondering whether to simply walk off. 'Why now?' she sighed, finally.

'A very good question, Elessi.'

'I was just forgettin' about him.'

Durnus looked a little pained by that, as if it were almost an insult. 'The rest of us have not. *Cannot*, even. He is like a son to me, and he is Tyrfing's nephew.'

'He's also a deserter, and the reason we're all 'ere today.'

'Considering you and Modren, I would hardly say that was a terrible thing.'

Elessi flapped her hands impatiently. Her shawl fell to the floor around her bare feet, forgotten. 'No, you know that's not what I meant. Stop tryin' to play your word games with me, Durnus. I've known you too long for that.'

Durnus sighed. He leant forward. 'I know what you mean, Elessi. I'm sorry.'

The maid crossed her arms. 'So. Why'd you do it? Why now, when we've just announced the wedding?' she demanded.

'Because of that very reason, Elessi. Your wedding could be the only thing that brings Farden out of his stubborn exile. Ilios refuses to tell us where he is, as does Heimdall. None of our messengers or emissaries have been successful. We need him, Elessi. Krauslung needs him. Tyrfing needs him, and now I need him,' confessed the old Arkmage. He had always needed Farden, he had just never admitted it. The loss of that mage was more painful than the loss of his eyes.

Elessi took a breath to try to calm herself down. 'Well I don't want him there.'

'He does not have to be there, as long as he is *here*, finally back with us, after all these years,' Durnus said, sounding wistful. 'Don't you miss him, Elessi? For all his faults? Don't you worry about him?'

'No,' replied Elessi, without even a hint of a lie. 'He hurt me.'

'It's been sixteen years, Elessi…'

'And it still hurts, Durnus. Modren may have agreed to this, but I 'aven't. And as usual, my opinions are ignored. Even when it's my wedding. I'm just a maid.'

Durnus nodded, and the conversation died. 'I am sorry,' he muttered, as she paced away. Before she left for good, he called out to her. 'Have you and Modren set a date yet?'

Elessi opened one of the giant doors with a heave. The guards behind it came to attention, even despite her maid's attire. They knew exactly who she was. 'Three weeks from today,' she said over her shoulder. She knew he would hear him. Durnus waved, and she left.

'I hope that's not too late,' he muttered to himself. The door shut behind her, and the Arkmage was left alone to ponder his own thoughts. There seemed to be so many of them lately. Guilt swam between them like tendrils of dark smoke, the guilt of an Arkmage's decisions. *Damn those gods and their counsel*, he inwardly cursed, slapping his palm on the throne's arm.

Counsel like using a certain wedding as bait.

Bait for a monster.

❦

The door slammed, and Modren came awake with a start. He had been asleep, and dribbling apparently, if the dark topography of wet blotches on his pillow was to be believed. He blinked blearily at the wall, and wondered where on earth he was.

'Bloody old vampyre, pale king, Arkmage... *bastard,*' somebody was cursing in the next room. The sort of hissing one does when in private. Modren winced as he rolled over, making the bed creak. He heard the angry slapping of slippers on stone pause, then somebody called his name.

'Modren?' said a female voice.

He had no choice but to answer.

'Here,' he croaked, voice thick with sleep. 'Bedroom.' Gods, he needed some water.

Elessi came to stand in the doorway. Her face was dyed a faint red by the sleepy coals in the cooling fireplace. It made her look even more angry than she already was.

'Something up?' Modren punched a pillow into a headrest. For some ungodly reason he was still wearing most of his armour. He must have been tired indeed.

'Somethin's up alright,' she snapped, coming to perch on the side of the bed. If it was possible to perch angrily, Elessi managed it. Modren put his cold metal hand on her back, saying nothing. Better to just let it come out naturally. He'd learnt that.

It took a while, but once she had begun, there was no slowing her down. Modren nodded along, his frown ever-deepening with every sentence that tumbled from her lips. '...and all he had to say was sorry. After all these years, all these bloody years, he has the bright idea to go draggin' him back *now*, on the cusp of our wedding. Finally happy, finally got us a date set, and who does he want to invite? Him. Bah, *invite*, as if he's a long lost nephew, or something. If he does ever rear his ugly head, he'll probably find a way to burn the whole place to the ground, or appear with a pack of ravin' bandits on his heels. Cursed, he is. And Durnus and the rest of you lot want him at my wedding.'

Modren suddenly found himself a target, just as he was about to remind her that it was in fact 'their' wedding. 'And you, you of all people, Modren, agreed to this madness!' She turned on him, slapping his hand away. She soon regretted it, and sucked the back of her hand, where it had connected with his steel.

'If he does come back, I will make sure he behaves, I promise you.'

Elessi strangled the air with her hands. 'I don't care if he behaves, I don't want him there at all! He hurt me, us, everyone. Why should he get to waltz back in when it suits him, sittin' in the front row, probably in a bloody cloak as well…' she trailed off, ending in an unladylike, 'Shit.'

'Did Durnus tell you we need him?'

Elessi nodded.

'Well…' Modren said. 'She's out there, Elessi. She will come. When she does…' It was a conversation Elessi had heard many times, he could see it in her face. He could tell she was bored of it. His wife-to-be sniffed, wiping her nose with a hand. The light glinted off a pale, polished, ring of whalebone on her finger. A promise, set in bone. It had cost him a pretty pile of coin.

'He asked me if I missed him. Durnus. He asked me.'

Modren pulled a face. 'And do you?' he asked, tentatively. He had never wanted to ask himself.

'Damn him for asking. And damn you as well. Should know better than that.'

'He broke your heart.'

'And then stamped on it.'

Modren stared at the blankets trying to smother him. His armour glimmered softly. 'The way you talk of him sometimes. So much hatred. So many years…' he was trying to get his words in order but his tired brain wasn't helping.'

'Sounds like I still love him. Go on. Say it!'

'Do you blame me?' Modren shrugged.

Elessi looked as though she was about to storm out, but she shook her head instead, and shuffled further on to the bed. 'There's only one mage for me. I just wish I'd met you first.'

Modren closed his eyes as she rested her cheek on his cold breastplate. Gods, he was tired. He felt like the air was trying to drown him. Eyelids heavy…

'Are you lookin' forward to it?'

'More than you can know,' he mumbled off a reply.

Silence for a moment. Light flickered softly. 'Are they planning something? Durnus and Tyrfing? Those… gods?' They gave her the shivers, he knew that. 'Planning something for our wedding?'

Modren rocked his head from side to side. Sleep was tugging at him. 'No,' he lied. So easy. So terrible.

Before he slipped away into nothingness, he heard Elessi mumbling to herself. 'Don't care if they are. Nothing's going to stop me. I'm having this wedding…' and so it went, until Modren fell into a deep, guilty sleep.

chapter 14

"Revenge is a dish best served cold, they say. I disagree. Revenge is a boiling vat of oil, ready to be poured onto the skins of those who trifle with it."

Words of Skölgard King Jarripick, in the year 687

Rain. It had come slowly at first, almost gentle, soft. But then, anticipating the night of darkness and dark doings to come, it had turned hard and brutal. It hammered and pounded until it became a deluge, borne by dark clouds and landslide skies. The earth was now a washed-out flagstone for the rain to have its wicked way with. Only the trees seemed to be appreciative of it, waving their new leaves and green buds to the wet wind. The trees, and one lone mage.

Creeping along the edge of a swollen canal, Farden hovered by a sturdy old oak, peering into the pouring sheets of rain. It battered him, but he didn't care. He found the feel of its incessant drumming on his back, shoulders, and head almost soothing. It was cold, but the air was warm from the last few days of sun. Day was teetering on the edge of night. By the time he reached Tayn's watchtowers, it would be dark.

Farden peered through the haze at a huddle of figures that were approaching. He slipped behind the thick trunk of the oak and waited for them to pass. Two men, one woman, and a motley dog, all hurrying along in silence with their heads down and their patchwork hoods up. No spears or armour, just humble townsfolk. Farden let them pass, and released his grip on his knife.

It had taken him over a week to walk from the Fleahurst moors to Tayn. Weak, shaky, and suspicious of every passing stranger, Farden had resorted to travelling mostly at night, avoiding the open roads. His body was still recovering, and over the last twenty miles it had begun to scream out to him, begging him to lie down and rest. His wounds were barely healed. His chest still oozed and burnt every time he crouched or jerked. His head pounded like the rain.

Farden put his head against the slimy, gnarled skin of the oak and rested for a moment. He had come too far now. He let the fiery desire for revenge tug at him. It lured him on with mental images of Kint and Forluss and Kiltyrin in varying stages of dying. It enticed him with thoughts of the feeling of cold metal around his wrists.

The mage peeked out behind the oak tree. He could just about glimpse the edges of the big town in the distance, its gates, and the dark shadow of the castle beyond.

When it came to defending Tayn, the Duke's purse-strings had grown very tight. Tayn was at the heart of his Duchy, why did he need to encircle it with stone and mortar, when a simple wooden palisade would do? Farden stared at it now. About twenty feet high, it was made from sharpened tree-trunks and bound with copper straps. Its points bristled with iron nails and wire. Ahead of him, the palisade had been cut away to make room for a thick oaken gate and an iron portcullis, hanging in a lopsided gatehouse of thatch and wood. It squatted over the road like a grinning wolf. Two wooden watchtowers sat on each of its shoulders.

Farden stepped out from behind the oak tree and crept along the road towards the town. The gate would be open until nightfall. He would have to time this right. His hood was down and low and his posture hunched like a beggar. His red cloak helped a little to hide his identity; its crimson red was very different from his trademark black.

His face, however, although a little more gaunt, a little paler, was still the same, and the guards would want to see it. In his pocket, he squeezed the little mistfrond thing that Loki had given him.

'This better work, Loki,' he muttered to himself as he trudged. Rain was dripping through the hole in his hood and running down his face in a little rivulet. He didn't mind. It was cold, and by tilting his head he could let the water run into his mouth and wet his nervous tongue. Why was he so anxious? Was it how weak he felt? Or was it his desire for revenge, making him eager. He had no idea, but he didn't like it. And gods, he needed to piss.

He hugged the woods until the very last tree. Then, crouching behind it and wiping the rain from his face, he examined the gates.

Teeming, was one word that described them. Teeming with guards. There were almost as many spears as there were sharpened stakes in the walls. Thirty men, at the very least, patrolled the gate and the gravelled courtyard behind it. Did he trust the mistfrond that much? 'Hah,' he snorted, grimacing. That was a no.

As he hid by the tree and pondered his next move, he noticed a smudge of brown creeping its way along the rain-dappled canal. It was a narrowboat, and an incredibly long one at that, piled high with barrels, boxes, and other things, all wrapped in tarpaulins. A lonely ox stood amidships, dripping wet and miserable. At each end of the boat stood a group of people, about ten or so, and each of them wielded a long oar. Instead of rowing with them, they were using them to push against the bottom of the canal.

Farden heard the metallic clank of a winch being turned. He shuffled around and stared at the palisade. There was a wooden frame suspended under the bridge; a sort of rudimentary gate for the canal. He had never noticed it before, but there it was. And it was being raised for the boat, with no questions asked. Farden was suddenly struck with an idea. It was so sudden it almost stung him.

He quickly fished the little mistfrond from his pocket and

looked at it closely. He couldn't quite decide whether it was a fruit or a seed. It was odd, whatever it was, and it smelled faintly of almonds. Farden grimaced. The narrowboat was drawing level with his hiding spot now. The forward team were busy steering the boat, while the aft team left their job up to momentum, and set about gathering mooring ropes. They were wearing waxed yellow coats to keep the rain at bay.

Farden readied himself to run. His body groaned at the very thought of running anywhere, but Farden brusquely told it to be quiet. There was knife-work to be done. He lifted the mistfrond to his lips and, with a wince, he took a bite and began to chew.

To his surprise, it tasted sweet like a pear, but its pink flesh had a rough, sandy texture that wasn't all that pleasant. It grated against his teeth as he tried to chew it into pieces he could swallow. Purple juice ran down his chin, mingling with the rain. But he need not have hurried, as the strange little fruit was already beginning to take effect.

It was a feeling that was beyond strange, and a sight that was slightly terrifying. His hands seemed to evaporate like mist on a sunny morning. Farden clenched his fist and was relieved to find he could still feel them. If he looked hard enough, he could see a faint outline of them against the rain, but only because of the droplets that clung to them. Farden swallowed his mouthful and watched as his shoulders and chest began to fade away. The mage couldn't help but gasp as the tingly feeling spread to his legs and feet. He got to his feet, but stumbled, immediately disorientated by his apparent lack of feet. He could feel them, but they were just trails of mist and rain.

Farden was just about to make a dash for it when Loki's words came crashing into his head. Something about being violently ill…

No sooner had he remembered them did his stomach lurch and bile begin fill his throat. Farden retched, but somehow managed to keep it down. The narrowboat was about to pass him, and he was running out of time before it reached the gate. He didn't know how long the fruit would last.

Fighting back the vomit, Farden sprinted to the edge of the canal, weak, invisible legs flying. As the ground fell away, he leapt as far and as hard as he could. The mage had aimed it perfectly. Arms wind-milling, he soared through the rain. The jump was perfect, it was just a shame about the landing. Having invisible legs tends to do that to a landing.

Farden crumpled to a painful heap beside the miserable ox, and slammed his head into the animal's leg. The poor ox, wide-eyed and more than a little scared, lowed gruffly and stamped its hooves, utterly confused. Farden winced as one hoof grazed his arm. He was still fighting against the powerful urge to empty his stomach.

He clamped his hand over his mouth and hid behind a crate as a shout rang out from the rear of the narrowboat. 'Easy girl!' it cried, but the ox kept stamping. One of the men began to climb over a mound of cargo to see what the problem was, but he needn't have bothered. The ox had fallen silent, relaxed by a misty hand calmly stroking its bedraggled flanks.

'Spooked, she was. Must be the noise of the gate!' called the man to his crew, crawling back to his spot.

As the blunt nose of the narrowboat slipped under the bridge and into the town, Farden kept one eye on the guards standing on the bank and one on the hand resting on the crate in front of him. The guards, surly and stony-faced, waved the boat through and tipped their helmets to its crew. They looked as miserable as the ox. Their leather and iron armour was dripping wet. The rain played little rhythmic ditties on their metal helmets and shields.

As the rest of the boat followed its nose and slid under the bridge, the water gate slowly began to lower. The winch that held its chains clanked and squeaked and moaned. Farden used the noisy opportunity to finally vomit down the side of his crate. His stomach felt as though it were having a fist-fight with the rest of his organs. He heaved and he retched until there was nothing left to spit. Farden slumped to the wet deck and took a deep breath, feeling his throat burn. *Damn that god*, he thought. *And damn that fruit too.*

The effects of the mistfrond lasted just long enough for the narrowboat to creep past the gate and get half a mile into town. Farden threw up twice more before the fruit was done with him. His hands began to materialise out of their wraithlike haze. He was still a faint shadow in the rain, but a shadow that was quickly growing skin, bone, clothes, and colour. Farden had to jump now, or risk reappearing in the middle of the street.

As the narrowboat crept past another that was moored beside a ladder, Farden bade the ox a swift pat farewell and leapt the murky, watery gap between the two boats. He landed with a soft thud, this time on his feet. Trusting the downpour to hide him, Farden scurried up the wooden ladder and onto the street, unseen boots crunching on the gravel. The street was empty but for a few brave souls hurrying back and forth in their cloaks and hoods. Lanterns had been put out to spare the torches, and the quiet street was bathed in a wet, lemon glow. Farden wasted no time in admiring it. He sprinted into the nearest alley he could find and caught his breath between the buildings. The noises of a nearby inn, maybe a cathouse, could be heard above him. The din spilt out of cracked windows.

The mage put his head against the cold brick of the building. The nausea was slowly dying away, and with it the mistfrond's effects. Slowly but surely, in the dripping darkness of the alley, the mage's limbs began to reappear out of their misty haze. Within minutes, he was solid again.

'Onward,' Farden whispered to himself.

No sooner had he taken a step forward, did he hear a very familiar sound indeed.

Hur-hur-hur-hur… came the laugh, echoing down the

alleyway.

Farden froze.

Fat Forluss.

Footsteps followed in the laugh's wake. Farden tugged his hood down and stepped back into the street. He jogged a short distance, and then turned to watch Forluss and a trio of his friends emerge from the very alleyway Farden had hid in. The mage shook his head. It was a lucky escape for him. Not so lucky for Forluss.

Farden's eyes burnt into the obese lump as he swaggered along the gravel road. Forluss stared at everybody he passed, challenging them, daring them to get in his way. They knew better than to try.

While Farden kept his head down and his hood low, Forluss led his friends to a nearby building that sat on the edge of a curve in the canal. It had a rain-washed and sun-faded sign hanging from a pole. *The Piebald Skald*, it said, with a crude painting of a man with a black and white face for good measure. Forluss went in, closely followed by the others. Farden narrowed his eyes, and ran his finger along the blunt side of his longest knife. It was time.

❦

'What's in yer hand, Forluss?' demanded an old voice.

Forluss looked up from his fistful of dog-eared cards, cheap cuts of parchment, coloured and varnished. 'Nothing for you, Isfridder. Keep your old nose out of it.'

'Well, you going to play, or not?' asked another.

Forluss glared at the other who had spoken. 'Shut up and wait your turn. I didn't bring you 'ere to moan.'

The table fell quiet and sipped their drinks while Forluss tried his hardest to figure out what he held, if anything. He flicked his cards with a greasy fingernail and scowled at their pictures for the hundredth time. Forluss sniffed, and took a thoughtful sip of his foaming mug of brimlugger, a dubious local concoction of pickled wine and ale. 'Fine,' he relented. He picked out four of his cards and slammed them on the wooden table. 'Two silver ravens, a half-moon, and an eight.'

The old man called Isfridder shook his head. 'That's a seven, Forluss.'

Fat Forluss shook his head. His three friends looked on with smirking faces. 'No it ain't. Look there, that's an eight.'

Isfridder tapped a gnarled old finger on the card, counting the tally-marks. 'No, that's a hair stuck in the varnish. What are you, stupid, as well as fat?'

Forluss stood up, shoving the table with his belly. 'You trying to cheat me, old man?'

This was a tense moment. Forluss may not have had The Fiend with him tonight, but he did have a little knife on his belt, and his hand was straying to it. Old Isfridder threw up his hands. 'Fine,' he whispered. 'Eight it is. My mistake.'

'Good man,' beamed Forluss, sitting back down with a heavy grunt. He swigged some more of his brimlugger. 'Now what have the rest of you got?'

Isfridder sighed as he put down his cards. 'A four and a measly copper-gate.'

'Dragon-tooth and a two.'

'A pair of sixes, and the silver jester.'

'Psh. Fools, lot of yer. I got a gold raven, a silver king, and a three-nail.'

Forluss stared daggers at the last man who had spoken. He was obviously new to this game; everybody knew you always let Forluss win. But the young man stood his ground. 'I win,' he cackled, cupping his hands around the silver and copper pile in the centre of the table. The others looked on, some smirking, others ashen.

Forluss watched for a moment, before cracking a wide smile and laughing. 'Well, Dern, you did well. Now, as you won, it's your round, ain't it?'

Dern looked up and opened his mouth to speak, but Forluss beat him to it. 'Women!' he bellowed over his shoulder. A pair of young women, mere girls to be exact, appeared from behind the thick red curtain that gave the room its privacy. They were wearing short dresses, and cheap copper jewellery around their necks and arms. They curtseyed to the men around the table, trying not to wrinkle their noses at the feeling of hungry eyes roving over their bodies. They smiled tightly. Forluss beckoned to the nearest, a tall girl with jet-black hair, with a single finger. 'Come here then,' he grinned. She smiled wider, hiding the disgust perfectly, and went to stand near him. Forluss wrapped a fat arm around her waist and pointed at each of the men. 'We'll 'ave fresh bottles of 'lugger all 'round. And a round of pig ribs too. And some of those little fried potatoes your cook does. A bowl for each. That's right, ain't it Dern?'

Dern opened his mouth as if he were about to complain. Forluss drummed his nails on the tabletop. Daring him…

'Course,' Dern sighed, as he shoved a good chunk of his coin-pile towards the edge of the table. 'Little potato things. Why not.' The second girl, a short little thing with a shock of red hair and freckles, quickly scooped it into her apron. The other men sniggered as they looked on. The two girls curtseyed again and managed to escape without too much groping this time. Leaving the men to go back to their cards, they ducked behind the curtain and shook their heads.

'Gods, he's disgusting,' shuddered the red-haired girl, as she fetched five bottles of the green-hued brimlugger from a cupboard. The noisy hubbub of the tavern below kept their voices quiet. A skald was halfway through a lively ballad, and half of the patrons were dancing. The black-haired girl peeked over a balcony. There was a look of longing on her face.

'We're bein' punished, I tell you. Hassfold is punishing us for something, making us look after that fat lump and his crowd.'

'I don't know why old Isfridder plays with them.'

'Company, I guess. He's an old guard ain't he?'

While her friend watched the dancing below, the red-head inked a series of scratches on a little scrap of parchment and folded it into a wooden tube. She slipped the tube inside the mouth of a nearby copper pipe and let it fall. There was a bang from far below, and a muffled voice shouted back up the tube.

'Thank yer kindly!' it called, dripping with metallic sarcasm.

The black-haired girl waited for a man in a red cloak to pass by before she went to stand with her friend. She leant up against the cupboard and shivered. 'His hands are like sweaty hams.'

'Well, he doesn't seem to fancy me. Just you.'

'Oh, joy.'

'I'm just prayin' Hassfold doesn't ask us to do anything else. You 'eard about Sall?'

Another shiver. 'I just wish he'd go someplace else.'

The man in the red cloak, who had paused near the balcony railing, stepped into their conversation. The two girls looked at him, wrinkling their lips slightly at the sight of his straggly black beard and his pale, thin face. He was dripping wet with rain, and there was a hole in his hood. 'Maybe I can help you out?' he muttered in a low voice.

'Help us with what?' asked the red-head, putting her hands on her hips.

The man nodded towards the curtain. 'There's a man in there they call Fat Forluss, am I right?'

'Yeah,' chorused the girls. 'Though try calling him that to his face.'

'I couldn't help but hear you want him to leave?'

'Maybe.'

'Well, I can make that happen. For good.'

The red-head narrowed her eyes. 'You a friend of his?'

'A long-lost acquaintance,' Farden smirked.

She looked dubious, but her friend stepped forward. 'Go on.'

The man lifted a little vial of brown-black liquid from his pocket and handed it to her. 'I've heard that this stuff can clear a room quicker than you can say *skald*. Drip some on him, and he'll be forced to leave. Make sure he goes out the back door, into the alley.'

'Why?'

The man turned away. 'Never you mind about that. If you don't want him to come back, don't ask questions. Deal?' There was a hesitant pause. 'He won't be back. I promise.'

The two girls swapped glances. The dark-haired one looked eager. The red-head wasn't so sure. 'It's your fault if Hassfold catches us,' she wagged a finger.

'He won't!' When she turned back to man, he had gone, leaving nothing but the little vial on the edge of the cupboard. 'Deal it is,' she muttered. She lifted the vial to her nose and gingerly cracked it open. She almost wilted under the stench that punched her nostrils. 'That'll bloody do it,' she wheezed, coughing and spluttering.

'Fine,' sighed the red-head. 'I'll take the drinks, and you put that stuff on him.'

It was a moment's work to slip the bottles onto a tray. One following the other, the girls pushed the curtain aside and walked back into the room. Forluss turned around to wink at them. 'There they are,' he said, beckoning to the dark-haired one once again. She smiled, and went to stand by him, even going as far to put her arm around his thick, sweaty neck. Forluss seemed to like that; his hand began to sneak up the front of her dress. While he was busy, she leant forward and with a quick and deft dab of her hand, she dripped half the vial down Forluss' back, between his tunic and the coat folded over his chair. The girl had to cover her mouth to keep from retching.

'My gods,' she wheezed, quickly making her exit.

'Oi! Where you goin'?' Forluss cried, as the red-head swiftly followed suit, covering her nose with her tray. 'Women!' he spat.

It didn't take long for it to hit them.

'Jötun's balls! What's that reek?!' coughed Dern, being the closest. He got up as quickly as he could and backed away from the table. The others did the same. Unfortunately for them, there were no windows in the little room. Forluss stayed put, confused, beginning to gag.

Isfridder had clamped his sleeve over his mouth. 'You shat yourself again, Forluss?' he challenged.

'You want to watch yer mouth, old man…' Forluss began, mouth flapping.

'It's not any of us!' yelled one of the men. He looked to be on the verge of vomiting. He left the room in a hurry, along with Dern and the others close in tow. Isfridder got up and gingerly edged around the table, trying to keep as far away from Forluss as possible.

'By the gods, man, that's vile!' he cried.

Forluss had gone a bright shade of crimson. Had he shat himself? He didn't remember… Gods, it truly was vile. He scrambled awkwardly to his feet and tried to cover his nose with his coat, but it made the smell even worse. In a panic he burst through the curtain, half-ripping it from its rickety pole and making the two girls shriek in the process. They scampered off down the balcony and ran down the steps to find Hassfold.

Forluss was utterly bamboozled. A couple stood by the railing. Was it him? Was it something in the room? He tried to paste an innocent look on his face as he slowly made for the stairs, a confused look on his face. The couple caught one breath of him and immediately began to gag. 'It's not me!' he bellowed, breaking into a stumbling jog. The brimlugger had gone straight to his legs.

Hassfold, the landlord, was standing at the bottom of the

stairs. The smell was beginning to spread, and he already had a damp cloth firmly clamped over his nose. He pointed at Forluss. 'You! Get out!' he shouted.

Forluss could do nothing but glare as he floundered on the bottom step. The skald's song was coming to a grinding halt. People were either staring or leaving. A woman had fainted. 'Don't you go shoutin' at me, Hassfold. It ain't my smell!'

'Gods, you reek, Forluss! It ain't anybody else but you! You need to leave!' Hassfold literally sagged as the man brushed past him.

'Out the back!' a female voice shouted, one of the girls no doubt.

'Yeah, send him out the back!' shrieked another. 'There's people here!'

The crowd soon joined in. Red-faced and fuming, Forluss pushed his way through a set of stiff doors and into a storeroom. The shouts chased him. He found a door and barrelled into it, finding himself in an alleyway, and the cold night rain on his sweat-licked head. The door quickly slammed behind him. Somebody locked it. Forluss scratched his head, bewildered, and began to try to wash his clothes in the rain. Even he had to keep from gagging, and he had smelled things in the torture chamber no man should ever smell.

As he bent for a puddle, a blade slipped under his chin and an iron hand seized him by his hair. Forluss didn't even dare to gulp. 'Move, and I'll gut you,' uttered a bitter voice. A voice from the grave.

'Farden,' the name was a cold whisper on Forluss' alcohol-swollen tongue. The blade was cold, colder than the rain drumming on their shoulders and the gravel under their boots. The alley was dark, light-starved, like the throat of a yawning monster. Forluss could feel hot breath on his ear.

'The very same.'

'But you're dead...'

'Then you can call me a ghost.' The blade tickled the lump

forming in Forluss' throat. The man took a few short breaths, trying to figure out what to do or say. All the while, all he could smell was his reek filling his nose.

'W... what do you want of me?' he stammered.

Farden tugged his hair a little harder. 'I'm not going to lie to you, Forluss, I want your head on a pole, along with the others. In a nice line, I think. You first, then Kint, then that Loffrey fellow, and then Kiltyrin last. It will look nice outside my shack. You remember it, don't you?'

Forluss nodded, immediately regretting it as the keen blade dug into his neck.

'Good,' growled Farden. 'But on second thoughts, Forluss, you fat lump, perhaps if you did me a favour I might be willing to spare your miserable life...'

Forluss would have dropped to his knees in an instant if it weren't for the blade. 'Anything!' he yelled. Behind every bully was a coward, and Forluss was no different.

'Keep your voice down!' Farden hissed.

Forluss clapped his rain and sweat-soaked palms together. 'Anything, Farden. Anything you ask. Just don't kill me!' he wheezed.

'Good,' Farden whispered. Further down the alley, somewhere in the darkness, a window closed with a thud. The mage pointed to a nearby puddle with his knife. As the sky rumbled overhead, he kicked out Forluss' knees and pushed him to the ground. 'Wash that stink off you first. Then we'll see what you can do.'

Forluss gibbered to himself as he crawled forward and into the puddle. Had the downpour from the stony sky above not churned the surface of the mud-laced little puddle, Forluss might have spied his true self in its reflection. He dipped his hands into the water, and began to wash.

Behind him, Farden took a length of rope from a pouch on his belt. His revenge was close. He could almost taste its bitter-sweetness in his mouth. Copperish. Metallic. A lot like blood.

❦

Castle Tayn was a shard puncturing the stormy sky. Night had truly fallen on Tayn. The worst of the rumbling storm had died away but the rain had stayed behind to bludgeon its streets and roof-tiles and chimneys and parapets. Everybody but the guards had retreated inside for the evening. Such weather was for fools.

Two figures sloshed up the steep steps towards the castle's mouth. The rain had made a tiny waterfall of the steps and the going was treacherous. Once or twice, the figure in front stumbled, and was shoved upright by the one behind. Puddles of yellow light lit their way. All the torches had been drowned. Only a precious number of lanterns had been spared to light the way. The rain pounded musically on their little tin roofs, pawing at the candles inside. The two kept climbing.

Before long, they came to the first gate of the castle and were immediately challenged by a trio of guards standing under its wooden roof. Spears were lowered.

'Who goes there?' asked one, a captain of the guard by the looks of his fancy armour. 'State your name.'

'It's Forluss, you idiot,' grunted the first man.

'And what have you got there, Forluss?' challenged another guard.

Forluss sighed and yanked the length of ship's rope tied about his wrist. The man had a cloak on. His hood had been pulled over his face and tied around his neck, like a sack. There was a hole in the hood, through which a wide and fearful eye stared. 'Trouble-maker,' Forluss explained. What he didn't explain was that the ropes were cunningly coiled around a blade, and it hovered inches from his spine. A steel-tip warning.

'Taking him to the rack, are you?' chortled the captain.

'Somethin' like that,' nodded Forluss.

'Make sure you show him a good time,' he laughed, and clapped the fat man on the shoulder. He was even brazen enough to give Farden a kick on the backside as Forluss dragged him forward. Farden stumbled, almost revealing the blade. It took all of his control not to lash out and bury it in the captain's neck. Somehow, he managed. *All in good time*.

Like the canals of its town, the castle had swelled with the rain. Dank and dark, the torches did their best to light the place. The ominous sound of dripping joined the echoes of footsteps and voices. Guards slouched against walls, idly watching Forluss drag his prisoner past. Some tapped their spears and chuckled. Some engaged the man in conversation. Nobody thought twice.

As instructed, Forluss led Farden into the upper reaches of the castle. Farden kept his eye pressed against the hole in his hood. Through one set of doors he spied a banquet hall full of dancers and diners. He strained his head to see if the Duke was at any of the tables, but it appeared not.

After a group of people in banquet attire passed, Farden leant forward to whisper in Forluss' ear. 'Take me to Kint first, understand?'

Forluss nodded. He led the mage up another spiral staircase and then along a corridor. Farden looked around with his one eye so that he could follow where they were heading. They were in the east wing. His hands were beginning to grow sweaty. The rope loosely looped around his wrists smelled faintly of brine. They kept walking.

'Are you goin' to let me live?'

'If you do what I say,' Farden lied, keeping him compliant. He could see the drips of sweat from the man's neck mingling with the raindrops on the collar of his raincoat. He was beginning to wheeze.

'Forluss!' A sudden and high-pitched shout halted them in their steps. Farden pressed up against Forluss' back, making him yelp as the knife dug into the fleshy part of his back. Farden kept his head down and sullen while Forluss turned in the direction of the shouter.

It was Moirin, the Duke's wife, borne by quick and urgent steps and shoes that tapped a frantic rhythm on the stone floor. 'Forluss!' she shouted again, even though she had almost reached them. She ignored the hooded man trailing behind him; Forluss was often seen hauling prisoners around Castle Tayn, taking them to and from his torture rooms, guffawing as the other guards kicked at them. Farden wondered why she was even talking to the man. As far as he knew, she loathed Kint and Forluss almost as much as he did. He stole a glance at her through the hole in his hood. There was a faint hint of disgust there, at the sight and smell of the man, but it was drowned by the expression of worry and panic she wore. *What was the matter?*

'Have you seen Timeon?' she panted. This made Farden frown. *She never let Timeon out of her sight.*

Words stolen by the fear of the knife in his back, Forluss simply shook his head.

Moirin looked around. 'Are you sure? Think, man,' she urged.

'No, I ain't,' muttered Forluss, turning away.

Moirin wrung her hands. 'Well, have you seen the Duke?'

'No.'

Exasperated by the useless man, she spared a quick and pitiful glance for the prisoner behind him, and then dashed off in the direction of the banquet hall, skirts flying. Farden watched Moirin go. Tonight was a banquet night, Timeon and Moirin should have been confined to their rooms. Farden pulled a face under his hood; he didn't have time to wonder. He prodded Forluss again, eliciting a whimper, and they moved off.

It didn't take them long to arrive at their destination. Forluss led the mage to the end of a carpeted corridor and pointed a chubby finger at a skinny oak door near the window. The rest of the hall was empty. Every other door was shut. The noise of the banquet was a muffled echo. 'He's in there,' he mumbled, pitiful.

Farden ripped the rope from around his head and threw back his hood. It took seconds to shrug the rope from his hands. He held his knife to Forluss' neck and pointed to the iron handle of the door. 'Open it,' he hissed.

Forluss bit his quivering lip. Farden could tell that somewhere deep inside him, some scrap of humanity was considering the weight of this betrayal, of giving up his only friend to Farden's blade. He could see the conflict on his face as that little scrap battled with the thought of saving his skin. It was a short battle.

Forluss pushed down on the handle and lumbered into the room, followed closely by Farden. They were greeted by a shrill shout.

'Oi! What's the meaning o' this? Forluss? I told you…' Kint's voice died at the sight of the dead man standing behind his comrade. A dead man holding a knife. A dead man who was very much a live man.

To give Kint credit, he wiped the look of confusion off his face pretty quickly. He had been lying on his bed, surrounded by pillows. There was a half-empty bottle of wine beside him, alongside a tray bearing a little bottle of ink, a cloth, and an array of bone needles. One still lingered in Kint's hand, its point smeared black and dripping. He was topless. A half-finished, badly-scrawled word sat on his upper arm, in amongst a crowd of others. It was bleeding slightly. It looked like a name.

Farden slammed the door and booted Forluss further into the room. Kint's was a tall room with oak beams spanning an arched roof. There was a crackling fire in the hearth and bottles of wine on a nearby table. Kint's collection of wicked knives was splayed on the wall, along with Forluss' Fiend, looking out of place hanging from a peg. Farden caught the fat man staring longingly at it.

'Not a chance,' he said, moving to grab the knives. The Fiend he had plans for. With a flick of his wrist, he tossed the blades on the fire, and their leather scabbards began to wither and crackle.

Kint had put his needle down. 'How?' he asked, simply. No fuss. 'How'd you escape that noose?'

Farden ignored the question. He jabbed at Forluss and pointed to the ground. Forluss did as he was told. He prostrated himself at the end of Kint's bed and mumbled something that sounded vaguely like a prayer into the carpet. Perhaps he was starting to realise that the mage had been lying. As Farden untied the rope from his hands, he looked up at Kint, and smiled. 'Well done, Forluss,' he said, loudly. 'You were right. He is alone.'

Kint turned his vicious little gaze at Forluss. 'That true, Forluss?'

Forluss simply moaned. It was enough proof for Kint. 'You fat, back-stabbing, treacherous, weaselly fucker,' he snapped, eliciting another moan. He looked to Farden. 'How, I ask you? I watched you die.'

Farden shrugged. 'The gods must like me,' he stated flatly. 'Now, on your feet, scum.'

Kint also did as he was told. Farden could see his skin ripple into goose-bumps, even in the warm air of the room. He hoped it was fear. He watched the man's eyes skip about. The door, the knives, The Fiend, the window that had been cracked ever-so-slightly ajar, they were all so far away. He could see the hopelessness in his eyes, the same as he had felt on the tree. *Good,* he thought.

Kint shuffled to the end of his bed. Farden tilted his head to read the half-finished word Kint had been tattooing into his arm. 'Far...' he said aloud. He chuckled darkly. 'I should have let you finish. It's the last name you'll ever put on your arm.'

Kint visibly gulped. Like Forluss, his wicked exterior hid a snivelling coward. The man fell to his knees and clasped his hands together. Farden curled his lip at the contemptuous sight. Kint began to whine in his shrill voice. 'Please,' he begged. 'It weren't our idea. The Duke told us to follow you to Wodehallow! He was the one who set you up. Not us!'

'No,' said Farden. 'But you did kill me, didn't you?'

Kint fell silent with a wretched sob. Farden could see through the act. It just hardened his heart against them. Forluss was still mumbling something into the rug. It must have been a prayer. He didn't sound very practised at it. Farden growled. If there was one thing he hated his victims doing before he dispatched them, it was praying. It meant somebody might be watching. Farden kicked him and Forluss whined. 'Shut up,' he ordered. 'Nobody's coming to save you now.

'Please…' begged Forluss.

But the words fell on deaf ears. 'Shut up!'

Kint spoke up again, trying to reason with the vengeful mage. 'You don't 'ave to do this, Four-Hand. You and I ain't so different!' he began, but Farden whirled on him.

'I am nothing like you!' he bellowed, flecks of spit landing on Kint's face.

Forluss began to whine again. 'What do you want from us? You want us to say sorry? You want us to beg? We'll beg. We'll do anything you say, just don't kill us!'

Farden shook his head at both of the men. Both of the spineless weasels were sweating profusely now. Their eyes were red with fear. He hadn't taken them for beggars. Fighters, perhaps, but not beggars. It made him hate them even more. All they cared about was protecting their own worthless hides, even if it meant killing the other to do it. As callous as a grindstone. As unscrupulous as a winter wind.

Just like you, said a tiny voice inside his head. It stung him like a bee.

Farden quickly silenced it. *No*, he told himself. He may have shared a master with these two, but he was not like them. These two had robbed and hanged him at the whim of a greedy, double-crossing master. They had rattled home and laughed between themselves at their deeds. Farden had never done that. Not the latter anyway. He looked down at Kint. This bastard even had the sick audacity to tattoo the name of his victims on his arm, like a lady wearing her jewels on her fingers. Shameless. Farden burnt with revenge and disgust. He wished he had the hours to draw it out and make them suffer. 'The difference between me and you wretched creatures…' he began, but he paused, suddenly unsure of what to say. On the walk from Fleahurst he had dreamt up a hundred different ways to put these two to death, but now, standing over them with a blade, he realised he hadn't decided on one…

What did men like this truly deserve? Did they deserve a quick death? That would have verged on merciful. Did they deserve to be strung up with the ship's rope like he had been? Part of him wouldn't wish that on anybody.

Farden thought of the ash tree and how his feet had left the earth, how he had felt his heart flutter to its last. Coming face to face with death had taught him that the fear of it was torture enough. The mage had spent years being tortured in that way. First it had been his uncle's madness. Now it was the grave. It was the fear of what lay beyond that made men beg, scream, and fight.

A cold river. A boat with a vulture's head. Millions pushing behind.

But that had been a dream. A gryphon's dream. He hadn't had a dream like that since the night of the Battle. Ilios was responsible for that beyond, not his death. There, standing over two men he was about to put to death, a realisation slowly dawned on him. On the beach, Loki had asked him why he had wanted to live forever. Why? He suddenly knew. The dream had been fake, but the darkness and the emptiness beyond it had been real. Farden had never feared dying; he had simply feared death because after any death came the other side:

the void where ghosts dwelt, where nothing spoke and nothing lived and nothing existed. It pained him to think of that, but it was true. A memory bubbled up of what he had said to Cheska on her death-bed. But she too was now nothing but memory. Farden didn't want to be nothing, he wanted to be something. Even if it was just a hired blade scraping a living in a shack by the sea, alive was *something*.

'Why don't you stop wasting my time and do whatever it is you're going to do,' spat Kint, staring up at the mage. He had found his balls then, it seemed. Farden realised he had been staring into space. He looked down at him and shook his head.

'I'm not doing anything,' he said, sheathing his blade. Kint's eyes widened, and Forluss looked up with a glint of slim hope in his teary coward's eyes. Farden walked to the wall and snatched The Fiend from its peg. He felt the sharp tip of one of its nails. What did these men deserve? Just death. Death and nothingness. *Let them rot in the void.*

Farden smiled as he tossed The Fiend on the carpet between the two of them. Then, he sauntered to the door and put his hand on the doorhandle. He looked back at the two men. Kint and Forluss were as still as frozen statues. Their eyes were still wide and confused. Farden put them out of their misery, in more than one way. 'Whichever one of you comes out of this room alive, gets to leave alive,' he explained, and with a casual whistle, he opened the door, scanned the corridor, and then closed it behind him.

Kint looked at the ugly weapon lying on the carpet, and then up at Forluss. Fat Forluss did the same. He blinked. 'You called me fat,' was the only thing he could think to say.

❦

Farden lingered outside the door, hood up and calm. He drew his blade and spun it around in his hand so that the blade pointed backwards. Its cold steel rested lightly against his wrist. Threatening. Hungry.

Farden let the stone wall hold him up. He crossed his feet and waited, listening to the muffled sounds of scuffling and grunting behind the closed door. Only once did the doorhandle rattle, and Farden tensed, but it was followed by a thud, and then a crash as glass met stone floor, and skull met club.

Silence. A silence that gave Farden more than an iota of satisfaction.

Moments later, the doorhandle rattled again and this time the door inched open. Out stepped Forluss, heavy of breath and of heart. There was a pained look in his eye, caused partly by the long gash along his forehead, partly by the dead body lying on the floor behind him. The Fiend hung loosely in his hand. He didn't seem surprised to see Farden.

'Well done,' the mage muttered. Forluss nodded vacantly. Farden swung his arm so quickly that Forluss barely even saw the steel before it slammed into his traitorous, leaden heart. Farden stepped back, letting Forluss take the blade with him. He watched him topple backwards into the room like a sweating tree, landing with a wet thud on the battered body of Kint. Farden took a deep breath. He had been waiting to do that for years.

He didn't waste time staring at the dead pair. The door was shut, the wretches locked away, and the mage moved off down the corridor, only half the night finished.

chapter 15

"Why is the moon scarred so? Because of the daemons and their claws."

A snippet from a classic Arka book of nonsense and nursery rhymes

The guards didn't believe it necessary to guard the upper corridors of castle Tayn, seeing as its lower regions were so heavily patrolled.

How wrong they were.

Padding as softly as his wet boots would allow, Farden crept from doorway to doorway. The rain drummed urgently on every window he flitted past. There was a fresh blade in each hand. One for Loffrey. One for the Duke. He would see them both stained within the hour.

As furtively as a cat-burglar's ghost, Farden dashed up the steps to the main tower. He hid in an alcove as a number of women passed by. Maids by the look of their smeared aprons. They nattered contentedly to each other. Apparently there had been a ruckus at the banquet. The Duke's wife had embarrassed herself yet again, yelling for the Duke. Who had ever heard of such a thing? She needed to be locked away in her room for good, and that brat of hers too.

Farden scowled and kept moving. His body felt like lead, but as always, Farden's stubborn mind whipped his muscles into action. There would be time for rest after this mess was cleared up once and for all. As much rest as a man could want for.

The spiral staircase led him up into the main tower, and he was pleased to find the corridors there as sparse as those below. The banquet must have drawn all of Tayn's nobility to the lower levels. It must have only just begun too, as there were not that many drunken stragglers wandering the halls. *Good*, thought Farden. That gave him ample time to have his way with Kiltyrin. There was a man who did deserve a slow death. Loffrey could wait, and watch.

As Farden passed a long set of steamed-up windows, he caught a glimpse of a shadow hurrying up the curving hallway towards him, thrown ahead of its maker by the hot torches in their stone alcoves. Farden looked about but found to his dismay that he was stuck in the open. There wasn't a hiding place in sight. More jittery shadows joined the first, a little behind but swiftly catching up. Farden could hear raised voices, the familiar jangling of studded armour and metal.

The mage cursed and threw his hand into his cloak pocket, fumbling for the second half of the strange little mistfrond. His stomach cried out in protest, but Farden told it to be quiet amidst another stream of curses. He couldn't risk raising the alarm. Not now that he was so close.

Wincing, Farden shoved the strange fruit into his mouth and chomped down as fast and as hard as he could. Just like before, the effects of the mistfrond were almost instant. Farden tucked himself into the nearest shadow as the voices and hurried footsteps came nearer.

Moirin burst into view, hair wild and eyes frantic. She looked distraught. What had happened? Was she being chased, or was she chasing something? Two guards followed in her panicked wake. Farden ducked instinctively, even though his skin and clothes had turned to fog. Luckily, they were too preoccupied with Moirin to notice the strange haziness crouching at the side of the hallway. They quickly caught up to her. Each grabbed an arm and wrenched her to a stop. Farden stood up, hackles rising. His knives folded out, blades no more than a whisper of water droplets. He could barely see them himself. Farden took one step forward, and then the sick began to rise in his throat. He clamped a hand over his mouth and fought it back.

'I said *stop*, Moirin!' one of the men barked in her ear. She didn't look at him. Farden recognised him as one of the more senior guard captains. The other was just a lackey. He was bent over, trying to catch his breath.

'I told you! He's with the Duke. And you ain't allowed in there!'

Farden took another step forward. Kiltyrin tried his hardest to avoid the boy as much as possible. For him to summon his son made no sense. Moirin yanked herself free. 'How dare you tell me what I can and cannot do!' she shrieked, her old fire sparking for just a moment. She wrenched herself free and sprang forward. 'If that bastard harms a single hair on my boy's head…!' her threat trailed away as she fled down the hallway.

Farden followed, knives ready. It felt as though his stomach was trying to escape up his windpipe. He skidded to a halt to spew in a doorway. It was quick, mercifully so, and the mage hurried on. His skin felt as pale as the mist that wrapped him. Dizziness had crept upon him like a lizard. He sprinted to catch up.

Moirin had found the Duke's doors and thrown them open. They were not locked, but the heaviness of the doors slowed her, and the guards tackled her to the stone floor. She cried out in pain and frustration.

Farden was on them in a second. He tried to imagine their confusion and abject terror as a pair of unseen hands grabbed each of them by their necks and dragged them aside, kicking and yelling. Farden quickly silenced them with swift thwacks from the pommels of his knives. The blades were not for them. Moirin was completely oblivious with panic. She scrambled to her feet and ran into her husband's room, all thoughts for her son. A scream split the air.

If Farden had hated the Duke before, the sight of him in that room drove him to sheer and utter loathing, a feeling reserved for the deepest, darkest pits of one's heart. A feeling he hadn't felt since he had faced Vice.

Timeon sat in a little wooden chair by the hissing fire. A glowing dagger hovered near his face. Moirin's screams may have halted Kiltyrin's hand but the hot blade loitered with intent. Timeon's face was tear-stained, streaked with brine and the dust of a boy's play. Another hand pinched Timeon's right ear in a tight grip and was pulling hard. A brat, Timeon may have been, but a boy all the same. The Duke's boy too. His own son, and here he was, about to slice his ears from his head.

Moirin rushed forward but Kiltyrin waggled the blade closer to the boy's ear. Farden thought he saw a glint of red and gold hiding under the ruffles of the Duke's emerald shirt-sleeves. That made him burn even more. 'What are you doing?' Morin was shrieking.

Farden stayed by the door, fuming and growling and squeezing his knife-handles so hard it hurt. The Duke was ignoring him. He didn't seem surprised to see him…

… Wait. He *hadn't* seen him. The mage was still invisible. He had completely forgotten in the tumult. He looked down at his arms and saw his hands slowly fading into reality. Two faint shafts of steel began to form out of water-droplets and catch the firelight.

The Duke was talking. 'What I am doing, Moirin, is teaching this wretched boy of mine a lesson he will never forget. Eavesdroppers! Even my own…' Kiltyrin faltered for a split-second. 'Even this *boy* thinks he can put his filthy ear to my door!' The hot dagger inched forward. Timeon whined with utter fear.

Farden grit his teeth as another wave of sickness came. He looked down again. His fist, knuckles strangled, white as snow, appeared from the haze that wrapped his body. It steamed as though the burning rage inside him was a real fire. Farden began to stride forward. The Duke was still talking. The words were hollow ramblings. Farden could only hear one thing, and that was the cracking of his knuckles as he put one of his knives away and clenched his fist as hard as he could. The rage poured into his arm as if it were his old magick. The mage broke into a jog, then a run, then a full-out sprint, fist poised, the arm of a catapult, steam trailing from it as it formed out of fading mist.

Kiltyrin looked up to see a spectre bearing down on him, and his mouth fell open just in time for Farden to swing his fist like a hammer.

The noise of knuckles meeting cheek was like a brick flying through a slab of meat. Kiltyrin sailed into a nearby desk, while Farden rolled with the momentum of his swing and tumbled to a heap near the window. The dagger spun to the floor. Moirin rushed forward and yanked Timeon from the chair. The boy was in deep shock. A ghost had just saved his life, after all. He trembled as his mother nearly smothered him with her arms. They both cowered behind the bed and watched in disbelief as a bedraggled man in a red cloak formed out of thin air, and then vomited behind a curtain. Moirin was as shocked as her son.

'Farden?!' she gasped. The name made Timeon flinch, and he lifted his head to see the mage stumbling over to where the Duke lay amidst the wreckage of an ornate pine desk.

'Four-hand?!' he whimpered, bewildered. Farden lifted his hand in dizzy reply, but he did not look at the boy nor his mother. His rage had glued his eyes to the despicable Duke that lay at his feet.

Kiltyrin was out cold. His eyes were wide open as though he were dead, but Farden could still hear the breath sliding in and out of him. The mage slammed his knife, point-down, into a section of desk near the Duke's head, making Moirin jump. She could guess what was coming, and she quickly covered Timeon's eyes with her hand again.

But the mage did not do anything except bend over to pick up the book that lay underneath the broken desk. It was a messy thing, crammed with scraps of cloth and parchment and bursting at its spine. It was his notebook, pilfered from his shack along with his armour. Farden thumbed through it. Some pages had already been ripped out, no doubt by Loffrey.

Just as Farden was about to toss the tome to the floor, his thumb landed on a page that stuck out from all the rest. A page he had spent many a sleepless, nevermar-tainted night on. Farden made sure to keep it close to his chest as he cracked the page a little wider.

It was his Book, faithfully recreated by ink, a pair of mirrors, and a lonely candle. Farden ran his fingers across it, glaring at every little rune and scrap of script. It had taken him many nights to scrawl. He had begun out of pure boredom and drunken curiosity, but the more he transcribed, the more he began to think he could unravel the secrets of why his Book was so different. He hadn't come remotely close to unravelling anything at all, but had let it remain in the notebook nonetheless, an homage to the hours he had spent copying it out. To his knowledge, such a thing had never been attempted, not by scholar nor Written. Nobody would be foolish enough.

Even written in simple ink, the arrangement of its foreign words and intricate runes made the page glisten with a faint power. All it lacked to make it thoroughly dangerous, like any spell, were its keys. Farden had known better than to transcribe them. They remained on his wrists, dormant, spurned, exiled like the rest of his magick. But that didn't stop particular words biting at his fingers as he roamed over them.

Tattooed or transcribed in ink, the strange script of a Book was one of pure magick. Farden had often stared at this page and wondered at how to translate it. A spell could be written and spoken in any language, and the language of the Book was a peculiar one. One that only the dead Scribe had ever known. The Arfell scholars would have given half their libraries to examine this page, Farden thought. And half their minds, too. It may not have been a true Book, but its words could still send a man's mind spiralling into madness. Not Farden's mind, however. Though the Written were forbidden to show their Books to anyone, even other Written, their own Books were safe to read. Farden was immune to his and his only. It was a curse and a useless blessing all at once.

Kiltyrin groaned at his feet as he slowly returned to the world of the conscious. It was at that moment, his thumb stuck fast in the open page, that a dark idea stumbled into Farden's mind. A very dark idea indeed.

Farden knelt down next to Kiltyrin's head, watching him come around. The Duke's eyes fluttered for a moment, trying to focus, before he recognised the man staring down at him. He flinched away and began pawing for his dagger, but Farden had already kicked it away. 'You,' was all Kiltyrin could say, the shock and pain and confusion all neatly wrapped up in a venomous, monosyllabic accusation.

'Me,' came Farden's reply. He leant closer to show Kiltyrin his notebook. Kiltyrin scrabbled weakly to get away, screwing his eyes shut.

'Get that away from me!' he hissed. His cheeks were already turning an angry red. Farden could feel the man's hatred emanating from him and clashing with his own. Failure and fear met revenge and wrath.

'If you know what it is,' said Farden, in a voice tight with anger. 'Then you'll know what it can do.'

'Loffrey told me all about it.'

'I'm sure he did,' Farden nodded. He stood up, let the notebook fall to the table, and wrenched the knife from the top of the desk.

'Farden, please!' cried Moirin. She may have hated her husband, but she wasn't quite ready to see him gutted on the floor. He was Timeon's father, after all.

'Don't worry,' Farden muttered. He put his boot on Kiltyrin's chest and reached up to cut the cord from the curtain. He then deftly looped it around the Kiltyrin's neck, much to his dismay, and dragged him into a nearby chair. Farden's tired body screamed as he manhandled the Duke but once again his anger spurred him on. It took little more than a moment to wrap the cord around the man's hands and legs and knot him to the little chair.

Farden had to give it to him. There was not a trace of cowardice to be seen in the Duke, simply a hot, glowering anger at being outmanoeuvred. 'I suppose you're going to make this slow and painful,' he spat. Farden smiled, saying nothing. It gave the mage immense pleasure to see him so helpless, so broken. A man usually so groomed and composed and spotless, suddenly no more than a dishevelled mess tied to a chair. Kiltyrin's expensive clothes were now covered in splinters and wood-dust. There was a little fleck of saliva dangling from his flame-red goatee. An ugly bruise was already blossoming on his cheek. His split lip oozed. Oh, how many times had Farden dreamt of this.

'Not before I get my answers,' he said.

Kiltyrin spat some more. 'Ah yes, of course. Your simple brain hasn't quite traced the steps yet, has it? I have to commend you, Farden. You're nothing if not consistent, in your idiocy at least. Let me guess. First of all you're going to get your answers, then you're going to lecture me on what a despicable sort of human being I am, and how, despite being at my bloody beck and call for the last, what is it? Sixteen years? That you're exempt from any sort of depravity or inculpation, due to the fact that you're now doing the world a favour by saving that brat and his mother, and stringing me up by my neck. All sins wiped clean, so to speak? Of course, not forgetting these too,' he laughed, snidely, as he rattled his wrists, ramping up his verbal onslaught. His eyes were wide with anger. 'You and I both know that the armour was the real reason you came back. Not some higher moral calling or righteous quest for revenge. Greed, Farden. Greed and another excuse to dip your hands in more blood. I'm assuming Kint and Forluss have already met their gruesome ends? I thought as much. Tell me, Farden, how many have you killed for me over the years? You're naught but a common murderer.'

A month ago, Farden would have quailed at the onslaught of sharp words and poisoned accusations. But now, the words fell on ears of stone. He laughed heartily, noticing how quickly the Duke's smile faded. 'Hundreds, probably,' he shrugged, putting another little crack in the Duke's ploy.

'Hundreds…' Kiltyrin echoed.

'Seems your tongue has finally lost its poison, Kiltyrin. And even if it hadn't, do you think that I would listen now, after what you've done to me? Another mistake made.' Farden sauntered to the door and turned its iron key, sealing the room. He then took an armchair from beside the fire and set it in front of the Duke. 'Now, about those answers…' he began.

Kiltyrin sneered. He tried another tact. 'And why should I give you the satisfaction of answers? You're going to kill me anyway, so I why should I bother myself? I have half a mind to let you drive yourself mad.'

'You flatter yourself. You're also wrong,' Farden tapped the Duke's knee with the tip of the knife. 'You see, I have no intention of killing you. Far from it. I know you're a man who puts a lot of effort into staying alive, staying on top. Why else would you go to some much trouble to steal my armour? I also know now that death is the easy way out. No. I'd rather you live on and have your final, pitiful years haunted by the fact that I'm still alive.'

For once, Kiltyrin looked indecisive. His face reminded

Farden of when they had first met, in the keep of Wodehallow, when the Duke had seemed so impetuous and young. 'And how do I know you're not lying?' he asked.

'You have my word.'

Kiltyrin laughed coldly. 'And what use is the word of a murderer like you?'

Farden nodded. 'You're right. I wouldn't hold a promise to you. But I would hold one to your wife.' The mage turned around in his chair and looked at Moirin. She seemed to have regained some of her colour. 'I give you my word I will not kill your husband,' he said. Moirin looked at him and bit her lip. He could tell that she was torn. Timeon struggled in her grip.

'Unhand me, mother!' he cried. Moirin just held him that much tighter. She licked her lips, and nodded. Farden turned back to the Duke.

'See?'

'Fine.'

Farden got comfortable. 'First things first. Where's Loffrey?'

'He's gone.'

'Where?'

'Are you going to kill him too?'

'That's between me and him. Answer the question.'

'Back to his master. Much the richer of course.'

'He's not yours? Then who is he? And how does he know so much about my armour?'

Kiltyrin glared. He was used to asking, not answering the questions. 'He's Rannoch's. Duke Rannoch's head servant and scholar. Like you, he's spent his entire life researching Scalussen armour. The man is obsessed with it.'

'How did he come to you?'

Kiltyrin remained silent. Farden waved the knife at him. 'Your life is conditional on me getting my answers, remember?'

There was a sigh. 'Loffrey found some book called the *Fable of the Nine*, written by somebody called Benton, or Binton, who cares. He became convinced that the Nine were real. So Loffrey went to Rannoch and asked for the coin to mount an expedition to find the armour, all in honour of the Duke of course. All Loffrey wanted was the fame of being the one who uncovered it. Fool. But Rannoch was unimpressed by his ideas. He dubbed it nonsense, so Loffrey came to me instead.'

'Why you?'

'Why not? I'm the richest Duke there is. Everybody owes me something. Loffrey came to me, and I heard him out. I thought he was mad at first, just like old Rannoch, but it cost me little to let him try. I would either reap the benefit, or have him hanged for wasting my time and coin.'

Farden waved his knife in a circle. 'So where do I come in?'

'Can't you figure this out for your…'

'Answer the fucking question,' the mage snapped.

'Loffrey was here when the Arka messenger came asking for you. A few had come before, but this one seemed desperate. He described you in perfect detail, the cloak, the scars, the red-gold armour you were never seen without. Scalussen, if the messenger wasn't mistaken…' The pieces fell into place as Farden listened. 'Then I remembered what you were wearing the day you came to Wodehallow. I remember thinking nothing of it at the time, thinking it was fake. Then, when Loffrey asked me about your age, your face, it all became obvious. We laid you a trap with that whore and a fake bit of armour, and you took the bait, like the fool you are. And you did me one last favour as well,' Kiltyrin chuckled. 'Wodehallow thinks I saved his life. He thinks you were young Duke Leath's assassin, and that he's to blame for all these "unfortunate accidents." My warning saved his life, and now we're moving against Leath. Together.'

Farden didn't care for the Duke's political machinations.

'What whore?' he asked.

Kiltyrin spied a weakness. 'Why Farden, you didn't know? The blind girl? Oh my. It seems you might not want these answers after all.'

Thump. Farden's left fist collided with the other side of Kiltyrin's jaw. 'What was her name?' The betrayal stung, if it was true.

The Duke winced. His eyes brimmed with hatred as well as tears of pain. 'Why should I care?' he barked. 'She did as she was told.'

'Which was?'

'She arranged for Loffrey to spy on you while you bedded her, to make sure you had the armour,' Kiltyrin chuckled. 'Betrayed you for a bagful of jewels, she did. Just like that.' He clicked his fingers behind his back.

It was then that a shout came from behind the door. 'Your lordship! Is everything alright?!' Farden whirled around, swearing darkly. He had forgotten to hide the unconscious guards.

Kiltyrin began to shout. 'They're in here! Help!' he yelled. Farden silenced him with another punch that split his lip even wider. Farden winced as his knuckle grazed one of the man's teeth.

'Shut it,' he snapped, but it was too late. The guards had heard their lordship's cries. Spearbutts and fist and elbows and boots began to hammer on the door.

Farden strangled the arm of his chair, wracking his brains for a plan. 'Quickly,' he shouted to Moirin and Timeon. 'Get under the bed! Hide!'

They swiftly did as they were told. Moirin lugged Timeon to his feet and pushed him across the floor. All the while he looked back at his father with a mixture of fear and indignant confusion. Moirin shoved him under the bed, and then followed herself. She couldn't help but watch wide-eyed from the shadows, like a stray cat in an alleyway.

With Kiltyrin still reeling from the punch, Farden grabbed him by the cord around his neck and dragged him towards the huge window at the end of the room. The feet of his chair squealed in fear. As the Duke dribbled blood, Farden whispered in his ear. 'I wish I had time to mount your head on your own wall, Kiltyrin, but it would appear that I don't,' he said.

Kiltyrin's eyes grew narrow when he saw where the mage was dragging him. 'But you swore! You gave me your word you wouldn't kill me!' he choked. The soft curtain cord was strangling him.

'What makes you think I'm going to kill you?' Farden asked. With a grunt, he spun the Duke around in his chair and pushed him up against the stone wall beneath the window ledge. Kiltyrin cried out as his kneecaps were rammed up against the stone. He looked out at the rain and the distorted lanterns of Tayn below. 'There are worse things than death, my good Duke,' said the voice in his ear.

Kiltyrin struggled for all he was worth. He felt Farden's rough and calloused hands fumbling at his wrists. 'Damn you Farden! What are you going to do with me?' he yelled frantically. His snide confidence had all but melted away. 'Help!' he began to shout. 'Help!' The banging at the door became a deep and slow thud of something heavy slamming against the wood.

Boom.

Farden ripped the Duke's silk sleeve from his shoulder and tossed it aside. He couldn't help but hesitate as his eyes met the red-gold sheen of his vambraces. He licked his lips, like a starving man discovering an abandoned banquet. His eager fingers grabbed at them, and as he pinched the hidden latches, they came loose with a metallic whisper and dropped to the floor. Kiltyrin felt them fall and struggled even more. 'Curse you, mage!'

'Where are the others?'

'As if I'd t...' A cold knife slipped under his chin.

'I've broken a promise before, and gods help me, I'll do it again. Moirin or not,' Farden growled, wrenching the man's head back by the roots of his fiery red hair. They stared at each other then. There was utter death in the Duke's eyes. Utter murder in Farden's. The mage sneered, and pressed the knife closer.

Boom.

The knife bit into his windpipe.

'Beside the bed!' Kiltyrin screeched.

Ignoring Moirin's panicked eyes, Farden rushed to the side of the grand bed and ripped open the door of a little cupboard that sat next to the wall. Its insides glittered with red and gold, scarlet and treasure. Farden snatched at it.

'Farden?!' cried Moirin. Timeon was struggling now.

'Father!' he was shouting.

'Stay there!' Farden ordered. 'And keep that boy quiet!' Farden tossed the gauntlets on the floor and threw his hands into their open mouths. They seized his fingers in their metallic grip and fused to the vambraces in seconds. The greaves would take too long, so Farden ripped the case from a pillow and made an impromptu sack.

The room bubbled with noise. Farden clutched his pounding head in his hands. The door creaked. The guards yelled. The Duke was screaming. Timeon was shouting. Only Moirin kept quiet. Farden knelt at the end of the bed and met her eyes.

'I'm sorry I can't take you with me,' he blurted.

Moirin looked scared. 'I wasn't asking.'

'I know.' Farden looked to the Duke, thrashing in his chair.

'Are you going to…'

'No. But trust me. You'll be safe.'

'Will you?'

'I'll manage,' Farden nodded. 'I always do.'

Boom.

He looked to the door. Its thick lock was beginning splinter.

The key was jangling loosely in its hole. The wood quivered as the guards struck it again.

Boom!

'Do what you have to do,' Moirin said, and reached for his hand. Farden didn't quite know what to do, but he grasped it all the same. A fleeting, cold, metallic goodbye.

'Close your eyes,' he told her.

'Father!' screeched Timeon, as Moirin clamped her hands over the boy's face.

Farden marched over to the window and his captive Duke. Kiltyrin saw him coming in the reflection of the rain-spattered pane. He could see the iron darkness of the mage's intent in his narrowed eyes. It terrified him to silence. Farden went to the desk and snatched up his notebook, still open at that most dangerous of pages. Kiltyrin soon found his tongue, bloody as it was. 'No!' he cried! 'NO!'

In a cold, slow movement that was far more frightening than if he had done it with speed, Farden ripped the page from the notebook and pressed it up against the damp windowpane so that it stuck facing the Duke. Kiltyrin looked up at the ceiling, at the floor, at the metal-eyed mage, anywhere but the Book.

Farden grabbed a loose end of rope and looped it around the Duke's face. One, twice, binding him still. Farden yanked it, and Kiltyrin's head snapped back. It was a moment's work to knot it tightly to his bound hands. He was stuck facing the dreaded page. 'No!' he shouted, clamping his eyes firmly shut.

Farden wasn't done yet. He grabbed Kiltyrin in a headlock, and held him tight against his chest. 'There are worse things than death, Kiltyrin, and I am one of them,' he whispered. Then, with a final glance to check that Moirin was not watching, he lifted up his knife, and began to cut.

The guttural screams rose higher than the rafters.

When the mage was done, he wiped his hands and turned

away, and headed straight for the fire. He reached inside his pocket and dug out the scraps of crumpled parchment Loki had given him. He held them over the flames for a brief moment until they caught light, and then sprinted to the door.

Boom!

It was not a moment too soon. 'Cover your eyes!' Farden snatched the iron key from its lock and wrenched the doors open. The guards staggered onto their faces as their rudimentary battering ram met nothing but empty air. Wide-eyed and panting, they gawped at the dishevelled man standing in the doorway, a piece of burning paper in each of his hands.

'Er…' was all one of them could stutter, as the burning papers exploded into twin balls of blinding light, miniature suns in their own right, fighting for space in the doorway. Farden screwed his eyes as tightly as he could and braced himself against the unfurling spells. His arms felt as though they had been hit by hammers. It took all of his might to stay standing. On the floor, the guards clutched at their faces, trying to shut out the blinding light.

It lasted only second, but that was all he needed.

Farden kicked his way through the dazed guards, slamming the door behind him and locking it tight. He left the guards moaning and pawing as he hurtled down the empty corridor, pillowcase of armour waving like a banner behind him. Steps flew past under his feet as he sprinted down the stairs. Soon he was flying through the hallways of the main castle, barging people aside in a mad dash for the main entrance. Nobody raised the alarm. Nobody thought anything of it. Just a rude man in a cloak. Not a murderous mage on the loose, busy escaping.

It was only when he reached the main doors that he encountered a problem: a dozen or so guards standing at the main door, staring dumbly out at the dripping gloom of the night. He was out of ideas, but he didn't let that slow his pace. The slapping of his feet echoed around the atrium, and the guards, one by one, began to turn. Farden opened his mouth, though what to shout he didn't know.

'Fire!' he blurted. That was a surprise and no mistake. A pleasant one too. The guards turned, wary. 'Fire in the banquet hall! Go help, quickly!' he yelled.

It was a stroke of genius. The guards, too bewildered to stop him, quickly began to take up the shout. They saw nothing of the blood-spattered pillowcase, his sooty and crimson hands. Instead they abandoned the door and jostled him aside, yelling 'Fire!' at the top of their lungs as they did so.

Farden didn't waste any time clapping himself on the back. Feet clattering on the slippery, rain-battered steps, a constant inch from stumbling, he flew down the precarious walkway and down into Tayn. The only thing he left behind was a long iron key, tumbling into the inky, wet darkness.

❦

'The sand don't lie, sir. Your time is up,' said Jeasin, as she tapped the little hourglass by her bedside.

There was a disgruntled sigh, followed by a rustle of sweat-laced bed linen and a muttered, 'Fine.'

Jeasin reached for her robe and swiftly folded it over her shoulders. She went to stand by the door and waited for the guard captain to dress himself. He was a regular; a portly, timid man, well entrenched in his later years. Many of her visitors were like him, sheepishly grasping at a long-lost youth well misspent. Wives none the wiser, of course.

As she heard the clomping of his tired boots come closer, she put one hand on the doorknob to her right, and held the other out in front of her, open and flat. The purse was swiftly deposited. She clutched it, weighing it. Heavier than usual. Jeasin smiled. 'Why thank you, sir. Now be sure to give the lordship his Duke our warmest regards. He and his men are always welcome here,' Jeasin said, gently shepherding him closer to the door. In her mind, she sniggered at the thought of the Duke coming to her cathouse for an evening. His men had been flooding through her doors these past three weeks, ever since... well. Since. The Duke's word had made business boom, and Jeasin was intending on keeping it that way.

'I'll be sure to mention it to him,' muttered the guard captain, unconvinced. He probably shared the same mental image. *Perhaps she could have her girls visit the castle instead*, she pondered...

'Be sure that you do, sir...'

Her hand resting gingerly on the captain's sweaty shoulder, Jeasin opened the door, and pushed him gently out. He didn't move. Jeasin was about to tut when she felt the presence of somebody else standing in the doorway, somebody wet, dripping, and breathing heavily.

The captain was fumbling for his knife. A rough hand pushed Jeasin aside and she heard the distinct wet thud of a fist colliding with a rather saggy jaw. It was swiftly followed by the bang of a head on a wooden floor.

'Hel...!' A wet, calloused hand clamped over her mouth. Another hand pushed her up against the wall. The door slammed and locked. Hot, tired breath wafted across her cheek and into her ear.

'Entertaining the guards now, are we? And a guard captain no less. That's a step-up for this house,' rasped a familiar voice. 'Must have been quite the favour you did the Duke.'

Jeasin hissed his name under his hand. It was a muffled hiss of fury, garnished with a sour pinch of guilt. There was fear there too. Whatever the Duke had done with Farden, he had survived it. He had come for his revenge.

She struggled against his tight grip. He didn't feel as strong as usual. There was a distinct smell of vomit on his hands. Soot on his clothes too. That coppery tang of blood, steel, murder. The fear grew. '*Mmhmm mmm!*' she mumbled. Farden parted his fingers so she could speak but she tried to bite him instead. The mage thumped her head against the wall for good measure. 'I s'pose you want to know why I did it? Why I sold you out?' she spat, breathless.

Farden shook his head. He watched her misty blue eyes look this way and that, searching for something to glare at. Her hair was tousled and tangled. Her perfume, as always, verged on the overpowering, even with the smell of sweat and sex on her. 'No,' he said a long pause. That seemed to take her aback. 'I know exactly why you did it.'

Jeasin lifted her chin away from the mage's hand. 'Well, good… and I'd do it again in a second,' she asserted proudly. 'For my girls.' Farden didn't reply. She stuck out her jaw. 'What did they do to you, anyways?'

There was a squeak of wet leather as Farden slowly released her. 'They killed me,' he said.

Jeasin spat again. 'Sounds like they didn't do a good job. If you're expectin' me to feel guilty, you've come to the wrong place. If you're 'ere to take your revenge, then bloody get on with it.' Behind her flinty bravado, she was quivering, but she didn't dare show it. 'Well, what you waitin' for? Do whatever it is you came to do!' Jeasin demanded, pulling open her robe and pointing to her heart.

'Such a small target,' remarked the mage. 'But I'm not here to kill you, Jeasin. Just to let you know I'm alive. And to wish you luck.'

Jeasin snorted, barely masking her relief. 'Luck? Luck with what?'

Farden kicked at the unconscious guard captain sprawled on the floor. He was rewarded with a groan. The sound of bells and horns suddenly began to emanate from the distant castle. 'After what I just did, and after *he* wakes up,' Farden kicked again at the limp body, 'you'll probably need it.'

Jeasin suddenly looked flustered. It was the first time Farden had ever seen her like that. 'What did you do?'

'Let's just say that whatever protection you had from the Duke has now been revoked. And I doubt the guards will look too kindly on you harbouring a murderous fugitive like me, or for assaulting one of their fine captains.'

'Murderous... wait! I ain't harbourin' you! An' you punched him!'

'Really?' Farden shrugged. 'The girls saw me come in. They saw me come upstairs. No screams. No cries for help. Not a mark on you. An unconscious body. Hmm, I wonder if they're as loyal to you as you are to them. Tongues wag when the knives come out. I should know.' The horns and bells were getting closer. Farden leant against the door and chuckled, chatting almost conversationally. 'Of course, you could get those hands of yours real dirty. Kill the guard before he wakes up and hide the body. Say I came for you, I killed him in a struggle, and then escaped. Strange though. I suddenly feel like sticking around. Or you could run, of course, but nothing screams guilty like running. All in all, it looks pretty bad.'

'You bastard,' Jeasin spat.

'I guess you're not the only one who's good at screwing. As I said, good luck,' said Farden, with a long sigh.

Jeasin pulled at her hair. She began to pace back and forth. Farden was idly picking his nails. She could hear it, ticking by the seconds. 'Oh, gods,' she muttered. Her little safety net had been pulled apart by its seams. Without her protection her girls were vulnerable enough, but now, thanks to the mage's meddling, they were more vulnerable than ever. The house would be torn apart. Their Jeasin, harbouring a fugitive, after all the Duke did for her. Double-cross they would call it. The girls would be locked up as traitors too. Beaten and worse. The half-empty bag of jewels in her bedside table would be all the proof they needed...

'You bastard,' she said again, venom dripping off her words. She considered going to her desk and fetching her little blade. Maybe she could catch Farden off guard, while he's weak. Nonsense. He was a trained killer. She wrung her hands, feeling that sour sting of guilt again. He wasn't the only one to blame here. She had brought this down upon herself. Her house. Her girls. All for a bag of bloody jewels.

Beaten. And worse.

'Take me with you!' she abruptly blurted. The girls could claim ignorance, claim they never knew. It would look like the mage had abducted her. She could hear the shouting of the guards in the street now.

'I travel alone,' said the mage, coldly.

Jeasin stamped her bare foot. 'Get me out of Tayn!'

She couldn't know, but Farden was staring deep into her misty blue eyes. Something made of old memories prodded his heart sharply, and he cursed it. Why did dead things refuse to stay in their murky, forgotten graves? He grit his teeth. 'Jeasin. The scapegoat,' he said. There was no trace of mirth in his words.

Jeasin nodded. 'My girls,' she gasped, barely a noise.

'Fine,' Farden grunted. 'Put some clothes on.'

Jeasin quickly felt her way to her bedside table and frantically fished out some clothes. While she dressed, Farden went to the window and peeked out. A swarm of wet guards brandishing lanterns and spears was surging down the street, yelling and braying for the blood of the mage. They were heading straight for the cathouse.

'If you're coming with me, then you're coming now,' Farden ordered. He marched across the room and yanked Jeasin toward the door. She did as she was told, but her face bubbled with anger, pain, and a dozen other feelings.

Farden quickly ushered her down the hallway and down a quiet set of stairs that led to the larders. They passed nobody. It was merciful in a way, thought Jeasin. Her ears told her the girls were busy staring at the guards from the windows, or downstairs watching them barge through the door. She would be their scapegoat, as Farden had said, and they would go unharmed. She repeated that to herself as she was half-pushed, half-carried through the silent wine larder and out of the little hatch that was the back door. Jeasin thought of little Osha's face then, her confusion. It took all she had to fight back the urge to shrug herself free and storm back to her room to confront the guards. She could tell them they had nothing to do with it, that Farden had broken in, held them hostage even. *No*, she told herself, the guards were too angry for explanation. They had already made their minds up. If she stood with the girls they would be seen as accomplices. Ignorance meant innocence.

Beaten. And worse.

Cold rain splashed on her hot face. She flinched. The cold quickly penetrated the clothes she'd managed to snatch from her drawers; a thin dress to cover up her thin robe. Farden led her onto the street and away from the cathouse.

'I've never left Tayn in my life…' Jeasin was saying. Farden gave her no reply; he simply pulled harder on her arm and broke into a jog.

Farden led her straight towards the nearest gate. The guards would be distracted at the house, but it wouldn't be long before they realised Jeasin and Farden had disappeared, and alerted the gates. The bells and horns had already done half that job. They stumbled along a rain-soaked knife-edge.

It didn't take long for a set of gates to loom out of the rainy haze. Smaller than those he had entered by, but bristling with guards all the same. Twenty, at a glance. Farden began to slow his pace. He began to wish he'd stripped the portly captain of his uniform. Shouting 'Fire!' wasn't going to work a second time, not in this blasted rain.

Exhaustion had finally pounced on him. His bones and muscles were weary. He still felt sick from the mistfrond. All Farden wanted to do was find a warm, dry place, and curl up in it. Sleep for a hundred years.

No, that felt too much like death.

'Where are we?' Jeasin whispered. She kept looking back, listening to the yelling and crashing of the guards, barely three streets away. It would not be long before they discovered they'd escaped.

'By the gates,' Farden gruffly replied.

'Guards?'

'Dozen.'

'What's your big plan?'

'Kill everything that moves?'

'Great plan.'

'You didn't have to come with me.'

'Didn't I?' came the hiss. Farden swore he felt spit on the back of his neck. Maybe it was the rain. He pulled his hood up just in case. Farden bit his lip. It was risky, but it might just work. 'You want to keep your girls safe?'

'Stupid fuckin' question.'

'Then do as I say.'

❦

'What's all that ruckus up there then, Cap?'

The captain swaggered through his bunch of men. There was mischief afoot, that was for sure. They could hear the bells of the castle clear enough. Lanterns too, in the streets up ahead. Like firefangs at dusk. 'How should I know?' he barked. 'Jus' you keep your mouths shut and your hands ready, understand?'

'Aye,' came a grumbled chorus.

'I bet it's Dunfoot and 'is lot. They always get to have all the fun,' muttered a voice in his ear. It was the sergeant.

'You ain't wrong Tirst, you ain't. That's what you get when your old father sits on the Duke's court.'

'What do you reckon the bells are ringin' for?'

'Mischief.' That was for sure. There was always mischief going on, and Captain Yaggerfell was damned if he ever saw any of it. That's what you get when your old father gets drunk and vomits on the Duke's best rug. *Shitty posts with the dregs of the barracks*, he told himself. Yaggerfell spared his guards a glance. Reprobates all. Half of them couldn't even put their armour on the right way round.

'Somebody's coming!' hissed one of them, the fat one. Yaggerfell had forgotten his name.

'Spears!' Sergeant Tirst shouted. Sure enough, a figure was coming out of the rain. A slim figure at that.

'Spears down, you morons. Don't you know a woman when you see one?' the captain snapped. Truth be told, with his lot, anything was possible. At the mention of a female, all alone and out in the rain, they perked up. Grins widened. Eyebrows raised. Elbows nudged.

A woman it was and pretty one too, albeit drenched to the bone. She clutched her soaked robes to her skin, betraying more than a hint of curve and bump here and there. A few of the guards began to edge forward. Tirst whacked them back into place with his spear. She was shivering, and she looked agitated. It was hard to tell through the rain and the bedraggled hair wrapping her face, but Yaggerfell still recognised her. That blind whore. He'd heard many a story of her over a mug of brimlugger.

'Please…' she began, teeth chattering. 'He's tryin' to kill me!'

Yaggerfell stepped forward, eyeing the rainy gloom behind her. 'Who is, m'dear?' He threw open an arm and the woman ran into it, clutching at him. A whistle or two came from behind him. More whacks of the spear.

'The man the others are chasing! The man who's killed the

Duke! He's after me, tryin' to kill me too!' the woman wailed.

The guards erupted into shouting. 'The what?'

'An assassin?!'

'Where 'is 'e?'

'Duke's dead?'

'I'll show him!'

Farden began at the back, knifing out of the hazy gloom. The blade opened the throat of the first, spinning him like a bloody top on the second. That one got the knife-point in his guts. It didn't take long for him to start howling. A man will do that when he unexpectedly finds a long blade in his midriff.

As the guards began to turn and yell, Farden sprang from one to the next, slicing at legs and arms and throats and hands before they could even wipe the rain from their eyes. Mud splashed as he kicked and darted. The rippled puddles turned golden as blood mingled with the light of the lanterns. Roars met whimpers as the mage's blades whirled.

There were three men left standing when the first spear caught him. Up high, in the shoulder. The other followed soon after, catching him just above his arse. Farden cried out as he twisted and knocked the blades aside. They had been frantic jabs, ill-aimed and desperate. He'd live, but their owners didn't. Farden grabbed the nearest by the neck and dragged his head down, at the same time as he drove his knife up. The blade popped through the back of his skull with a sickening crunch.

Before Farden could drag the knife back out, the last two were upon him. Jeasin was screaming something about being abducted. Fine little actress she was. Farden was half-surprised that she hadn't grabbed a spear and tried to skewer him herself.

Farden felt the breath go out of him as the two men bore him down. His other knife was being wrestled out of his hand. The one that Jeasin had spoken to was trying to force the mage's head into a puddle, and winning too. Farden coughed filthy, bloody mud.

Through the corner of his eye he spied his chance, and took it. He reached up, grabbed the man by the roots of his hair and yanked him down with all the might he had left, straight down onto the knife-point protruding from the dead man's skull. The man screamed as the blade took his eye. It was enough to make the second man pause, and Farden drove his other knife into his neck.

Yaggerfell rolled in the mud, clutching at his face. He was screeching like a tortured eagle. Farden put his boot on his neck, making sure he was paying attention for the finale of their little escape, and for Jeasin's little ruse. Yaggerfell still had the one good eye.

'Come here!' Farden yelled hoarsely, still spitting mud. Jeasin struggled as he grabbed her, feigning horror.

'No! No!' she cried. Farden seized her by the wrist and yanked her forward, almost tearing her hand from her arm in the process. He could hear boots. She yelped, but followed, and together, Jeasin still screaming at the top of her lungs, they barged through the gate and out into the soaking darkness.

❦

When the castle guards finally managed to break down the door to the Duke's room, some time early in the half-dawn morning, they were presented with a sight that would haunt their dreams for the rest of their lives. They didn't dare touch him. They didn't dare come any closer than they had to. Some even had to run from the room, hands clamped over their mouths. For, at the window, tied to a chair with a curtain cord, sat Kiltyrin, a rich and powerful Duke of Albion, reduced to a gibbering, foaming madman, both his eyelids lying on the floor beside him.

chapter 16

"As requested, Arkmages, we enclose our findings. I must say, we scholars find ourselves both excited and fearful. We have glimpsed the strange things of the new magick markets, but we confess, things are no less strange nor outlandish here in the libraries. Long-lost tomes are coming to life before our very eyes. Texts and scrolls we thought lost to decay and faded script are seemingly repairing and rewriting themselves. Only the other day, a colleague was reading aloud from a smithing manual, only to have the script burst into flame as he read it, the very words burning themselves from its pages!

I beg you again for more staff. We suddenly find ourselves in an age of discovery the likes of which have been lost to history. Forgive me if my words exceed my station, but it seems as if magick is reinventing itself, and I implore you to allow us to keep up with it. My utmost regards, Fontin Carga, Scholar of Arfell."

Excerpt from a report on the Arfell Libraries, year 903

'I'm beginning to wonder if he's dead,' said a ponderous voice to the sighing sea. It was quickly reprimanded by a sharp clacking of a beak and an irritated whistle. The gryphon was beginning to tire of the god's pessimism. Ilios clawed at the empty shell of a crab that had washed up with the tide. He whistled again.

Loki shrugged. 'So you keep saying, but I'm not like the others. I will reserve my judgement until I see him.'

Silence, save for the sea and the crying of a few gulls on a nearby rock. In the distance, a fishing cog plied the waves; its yellow sail chasing after the breezes. Loki and the gryphon watched it disappear around the headland.

It was a while before either of them made any sort of noise. Neither were truly worried about the return of the mage. Ilios had his dreams and his sight to calm his concerns, while Loki had his indifference. Whether it was a cunning front or genuine insouciance, even the gryphon couldn't tell.

He didn't have much time to ponder that question. The sounds of tired feet on flint pebbles wafted to his sensitive ears, and he sniffed at the salty air. Without so much as a whine or a whistle, Ilios got to his feet and launched himself into the air. Despite the down-draught of the gryphon's wings almost knocking him flat, Loki barely spared an upwards glance.

❦

Jeasin, on the other hand, was terrified.

It had been over a week since Jeasin had been wrenched from the gates of Tayn, and she had barely let a single word fall from her lips. Silence seemed to be the order of the day with her. An angry, sour silence. Farden counted his lucky stars her blind eyes couldn't catch him. The look she perpetually held in them was as sharp as hot swords.

They had travelled by night, sleeping in ditches and deep forest by day. Only once did they encounter a guard patrol, and only Farden had been awake for that. His hands had hovered over her mouth, ready to stifle her should she cry out in her sleep or awake suddenly. Thankfully, the light had been fading, and the guards marched on, completely oblivious to the fugitives hiding in the ditch, inches from their boots.

Fortunately, Farden's actions had left a tantalising power vacuum in Albion. A certain raving mad Duke had been quietly ushered into the a secluded wing of Castle Tayn and locked up for good. With only the young brat Timeon for an heir, the duchy was declared fit for the taking. Claims to Kiltyrin's throne fell from the sky like ripe fruit in an autumn gale. The court descended into uproar. Every noble, lord, and count in the duchy whipped their carriages into a frenzy and made a beeline for the city of Kiltyrin proper. Even a few neighbouring Dukes arrived to lay claim to the right to rule from its vacant seat. Kiltyrin's duchy was a fat calf delivered for slaughter, and it provided the perfect distraction for Farden and Jeasin. After all, why waste time pursuing the murderer whose hand had delivered it?

After a few days of skulking in the wilderness, Farden finally realised that nobody was chasing them, and they began to follow the flint roads east towards the coast and Fleahurst. She would occasionally make a sulky, bitter mumble of a remark, but nothing more. He could feel her storing up her venom, ready to unleash when they finally reached safety. Farden only wished he had some mistfrond left.

And so it was that after nine days of ditches and roads and sulking, Jeasin came face to face with a most terrifying creature indeed.

It swooped down from the striking blue sky with a screech that made her ears hum for hours afterwards. The monster, half ferocious eagle, half giant lion, flared its wings a mere moment before it crashed into the ground, flapping so hard that she had to cling to Farden to keep from toppling over. Jeasin didn't need her eyes to know there was a monster in their path. Her blood had already run cold from the sound of it.

Farden stood perfectly still as the creature came to a scraping, whistling halt on the flint road. He stood right in the creature's path, arms crossed and eyes closed as the road dust flew in his face. He sighed and waited for the gryphon to sit down. Behind him, Jeasin trembled.

'What is it Farden? Farden?!' cried Jeasin, looking around frantically.

'It's fine, is what it is,' replied Farden. Ilios also caught the edge of his dry tone and whistled warily, yellow eyes squinting at the long-lost mage. His claws tapped rhythms on the stones.

'What is it?' she hissed.

'A gryphon.'

'A what? Oh, I don't want to know. What's it doin' here?!'

Farden sighed. 'Gods only know,' he said. The gryphon was just as his murky memories recalled him. A few grey feathers hiding amongst his tawny plumage. His tail swished back and forth, unsure of itself.

'Is it dangerous?' she asked.

Farden shook his head. 'Not to us.'

Ilios warbled a polite little tune and leant down to nudge the mage's elbow with his beak. Farden didn't respond. Jeasin just flinched away. 'Keep following the road, you hear me? I will be right behind you,' Farden told her.

'Not a chance. I'm stayin' with you. This thing sounds like it could eat me whole.'

'He won't hurt you,' Farden sighed. As if to prove his point, Ilios gently touched his beak to her shoulder. Jeasin tentatively held out a hand, and the gryphon let her touch his beak.

'Bloody hell,' she muttered.

Ilios fixed Farden with a worried stare. The mage narrowed his eyes in reply. 'First Loki, now you. Is Durnus at the shack?'

Ilios shook his head.

'Don't tell me, my uncle's on the beach?'

Another shake of the gryphon's feathery head. Farden didn't know whether to be relieved or disappointed. 'Well, I'd say it is good to see you,' he said gruffly, 'but I'd be lying.' Ilios whistled a low note and shuffled aside to let Farden and Jeasin pass. 'Oh, and stay out of my head.'

With a silent, and confused, gryphon in tow, Farden stalked along the road, Jeasin stumbling behind him. She kept asking him about the gryphon. He wasn't in the mood for her questions. He had enough of his own.

It took them mere minutes to reach the ash tree and the lip of the hill that hid his shack from the rest of the world. A shiver ran through the mage when he saw the tree. He had ignored it on his outbound journey. He hadn't the courage to look at it. But now face to face with it once more, he couldn't spurn it. The tree swayed gently, innocently, in the breeze. Its slate fingers caressed the sky.

Half of him wanted to hack it down and burn it to its very namesake, right there and then. The other half didn't know what to do but stand in its shadow and stare up in dull horror at one bough in particular, a dozen feet up its trunk, where a frayed knot of rope danced on the wind's back. *That will be the only gravestone I will ever have*, he promised himself.

With a tired grunt, he led Jeasin and a sulking gryphon over the stubbled lip of the hill and down to his shack and beach. Loki was nowhere to be seen, presumably in the shack. A pair of scrawny rimelings had set up camp on the roof. They mewed boldly at their newcomers and the strange creature that padded along behind them. Ilios screeched at them, and they beat a hasty retreat, leaving nothing behind but their dung.

As it turned out, Loki was on the beach. Farden marched straight through his shack as though it were nothing but an archway, pausing a bare second to toss his haversack onto the floor. Striding across the pebbles and grit, he headed for the sea. He barely cast the god a second look as he passed him. Farden's feet met the gentle water, cold in the wake of winter, and kicked it aside. He marched straight in, clothes, cloak, boots and all, right up to his waist. He stood there for a moment before ducking under. He didn't come up for a long time. When he finally reared his head, he took a deep breath and went under again, scrubbing the dirt and blood from his long hair.

The mage stayed in the water for almost an hour, shedding his clothes and his filth, until his bones felt as though they would shiver right out of his skin. When he was done, he marched back up the beach, a little slower this time, and slumped into a heap on the straw-strewn floor at the foot of his bed. Jeasin was perched on a crate near the door. She hadn't moved. Her nose had told her to stay put, and not touch anything.

'The bed's good, if you want it. If not, use the chair. Make yourself at home,' the mage muttered to her, as exhaustion finally began to take him. Its hooks pulled at his tired muscles, his aching bones. His fingers stroked his eyes shut. His breathing grew heavy, leaden. Darkness gathered, and swallowed.

❦

The smell of burning awoke him. An acrid smell that burnt his nostrils, made his throat sting. His eyes fluttered and found his world at a precarious tilt. Everything was on a slant. He had somehow found his way into his bed in his sleep, and propped himself up on its straw pillows.

Roasted fish. That was the smell. Greasy, salty, roasted fish. As he sniffed the air, Farden became aware of the deep emptiness his stomach had been harbouring. It felt as though he had gulped down a sharp lump of rock in his sleep.

Farden could hear voices too, and a low whistling. He tried to shut his eyes but his hunger pried them open. It was no use. He tried his legs. They were there at least, but they were tired, aching, and barely working. His arms were the same. His whole body felt borrowed and foreign. It took him a full minute to fling himself into an upright position.

Step by shuffling step he made it to the door. The others were sitting in a circle under the blanket of stars. Jeasin was lying on a filthy blanket in the sand, probably asleep. Ilios lay like a cat, with his forelegs curled underneath him and his tail wrapping around him like not enough twine around a present. Loki was prodding the orange fire with a stick, his back to the mage. It was dying with the night; dawn was beginning to claw its way to the top of the horizon. *How long had he slept?*

Farden stumbled his way down to the fire. His stomach announced his arrival with a gurgling rumble. Loki and Ilios looked up.

'Have you even moved since I left?' he muttered hoarsely to Loki. The god shrugged. Farden took the stick from him and poked around in the fire, where a pot of fish stew had been left to keep warm in the coals. He knelt to pick out some nondescript vegetables and a morsel of oily fish with his fingers. They were lukewarm, but he gobbled them down hungrily while he eyed the god. Loki looked as fresh-faced as ever. Only a slight dusting of sand clung to his youthful skin. His eyes glistened in the fading light of the stars and the fire. 'Do you even sleep?' he asked.

'Of course not. Gods don't need sleep' he said, in a quiet voice. He seemed wary of waking the woman. She snored gently, twitching in whatever dreams she was having. Ilios was staring at her intently.

'Mhm,' Farden mumbled around a mouthful of fish, watching the gryphon. 'You'd better not be doing what I think you're doing, Ilios. She doesn't need your dark dreams.'

The gryphon looked up and fixed Farden with his golden eyes. Farden couldn't hold them for long. Something in those eyes was sorrowful, and he couldn't meet it. He occupied himself with his stew instead.

'Sleep well?' Loki asked.

Farden nodded, manhandling a half-warm potato. 'A dreamless sleep. As they should be.'

'You deserve a nightmare or two, if'n you ask me,' whispered a quiet, cold voice. It was Jeasin. She rolled over. Flecks of sand in her hair caught the orange glow of the embers. 'After what you jus' put me through.'

'Quit your whining, whore. You had a choice.'

'Choice? Don't remember having a choice, you swindlin' bastard. You forced me into it. 'aven't you pulled enough lives into your shit-trough already?' she hissed, deep in her throat.

Farden spat a bone out. 'You made your bed when you sold me to the Duke.'

'I thought you were used to me fucking you.'

'Normally I pay.'

Loki looked up at Ilios. 'What a lovely gathering we have here…' he whispered.

Farden flung a tough bit of gristle in his direction. 'And you're no better, Loki.'

Jeasin turned her sharp tongue on the god. She had ignored him so far, too angry to do anything but sleep. 'So that's your name is it? Sounds familiar. Where 'ave I 'eard that before?'

Loki sat a little straighter. 'On the lips of countless worshippers prostrate before shrines, perhaps? Or written in the long list of deities passed down from generation to generation? Or, if Farden's whore comment is anything to go by, perhaps you've heard it in the whispered ecstasies of your many clients?'

Jeasin pulled a confused face. She jerked a thumb at Farden. 'Is 'e a halfwit? Because it sounds like 'e is.'

Farden shook his head. 'Go back to sleep, Jeasin,' he growled, turning his back on her. 'If you want to shout at me, do it in the morning.' For half a moment she looked as though she would pounce on him, but instead she blew an exasperated sigh, rolled over, and muttered something dark under her breath. It wasn't long before she was snoring softly again. Exhaustion quenched anger for the moment.

'While we're on the subject, why did you bring her?' whispered Loki.

Farden rolled his eyes. 'I would have thought an omniscient being like yourself would have known?'

'I'm not Heimdall, Farden,' reminded Loki.

'She sold me to the Duke for a bag of jewels. Let one of his men spy on me from the next room. Set me up to die, so she could reap the profits.' The mage's tone was beyond bitter.

'Why?'

'To protect her girls, the other whores she had taken under her wing. She's a molly. She's in charge of her house. The Duke offered her his protection and she took it.'

'And you blame her for that?'

Farden thought for a moment, staring up at the hazy stars. Did he blame her? Could he, knowing how she had cared for her girls, worried for them, fought for them? Farden had already spelt it out for himself. The question was, would he have sold her to keep his armour safe? He already knew the answer, and it was a cold, resounding *yes*, clear as a bell on a winter morning. Farden felt the teeth of guilt bite at him. 'Yes,' he lied, more to confuse Loki than to mask his own regret. 'Yes I do.' Ilios saw the hard look in Farden's eyes and whistled plaintively.

The god raised an eyebrow. 'What a strange world you humans have carved for yourselves.'

Farden narrowed his eyes. 'I would blame the gods, but I know better now.'

'You think we don't care?'

Farden chuckled loudly. 'Hah! If this world was on fire, I

don't think you'd spare the piss to put it out.'

Strangely, Loki chuckled too. 'And who would pray to us then?'

Farden scowled. 'And that's the golden question, isn't it?'

Silence passed between the two of them. Farden concentrated on filling his empty stomach. Ilios let his gaze rove from one to the other, trying to read their eyes. Loki echoed his earlier question. 'So, why did you bring her here?'

'It wasn't part of my plan.'

'Which was?'

'Just teach her a lesson… somehow. This wasn't part of it.' Farden felt another nibble of guilt. Barely a month ago he had been watching her sleep, even daring to stroke her hair, like he had with Cheska. Had he needed to punish her? Yes. No… Farden bit his lip. 'She brought this on herself,' he told himself again.

'What will you do with her?' Loki echoed the question.

'Traffyd and Seria, maybe,' mumbled Farden. 'They need a hand around the farm. She may be blind, but she's resilient. Maybe that'll work.'

'Good with her hands, is she?'

Farden shot him a dark look.

'And what will you do?'

Farden looked up at the stars, frozen in their slow dance. 'Go north, probably. I know Leath duchy like the back of my hand. Ness and Rannoch too. I can disappear there.'

'I'm not workin' on a bloody farm, while you *disappear* wherever you please,' hissed Jeasin. She'd awoken again, feigning sleep.

'You are free to go wherever you want.'

The mage's words were like sparks to tinder. Jeasin sprang upright and slapped the sand. 'You promised to take me with you!'

Farden stared at the sharp edges of a broken promise, feeling yet another stab of guilt. *Damn those feelings of his*. 'No, I promised to get you out of Tayn,' he coldly reminded her. Even though she couldn't see the gesture, he waved his arm towards the black sea and the stars. 'This doesn't look like Tayn to me.'

'You've ruined my life!'

Another in a long line. 'And you ended mine!' snapped Farden, resisting the urge to put a hand to his neck. 'My friends will take you, if you can stomach some real work for a change. If not, I know a lovely place to stay with a great view.' Farden pointed in the direction of his dilapidated shack, and then got to his feet. He'd had his fill of stew and sour conversation.

'How can you be such a heartless bastard?'

Farden snorted as he left. 'I've spent a long time practising,' he said, drily.

'That he has,' added Loki. He too got to his feet and followed the mage, leaving a furious Jeasin to strangle the sand and kick her feet in rage.

Inside the dark shack, Farden rummaged around for fresh flint and tinder. It was a fruitless search. Loki stood in the doorway. *What did he want now?* Farden sighed. He hated to ask the god for help, but he was tired. 'Have you got any fire in those endless pockets of yours?'

Loki nodded and produced a fresh flint, a steel, and a box of wood shavings. Farden proceeded to break up a crate and stuffed the splintered bones of it into the dirty stove. It took him a moment, but he soon had the crackling beginnings of a fire. As the light began to grow and flick back the dawn-lit and dusty gloom, Farden found a seat and his discarded haversack. Something heavy and metal clinked inside it. It was the flail.

'You'll have to wait your turn,' he told it, and put it on the floor. Following in the weapon's wake came a large, empty notebook, a spare. He propped it upright on his lap, open at a vacant page. He sucked his teeth as he cast around for a quill or fine stub of charcoal. He looked up at the god again, reluctantly.

No sooner had he met Loki's eyes did the strange god hand him a quill.

'Ink?' asked the mage.

Loki shook his head. 'Oilamander quill. Feathered lizard. Makes its own ink. That quill will be good for a few hours or so.'

Farden contemplated thanking him, and then thought better of it. He found a large chunk of his shattered mirror and leant it against the notebook. Then, he picked up another, smaller shard and placed that on his knee. After rubbing the dust from it with his thumb, he grabbed the hem of his shirt, hesitated, and then pointed to the door. 'You might want to leave,' he warned.

But Loki had already guessed what was coming. He shut the door but remained in the shack. He even had the nerve to sit down on the floor, ready to watch. Farden raised an eyebrow. 'As if I need to fear a Written's book,' Loki beat him to it. He could barely contain his superior tone.

Farden shrugged. 'You've been warned,' he said.

Wincing as his aching muscles set fire to themselves, Farden pulled his shirt over his head and tossed it to the floor. He clicked his neck from side to side, rubbed his eyes, and leant closer to the growing light of the stove. It would do.

With the quill in one hand, Farden lifted the shard over his shoulder and angled it so he could see his Book emblazoned on his bruised and bony back. He could see the ridges of his spine leading a malnourished path down to his hips. See the scars weaving in and out of the black script. He sighed, and with a steady hand, he began to transcribe.

Loki was transfixed. He couldn't see it all, but what he could see was like nothing he had ever seen in his entire existence. To Farden, the script was meaningless; a foreign tongue that had been lost to time and forgotten tomes, but to Loki, it was a song. A song that wove back and forth between the scars and old wounds of the mage's skin. A song that he had heard Evernia sing snatches of when she thought she was alone. A song that had been butchered and twisted into this Written's tattoo. Loki let its words parade through a cavernous hall of his mind's construction and sing out as they passed him by. Even though the words stayed dark and dead in that little shack, in his mind they flashed and pulsed with a light brighter than the sun. The god was hypnotised.

It was only when Farden's tired arm began to sag, a good few hours of unblinking bewitchment later, that the god moved. 'Let me,' breathed Loki. Dawn had risen, and the daylight had begun to creep through the splintered windows of Farden's shack.

The mage flinched at the words, as if he had forgotten he had company. The Book was only half done. He rubbed his eyes, and put his work aside as he stood up to stretch his back. After a moment of silent thought, his fingers and thumbs circling each other slowly, he reached down to the side of the stove and retrieved his bag of nevermar. Loki had already picked up the quill. Against his best judgement, Farden sat back and handed his notebook to the god. Loki didn't need the mirrors. Farden hunched over and listened to the nib of the quill scratching on the paper. A god, scribbling out his own Book. He ignored the bizarreness of the situation and fished a tiny morsel of nevermar from inside the bag. Slowly, tentatively, hopelessly mindful of his last time with it, he slipped it into his mouth and began to chew.

The sweating began almost immediately, even before the numbness had a chance to spread past his tongue. Farden put his head in his hands and clamped his eyes shut, trying to ride out the panic that had clutched him in its iron fist. Loki could sense his sudden shift in mood, but he didn't dare pause. He worked as fluidly, as swiftly as any scribe or scholar could dream of. 'Why do you insist on poisoning yourself?' he asked.

Farden didn't answer for a while. When he did, it was in a small and strangled voice. 'Because I have things inside of me that I need to kill,' he whispered.

'It doesn't look like…'

'Just shut up and keep scribing.'

Loki didn't say another word. He melted back into his task, eager to let the song flow through his head again. The dark ink set into Farden's skin began to glisten as the light grew and the sweating became more profuse. Farden tossed the nevermar to the floor and grit his teeth until they squeaked. His breathing came in strangled grunts. His skin pricked. It felt as though a snake had made its home in his stomach.

Even in the hours afterwards, when the sickening bite of the nevermar had passed, the panic remained. It was now solely Farden's. His faithful crutch had suddenly deserted him. The sweet release had turned to choking ash. Without his nevermar, the memories he had spent so long burying would begin to bubble to the surface once again, like the pus of a festering wound. The imagery of that thought was not lost on Farden. He looked down at the spear-wound in his side, the other on his shoulder. They were still trying desperately to heal. The mage could imagine his mind doing the same in the coming weeks. The stitches and bandages he had put in place would be swept away, and he would be defenceless. Farden mumbled questions and fears to himself as a whirlwind of worries set about corroding him. Farden twitched and convulsed as the panic ebbed and flowed. His mind rambled on…

This is just temporary, he told himself, over and over. *Just temporary*. That echoing thought stayed with him until he heard a door slam, shattering his clammy reverie. He wiped the sweat from his eyes and turned around to find that Loki had gone. He had left the notebook on the floor, open at a page now emblazoned with a perfect copy of his Book.

Trembling fingers reached out to close the notebook and slide it back under the seat. Farden crawled into his bed. Whiskers appeared from the shadows and curled into a ball on his chest, listening to the mage's heart thundering behind his ribs. Slowly, painfully slowly, the storm subsided. His heart ceased its senseless battering. His mind let tiredness come, and Farden fell into another mercifully dreamless sleep.

❦

The same could not be said of Loki.

The god awoke with a start, several hours later, just as the sun was reaching its lofty zenith in the faint blue sky. Loki sat bolt upright and looked around, wary and uncomfortable. Jeasin was still fast asleep. As was Ilios.

Loki tucked his legs into his chest and rested his chin on his knees. He stared out to sea and frowned at its calmness. He couldn't pretend it hadn't happened. How had he fallen asleep? He had been lying on his back, watching the bruised sky change from dawn to morning, when suddenly… No. It was impossible. Gods did not sleep, he asserted to the silence and the waves.

'Gods do not sleep,' he blurted the words, unbidden.

But the thing that had unsettled him the most was the fact that if gods didn't sleep, they definitely didn't dream. Loki narrowed his eyes at the sea.

He had done both.

A darker dream had never been dreamt.

part three

to the found

(revelations)

chapter 17

"What strange creatures they must be, to spring from eggs fully formed, as though it were a chicken, or a monstrous goose! Be wary, in your travels, of stumbling across a dragon breeding ground. Closely guarded are they, and hold vicious retribution for the unwary trespasser! Be wary also of the eggs themselves, as rumour has it that they burn with a mystical and cursed fire. If ever you are unfortunate to come across an unprotected one, leave it be, for the infant dragon may sprout at any time, and emerge hungry and ready for its first meal!"

Excerpt from 'Dragons and their Features: Lessons in Identifying the Siren Beast' by Master Wird

'I'm beginning to wonder if he's dead,' said a ponderous voice to the morning breeze, unknowingly echoing her brother's words.

'Nonsense. Loki would have returned already. He would not waste time dawdling in the countryside, keeping watch over a corpse.'

'I am not so sure. Our brother brims with curiosity.'

'And do you not? This is your first time here also.'

'Curiosity can wait until after. If there is one.'

'The humans are right, Verix, sometimes I wish you'd learn to temper your truthfulness.'

'What is the truth, if not untempered?'

Heimdall had no reply to that besides, 'Irritating at

inopportune times.' These younger gods sometimes needed guidance. The others had been quick to doubt his choice in bringing them along, but what they lacked in wisdom, they made up for in eagerness, in passion. Besides, they used up less prayer. Three was better than one, especially when reserves were tight. The gods had to be wary of what was to come…

Heimdall and Verix stood alone in the Nest. It had become their favourite haunt over the last few weeks. It reminded them of home, and, especially for Heimdall, afforded them an uninterrupted view of the city. He had spent long days staring at the city and its dark mountains, searching and straining for that first glimpse of the girl. She was coming for them. He and the others could feel it.

'How do you expect to find her when you don't even know what she looks like?' the Arkmages had asked.

'I can see more than what is visible to the eye, mages,' Heimdall had replied. It was true. He could see much, much more.

If he turned his eyes truly loose, the world vibrated in front of him, shedding light and colour in ways that were indescribable, painted with spectrums that no artist could ever dream of. Magick itself lurked in one of these spectrums, and if he concentrated, Heimdall could watch it billow in waves around the patrolling mages, or dart back and forth over the merchants' wares. Sometimes it clung to certain people like a draping fungus. Other times it crept like fingers of water through a sinking ship; probing, testing, seeping. If he looked up, he could see it wrapping the mountains with its strings. It was never the same colour for long, if colour was really the word for it.

It was how he expected to find her. From the stars and their shadowy void, it had proved impossible. She was a ghost on a misty morning, silent and deadly. But down here, under the clouds, it might be different.

At least, that's what he hoped.

'Nothing?'

'Nothing,' said Heimdall, wincing as he lost concentration for a split-second. He closed his eyes and switched to using his ears. The sound of the city flooded in, and he began to trawl through it.

Verix sighed. She was becoming impatient. She turned to face north where a little forest of white tents had appeared on the hillside, near a growing building. There was a little train of people going to and from the city gates, bearing sacks and tables and flowers and chairs and clothes and food and rope and many, many other things that were apparently required for this upcoming festivity. A wedding. Verix had never seen a wedding. Her kind had no such thing. She had to admit, she was a little baffled. 'On the brink of a war like no other, and the maid insists on her wedding,' she mused. 'How decidedly foolish.'

Heimdall barely heard her over the tumultuous noise. 'Better it happen sooner, than later, do you not think?'

'Better it not happen at all, brother. What target could be more tempting than a wedding where the guest list consists of every powerful mage the Arka have to offer? If I were the spawn, I would attack.'

Heimdall raised his chin a little. 'Do you not think they know that? Elessi is adamant it go ahead. Why should they hide and cower? If the spawn is indeed capable of what we think she is, what the Lost Song says, then wedding or not, it will not make a difference when and where she strikes. Besides, they have prepared accordingly. The new Spire's cellars are as fortified as the Arkathedral. The Written will be elsewhere, expecting the worst. As will the army, and the rest of the mages. Better to be wary, than to be surprised.'

Verix tilted her head, as was her habit. A flash of flame in the distance, to the east of the new Spire, caught her eye. In the training yards. 'True indeed,' she said. 'It's almost as if this wedding is bait.'

Heimdall hummed. 'I knew it would be a matter of time before you guessed our plan. You are not the goddess of truth for nothing,' he said.

'Why did you not tell me? Am I not here to help?'

Heimdall wagged a finger. 'You are, in other ways. Truth has its downfalls, Verix. We could not afford an honest tongue in the wrong place. 'But if you value your life, I wouldn't mention it around the maid. She doesn't know.'

'AGAIN!' came the deafening, rasping order of the drill sergeant. A hundred hands punched the air with a shout of a spell. Flame roared. Smoke puffed. The air flexed and bowed as the heat rose.

'ONE MORE TIME!' The man's guttural bark had the tonal quality of two rusty saws duelling. The mark of a true School instructor.

Once again, a hundred lips moved in unison, and a hundred palms threw bolts of fire into the azure sky. All except one. There was a cry as two recruits were soaked with ice-cold water. The sergeant found his prey and pounced.

'By Njord's festering ballsack!' he yelled, stamping his way across the dusty training yard. The gathered recruits stood as still as they could possibly manage. They were the very epitome of mismatched miscellany. Any handful could have been dragged from their lines and not a single one would have anything in common with the next. They were farmhands, goatherds, veterans, butcher's apprentices, travelling merchants, bored sailors, toothless brawlers, council members' daughters, and freed slaves from across the sea. They were old, young, fat, malnourished, poor, rich, muddy, perfumed, bald, and coifed. Some had never seen the city before, some had never bothered to leave the comfort of their velvet-clad houses. Even their clothes were at odds. The pure, mind-boggling variety was an assault on the eyes.

But all of them, every single one, had felt the stirrings of magick in them to some degree or another. Down to the last hair on the very last head. Not in the history of the School had such an odd assortment of recruits been allowed through its prestigious, brutal doors. A blessing and a curse, all rolled into one.

'Stand still, all of you!' barked the sergeant. He had made his way to the back of the ranks, homing in on his quarry like a falcon, a red-faced and muscular falcon at that. Had the man not stood over six feet tall, had he not been built like the broad side of a house, his stormy face alone would have set the recruits quaking. His nose looked as though it had been on the wrong side of a row of knuckles too many times. Burst blood vessels decorated his cheeks. His russet hair was shaved into a wide, waxed line that ran from his brow to the back of his neck. Paraian fashion.

Had all of that failed to strike fear into the hearts of a recruit, then the man's reputation would have finished the job up nicely. Exclamation was his middle name. Expletive his last. School rumours had it that Sergeant Toskig had once strangled a minotaur to death with his bare hands. It was also widely known that, while he had never been directly responsible, many a recruit had died under his instruction over the years. Learning magick was a dangerous game. The School was a dangerous board to play it on.

Toskig hauled a man out the furthermost rank and clapped him hard around the head. A man equally as tall and muscular, but with a fair face and a glum expression. It was the third time that day. He was beginning to bruise.

'Gurmiss, you fecking idiot. For the last time! Get. Your. Spells. *Right*!' bellowed Toskig, right in the man's face. Each word was a slap in the face. Gurmiss nodded. He must have only been about twenty. From a privileged background too, by the looks of his clothes. 'You a water mage, Gurmiss?' demanded Toskig.

'No, sir,' replied Gurmiss.

'Then why are you casting a water bolt spell in my fire class?'

Gurmiss made a face. He didn't seem to be the brightest fish in the net. 'I don't know, sir.'

'Cast it again. Just you. Right now.'

'Now?'

'By Evernia's wilting tits! *Now*, Gurmiss!'

Gurmiss began to mutter something and held his hands out in front of him. The men and women around him began to scatter. Toskig smacked him on the arm. 'Back in line, gobshites! Point it up, you fool. Up!'

Gurmiss bit his lip and put his hand in the air. He cleared his throat, closed his eyes, and began to mutter anew. Seconds later his hand began to tremble. He planted his feet as instructed, and a fountain of orange flame burst into the air above his palm. Gurmiss' glum face broke into a wide smile. Several of his nearby compatriots cheered quietly, relieved. Some of them were soaked to the skin.

Toskig clapped a hand to his head in exasperation. 'Thank the bloody gods for that! Back in line!'

The recruits scrambled to do his bidding, readjusting their ranks as quickly as they could. They weren't fast enough, and Toskig began laying about with the back of his hand again. 'This is a military school for military recruits, not a dancing class, you sorry sacks of septic entrails! Start acting like it!' Toskig took his place at the front of the formation and put his hands by his sides at attention. He stamped his foot, and the hundred recruits did the same. They tried their best to be snappy about it. Most failed. Toskig looked up to the heavens for help. He need only have looked behind him.

'Working them hard I hope, Sergeant Toskig?'

The sergeant turned and immediately saluted the shorter man standing behind him. 'Undermage Modren, sir!'

'Sergeant,' smiled Modren. He was wearing a suit of armour

that defied the very definition of polished. Its overlapping steel plates veritably glowed. Toskig, clad in his own leather and iron half-plate for training, couldn't help but gawp. Neither could half the recruits, but Toskig's trained ear could hear the slackening of a recruit's jaw at a hundred paces. He whirled around and glared at the front rank. 'What are you drooling idiots gawking at? Twenty press-ups followed by three fire bolts! Quick as you can! Upright and thoroughly in the air! And if any of you stop before I say, I'll flay you alive! Gods help me, I'll make a tablecloth out of your hide and eat off it at the good Undermage's wedding!' he barked, clapping his hands to set the pace.

The recruits knew he wasn't joking. They leapt to follow orders. Some of the more overweight recruits struggled, but they didn't dare complain. Toskig turned back to Modren and pointed at the etched breastplate hugging his superior's chest. The design of a gryphon was emblazoned there. 'Arkmage Tyrfing's handiwork?'

'Indeed it is.'

'He isn't showing any sign of slowing down, is he?'

'Just broke a new spell this morning.'

'What kind?'

'More of the same. Anti-magick stuff, courtesy of our dusty friends of Arfell. Gods only know what's going on in their libraries.'

'Probably the same magickal malarkey as what's going on here.'

Modren nodded. He took a step forward to stand beside the sergeant and together their narrowed eyes roved over the panting, sweating formation in front of them. They were hardly impressed.

Toskig doled out some encouragement at the top of his lungs. 'To the dirt, Hoskis! I want to see a dust-print on that big nose of yours! You there, woman in the grey! Good work! Gurmiss, you lump! Faster, man!' he yelled, and then bent down to whisper in Modren's ear. 'Truth be told, Undermage, I've never seen a group of recruits like them. I've never known six-monthers to suffer this much magick.

Their spells might not be smooth yet, but their endurance is up there with one-years, maybe two-years… ' he paused to shout as a little puff of smoke wafted into the air. 'That'll teach you not to roll your sleeves up, Shariss! I hope that tunic was expensive!'

Modren stifled a dry chuckle. He could remember the sergeants of his day. They were all the same. Tough, brutal, and dangerous, but fair, somewhere deep down. He still had the scars with their names on, and from other days at the School. It wasn't a gentle place, and it wasn't just the instructors that the recruits had to be wary of. Given the tough selection processes, competition had been fierce in his day. Fierce, and often deadly.

But now, with the huge surge in recruits, the selection process had slackened to accommodate them all. The Arkmages couldn't risk prospective mages slipping the net. Looking around, he could still spy a few bruises hiding in the hollows of tired eyes, the split lips lingering at the corners of mouths. The old ways still lingered, but now there was a new sort of trouble: accidents, over-crowding, under-staffing, inexperience… The list went on. But still, it was better than the alternative: even more accidents, people trying to train themselves; loose cannons, rogues… the list went on again. The Arka had to regulate this strange surge in magick users or suffer for it, pure and simple. The coffers were nearly drained because of it. Cuts had been made. Complaints issued.

Toskig spoke some of them aloud. 'I'm used to training recruits from well-known families, your Mage, families with long-lines of magick and battle in their blood. I'm used to recruits who already know which bit of a sword you use to stick a man with, who already known how to spar and how to march. Those are the recruits I'm used to,' he sighed. Toskig waved his hand towards a corner of the formation, where a score or so of fit-looking, grim-faced recruits had been clumped together. Modren's keen eyes had already picked them out. Everything about them screamed future mage. These were the sons and daughters of soldiers and proud families and long lines. Even their tunics were noticeably sharper. They had most likely been training since they were children, always destined for the School. Modren had been one of them. In better days, some of them would have gone on to be Written.

‘But these,’ Toskig sighed again, ‘these people aren’t soldiers. Magick aside, they’re as useful as tits on a bull. If I had my way, I’d kick half of them out tomorrow and half again the next day.’

Modren shook his head. ‘Room must be made,’ he said firmly. *Especially with a war crawling its way towards us.*

‘But can we afford them all? We’ve already taken two cuts in coin. There’s barely enough food stockpiled for the next few months. It’s not just me that thinks this, Modren, it’s the rest of them too. Sergeant Haverfell and his mages say the same. The griping in the taverns at night is near deafening. Not to mention half the instruct…’

Modren cut him off sharply. He had heard the griping firsthand. Over the last three years, complaining seemed to have become the Arka’s national sport. ‘Orders are orders, Sergeant. I don’t like it any more than you do. The Arkmages have spoken.’

Toskig bit his tongue and nodded, and was about to apologise for speaking openly when Modren shrugged off his Undermage’s cape and threw it to the dust. As he unfastened his gauntlets and glittering vambraces, he rubbed his hands together, and the keys on his wrist flashed in the afternoon sunlight. ‘I know you’re only speaking the truth, Sergeant,’ he said, cracking his knuckles. ‘My hands may be tied, but they still know a spell or two. If I may,’ he gestured towards the ranks. Toskig let his sour face fall and began to grin from ear to ear. He took a deep breath and painted the air blue with it.

‘Right, you ugly cluster of clod-hopping gob-shites! Stop whatever it is you’re doing and salute Undermage Modren accordingly!’

There was a rustling applause of heels snapping together and hands quickly rising to temples.

'At ease!' barked Modren, testing his parade lungs. Rusty, but still there. He strolled up and down the front rank whilst Toskig introduced him, eyes hard and dangerous. He let his magick unfurl. He could see some of the recruits wince.

'The man standing before you is as good as they come! A real mage. A Written no less! It's a pleasure to have him on my training yard,' shouted Toskig, following in Modren's wake. 'He's going to show you a gods-damned thing or two, so clean out your ear holes and pay attention, or so help me I'll end you right here in this yard and make the others do laps around your pyre. Do you hear me?'

A resounding blast of, 'YES SIR!' followed, and Toskig let Modren have the floor.

Modren took it with a will. He clapped his hands and lightning shivered up his arm. The recruits' eyes widened. 'Magick doesn't make a mage,' he began, quietly at first, 'a soldier makes a mage.' Modren let the lightning trickle down his arm, breathing in the hot smell of burning air wafting on the breeze, and then let it flow into his palms. With a clasp of his fists, the lightning died. The Undermage looked up and met the gaping eyes of the sweaty, gasping, and dusty recruits. Modren took a deep breath and readied himself to shout his lungs out.

❦

The hammer kissed the glowing metal with its blackened face. A burst of flaxen sparks skidded along the anvil.

'That will do,' Tyrfing muttered, partly to himself, partly to the trio of scholars that stood patiently behind. The forge-room was blisteringly hot and clad in their thick Arfell robes, the scholars were sweating buckets. They held cloths to their foreheads as they watched the Arkmage pick up the hot steel plate with his bare fingers and place it back in the glowing firepot of the forge.

Tyrfing rubbed his fingers together to refresh his protection spell as he reached for a nearby glass of water. He stared pensively into the coals of his forge-fire, watching the yellows, the oranges, the dancing of the black and red.

'Are you ready, Arkmage?' One of the scholars piped up, a young man who seemed to be trying very hard to grow a beard, but somewhat failing.

'Almost,' replied Tyrfing, scratching at the itchy skin beneath his own beard. It was strange to think that Written, for all their fighting prowess, were actually perfect blacksmiths. Tyrfing wondered, with a wry smile, if their calling had been misinterpreted.

He sipped his water and rubbed some of the soot from his face. He had been in his forge all morning and for a sizeable chunk of the afternoon. He turned his gaze from the coals to the far wall, where sets of armour hung on nails and hooks. It was a vast wall, long and sparkling with the reflections of flames, bedecked with metal of all shapes, colours and sizes. There were some there that sparkled more than others. Only Scalussen armour could caress the light like that, as if longing for the flames that birthed it.

Scalussen armour cost an unspeakable amount of coin. Tyrfing's ever-growing collection, spurred by the desire for his nephew's return, had nearly drained the Arka coffers. It wasn't all for Farden, however. Tyrfing had kept the other Written in mind. Almost every piece in his collection was spoken for. Nothing but the best, for the best. And the last.

It also hung there to inspire him. Scalussen armour and arms were near-perfection in metal form. Relics of a long-lost art. Tyrfing had challenged himself to breaking its secrets, secrets that most blacksmiths in Emaneska would gladly have cut off their own limbs for. Too long had they been lost. It was time to rediscover the Scalussen skill.

That was where the wise men of Arfell came in.

'So,' began Tyrfing, savouring the coldness of his water. The glass it swished around in was a trinket from the magick markets; a glass which kept its contents ice-cold no matter what, no matter how close to the forge-fire he left it. Tyrfing smiled as he placed the glass down. Nuisance or not, the magick markets produced some intriguing things. 'You say that I have to burn the actual spell itself?'

'It would appear so, Arkmage,' replied the oldest of the three. A great, wizened fellow, part man, part beard.

'Speaking aloud and burning seem to have the same effect. We thought it heresy when we first clapped eyes on a merchant burning cantrips in the main square of Arfell. We almost had him arrested,' said a third, a plain fellow with the pink scars of vanquished acne splayed across his cheeks.

Tyrfing reached for his hammer. 'Well, I'm glad you didn't.'

'It takes young eyes to see past old tradition,' said the young scholar, with a cheeky smile, garnering a glare and an elbow in the ribs from his colleagues. He winced.

Tyrfing smirked and turned back to his forge. He rubbed his dusty fingers together, feeling them go numb and cold, and then leant into the hearth to adjust the position of his glowing breastplate. 'The spell?' he asked, and moments later a pair of quivering tongs appeared by his side, a narrow strip of parchment clasped in their soot-laced teeth. The young man clutching them was leaning as far back as his short arm would allow, shielding his face. The air was so hot there it was barely breathable. Sweat dribbled down his cheeks in rivers. 'Thank you,' said Tyrfing, snatching the spell from the tongs and putting the scholar out of his misery. He scampered back to join his elders.

It felt odd to simply toss the spell into the fire. Tyrfing scanned the ink-spattered page and found it to be in an old Arka dialect, on the cusp of ancient. He resisted the urge to read it aloud, and pressed it into the coals to let it burn. And burn it did, like any paper would when faced with a forge.

With a puff of white smoke and a flash of green light the parchment was consumed. While the smoke quickly evaporated into the huge iron vent hanging above the forge, the green light lingered, swimming to and fro amongst the coals like tendrils of seaweed. It was hunting for something, sniffing it out. It didn't take long to discover its prey. The light wrapped around the breastplate and vanished. There was a twang as the metal contracted. It darkened, cooling ever so slightly. Tyrfing bent to pick it up. He could feel the magick throbbing in it, and flicked it with his nail. It sang to him with a deep note. 'It worked,' he muttered, impressed.

The scholars exhaled a sigh of relief. The oldest two bowed hurriedly and made for the door, leaving their junior behind to make their excuses. They couldn't wait to escape the heat. The young man was positively trembling with excitement. 'With your leave, Arkmage, we will head straight back to Arfell. This discovery has given us much work to do!' he said, sliding towards the door with each word, bowing more than once.

Tyrfing nodded and waved him away. 'You and I both,' he said quietly, as the door shut behind them. Peace and quiet, all his to fill with hammer-clangs and the screeching of metal. Tyrfing cleared his throat but ended up coughing instead. He winced as the pain spread from his throat to his lungs. It lasted only a moment. Spitting something into the forge-fire with a hiss, he reached for his cool water, and growled something under his breath.

❦

A shout rose above the hubbub, ringing through the little city square. 'The gods are displeased with the lax attitude of humanity. They require sacrifice and repentance!'

'And action too!'

'That is not what I said…'

'Just a minute here. What do you mean by *sacrifice*? You're not suggesting some blood-of-a-virgin rubbish, are you?'

'No, I…'

'Then what?'

'*Personal* sacrifice. Holy lives. Prayer. A righteous life.'

'And coin, too, no doubt?'

A murmur of agreement rippled through the little crowd, stalling the debate for a moment.

'If you ask me, mates, I don't think the gods are that fussed with us. They didn't help us in the war, why should they help us now?'

'*Fussed*?! You make them sound like skinny damsels picking over pastries!'

'They didn't help us, dear boy, because we weren't praying enough!'

'Or praying to the wrong one!'

'Heretic!'

'Evernia is our goddess.'

'Njord. Always has, always will be!'

'You're a sailor, you would say that. I say Thron is overlooked.'

'Siren-lover!'

A fist banged a table, jolting pint glasses and bottles. 'The Arkmages are the problem. They're the ones letting this get out of hand. Lax attitude you say? They're the lax ones, I tell you!'

Another murmur of agreement then, louder than the first. The arguers had finally found a common ground.

'Aye! They're deaf to our shouts, they are!'

'Incompetent!'

'Taxes are going up again, I hear.'

'UP?!'

And so it went. Religion, so they called it. It would never stir a man like taxes can.

Sitting on a step in a nearby doorway, Malvus Barkhart sipped his cragleaf tea with smiling lips. He was watching the growing gaggle of vehement debaters with a happy eye. He had seen this a hundred times in a hundred tavern courtyards. The arguments were almost scripted now. The lines had been drawn. Camps chosen. The battlegrounds? Public places. Taverns. Boardwalks. Market stalls. The weapons? Opinion, discontent, and loud voices.

Malvus caught the eye of one of the men and winked. The man nodded in reply and went straight back to his ranting, decrying the marble thrones and the useless fools that dared to occupy them. It was music to Malvus' ears, music that was coin well-spent.

He finished his tea with a gulp and got to his feet. The dregs of the cup left a bitter taste in his mouth, and he grimaced. He looked down into the cup and wrinkled his lip at the sludge that had gathered there. He had half a mind to complain to the tavern owner, but he was already going to be late.

'Read your leaves, sir?' A nearby voice slithered into his ear.

Malvus turned to find an ageing, obsidian-haired woman standing very close to him. She was clutching a withered arm to her chest. She was reaching out for his cup with the other. Malvus pulled a face and shoved her hand away. 'Out of my way, beggar. I'm not interested.'

'Are you sure, Council Barkhart?'

Malvus paused. He was well-known in the city. She could have picked up his name from anywhere, but the way in which she croaked it plucked ponderously at the superstitious string in his mind. *With so much familiarity.* 'How much then?' he asked. 'State your price, beggar. And let's not make it too extortionate, shall we?'

The woman tapped the side of her nose. 'What's a future

worth to you?'

'That depends on the future.'

The woman chuckled, a hoarse cackle. 'And your future depends on the questions you ask.'

Malvus narrowed his eyes, wondering if he was wasting his time. 'How decidedly odd. I was under the impression my future depended on my actions.'

The woman cackled some more, louder this time. 'Hah! Every man is a book, Barkhart, and every book has a beginning, an end, and the chapters in between. They're already written, m'dear, you just have to turn the pages.'

'I disagree. A man makes his own fate, as I have made mine.'

'Whatever you say, Council, whatever you say!' The woman smiled and pointed at the cup. 'But say that you did 'ave a book, you fancy skipping a chapter or two?'

The woman's words made Malvus wary. 'I thought your kind read stones, not leaves?'

The woman beckoned to the cup with a handful of long nails, as if willing it closer. Her voice had become quiet, urgent. 'Leaves, stones, feathers, guts. It don't matter to those with the skill to read,' she whispered.

Malvus contemplated. He looked deep into the woman's grey eyes and patted the coinpurse at his belt. 'Your words will decide my payment.'

'A fair deal,' she said. She pulled her skirts around her knees and settled down on Malvus' step. Malvus did the same, but made sure to keep his distance. Beggars carried diseases. This one looked particularly filthy. Her skin was that of cheap leather.

Malvus handed over the cup and she snatched it away. She held it to her breast and began to whisper to the greenish sludge sitting at its bottom. She shook it, once, twice, then again, and then began to whisper to herself. She seemed genuine enough, and that got Malvus' heart beating. He had seen enough seers to know. He leant forward to try to catch the words, but they slipped away from him. He licked his lips impatiently. His future was constantly at the forefront of his mind these days. He had his dreams, his plans, his grand designs, but there was nothing like having a seer lie them out for him to make the blood rush.

'What do you see?' he asked. Several moments went by without an answer, so he asked again. 'What do you see, woman? Tell me!'

So she told him.

It took several minutes for Malvus to take it all in. Council Barkhart was not a man who often stammered, if ever at all, but on this one occasion anything was possible. 'W… why are you telling me this if my book is already written?' he squeaked.

The seer squinted at him. 'Because a journey is always quicker if the traveller already knows the road. Besides, everybody reads books different, see? You might skip an important line, read too eagerly, miss the plot.'

Malvus tried to shake himself from his daze. Her metaphors were getting muddled up. The blood was rushing indeed. 'I am not fond of riddles, woman. Tell me, why you? What interest have you in my future?'

The seer ran a hand through her dark hair. 'Revenge,' she said. 'And repayment.'

Malvus drew back. 'For what?'

'For my death,' she smiled a wry smile, one that had no trace of humour in its curves. My life has its own book, Barkhart, and like most stories, it ends. Our fates may already be written, but you can read slower, if you catch my drift. Stave off the ending, so t'speak.' A look of disgust came over her face. 'I've staved off my ending long enough, it seems. But I ain't done there. I want revenge on the one who ends my story, understand? Kill the man who kills me. It's simple. I help you. You help me.'

'And why would I do that for a mere beggar?'

'Because in return,' the smile returned, this time with humour splashed all across it, 'I'm going to tell you how to live forever. Now is that worth your pretty coin, Malvus Barkhart?'

The smile that spread across Malvus' cheeks was so wide it actually hurt. Not only had his hopes been confirmed, nay, *ameliorated*, by this woman, but now his dreams, and most private desires, were being dangled in front of his face. *What a lucky day it was*, he thought. *Thank the gods for cheap cragleaf tea.*

With a slow and steady movement of his hand, Malvus reached down and untied the strings of his purse. He took the cup from the woman's palm and tossed it into the street. Then he took his purse and upended it over her hands. Coin poured from its mouth like a butchered pig spilling golden entrails. The seer counted them as they fell.

'Tell me,' he told her. 'Tell me everything.'

❦

In a dark and sodden hole, underneath the salty boardwalks of Port Rós, where the sewer pipes met the sea, a young girl squatted in the dark and held her nose against the stench of Krauslung's piss and shit. If she cared, she didn't show it. She didn't grumble. She didn't moan. She just held her nose and poked the dead rat once more.

The brown rat was the size of a hunting dog, a sewer monster. She hadn't killed it, merely uncovered it in the seeping effluent that was trying its best to invade her sturdy boots. It lay on its back with its legs in the air. Its head was tilted back and its mouth open, revealing rows of black, needle-sharp teeth. A trio of maggots were having a picnic on its grey snout.

Samara prodded it in the chest one last time, wrinkling her

nose at the feel of its sagging ribcage. It had been there quite a while.

'Come on,' she urged it. 'Hurry up.'

It did just that. Its tail twitched and its feet trembled. Much to the maggots' dismay, an unseen handed guided the rat's head up and over with a squelch. Its mouth jiggled, trying to find its tongue. Its black, dead eyes began to blink. 'Where are we?' it hissed, with a voice no rat could ever muster. Nor any human for that matter. It was a voice made up of many speaking in unison. For anyone else but Samara, it was blood-chilling. She'd heard it before.

'Krauslung,' replied Samara, with a smirk of satisfaction. They may have been lurking in the sewers, but they were finally here. Every time she entertained that thought she got a little shiver of anticipation.

'Ahhhhhh,' the breath slid from between rat-lips. Even though it sighed and gasped, its chest never quite moved. 'Finally. The time is near?'

'Tomorrow night.'

The rat smiled. 'Tomorrow night. It will be our pleasure. What is the occasion?'

Samara cracked her knuckles. 'Some sort of wedding. The Undermage's, Lilith says. Ruin will be there, and Tyrfing, and all the other mages. It's perfect.'

'More than perfect.' The rat turned its head then, as if listening to something faraway. The dead rat sniffed, its whiskers twitching. 'He asks of Farden?'

'No sign,' the girl replied. She couldn't help but glare. 'Lilith said he'll be there. I hope she's right this time.'

'Then guard yourself until the last moment. We can taste the stench of gods in that city. Do not alert them.'

Samara couldn't help but look confused. 'Gods? Here?' she asked.

'Shades, shadows, apparitions of prayer. Mere ghosts. But

they may still raise the alarm. Hide your magick.'

'I already am,' Samara replied. It was a constant effort but she was managing. It felt like a thunderstorm was trying to burst out of her chest.

The rat looked away again, and then turned back. It gazed at her with its beady eyes. They were so narrowed that in the dark they looked closed. 'Are you afraid?'

Samara was taken aback. She wondered if she should lie. She realised she didn't have to. 'The only thing I fear is failing.'

'Ahhahaha,' the rat convulsed as the voices chuckled. It was haunting. 'Two millennia of waiting come to an end tomorrow, child, and you shall bring the end crashing down. Until then,' it said. As it spoke, its head fell slowly back into the slop gracing the floor of the pipe. Samara left it to the maggots and shuffled back the way she had come.

'Until then,' she said to herself, trying to calm her beating heart.

When, at long last, she made it back to their hiding hole, a little alcove in a larger tunnel, Lilith was waiting for her. She looked out of breath, greased with slime.

'What is it?' she asked.

Lilith flicked a drop of something black from her nose. 'He's here,' she said, in a low tone.

❦

Right above their heads, where the boots paced the cobbles, where a market had squeezed itself into a tiny square between three streets, Malvus Barkhart felt a tapping on his back.

'Council Barkhart?' asked a high voice. Malvus turned to find a skinny messenger, no more than a boy, standing behind him. He was dancing from one foot to the other. Dartsoles, yet another gift of the markets, designed to allow their wearer to move twice as fast as normal. According to the messengers, they were incredibly painful to wear, but least they got the job done in half the time.

'What?' asked Malvus. There was an unusual smile still pasted on his face. Had the messenger had time to think, he would have found it rather unsettling.

'Councils Bort and Anviss request your immediate presence,' blurted the skinny boy.

'What ever for?' Malvus frowned.

'Somebody is arriving in the city. A mage they said. A Written. Arkmage Tyrfing's nephew.'

Malvus' smile faded.

❦

Tyrfing barely heard the shouting over his vicious hammer-blows. When he turned around, he found Durnus standing in the doorway of the forge. He was beckoning to him with one hand and holding a fresh Arkmage's robe with the other.

Tyrfing wiped his soot and sweat-stained brow. 'What is it?' he asked.

Durnus didn't have to say anything at all. His look spoke for him. As did his grin. Tyrfing threw the hammer and the ingot he had been battering to the floor and darted for the door.

❦

'And that's how it's done, you bunch of ingrates! Off to the water trough with you, before you vomit over my nice, clean training ground! Dismissed!' Sergeant Toskig yelled.

The recruits could barely raise their arms to salute Toskig and the Undermage. Rank by sweaty, exhausted rank, they shuffled off towards the low building at the end of the training yard. Some of them were bleeding from several cuts, others had fresh, blossoming bruises to nurse. Others looked like the walking dead.

Toskig clapped the Undermage on the back as he picked up his cape. Even he was sweating. 'Maybe I'll come back again tomorrow.'

'We may need all the help we can get, but you, sir, have got a wedding to attend.'

Modren smiled. 'That I do, Sergeant. You are invited, you know?'

'It would be an honour, sir, but these recruits…' he trailed off. Modren understood. Toskig was a good soldier and an even better instructor.

'We'll save you some boar, then,' Modren said, fastening the straps of his vambraces with his teeth.

'Ale would be better, your Mage.'

Modren was caught mid-laugh as a red-faced messenger darted across the training yard and skidded to a halt. He barely saluted before the words came tumbling out of his mouth. 'Undermage Modren, sir, he's back.'

Modren crossed his arms and furrowed his brow. 'Who's back?'

The messenger looked confused. 'Arkmage Durnus said you'd understand…?'

The realisation struck like a sling-stone.

❦

Heimdall rubbed his eyes and looked again. He had never needed to look twice before, not in all his uncountable years, but now he was doing exactly that.

It was absolutely unmistakable. The gryphon swung low over

the matchstick masts of the port and then climbed into the air with several huge beats of his wings. Heimdall could already hear the screams in the streets as Ilios skimmed the chimneys and rooftops.

Heimdall could already pick out the fair face of a young god, and the bloodied, gaunt face of another sitting behind him, stubbornly refusing to hang on. His arms were crossed tightly.

It could be no other.

'Verix…' he began, but she was already moving.

'I'll get the Arkmages,' replied the goddess, as she quickly jogged down the marble steps, leaving Heimdall alone to shake his head, partly in awe, partly in trepidation.

Farden had finally returned.

1568 years ago

the world was a bucket of mud, tipped on its side. Heavy-footed and uneasy, Korrin stood in the middle of it, like a hatted statue presiding over an overflowing delta. Rain dripped down his nose from a hole in his hat. Rivulets pestered his boots. Pebbles rattled past as the rain chased them. He lifted his head from studying his feet. Lightning scorched the glum sky in the east and showed the fractured islands in the bay. He was thankful for the dark. He had yet to recognise any of the men, or to be recognised himself.

The rain did its best to keep the mudpigs in their huts and the farmers in their cottages, but the day's work had not finished with the coming of the storm. Troughs needed to be filled. Fences hammered. Gates repaired. It would be a while before muddy boots could be kicked off in front of the hearth, welcomed with a cup of warm ale and a fire to help the cold.

Korrin took a hesitant step forward, his first in half an hour, towards the most familiar of the cottages. There were eight of them altogether, all in a semi-circle around a fat cluster of pig pens. The oil lanterns did their level best to light their muddy doors and porches. In the pens, mudpigs waddled to and fro, fat and glistening with the rain. Korrin could feel the kiss of cold snouts in his palms as his eyes ran over them. He could hear their snorting and snuffling against the rain.

Korrin.

He made a sour face.

Korrin could wrench a man's arm from his socket with a simple twist of his fingers. He could run for miles across ice and rock and never fear for tiredness. He could splice a hair down its centre with a throwing knife. He could even topple the giant they called Balimuel. And yet, standing in the mud outside his father's hut, he was frozen and clumsy. He was cloth-tongued and scrawny. He was a boy again. Just like he had expected.

He looked back the way he had come. The Pens weren't here. They weren't to know. With that thought in his mind, he turned to leave.

The man who shouted to him had other ideas. 'Ho, young sir! Lad!' Korrin grit his teeth and turned back. A man was struggling with an empty trough. His back was bent nearly double with age and the others were too busy helping themselves to aid him.

'Lend an old farmer your young muscles, could ye?'

If his father had instilled anything useful in him, it was that Korrin didn't have an impolite bone in his body. Even though his mind sighed and threw up its hands, Korrin trudged forward to help the old man.

'Thank ye, lad,' said the old man. Korrin picked up the corner of the trough. The man brandished a sack of rotten vegetables, and Korrin hefted it into his shoulder. Old practice moved his hands, untwisting the wire, spilling the pig-slop in even piles, not a spot falling on his clothes. Not that it mattered, in the mud. The man patted him on the arm. 'You've done that before.'

Korrin just nodded and smiled. He turned to leave, but the old farmer caught him by the elbow and turned him into the lanternlight. 'I know you,' he said, squinting. There was a sword hanging from Korrin's belt. The man tutted at that. Swords were foreigners in this place. 'At least, I know your eyes.'

'I think you've made a mistake. I'm just passing through...' he mumbled.

'You don't pass through *Pollokstead, lad. This here's the end of the road. Or the start of it,' he tapped his nose. 'Depending on how you look at it. Does your father know you're here, or your grandfer?'*

'I...'

The old man suddenly called out to the others bustling through the mud with rope and tackle. 'Ho, Ust!' he called, looking about.

One of them, standing at the door of Korrin's old cottage, tipped back his waxed hat. 'What?' he yelled over the drumming of the rain.

'This lad looks a lot like your son!'

'Can't be. My son done run off!'

'Well, come and 'ave a look!'

Boots met mud, and there he was, Korrin's father, framed by oil-light and flecks of rain. He left his door and strode forward to confront the two. Already his arms were crossed. Already his face had creased into its stern glower. A hard man, was Ust. Korrin stood as tall as he could and folded his hands behind his back, naturally, and rather unconsciously, coming smartly to attention.

Ust stopped short, and thumbed the rain from his nose. 'Ain't no son of mine that wears a sword,' he muttered. The old man felt the hard edge to Ust's words and shuffled away.

Korrin stood alone with his father. He too could feel the jab of his words. It was that same tone that had first stoked the fires of escape and resentment several years ago. His only reply was to bow his head. Korrin stared at his boots again, feeling as though the last year had never happened.

'So what fort-lord did ye swear fealty to? Hmm, to get that sword, boy? Which one took ye in?'

Korrin shook his head. 'None.' He could almost hear his father's sea-washed face creaking as his glowering deepened.

'Tell me you ain't no sell-sword then.'

'No.'

More glowering. 'A bandit? A rogue? Is that what my son left his father for?'

'No.'

'Then what? What cursed life did ye run to?'

Korrin frowned at that mud. His father's tone made him flinch from practice. Ust was as tough as his pig-wrangling hands. He had beaten fear and resentment into Korrin with more than just words.

But despite it all, Korrin couldn't help but chuckle at the question. He hadn't the faintest clue. He said as much as he looked up and met his father's stern eyes, forcing himself to meet them, as he had forced himself from his bed every day for the past year. 'I don't know. But by Jot's roots, I'm good at it.'

'Well at least yer good for somethin', I tell ye,' said Ust. It was in that moment that something clicked for Korrin. As he looked at his father, the small, tough man with hard eyes, at the mudpigs snuffling in their pens, at the mud running between his boots, he realised none of it mattered. The world was so much bigger than this, this place, this wiry little man. He knew more of it than any of these farmers. How dare they judge, when their horizons are so small.

'Yes,' Korrin smiled. 'I am.'

chapter 18

"Do I police them or ban them? That is the question.
I once heard a tale of giant wild fires in the forests of the east, far beyond the Fool Roads. They say that these fires are not natural, but man-made. They ravage miles of land and belch smoke higher than the mountains. The tribes that set these fires shepherd them by scorching the earth in their path, guiding and leading them on. Why do they set these fires? Once the fires have died, the strangest fruits appear from the ashes. It appears that there are strange seeds buried in the eastern earth. To flower they need the scorching heat of a forest fire to wake them into sprouting. These seeds produce trees that are food, oil, husk, and wood to these tribes. Life, in seed-form.
The magick markets are like wild fires. Do I allow them to ravage this city, in the hope that they will bear fruit, corralling them as and when I can? Or do I refuse to light them at all, and go without these fruits? One thing is certain, whatever our decision, the Councils will disagree."

Excerpt from the diary of Arkmage Durnus, dated Frostfall 899

3 days earlier

Farden cracked an eye and stared at the bowed ceiling. He tested his mouth. His lips were dry and cracked. He lay in silence, waiting to see if the panic had truly died in his sleep. Mercifully, it had. Its corpse was a numb ache right between his eyes.

Farden sat up and groaned as the headache blossomed with his movement. A hangover times a hundred. It would subside as soon as he was on the road, he told himself.

The mage swung his legs over the bed and hoisted himself upright. There it was: a bag of nevermar on the floor. Farden shot it a dark look. It had deserted him, just when he needed it most. Just when his past had come back to haunt him. Come to taint his beach. Farden looked out the window. There he was, sitting cross-legged and pensive by the fire, still wearing his strange leather coat. Ilios was nowhere to be seen. Jeasin was in the water, cleaning herself with sand and clumps of sea-grass.

It was a soft day, its edges blurred with early sea-mist. The sun was a good height above the horizon and already the air was warm, tempered only by the crisp breeze coming off the rippling water. It would be hot later. The wispy clouds hovering high overhead might have spoken of evening rain.

There was a whooshing sound as wings passed over the shack, making the roof rattle in their wake. Farden watched Ilios land softly on the beach. There was an enormous fish stuck in his beak. Loki looked up as the dripping gryphon stood over him. Ilios dropped the fish right in his lap and the god cried out. Farden couldn't help but snigger.

Farden realised he was still shirtless and dangerous, so he cast around for his shirt and quickly put it on. His stomach growled angrily at him. The weakness in his limbs was still very apparent. His body had a long way to go before it was healed. Farden could feel the clamminess of last night's sweating on his skin, and he glared at the nevermar again. That hadn't helped matters.

How had it turned to poison? He wracked his brains, searching for some excuse or a rational explanation, anything that could save him the pain of it failing him.

Maybe it had soured.

Maybe it was a bad batch.

Maybe Bastio had tricked him.

It had worked before.

Maybe he was too tired.

That had never been an issue.

Maybe his body was too weak.

Neither had that.

Maybe Loki had poisoned it.

He couldn't have.

Arguments and answers battled to and fro. Farden shut his eyes and silenced them. The true answer was inevitable. His body had had its fill of it. Farden clenched his fist, grit his teeth, and stamped on the little bag of traitorous weed. Once, twice, three times, and each time was more vicious than the last. When the floorboards began to splinter, he stopped, letting the headache and weakness congratulate him. The mage took a deep breath and sighed.

At least Farden still had one last crutch. Out of the corner of his eye he spied a mud-covered pillowcase leaning up against the door. His armour.

He had worn his vambraces several times since the escape from Tayn, but only for short periods during the day when Jeasin had been sleeping. The feeling of their cold caress was almost euphoric, but Farden had promised himself he would wait to don it all until he and Jeasin were completely safe.

Farden peeled back the crusty pillowcase and revealed the glittering metal underneath. He quickly slid the vambraces on, then the gauntlets, and lastly the greaves. He could feel their cold touch even through his grubby cloth trousers. The metal slithered and whispered as it hugged him. The mage stayed crouching beside the door for a little while as he savoured the strange, yet familiar, sensation spreading through his veins and tired muscles. How he'd missed it. A little smile hovered on his lips for a short while. It looked foreign on his face, given the circumstances.

When he had finished relishing the feel of the armour, Farden left the shack and strode onto the beach. The metal around his limbs glittered in the late morning sun. Loki and Ilios looked up. Jeasin was busy washing. He came to a halt by the fire, which Loki was busy trying to re-light.

Farden didn't waste any time getting to his point.

'Whilst I'm sure your message is utterly thrilling and of the utmost importance, Loki, I'm afraid you've wasted your time coming here. You too, Ilios,' Farden stated. The gryphon growled softly. 'I'm leaving at midday. Don't follow me.'

Loki shrugged. 'Suit yourself,' he said.

That wasn't the answer Farden had been expecting. 'You hear me, god? You've wasted your time. I'm not interested in whatever message they've asked you to deliver.'

'I knew you wouldn't be,' Loki nonchalantly replied. 'I told them the very same thing. But they wouldn't listen. I said you'd want to be left alone to your pitiful existence. In your shack, with your nevermar and your armour. Killing things for coin. That after all this time you wouldn't care about her.'

Farden raised an eyebrow. 'Who?'

But Loki held up his hands and shook his head. 'No, no, I've said enough as it is. You're not interested, Farden. I'll save you the trouble. Wouldn't want to add any more bad memories to your growing mound.'

The mage shot him a murderous look and sat down. Ilios took a few steps back and sat down. Farden met his eyes. 'And you can stop looking at me like that, Ilios. My decision is final.' Ilios warbled something and looked away.

Loki took a little knife and a grubby potato from one of his pockets. He began to slice it into chunks, making a musical thud every time they hit the bottom of the rusty stew pot. The resurrected fire slowly began to crackle and lick at its sides. 'I think you've offended him,' he said, nodding towards the gryphon.

Farden pinched his aching forehead between his fingers. 'What do you expect from me? What do any of you expect from me?'

'Nothing. We're just extending a simple invitation, that's all,' Loki said with an innocent face.

'Stop it. Your games aren't going to work on me, god.'

The three sat in silence for a moment. Jeasin had escaped the icy cold of the water and was trundling slowly up the beach. Her sandy hair was even sandier than ever before, and tangled with the salt. Her face and eyes were red from where she had scrubbed them vigourously, almost like she had been crying. Almost. Her robe was wet from the sea, and barely clung about her.

She'd heard the mage's voice. 'You're alive are you? Shame,' she called.

'Only just,' came the muttered reply.

Jeasin shuffled forward with her arms outstretched. She stopped when she heard the thud of another chunk of potato in the pot. 'What are you talking about?'

'Farden is leaving. Alone,' Loki informed her. Farden glowered. He resisted the urge to punch him. Loki could see the intention in the mage's dark eyes and got to his feet. 'Need some water for the stew,' he said, announcing his retreat to the water's edge.

'You're leavin' then,' she stated, her anger simmering just under the surface. Farden could see it waiting to erupt.

'That I am,' he said.

'Heartless.

'I told you. I prac…'

'How'd you do it? How'd you cut out bits of your heart and toss 'em away?'

'I…'

'How'd you turn your back so damn coldly? It ain't human.'

Farden didn't reply.

Jeasin walked a little closer. 'You told me what you left behind once, when you were drunk. Krauslung. Arkmages. Magick councils. You don't remember it, I know you don't. I didn't believe you. Thought it a story for the pillow, like all the other men tell. They make 'em up just for somethin' to say. Make 'emselves sound bigger and better than they really are. Sad, really. I took you for one of them.'

'And do you believe me now?'

Jeasin spat. 'Not in the slightest. Arkmages. Arkathedrals. What rubbish. But the bits you told me about you leaving your loved ones behind, turnin' your back on them? I believe that bit. Now that I'm seein' it in action.'

'You're still not coming. I'm a curse.'

The anger bubbled up. 'You're damn right you are, but you're still takin' me with you! I ain't going to be another one of those,' she waved her hand, 'those you left 'cross the sea, whoever they are. I'm going with you!'

Farden tried to stop the words from coming, but they forced their way out anyway. Truth always did, just like it always hurt. 'I've no need for a whore any more, Jeasin. There are plenty of those in Krauslung!' he shouted at her.

Jeasin turned away. After trilling something damning, the gryphon did too. He followed her to the shack, sitting down next to its step like an odd-shaped door. Farden punched the sand with a red-gold fist, eliciting a futile thud. He looked around for something to break. Loki was returning from the sea, bearing a pot full of water. *That might do*. 'You didn't handle that very well, did you?'

Farden got to his feet. 'Go fuck yourself,' he cursed.

Loki let him storm two strides before delivering his killing strike. 'She's getting married, Farden,' he said, stopping the mage in his sandy tracks. Loki continued. 'Elessi. She's getting married. Three days from now. She thought you might want to be there.'

It took Farden a full minute to turn back around. When he did, it was with his fist. He struck Loki hard in the face, just to the right of his nose. Surprisingly, Loki didn't stop him. He took everything the blow had to offer and more besides, landing hard on his rear. Farden may have been weak, but he was angry, and that made up for whatever his knuckles might have lacked. Loki scrunched up his face and blinked, tasting the odd sensation the fist had left in his face.

'I hope that was a new experience for you,' Farden spat on him. His armour clinked as he stormed up the beach. It felt good to hit a god.

Loki simply smiled as Farden disappeared over a ridge of boulders. His message had been delivered. It would work its magick on him, slowly but surely. Like a worm gnawing through an apple. Loki rubbed his face, and then tested his nostrils and lip for blood. He needn't have bothered. After all, shadows didn't bleed. He couldn't help but wonder what colour it would be if they did.

❦

Two hours later, and Farden was still sitting under his ash tree at the lip of the hill. The bark was sturdy and warm behind his back. The wind tasted of salt. A few seagulls wheeled overhead. In the branches above him, a sparrow sang to the afternoon.

'What do I do?' Farden voiced the question aloud to the barren wilderness. The only answer he got was the little slap of a winged seed falling in his lap. Farden looked down at the tiny thing and picked it up. It had one solitary wing like that of a dragonfly, with brown veins running through its translucent paper. At the end of the wing was the seed itself. Again, brown, wrapped in a husk. Farden held it by the tip of the wing and looked up. From what he could remember of spring, trees needed leaves before they could sprout fruit. There were no others hanging from the branches or dangling from the brittle grey twigs. *Ambitious little thing*, he thought.

Farden twirled it around in his cracked fingers and watched how the sunlight shone through its wing. *Spinning Jennies*. The name floated up out of the misty depths of his memories, a trickle of silliness. That's what the other children had called them. Spinning Jennies. He faintly remembered standing on a rock and tossing handfuls of them into the air. Farden could hear delighted little screams echo in his ears.

His childhood had been locked away with the other memories, though not on purpose. A memory grew mould and eroded just like every other relic. Time had done the groundwork; nevermar had finished the job.

'Ugh,' sighed the mage, and for the third time that hour, Farden tried to make sense of it all, splayed out in front of him like the crumpled landscape.

For years he had been living in self-induced shadow, crouched and hidden in a fog of his own making. The road he had taken there had been swallowed up and forgotten. He had enjoyed the numbness of it. It had been dark and cold of course, but it was his. Now he could feel the fog lifting and the sunlight barging its way in. He feared it. Despised it. It was a big beaming ray of change, and what had already been burnt away could never be found again. His fog had been permanently cleared. He had cursed it, fought it, and clawed at it, but to no avail. Something had changed. The Duke was gone. The nevermar had abandoned him. Krauslung had climbed back into his thoughts. He sighed again. Like it or not, his little world had crumbled.

Farden rubbed his grizzled chin. The mage looked up at the frayed rope dangling above him, and he remembered what he had told himself, standing knife-drawn and ready over Kint and Forluss: *alive was something.*

'Well,' he said, beating the wilderness to an answer. 'Alive is something. But am I living?' *No*. He was merely existing. He thought of the leper of Wodehallow, and the wise words he had spoken on the way to the keep. Of life and how a man could squander it. How the very gift of living deserved better. Gods, what was his name? Farden scrabbled to remember it, but it evaded him. He scrunched up his eyes.

Elessi was getting married, and according to Loki, she had invited him despite everything. She deserved better than another stab of disappointment on her wedding day, he thought. They all deserved better. Traffyd and Seria. Durnus. Tyrfing. All of them. The thought of that almost made him laugh. It would have been a laugh without a trace of pleasure. He had spent countless evenings vowing exile and solitude, all the while obliterating his old life with blood and drugs. They had sent countless messengers, innumerable scouts, they had even sent a god to fetch him! But after everything, Elessi was the one who could finally do it. Farden had always harboured the secret fear that a certain female would one day haul him back to his old life. He had never expected it to be Elessi. Somebody else. He clenched a fist and shivered at the thought of *her*.

Farden let another memory drift down onto his tongue. He spoke it aloud. 'We could have buried ourselves at the bottom of the ocean and fate would still have dragged us ashore by the scruff of our necks,' he muttered. Durnus had said that. Farden closed his eyes and took several deep breaths. Was this it? He would have nowhere to hide. Questions would be asked. Painful subjects would be raised. He would be naked, strung out on a rack under a desert sun. Was it finally time?

'Shit,' he said to the wilderness. He looked up at the rope again.

This life had nearly killed him. It was time to find another.

Farden put the seed in his pocket and got to his feet. He looked at the little flint cottage in the distance. He could just about make out the sandy furrows of Traffyd's little fields. If he squinted, he could imagine a little cloud of pipe-smoke hovering over the back porch. Farden shook his head. That was not for him. He looked down at his wrists and metal hands. Farmers had no need for armour.

With feet that moved more eagerly than he would like, Farden went down the hill and kicked open the door to his shack. He looked around at its discoloured, pilfered walls and its rusty iron nails bent into hooks. He looked at the splintered floor and the scattered mouldy straw. He looked down at the bed where Jeasin wore a face like thunder.

'We're leaving,' he announced, in a low voice.

'*We*?' Jeasin echoed.

'Yes, we. Us. Plural.'

Her icy expression didn't change. Farden didn't blame her. 'Where?'

'We're going to a wedding.'

Jeasin couldn't have looked more contemptuous. 'A wedding? Who would dare invite you to a weddin'?'

Farden stopped in his tracks, halfway to the back door. 'An old friend that I once hurt very much,' he said.

'And what made you change your mind, jus' like that?' Jeasin snapped her fingers.

'A rope and an ash tree,' he replied with a shrug. Jeasin looked confused, but Farden couldn't elaborate even if he'd wanted to. It was hard to put it into words. Voicing his thoughts had never been his strong point. 'That, and she deserves better from me, after all these years. She always did. They all do,' he said, as he dug what belongings he deemed necessary from under the mess. He almost forgot to grab his notebook.

'Who's she?'

'You'll see,' Farden answered.

'You promise? This ain't no trick?'

Farden looked her right in the very centre of her blue eyes. 'I promise.'

Jeasin crossed her arms. 'Why should I trust you, after what you said to me?'

'You don't have to trust me. I'll send the gryphon back for you as soon as I arrive,' Farden called as he hopped out of the back door.

'Wait!' Jeasin felt her way out of the shack. Farden was already on the beach, saying something about Whiskers. Ilios and Loki watched with blank expressions. Jeasin stamped her foot, almost driving her heel through the wood of the doorstep. 'You're coming *back* for us? No, no! I don't think so. Not after your little speech! This is a trick!'

'I made a promise, Jeasin. This one, for bloody once, I'll keep.'

'Gods curse you if you're lyin', Farden. Gods curse you.'

'We'll see to that,' Loki called from the fireside.

A finger jabbed in his direction. 'I'm holdin' you responsible if he don't, stranger. And that creature too, whatever it is.'

'Gryphon,' Farden muttered.

Loki stood up, not bothering to hide his contented smile as he dusted off his hands. He went to stand by Ilios and watched the beast preen his feathers, ready to fly. Farden was scrambling about in the doorway, busy packing a haversack. 'So what changed your mind?' called the god.

Farden glanced at him over his shoulder. The god's face hadn't even bruised. That nettled him. 'You know perfectly well what did, Loki. Now shut up and climb on that gryphon,' Farden ordered. Loki buttoned his leather coat and did as the mage had so politely instructed. He didn't care; he had won. The smile loitering on his face said so.

'You not saying goodbye to Traffyd? Seria?' he asked.

Farden spared a moment to bite his lip. 'I'll send a hawk.'

Loki shrugged, and clambered on to the gryphon. Before Farden did the same, he knelt down and reached under a certain floorboard, feeling around for a little wooden box. His fingers soon found it, and he prised it open in the mouldy darkness. There it was. Forgotten, but not lost. Something hard and rough, wrapped in a skinny metal chain. Farden lifted the little thing from the darkness and fastened it around his neck. It was a little dragon's scale on a necklace, an old gift from a one-eyed Siren. It glittered briefly in the sunlight before he tucked it under the collar of his dirty shirt. 'I'm going to need all the luck I can get,' he whispered to himself, marching back onto the beach. It was the first time he had worn it in a decade. Up until now, he hadn't felt worthy of luck.

Grunting and heaving, he pulled himself onto the gryphon's back and sat down behind Loki. He looked back at his little shack. Jeasin was leaning against the wall. She was pouting, her arms firmly crossed. He shook his head. She would eat her bitter words. This was one promise he wasn't going to break.

Just before he turned away, a small black object emerged from the door and scurried over the pebbles and sand towards them, a little blur of feet and fur. Farden couldn't help but cheer quietly to himself, and chide himself too, for almost forgetting. Holding tightly to a clump of Ilios' feathers, Farden leant down and Whiskers jumped into his open gauntlet. He quickly stashed him inside his haversack and yanked hard on the straps around his shoulders.

I'm going back, he realised, in a flash-flood of unease. *I'm going back*.

Farden took a very deep breath indeed.

'Krauslung, Ilios,' the mage called to the gryphon, biting down on his fear. He gripped Ilios' sides with his legs, and held on tight to the ridge of feathers and fur running along his spine. The words felt very odd on his lips. He couldn't quite figure out if he was returning home or leaving it. It would all depend on what awaited him.

After trotting around in a circle, obviously pleased with the calibre of his passengers, Ilios spread his wings high. The breeze rustled in his pinions. He hunkered down briefly before exploding into the air like a bolt from a bow, leaving a cloud of sand in his wake. Soon they were flapping high into the blue sky, heading east to a wedding, and gods know what else.

chapter 19

"Admissions Notes - Summer 852. Written Class. Applicant - Male. 18 years. Existing skill - High. Potential - High. Family - Everwit's son, mage of some repute. Notes: Blacksmith's boy. Old, for an applicant. Master Rufellish believes him to be too old, but I believe he demonstrates the exact qualities young Vice is looking for. Tenacious. Fast-learner. Not a leader, but a fighter. He will have to be tamed, however. I will put his name before the others - Tyrfing."

Found in the desk of Master Wust, in 877, during the trial of the Written mage Tyrfing

As the tired gryphon's claws scraped against the smooth marble floor of the Nest, Tyrfing and Modren took a sharp intake of breath. They couldn't help it. Call it shock, call it sadness, call it downright relief that he was even alive, Farden was a sore sight for sore eyes. Only the gods beside them remained emotionless and still.

Farden looked like a dead man in a stolen body.

It was probably a mercy for Durnus that he couldn't see the gaunt mess of a mage that slid down from the gryphon's back. He heard the sound of boots hitting marble, and an uneasy clearing of somebody's throat.

Farden wasn't sure what to do with himself, a feeling he hated immediately. He stood there like a statue of embarrassment and just scratched his sandy scalp. Scanning the faces standing before him, he was unsure of whether they were happy to see him, or angry, or upset, or just being polite. His headache pounded mockingly.

Durnus could sense the awkwardness in his old friend. He smiled and stepped forward, one hand outstretched, and waited. After several moments, a familiar yet weary voice spoke to him through the darkness. 'I never thought I'd see you in an Arkmage's robe.' Farden sounded tired.

'Well at least one of us can,' he smiled, pointing to his eyes. He could hear Farden biting his lip. Footsteps approached, and a cold metal hand embraced his. Durnus used his other hand to trace the armour up his wrist and then to his arm. He followed the contours of his knotted shoulders to his grimy neck, and then to his face, where the sharpness of the mage's cheekbones and the rough patches of dry skin and scratches almost made him wince. The years had beaten Farden into a scarred pulp. And yet, there was a strange element to his skin that softened the blow for Durnus. Feeling a little uncomfortable, Farden closed his eyes as Durnus' fingers probed his forehead and the corners of his face. No matter where he touched, there were no lines nor creases of age to be found. Durnus smiled and patted the mage's armoured wrist. 'The years have been kind to you,' he said, with a sigh.

'Kind isn't really a word I'd use,' muttered Farden, staring back at his old friend. Old was truly the word. Although Durnus had barely aged since they had last parted, Farden had completely forgotten what he'd looked like. It slowly crept back to him as he took in Durnus' wispy silver hair, his pale face and thin, yet clever lips. Only his eyes had changed; their once pale hue had been wrapped in grey mist and hidden away behind blindness. A lycan's goodbye kiss.

Farden turned to face the others. The first two he didn't recognise. One was a very tall man with tawny eyes. The other was a willowy woman with strange sea-green hair. The last two he did recognise, but only just.

Fifteen years was a long time for any man. For Tyrfing, already in the latter years of his life, it was a very long time indeed. Farden felt a twinge in his chest as his eyes roved over his uncle's face. Tyrfing's black hair was now streaked with grey, like veins of silver running through seams of coal. The same was true of his beard. His blue eyes were beset on all sides by lines and the bruises of tiredness. Webs of wrinkles had crept into his hands and neck. They looked intent on staying. He too wore a white and gold Arkmage's robe. Farden didn't know which was more surprising: a pale king on the marble thrones, or a once-banished Written.

Farden didn't smile, but instead walked forward with his arms wide. Tyrfing met his embrace eagerly. It was quicker than he'd liked. As Tyrfing stepped back, he looked down at the armour wrapped around his nephew's limbs and then back to his face. He could see that despite the grime and scars of his exile, he hadn't aged a day. Tyrfing chuckled drily. 'So, the rumours of Scalussen are true. I didn't quite believe them until now,' he remarked.

Farden nodded and shrugged. He felt a strange sort of guilt then, a guilt at having the blessing of the armour. Tyrfing had gone on ageing while Farden hadn't. Farden tried to ignore it. 'I told you,' he said.

'You're making the rest of us look bad,' stated Modren. Farden turned to him and weakly tried to match his smile. Modren looked good. The mage had grown out his white-blonde hair, and even sprouted a matching goatee. He positively glittered in his suit of silver armour. He had a black and green cape fastened to his shoulders. It wavered and crackled in the wind.

Farden scratched his head again. 'Looks like I have a lot to catch up on,' he mumbled. 'Undermage.'

'All in good time, Farden,' said Modren, reaching for his gauntleted hand with his own. Farden hesitated, but Modren had already seized him in a tight, friendly grip. Underneath their armour, only one set of keys glowed. Modren could feel the lack of magick in his friend. His smile faded at the corners, but he held his tongue. 'All in good time.'

'Well!' Durnus clapped his hands to shatter the mood. 'This is all a bit too serious, isn't it? Not to my liking. We should be celebrating your return, Farden. This feels more like a funeral.'

'Well that would be fitting, considering,' said a dry voice from behind the Arkmage. They turned around to see Loki leaning against one of the marble trees. His arms were crossed, and his face impassive. Farden glared at him. He had hoped that his punch had knocked some silence into the god, but his ability to annoy persisted.

Farden held up his hands to his uncle and old friends. 'No celebrations, please. I wouldn't be able…' he trailed off, his tongue dry. 'I can't explain… I don't…'

'We understand,' said Tyrfing. Farden nodded. He was probably the only one who did.

'What would you like?' asked Modren.

Farden rubbed his wind-numbed face. It took him a moment to decide. He looked down at his drab, ripped, and sandy clothing and shrugged. 'A decent cloak. One with a hood,' he muttered through cracked lips. 'And a bath.'

The others couldn't help but chuckle. Farden, whatever little of him remained, had finally returned.

❦

The bath, it turned out, was too long in coming. Farden paced about the room like a caged sabre-cat, not sure whether to sit, stand, or slump. As he sauntered past the tall window, he stared out at the city for the hundredth time. He had insisted on a room in the lower level of the Arkathedral, away from the prying eyes of the magick council, away from the hustle, the bustle. His humble room stared right out into a forest of lofty chimney pots. Some shone in their virgin placements. Soot and moss slicked the rest.

Farden looked out and scratched his beard. What was he waiting for, besides the bath? For it all to sink in? Or for the dream to subside and fall out from under him? He was waiting mainly for his headache to disappear, but he knew it would be pestering him for a while yet. The nevermar was still having its way with him. Was he waiting to feel better, or to feel worse? He was waiting to feel something, that was for sure. Something that nudged the needle, to tell him whether he had made a mistake or not. Whatever it was, it was taking its sweet merry time about it.

Farden had never been one for waiting.

Looking out on his long-forgotten city, Farden decided he would wait no longer. The city's innards were calling to him, and the urge to melt into them grew unbearable. The bath could wait.

Farden turned on his heel and wrestled his way into the new clothes that had been draped over the corner of his borrowed bed. They felt soft, and that softness was a foreign quality that made him wary.

'Little steps,' Farden said aloud. He shimmied out of his armour and laid it aside, then shrugged off his torn crimson cloak and his road-ragged shirt. The trousers fell in a heap next to them. Moving quickly to ignore the bruises and scars, he put on the new clothes and made for the door.

❦

Half an hour later and he was standing on the cobbles of a city he barely recognised. The nevermar wasn't to blame for that. Fifteen years was a lifetime for a city as well as a man, especially for one he had left in a state of corpsehood and destruction.

Farden hoisted up his hood like a shield and struck out for

Krauslung's very centre. He took his steps slowly; partly to take it in, partly for the sake of his aching legs. The day was cool. The sun warm. The city was in the busy throes of a dying market day.

Krauslung was a honeycombed madness. Its alleys and curving streets seemed narrower and deeper than he remembered. He felt as if he were an ant in a canyon of doors, gutters, awnings, and criss-cross windowpanes. Farden didn't really mind. Here he could disappear in plain sight. He remembered liking this. It had been his first and favourite hobby in his younger days.

As he stumbled into the first of the countless market squares, Farden also encountered his first preacher.

At the corner of two alleyways, a man stood tall on a little wooden stage. He was all forehead and nose. A confident man, burly, with a sense of a brawler about him. His hair had been dyed a purple-red, like an angry bruise. There was a Siren tattoo on his cheek, and cheaply done at that. He was being heckled between sentences by passersby, sentences that he delivered in a deliberate drawl, as of speaking to an audience of morons. 'Thron,' he droned. 'Is a god above gods!'

'Someone better help him down then!'

'A wise and powerful figure, half god, half mighty dragon.'

'And he ain't half ugly-looking, neither! Bahaha!'

Farden was confused to say the least. A pair of guards stood nearby, in Evernia colours. He was surprised to see them ignoring this preacher. Nobody would have dared do such a thing a decade or two ago. Farden considered heckling the man himself, just to be belligerent, but he thought better of it.

As Farden walked on, he quickly realised the man was not alone. His competition stood on every other street corner, each bellowing their own brand of neurotic nonsense. Every step Farden took towards the centre of the city, the louder Krauslung became. As the streets widened, so did the crowds. Taverns spilled out onto the road in colourful umbrellas and fenced areas, replete with tables and chairs, packed with drinkers soaking up their fair share of beer and the last of the day's sun. Many of the men were smoking pipes. Farden ached to join them, but he had no coin nor pipe. He wandered on.

He soon encountered a magick market. He had scowled at them before, and he scowled at them now. *Meddlers*, he thought, eyeing the wares of a passing table. "Wigs! Fine Heifer-tail wigs that change colour with your mood!" screamed a painted sign. The man at the stall seemed to be wearing no less than four wigs, all on top of each other. The merchant must have been either a halfwit or deeply confused, for they all cycled through a various array of colours before the crowd stole Farden away.

At another stall, a woman in short skirts was trying on a brass shoe etched with flames and feathers. She put one foot on the floor and it began to vibrate, and violently too. She barely managed to get the thing off before it clattered down the street. The merchant chased after it, much to the laughter of a nearby tavern-crowd. Farden shook his head. Magick was for the trained or for the trinket, not for everyone. It angered him to see it so available, after all he had done to attain it.

Farden escaped to where a little hill rose under the cobbles, like a ripple in a grey carpet. There the buildings cleared just enough to allow a wanderer like him to stare out at the busy port. It seemed as though the water had been replaced with ships. There was barely enough room for them to manoeuvre out to open water. Krauslung truly was a hive, he thought. More so than ever. Farden then turned to gaze back at the mountains, and that was when he saw it.

He began moving almost immediately, heading directly north like an arrow with a hood. Pushing men and women aside and not caring for their complaints, Farden pressed on through the crowds and gawpers. The day was drawing its smoke-blue curtains. The night was coming, and with it the evening crowds: those off to see the twinkling of the ship-lights, those heading to the night-markets, or to a feast, those in need of pockets to pick, and those in need of ale or meat or whoring or all the above. Cities were all the same, at their hearts, fifteen years or no.

At the gates the guards were warning the passers-through that they would soon be shutting the city. As he wandered out into the field beyond, Farden gazed up at the thick walls and the giant gatehouse, every part of it bigger and deeper and taller than he remembered. The spear-tips of the portcullises, tucked up neatly in their grooves, caught the fading sunlight. Farden gazed up at the runes hammered into the stone of the arches, in the hinges of the gates, thick as a man is long. Whispers in his mind read them to him. Lock spells, slip spells, slow spells, and more… The Arkmages' handiwork, he presumed.

Farden stepped out from under the shadow of the monstrous gates. He had to smile wryly to himself; not an hour in the city and already he was leaving it. He paused and turned to take in the span of the walls once again, and caught sight of eyes watching him intently. They blinked and looked away. Their owners slipped back into the lines filtering through the gates. Farden shook his head. They didn't trust him quite yet, and Farden didn't blame them.

The mage set his feet to the well-trodden dust of the road. One half of its width led people into the battlemented maw of the city, while the other half pointed north to the green hill, the brown smudge of Manesmark, and the snow-capped mountains beyond. Along the road and around the gate, tents sprang up from the grass like brightly-coloured boulders. Campfires were already roaring. Even an impromptu market had cleared a space for itself and was busy enticing last-minute buyers before they escaped north.

A clatter of feet rushed up behind him. A hand caught his arm. Farden raised a fist, but he stopped himself when he found Modren standing beside him, a concerned look on his face.

'Farden,' began the Undermage. His brow was furrowed like a

spring field. His eyes flicked up to the Manesmark hill. ‘Where are you going?’

Farden chuckled drily. ‘Don’t trust me?’ he asked.

Modren let him go. ‘I trust you. I always have. Why don’t we go find a pair of stools in a tavern somewhere? We’ve got some grog to catch up on.’

The mention of ale set Farden’s mouth watering, but he shook his head. ‘There’s somebody I’ve got to see first,’ he said. He turned his back but Modren caught him again.

‘But evening’s falling. You must be tired.’

Farden blinked at his friend. ‘What’s wrong, Modren? What are you up to?’

It was his friend’s eyes that betrayed him the most. They flicked again to the hill and its new Spire, to the white specks at its base. Suspicion crept into his mind like a bony spider. ‘Is there something I should know?’ he asked.

Modren swallowed, then shook his head. ‘No, it’s fine.’ He released Farden a second time, and it was his turn to move away, towards the gate. ‘If you want me, there’s a tavern, on Friedja Street. It’s called the *Captain’s Folly*. I believe you know the place; it was once called the *Bearded Goat*. I’ll be there.’

Farden nodded, watching his friend leave. His narrowed gaze faded, but the spidery suspicion remained. He kept moving, feeling the ache settling into his calves and thighs as he set his feet to the hill. He knew it would be a long walk, but he willed himself into it.

And a long walk it was. Two hours it took him, with plenty of rests in between. Farden played catch with his breath while he leant against a boulder at the top of the hill. The past few weeks had beggared his muscles. If there was a god of fitness, then he must have been laughing from the firmament, thought Farden. His lungs were full of hot coals, and his armour made him feel as though bags of lead had been strapped to his limbs.

Wheezing, Farden assessed the path ahead, where the dusty road levelled out and then rolled straight down into the main thoroughfare of Manesmark. Her cobbles swallowed up the road like a cannibalistic snake.

Manesmark was a military town. It was easy to see that in the way the buildings kept each other at arm's length, and in the angles of the alleyways and roads. It may have been a military town, but that didn't mean it was blessed with quiet and order. Like the city behind him, it was a whisker short of crowded. Where Krauslung's port brought travellers and sailors, Manesmark meant soldiers and mages, and they too had coin to spend on ale, women, and trinkets. Their coin had brought the innkeepers and the traders running. The town had grown fatter and taller in his absence. Manesmark may have had town boundaries but it had city dreams.

Farden wasn't interested in Manesmark proper. His attention was firmly fixed on the little path that splintered from the dusty road and led towards a great stump of a building.

Wearing a crown of pine-wood cranes and scaffolding, the new Spire was a shadow of the old tower he could recall; a ghost pencilled in block-stone and granite. Its sleek sides were young, yet to be matured by ivy or storm. It was barely more than half-a-dozen windows high, but he could see it would be every inch the size of its predecessor. Farden pulled a sour face as he took in its lines. To him it was a grandiose gravestone. His thoughts were too tired to know what to truly make of this new building.

He was fortunately distracted by a splash of ivory white at its base. Bunting, tents, marquees, all gathered in a ring like a patch of eager daisies. People buzzed around them like urgent bees, desperate to make the most of the fading light. Farden put his hands into his pockets and followed his feet. He felt agitated. Uncomfortable. *Intrusive* sprang to mind. Nevertheless, he strode bravely into the ring of white tents, searching for her. The bunting stretched overhead flapped and flounced like bleached trout on a line. The people paid him no mind. They were too busy. Only one of them stood rock-still amidst the whirlwind of activity. A pillar of order standing on a wooden pedestal, all auburn curls and smock. Farden recognised her from a mile and a decade away. Farden couldn't help but crack a smile, albeit a foreign little thing, dragged by its heels.

Farden waded through the crowds of servants running amok, toting barrels and packages and bundles on their weary shoulders, and walked straight towards Elessi, smile and all.

❦

'No, no! The bunting needs to be put up before the lanterns, otherwise what will they hang from? Yes, white bunting, not the red. This isn't Frostfall, now is it?'

Elessi wiped away bead of sweat and took a well-earned breath. It felt like her mind had been invaded by squabbling seagulls, all chattering for her attention. So much to do! So much to think about! She sighed as a trio of servants edged past her with a table. 'Make sure it's clean afore you put the cloth on it!' she told them. *Damn, but this was hard*, she thought to herself. Weeks, she had been at it now, with barely a glance at a bed, nor a moment of peace. The women and wives of the court had been helpful at least, lending their finest servants and housemen to aid her. Like a seasoned general, Elessi had deployed them in battle formation, but the description of 'finest' servants had left much to the imagination. They were a docile, snooty lot. She was only really a maid herself, after all. It was only due to the orders of their mistresses and the status of Elessi's husband-to-be that made them listen at all. Thank the gods for that at least.

Elessi was shaken from her inner monologue by a voice from behind her. 'I hear congratulations are in order,' it said, tentatively, in a tired, raspy tone. But even despite its rough edge, it hadn't changed a bit.

Elessi couldn't help but freeze. She didn't turn, the world revolved around her instead, until somehow she was gazing down at what appeared to be a dead man. Skin paler than her precious bunting, beard thick as brambles, hollow-eyed, and thin, Farden looked a mess. A rough sketch of a dead memory, but it was him, nonetheless, standing there as sheepishly as a man could manage. Smiling, of all things.

Elessi didn't smile. She wanted to, a brief wish to appear polite. She tore herself away from his slate-moss eyes and buried her gaze in the grass. 'I'm glad you could come,' she said, in a little voice, one that did nothing to hide her lie.

Farden took a deep breath and stared up at the sky-bitten edges of the new Spire. His breath came out as a rasping sigh, and ended in a chuckle. 'I knew it,' he said, flashing teeth. 'I just knew it. Those bastard gods and their puppet strings.'

Elessi shrugged. The ruse had been a weak one anyway. It lay in the grass, with her gaze, shattered like cheap pottery. 'If you knew, why did you come?' she asked.

Farden looked around at the bustle. 'Because you all deserve better than a bitter memory. Especially you, Elessi, on your wedding day,' he said.

'My wedding day was fine before…' she stopped herself, but it had already been said.

That burnt Farden. He took a step back and half-turned away. 'I see,' he said. Elessi pursed her lips.

'I…' she began, but the mage held up a hand.

'It's fine,' he said. 'I understand, for once.' And he did, to tell the truth. He had abandoned her in a bloody mire. Why would she want the stains of that old memory besmirching the white cloth of her wedding day? *The gods and their tricks*, he thought. He should have known her better. Known them better. Farden began to leave. 'I wish you all the happiness all in the world,' he said over his shoulder.

Elessi watched him go. She didn't say a word. This moment had been rehearsed for years, and the scene was exactly as she had imagined it; the mage admonished, guilty, back turned. It was strange, though, that the satisfied smile she had imagined emblazoned on her lips was utterly absent. Elessi almost stamped her foot. Servants had begun to cluster around her, clamouring for her attention. Just before Farden left, he threw one last question at her.

'Who is it, anyway? The lucky man?'

'You don't know?' she called, genuinely confused.

Farden's reply was to shake his head.

'It's Modren.'

The mage nodded, turned, and walked away, boots squeaking on the evening dew hiding in the grass. 'Figures,' he muttered, feeling his anger and confusion grow with every step.

Farden was blessed and cursed with many things. Empathy wasn't one of them. Even after all these years, he was still oblivious to the fact that Elessi had once harboured feelings for him. Sauntering down the hill towards a darkening sky and twinkling city, her true resentment escaped him. As did the irony:

Elessi had gotten her Written in the end, just a different one.

❦

Durnus was contemplating flames. Tucked deep in the shadows of his rooms, nestled in a marble corner, the old Arkmage stared into the gloom of his blindness, watching the faint wisps of light ebb and flow with the crackling of the fire in front of him. Its heat fanned his face. A skinny bottle of wine balanced half-clutched in his lap. Thoughts danced through the darkness for him, as they did so often these days. So lost was he in his contemplation in fact, that he barely noticed the brushing of feet on the marble. It was only when their owner spoke that he realised he had company. He didn't flinch, he merely looked up.

'I finally did it,' said Farden, in a quiet voice.

Durnus smiled, a little confused. 'Did what?'

'I finally managed to sneak up on you. After all these years,' he muttered.

Durnus chuckled. 'That you did.'

Farden found a chair and dragged it to the fire. Durnus held up the wine, and Farden couldn't help but snatch it. He put its neck to his lips and gulped a good measure of it down. If he couldn't have nevermar, at least he had alcohol.

Durnus sensed the eagerness in Farden's drinking. 'It must be difficult for you.'

The mage took a moment to wipe his lips and place the bottle back into Durnus' hand. 'You have no idea,' he said.

'How was Elessi?'

'I see your spies did their job well.'

Durnus held up his hands. 'My idea alone. I just wanted to see what you'd do,' he replied. 'I have to rely on the eyes of others now.'

'I see that,' said Farden, and then winced at the unintended pun. He reached for the wine again, and Durnus let him have it. 'Elessi seemed pleased to see me,' he added. Durnus turned at that.

'Really?'

'No, of course not,' snapped the mage. His friend's silence made it obvious he had revealed the truth. 'Refused to play along, I guess. I've got a mind to go and see how that Loki feels about a knife in the face. The bastard lied about her wanting me at the wedding. She could barely stomach the sight of me.'

There was a hardened edge to Farden's threats that made Durnus' heart fall. The long and distant years, it seemed, had filed his friend to a sharp and brutal point. He had seen Farden's dark side before, but never as dark as this. Yet he knew how to deal with him.

He pulled himself upright in his chair. 'Then while you're at it, why not stick a knife in Heimdall, and Verix, and your uncle and me too. And don't forget Modren, while you're at it.'

Farden said nothing, he only glared. Durnus could feel the heat of his eyes. Nevertheless, he leant forward. There was urgency and emotion in his voice. 'Yes, we're all guilty of sending Loki to lie to you, Farden. We all wanted you back so desperately. Lies or truth, we would have told them both to make you return. Heimdall suggested it and we agreed, all of us except Elessi. And here you are.'

Farden shook his head. He could tell Durnus was elated by his return, Elated, but trepidatious, even though he hid it well. 'Here I am,' he echoed.

There was a question burning at the edge of the Arkmage's tongue. He turned it loose. 'So, you're here to stay?' he asked.

Farden was silent. He had been tricked, duped, coerced… sold a promise of stone that crumbled like chalk. Nonetheless, he *was* here. He had come back, after all this time. Farden rubbed his eyes. His exhausted mind was too fuzzy to grasp at a decision. Willingly or not, Elessi had been the catalyst that had dragged him from the mud. Now he stood, naked and filthy, amongst old friends, and strangely the only eyes that made him feel shame were hers. He would stay, if only to make it up to her. 'I suppose I will,' he mumbled.

Durnus leant back, trying to hide his relief. He did a good job of it. Farden finished the wine and put the bottle on the floor. The Arkmage clasped his hands together. 'So many years to catch up on,' he sighed. 'Where do we start?'

'Let's skip to the end,' Farden said. It hadn't ever been shame or guilt that kept his lips from talking about what he had done; it was the simple truth that others didn't need to know. Least of all Durnus, Tyrfing, and the others. Those dark nights were for him and him alone, and for the bloody ghosts that no doubt followed in his wake. Darkness that was best left alone. It had a habit of spreading, did darkness.

Durnus held his tongue. He and Tyrfing had sworn to let Farden settle in, to let him come to them with his explanations. He shrugged. 'Then what shall we turn our tongues to, if not the past? The future? The wedding? Krauslung? Or to the bastion in the room?'

'*Her*?' Farden asked. Durnus nodded.

'I was wondering how long it would take to broach that particular subject.' Farden looked out at the dark sky behind the windows. 'Six hours. I should have placed a wager.'

'We cannot ignore her.'

'No, but she can wait until the morning.'

'And I've prayed that every night since you disappeared,' said Durnus, then he shuffled around in his seat, uncomfortable because of more than just the chair. The carved and inlaid wood of his chair creaked as he fidgeted, like a musical accompaniment. 'The subject is a wound with you,' he said. 'Better to let it breathe, than to let it fester.'

Farden snorted. 'It's been festering for fifteen years. If this subject was a wounded leg, then a healer would cut it off and be done with it.'

'Well you tried that, and quite obviously it did not work, otherwise you would not be sitting here with me,' Durnus countered with a snort of his own.

Farden went to stand. 'Oh, it works alright. Let me show you.'

'Sit down, Farden! I thought your exile might have changed you, like it did your uncle, but that stubborn streak of yours still burns brightly, doesn't it?'

'I came back because of Elessi,' Farden replied, a half-lie, but a half-truth too.

'Well, that hurts,' said a voice. Another pair of feet had crept into the room, unnoticed in the heat of the conversation. The figure took a step out of the gloom. It was Tyrfing, arms crossed and stony-faced. He was wearing a blacksmith's apron over a thin shirt and starched trousers, military-style. Beads of sweat glistened on his forehead, trekking down from his tangled hairline to his overgrown beard. He did not look happy. Farden didn't blame him, but all he could do was shrug.

Tyrfing strode forward and found his own chair by the fire. He swivelled it around and sat backwards on it so that his elbows rested on its back. He stared straight at Farden, as if waiting for an answer. It was a while before anyone said anything.

Tyrfing finally broke the silence. The pained look hadn't left his face, but Farden could tell he would leave the subject alone. 'You look like hell, nephew.'

Farden had to smirk at that. 'I probably do.'

'And it smells like that bath never found you.'

'No, I don't think it did.'

'And your finger…?' Tyrfing's voice trailed off.

Farden looked down and waggled the fingers of his left hand, all except one. 'Vice's goodbye.'

Tyrfing sighed. 'What happened to you, nephew?'

Farden shook his head and let his eyes glaze over. A hundred scenes shuffled past his vision, dripping with blood and oily shadow. Scenes of gristle and bone and his knife tickling both. Scenes of guts and little glory, of all the different colours of flesh a blade could bare to him, red, pink, white and fatty yellow… of his knuckles embedded in crushed faces, of knife-points idly carving shapes in innocent stomachs, foreheads, cheeks… of teeth lying in puddles… He slowly moved his head from side to side, counting them all. He soon lost count. 'Let's leave that conversation for another night, shall we?'

Tyrfing looked to Durnus and the blind Arkmage nodded, somehow sensing Tyrfing's questioning look. He sighed and threw his hands up in the air. 'Fine.'

Farden quickly found another subject. 'What's with the

apron?' he asked.

Tyrfing pulled a confused face. 'Don't you remember?'

Farden scratched his nose. 'There're a lot of things...' he trailed off. 'It's been a long time...'

Durnus interjected. 'That it has.' He reached out and grasped Farden by the shoulder. As did Tyrfing. Farden looked rather uncomfortable for a moment, sat there, being clasped by the shoulders by two men. But they were his oldest friends. Family. By every right they should be fuming, reading from the same script as Elessi, and yet here they were, simply happy to be in the same room as him for once. Farden let the weight lift slightly. He knew it would reappear by morning, but for now, he could let it go. He sighed.

'We're so glad you're back, nephew,' Tyrfing whispered hoarsely. He sounded tired. He coughed then and quickly turned away, covering his hand with his mouth. Durnus patted Farden on the shoulder.

'Let us call it a night, shall we? We shall wait until tomorrow to wag our tongues.'

Farden nodded. He suddenly realised how tired he was. He got to his feet and felt the weakness in them. His body felt borrowed again, beaten.

Tyrfing also got to his feet. He put his hands in his pockets. 'Ilios should have returned by then, with that friend of yours. Loki mentioned her.'

Farden had completely forgotten about Jeasin. He wondered how Ilios must have been faring. The poor gryphon would be exhausted by the time he returned. 'Oh, she's just a lump of baggage that I can't get rid of,' Farden had to chuckle to make it sound light-hearted.

'How charming,' smirked Durnus. As Tyrfing and Farden turned to go, Durnus raised a hand. Enclosed within a cage of bony fingers was a candle. 'Farden?' he asked. The mage turned. Tyrfing too. He looked at the candle and ran his teeth over his bottom lip. 'Before you go,' Durnus began, 'could you light a few candles? For the maids, should they decide to disturb me.'

Farden looked at the candle as if it were a knife plunging into his side, wiggling its way through his ribs to nick his heart. 'Er…' he said. Durnus held the candle out so he could take it. Farden grudgingly did so. It felt like a bar of lead. He looked to Tyrfing, who was trying hard not to look utterly crestfallen. They already knew.

Farden grit his teeth. He pinched the greasy wick of the candle between his finger and thumb. For a moment, Tyrfing looked as though he were about to blow a great sigh of relief, but then Farden dashed his hopes by dropping to his knee and touching the wick to the dancing embers of the fire. Tyrfing could only stare dumbly into the flames. Durnus folded his hands on his lap and pursed his lips.

Farden wished the candle was a knife. He might have been able to cut the tension. He placed the candle in a nearby holder, jabbing it downwards onto the little spike, as if it was all its fault. The weight that had lifted so graciously began to pile back on with a vengeance. Without a word, Farden shuffled past his uncle and went straight for the door.

'Goodnight,' called Durnus. His voice was small, strained.

'Night,' replied Farden, an inch before the door clicked shut.

For an age, Durnus and Tyrfing did not move nor bring themselves to speak. Then Durnus, raising his head ever so slightly, forced himself to take a breath, and slowly released it, like a shameful prisoner. Words came with it. 'That man has about as much magick in him as a lump of coal.'

Tyrfing glared at the floor, sadness and anger both jostling in his eyes. 'No, Durnus. Coal would at least have the decency to give us some warmth.'

chapter 20

"You may be favoured by the Arkmages, Chasferist, but you're still just a council member. You, like the rest of us, have backs. Backs are for knives to hide in. This is my final offer. Join us, or suffer the consequences.
Signed, The Copse."
From a letter found in the rooms of Council Chasferist, shortly before he gave up his position as Council in the year 901

Farden awoke with a pounding headache. His dreams had been full of ice and colossal shadows, mountains hurling themselves from their own cliffs, and cold, enveloping water. *Gryphon-borne*, Farden whispered inside his own head, barely audible over the pain. It drowned out every sensible thought he could muster, almost as if he were shouting in the mist and waiting for an echo.

'Bastard bird,' Farden whispered through dry lips.

Farden manoeuvred his legs out of bed and his body reluctantly dragged behind it. His body creaked like his old shack in a gale. Nevermar would do that to a man, if it was trifled with, flirted with and then ignored. It was a jealous mistress.

The mage ignored the mirror by the bed and went to the window to assess the day. It was bright, for a start, too much so for his sleepy eyes. There was a hot sun on the mountaintops, and the daylight was beginning to pour into the city's valley. One of his windows could be tilted outwards to let in the air. Farden had cracked it open in the night to save him from drowning in his own hot sweat. Now the smell of fresh bread and last-night's perfumes wafted through the gap. It was strange. It didn't smell of seagulls and smoke-stains. It didn't smell of loneliness and filth, of cracked mud and week-old blood. It didn't smell like the mildew of a castle, nor the salt-tang of a quiet shore. It actually smelled like home.

This was the feeling he had been waiting for. It rolled in the wake of Krauslung's fragrances, distracting him momentarily from the headache and the night's clutches. Farden nodded at the window's view. A simple waft of air had made his mind up. He had made the right choice. It was now Albion's turn to be buried.

Farden dragged himself from the window and into some clothes that smelled moderately acceptable. As he dressed himself, he caught sight of a scrap of parchment that had been wedged in between the door and the frame. Trousers half-belted, he shuffled over to read it, muttering the note's words under his breath:

NEPHEW,

COME TO MY FORGE. NO ARGUMENTS.

UNCLE.

'Hmph,' Farden exhaled. That much he had expected, given the display of kindness, or rather, the lack of which, he had displayed in Durnus' rooms last night. His aching body suggested he go back to bed, but he knew if he did he wouldn't rise until sunset. The nevermar was leaving his body, a whole, stinking decade of it, and it wasn't about to leave quietly. The jealous mistress had a poisonous tail. Farden knew exactly what was coming, and he would make his exhausted body fight it out until the very last moment. He had already promised himself he would see Elessi married whether she liked it or not.

Just as his uncle's note had demanded, Farden ordered his legs to take him up the many stairs to the upper echelons of the Arkathedral. Old habits kept his hood low and over his face. He caught the eye of many a guard, but they had been given their orders, and they let him roam.

Farden caught other eyes too, and the higher he climbed in the Arkathedral, the more suspicious and narrowed they became. Eyes beneath perfectly trimmed eyebrows and balancing between combed lashes and painted lids. Farden peeked out from beneath his hood and stared at their owners. Magick council members mostly, on their way to the morning's gathering. Others were nobles and rich influencers who had bought rooms in the Arkathedral fortress, off to the breakfast table perhaps.

Farden didn't blame them for their staring and their whispers, but he didn't have to like it. If they forgave his rumpled clothing and hooded appearance, then they soon changed their minds as he brushed past them, and caught a whiff of his most intriguing odour. One woman looked as though she were close to vomiting. Farden hid a smile. He might have even slowed his pace a little to allow them to truly savour his passing.

Legs burning, head pummelling, Farden made it up to the second-highest level of the Arkathedral, where the windows stretched from white floor to white ceiling. Farden headed towards the muted clang of metal on metal. As he turned every corner, he hesitated slightly, expecting at any moment to spy the black scar of an old fire on the pure marble ceiling.

But there was no such scar. It had been covered up by chisel and dust and fresh-cut stone a long time ago, just like the others in the hallways. Farden shrugged. After all, what was home if not a harbour for a few scars? So long as their depth and length could be tolerated.

Farden turned a milk-white marble corner and found the source of the clanging. A cloth-padded door filled an ornate doorway. It was slightly ajar, and somebody behind it was clobbering some hot metal. Farden put his hand to the doorknob, and the clanging paused. Pushing forward, he stepped into a dark and smoky room, thick with the smell of scorched metal, sweat, and charcoal. There was cloth and straw cladding fastened to the walls to hamper the forge-noise. The shadows at his feet were hemmed with the orange threads of a fiery glow.

'Tyrfing?' Farden called for his uncle. There was no reply. Farden stepped deeper, following a curving corridor that led towards the light and warmth.

In the forge room, the daylight was muted and tanned grey by the soot hugging the window panes. Only the crackling fire and a smattering of whale-oil lanterns about the room gave it light. But it wasn't the light that mesmerised the mage, but the colours that it eked from the wall behind him, and tossed on the floor like handfuls of discarded gems.

Farden turned as quickly as his tired body would let him. The wall was long and curved again, and it stretched around the forge hearth like a guiding arm. It positively bristled with metal, as if it had grown scales and barbs to defend itself against the heat. Had the myriad pieces not been deathly still, Farden could imagine the wall as the advancing ranks of some glittering, insectile army.

Every colour swam on that wall, and every shade of light with it. Razor edges mingled with burnished scales, miniscule mail links, and stout blades. Farden stepped forward, hand already outstretched, as if his vambrace and gauntlet longed to be with its own kind. Scalussen. Almost an entire section of the wall devoted to it.

Licking his lips, the mage stumbled to the wall and ran his fingers across a chestplate fringed with gold mail. It had the unmistakable glint of Scalussen about it. A trail of old runes surrounded its flared collar. Farden ran his calloused fingertip across them, but felt nothing. He wondered what magick this armour hid.

A glint of red and gold caught his eye, hanging from a higher hook, and Farden held back an eager gasp. It was a lone sabaton. Forged in autumn gold and apple-red, it was a near match to the metal around his own skin. Farden clutched it with both hands, but still nothing. No familiar tingle shivered up his fingers and made his skin shiver. He grimaced, disappointed, and moved on.

With every step, the disappointment began to grow. Colours paraded past him, frozen in metal and paint. Blue, sea-green, emerald, red, cinder-orange, gold, white, black, and silvery steel. Even after all his years of research, Farden had never imagined the smiths of Scalussen could have forged armour in so many hues. Farden shuffled on, touching and caressing and clutching every single piece of metal he could see, dying to feel a familiar whisper.

It was only when he came to a dull-looking suit of mail that he stopped and let himself breathe. Nothing. The Scalussen section faded into lacklustre normality. The jagged border on the wall was stark. The dull, unpolished neighbours paled in comparison. Scalussen armour glowed in ways that other armour could only long for.

'How do you know?' said a cracked voice. Fissures of tiredness made it hoarse. Farden didn't have to turn to know it was his uncle, lingering in the shadows, hammer in hand. He had wanted to watch Farden and the wall.

Farden moved back across the armour, hoping that he had missed something. 'I just do,' he said. 'Not everyone can.'

'Almost like a selection process,' mused his uncle. He was watching intently.

'Perhaps,' Farden distractedly replied. 'Or protection.'

After a few moments, Tyrfing voiced his burning question. 'And is any of it… is any of that, *them*?'

Farden had to force the answer out. Fruitless as a desert. 'No.'

Tyrfing sighed. 'Good coin well spent then,' he said. He had never really believed that any of his collection was of the fabled Nine. Hoped, perhaps, trifled with optimism. But the wall had been gathered for other reasons than just simple myth, and so in truth, he was not disappointed.

Farden tore himself away from the Scalussen armour and wandered further along the wall, past the strip of dun-coloured scraps and spares, the practice pieces, the half-finished, and the rusty repaired, to where a wide band of new armour hung glittering. His uncle had been busy indeed. Some he recognised from wispy recollections of a store-room in Tyrfing's old sandstone cave, while others were new, polished, and very impressive. Mimics and copycats they were, built in the style of Scalussen with Tyrfing's own twists worked in. Farden looked closer at a few of the cuirasses. Cogs and springs hid beneath their plates, poised and ready to release blades or darts or whatever cunning viciousness he had managed to dream up. Others were simpler, with strings of runes following their curves, like the Evernia and Arkathedral guard armour. These however, looked twice as intricate. Quite advanced. Busy indeed.

'You did all this?'

Tyrfing chuckled. 'I've had the time.'

Farden waved his hand at the Scalussen collection. 'And you bought all of that?'

'Much to the displeasure of the council and the coincounters, yes.' Tyrfing pinched the sides of his dirty Arkmage's robe with his hands and lifted it off the floor. 'This comes with a few benefits.'

Farden rubbed his eyes and looked for a seat. His legs moaned when he couldn't see one, so he perched on the edge of a chisel-bitten bench, arms crossed once again. 'So then, Arkmage Tyrfing, what is it you wanted to talk to me about?' he asked.

Tyrfing put his hammer down and went to mirror his nephew's stance at the windowsill. 'I think you can guess, after last night.'

'So my magick is dead. Good riddance. It's like mourning a murderer.'

'And how many times have you repeated that to yourself on the dark nights?'

'You know nothing of my dark nights, uncle, and I'm not about to enlighten you.'

He could see that hurt his uncle. Tyrfing set his jaw. 'Really, Farden? Have you forgotten where you found me? I know a lost man when I see him. I know the weight of loneliness. I saw plenty of that in the desert, and most of it in the mirror. Of all of the people in this world, I was hoping that you might trust me to understand what you've been through, and trust me enough to let me help.' He took a breath. 'You're a different man than the one that left, and in truth, it scares me to meet you.'

Farden shook his head, still adamant. Why couldn't they just leave well enough alone, rather than bother him with these awkward, festering topics? He had returned. He was staying. That should have been enough for them. 'Durnus seems to think I haven't changed. Maybe you're just meeting the real me,' he said.

Tyrfing stared at him for a moment of silence. He blinked. 'I refuse to believe that.'

His nephew shrugged. 'It's not my problem,' he said. That made Tyrfing look at the floor. Farden narrowed his eyes, feeling guilty again. His uncle looked so old, and to tell the truth, he had missed him so much. He tried to keep his voice on the kinder side as he let his tongue loose, not really sure what words his muddled mind would find. 'Listen, you're obviously not content with the mere pleasure of my presence, uncle, otherwise this reunion would have been smoother, and quieter. There's obviously some higher purpose you had in mind for me. I would hazard a guess at helping you defend against my daughter, but now that you've discovered I've got about as much magick in me as a halfwit has philosophical ideas, I suppose you're disappointed, and angry,' he said, and then let himself sigh. Farden was many things, but not an idiot. He knew that his demeanour had taken a nasty fall. He knew he oozed violence, bitterness, and the rest. 'And probably scared too, given my mood,' he added quietly.

Tyrfing nodded.

'I don't blame you, but the pressure is making my head want to explode. You're lucky I'm still here, given your lies and the gods' ruse. Please don't push it. I am whatever I am.'

Tyrfing repeated his nod. Farden took a breath and ended his gentle tirade. It felt good to unchain his words. He was surprised he had unleashed them without shouting. Perhaps his mind was already starting to drag itself from the mist. It certainly didn't feel like it. Farden put a hand to his temple and jabbed hard. It was a stupid thing to do. His brain fought back with passion. It felt like a jellyfish had crept into his skull in the night and set up shop.

'Don't you miss it?' His uncle's words interrupted him. He meant the magick.

Farden shook his head, adamant. 'Like a knife in my back. Literally.'

Tyrfing tutted. 'You don't know what you've been missing,' he said.

Farden groaned. 'Uncle…'

Tyrfing held up a hand. He too spoke quietly, and gently. 'Now you listen, nephew. I *am* angry. I *am* disappointed. And I *am* scared for many a reason and not just because of you. Yes, one of the reasons we wanted you back was to help us fight your daughter. Yes, we lied, but such times call for such lies. But right now I can see you're no use to anyone but a bed. You're sweating, exhausted, and I can smell you over the charcoal, Farden. It hurts to see you like it, all things and magick aside, it's painful to see you like *this*, this pale, gaunt wreck that you are, burning with anger. I can feel it from here. So I'll promise not to push so long as you promise me you'll sort yourself out. We've got a vicious mess to clear up, and magick or no, we would rather you help us than hinder us, and right now, the sight of you is hindrance enough. The Arka have never been in a more desperate situation. I know that's hard to believe, after Vice, but we are. We balance on a knife-edge, as the old saying goes. We've never known so many enemies. Never known so many dogs baying for our blood. All it takes is one thing to go wrong…' Tyrfing trailed off. 'It's hard, Farden. It's so very hard, wearing this robe. I can't manage you making it any harder for me. Promise me that.'

Farden's first response was grit his teeth and bare them, but he suppressed that, and hard too. *Deserved better*, said an inner voice, a fraction from drowning under the hammering of his head. *They deserve better*. 'I make no promises,' he grunted. 'But I'll try.'

'I guess that's as good as I can hope for,' replied Tyrfing. As foreign as this new nephew was, he still understood. The others would want more, he knew that. They were lucky he was back at all. 'Let's walk, shall we?' he said, motioning to the door.

Farden nodded. 'Let's.'

Tyrfing led the way with slow, swishing steps. Farden trudged behind him with his hands buried firmly in his pockets. The fresh clothes felt itchy, strange, *clean*. His hood had the green-grass smell of crisp washing. It made him want to sneeze, but it was a welcome change from the smells hiding just beneath them.

They walked for a while in silence. Tyrfing was bowed and nodded to by every council member they passed, and just from that movement Farden could sift the loyal from the disloyal. Even as fuzzy-minded as he was, Farden could taste a tension in the Arkathedral. He wondered what was causing it. He found himself with a sudden desire to see Durnus and his uncle in action upon the twin thrones.

His chance came sooner than he had hoped. Tyrfing led Farden along the rebuilt corridors of the Arkathedral. If he remembered correctly, they were heading towards the great hall, and right he was. The number of guards increased with every corner, as did the echoes of voices and eager chatter. When they finally came to the great golden doors, they found a veritable crowd standing in their way. It seemed a polite crowd, at first glance, but in their keen gossiping and whispered hisses, there was a finger-rubbing sense of tense urgency. It didn't take long for the crowd to notice Tyrfing and his hooded companion. The rustle of conversation died away. Farden noticed his uncle's jaw tense from the corner of his eye.

'Eager this morning, aren't we?' Tyrfing said to the nearest clump of people. One of them stepped forward, a man with slicked-back hair and quick eyes. His smile dripped like poison from a knife.

'We wouldn't want to keep your Mage waiting, now would we?' he replied. Farden found himself instantly disliking the man. Council members had never been his preferred company, and this one wasn't about to shatter that rule. Tyrfing looked particularly perturbed by his smile.

Tyrfing went to speak but was interrupted by a cough. He held his hand to his face for a moment and then clenched it tightly by his side. Malvus' eyes followed it down. 'Malvus, you never fail to dampen the brightness of my day,' he replied, keeping his tone formal. Farden was impressed. At least someone in his family had learnt some restraint.

This Malvus character bowed low. 'I aim to please, Arkmage,' he said, and then he turned to regard Farden, wearing the same dripping smile. His eyes weren't the only ones that turned on the mage. Farden could feel the stares of the others standing in the hall. 'And I believe this is your fabled nephew, Farden, the self-professed exile. Why, just what we need; another loose cannon in the Written ranks. We haven't had the pleasure.' He even had the audacity to thrust out a hand.

Farden tried to keep his face impassive, but these days it had a mind of its own. Politeness had died of loneliness some time ago. With a sneer, Farden gripped the man's hand and tried to squeeze it as hard as he could, hoping he might bruise a bone or two. Maybe even break one, if he was lucky. To his dismay, he was weaker than he thought. Malvus was stronger. The man smiled and slowly squeezed back, and Farden found himself irritatingly outmatched. 'Pleasure's all yours,' he muttered.

'I'm sure,' replied Malvus, keeping his tone cheery.

Tyrfing quickly interrupted them. He looked to the golden doors. 'I believe Arkmage Durnus is already in the hall,' he said. Before Malvus could say anything, Tyrfing took a step forward and he quickly moved aside. Farden followed, making sure to nudge the man with the sharp point of his shoulder as he passed. He heard the almost imperceptible sound of Malvus wincing and had to keep himself from smiling.

'That's a snake in the grass if I've ever seen one,' he whispered. The crowd slowly parted before them, like reluctant reeds before the keel of a narrowboat.

Tyrfing nodded and hummed, wary of their surroundings. *And the grass welcomes it.*

Farden voiced another question. 'How did you know?' he asked.

'Know what?'

'Durnus was in the hall?'

Tyrfing looked back at his nephew as the guards set their hands to the great golden doors. 'Can't you feel it?'

'Feel what?'

Tyrfing marched forward into the hall, towards his throne. Durnus sat waiting for them, alone save for a thin woman standing by the kaleidoscope windows. 'Oh Farden, you're missing so much,' he sighed.

Farden simply grunted.

The great hall was bathed in soft light, pouring through the rainbow-stained glass of the huge windows around its edges. The marble floor, usually pale and milky, had been turned into pools and lakes of colour. The patterns washed lazily over the carved benches and marble tree roots, like a lazy artist clumsily spilling paint. As Farden followed his uncle's steps, he could almost imagine the colours rippling and splashing around their feet. Farden looked around again for scars of a long-lost battle. He looked around for a scorched tile, or a cracked window, anything that might hint that a dragon and a tyrant had fought and died here. There was nothing, save a gold dragon-scale plaque on a marble pillar, saying only two words: *For Farfallen.* Even the statue of Evernia had been repaired and reassembled. Some scars did heal then. At least on the surface.

The men and women of the council followed behind them, still rustling with conversation. Something was afoot. Farden could feel it. He just had no idea what.

Tyrfing went directly to his throne. Farden went to stand by the windows, where Jeasin was standing alone. She was trying to make sense of the marble under her fingers as she stroked one of the pillars. She heard his footsteps and turned.

'Told you I'd send Ilios back,' he said. Jeasin was shrouded in a green woollen blanket. Despite her dishevelled and wind-tangled hair, the furrowed and impatient look on her brow and lips, she looked beautiful dyed by the colourful light. Farden couldn't help but smile at her. He was glad she couldn't see him. Her tongue would have whipped the smile right from his mouth.

'This place must be bloody huge,' she said, rubbing the marble.

'That it is,' replied Farden. He watched Jeasin looking about, trying to count how many feet were striding into the hall. She looked thoroughly bewildered.

'I suppose I should thank you for keepin' your promise,' she said.

'I suppose you should.'

And that's where politeness ended. She crossed her arms. 'Well, that thing took its time in coming back to the beach. Had to wait in that grotty shack of yours. Then I almost damn near froze on the winged beast's back, headin' gods know where. Then we were welcomed by some frail-feelin' old man. Said he was blind too. And an Arkmage. Never heard such ridiculous piss. Where are we, Farden? Where have you taken me?'

'A little place called Krauslung. Heard of it?'

Jeasin pouted, still unsure. 'Of course I 'ave. And I still don't believe a word of it. Pillow stories, like I told you! Where are we?'

'Suit yourself,' Farden muttered.

'Fine. If you won't tell me where we are, you can at least tell me what's goin' on!' she hissed, listening to the hubbub. Her fingers found a bench, and she sat down. Farden sat down next to her, feeling his bones creak and a shiver of dizziness run through his chest. He hoped he could get back up without passing out. He looked to the two thrones and to the two men perched on top of them. As he looked, a man in bright armour emerged from the growing council crowd and took his seat on a smaller throne at their feet. He didn't look happy. He tried whispering to the Arkmages but they waved him away.

'There are two thrones, and two Arkmages. Arka tradition. The one on the right is Durnus, an old friend and a very, very old man, and the one on the left is my uncle, Tyrfing. And the man sitting below them is Modren, a mage like I used to be. He's the Undermage, and he sits on the Underthrone.'

'Your uncle?' She made a fist against the smooth, polished arms of the bench. 'Stop lyin' to me Farden, tell me where the f…'

'Magick Council! Be gathered!' a shout thundered across the hall, and it was then the truth dawned on Jeasin. She turned, open-mouthed to face him. Krauslung. The Arkathedral. She had heard the rumours of this place, from her travelling customers. They had told her the stories of the marble forest and the city below it. She couldn't help but gawp.

Farden had spied Malvus moving to the front of the council members, that satisfied smile still firmly plastered to his face, like mud onto the wall of a Paraian hut.

'What's goin' on?' Jeasin whispered again. Farden took her cold hand in his gauntlet, making her flinch. A loud bang echoed around them as the golden doors of the great hall slammed, sealing them in. He could see council members staring at them, wondering by what means such peasants had sneaked into their hall. Farden ignored their looks.

'Try to keep quiet,' he said. 'It looks like we might be here for a while.'

'Why?!'

But Farden didn't answer. He went to stand near the front of the hall so he could see Malvus and his patch of fawners at the front of the council. There was something about that man that stirred up crimson violence in Farden. He desperately wanted to know what it was.

'Silence!' boomed Modren. When his echoes faded away, the magick council stood in complete silence. Farden looked down their jumbled ranks. Some of their faces tugged at his memory, others were foreign as grass was to a fish. They were a silk-cloth crowd, bristling at the edges with jewels and trinkets and exuding sweet perfumes. Farden could see a few fat coinpurses dangling from a few nearby belts. Old habits made him weigh them in his mind.

Tyrfing tapped his throne with the ring on his finger, his old rainring, and began the day's proceedings. 'Esteemed council members,' he began, reciting the old oath of the council. Its formality was like lead on his tongue. 'We are gathered to weigh the choices of our city, and indeed our world. In one hand we balance magick, and in the other our people. Let our balance be true and our scales just, and may Evernia judge us if they are not.'

Even in the times when Farden had stood in the great hall as a soldier, that oath had already been ancient. He wondered if there were any men and women in this council that still truly believed in its words. By the rolls of their eyes, he could tell there were few, if any.

Durnus looked distracted, so Tyrfing continued for him. He looked down at a little list somebody had left on the arm of his throne. 'Firstly, we need to discuss the expansion of the port for the ships that have been designated for the navy s…'

'I believe we have more pressing issues than that, Arkmages?'

'Pipe down, Malvus,' somebody shouted from the back of the council. The man was quickly shushed.

'You will wait your turn to speak, Council Barkhart,' warned Durnus.

Malvus stepped forward, bold as summer snow. He folded his hands calmly in front of him. 'Actually, Arkmage, I will not,' he said.

Modren immediately got to his feet. To his credit, Malvus didn't falter. He barely even spared a glance for the Undermage. Farden edged closer to watch, as did half the council.

'What is the meaning of this, Malvus?' demanded Tyrfing, too tired for formality. Durnus looked about with his misty eyes. A look of dread had come over his face. *No, not now*, his face seemed to say.

Malvus raised his hands to the audience at his back, the audience he had bought, paid, and bargained for. They gave a little cheer. 'I will not be stifled any longer,' he began, 'and neither shall the rest of this council.'

'Speak for yourself, Barkhart!' shouted the same voice as before. It sounded old, wizened. Strangely loyal. There was a gasp and a cry from somewhere in the crowd. The guards at the doors moved forward, but the council held its ranks, suffocating any more complaint. This was Malvus' crowd now, whether they liked it or not.

'What on earth are you blabbering on about, man?' Durnus demanded. The air grew hot around the twin thrones. Hot and dangerous.

'Oh, I'm not blabbering, Durnus, I am speaking very clearly indeed.'

'You watch your tongue,' growled Modren. He took a step closer.

'Heel, lapdog!' one of Malvus' cronies shouted, too cowardly to show his face.

'Modren,' Durnus whispered, and the Undermage let the globe of sparks he had been nursing in his hand fade.

'It looks as if my fears are well-founded, council members,' announced Malvus. There was another cheer of assent. With great ceremony, Malvus dug into his long cloak and brought forth a tightly coiled scroll. A flick of his hand and it unfurled like a yellow waterfall, its emerald ribbon fluttering. 'I have been speaking closely with the wise men of Arfell. With the magick increasing in Emaneska, they are delving deeper into their libraries than ever before. They have shown me many a forgotten record detailing the foundation of this council. Records from the time of the very first Arkmage, when this council floated upon the sea, on our ancestors' ships.'

Durnus and Tyrfing both got to their feet. They could sense where this was going. Formality had all but vaporised. 'Coin can't buy you the thrones, so you're citing ancient law instead, are you? Why am I not surprised?' challenged Tyrfing.

'The thrones were never my concern. Just the people and the members of this council who have to suffer for their occupiers' decisions.'

Modren almost laughed. 'Don't you dare pretend this has to do with Krauslung's well-being, Malvus. We know you b…'

But Malvus cut his sentence off at the knees. 'This document,' he said, waggling the decrepit old scroll in the Undermage's face, 'instructs that should two Arkmages come to the throne and consistently ignore the good pleas of its council, then there is cause for them to be, shall we say, *removed.* I move that your rule has irreparably damaged this nation's proud history. Not only that, but you have turned a blind eye to every effort this council has made to protect its people. You have drained our coffers for private means, saturated the pride of our School with commoners and pretenders, allowed magick markets to run rife, ignored important trade delegates at the expense of your own ambitions, and last but definitely not least, have shown absolutely no determination to secure this nation's future in Emaneska. You have been negligent. Ignorant. We will have it no longer!'

A mighty cheer went up from the crowd of council members. Malvus played the victorious general. All he lacked was a bloody sword to wave.

Farden had never seen Durnus' parchment face so crimson with indignation, anger, and a swirl of other emotions that didn't have names. 'We have done nothing but seek to protect this city and its people since the moment we were appointed. You have no idea what you are dealing with, Malvus,' the old Arkmage yelled over the noise.

'That is right, Durnus Durnus, I do not.' He turned to face his magick council. 'I have dug deep into the archives with the men of Arfell. For such a powerful mage as he,' here he pointed casually at the thrones, 'you would think that he attended our proud School? Would have thought a record of him exists. But, most strangely, there is no record of him there whatsoever. It seems we have a rogue mage here, ladies and gentlemen. The only mention of any sort of Durnus I can find is a quiet mention of a vampyre in charge of an Arkabbey in northern Albion. In the Leath duchy. An Arkabbey that was abandoned the very same month that Vice came to power, and low and behold, almost a year later, you wander into our lives.'

'Lives that he saved, you ungrateful bastard!' Modren

countered. Behind him, Durnus made to descend the steps of his throne, ready to show the man his lack of fangs, but stumbled slightly as he misplaced his footing. The magick council rustled with laughter. Malvus sneered. Farden wanted to silence every single one of them with a dozen well-placed fists. His anger pounded in unison with his headache.

Malvus, it seemed, had a few more cards to play. 'Suspicious, no? And let us not get started on our good Arkmage Tyrfing's history. We've all seen the scars beneath the sleeves of his robe. They are both unfit to rule!'

In reply, Tyrfing slammed his hands together and a thunderclap deafened the council. He bellowed over its dying, booming echoes. 'That's enough, Malvus! I want your traitorous backside hauled out of this council. Guards!'

By the door, the guards looked downright bewildered. Instead of running to the Arkmages' aid they clumped together, as though stuck in treacle. Coin, clashing with loyalty. Malvus produced another scroll, a fresher one this time, the ink barely dry and the paper a bleached yellow. He shook that out and let it fall with the other onto the marble.

'What I have here are the signatures of a shocking majority of this council, every single one of which proclaim that you are unfit to rule us any longer.'

Durnus glared with his blind eyes. 'Malvus, you are deluded. Not in the history of this council has anybody dared to attempt what you are attempting now. There are measures in place to stop poisonous ambitions like yours from seizing these thrones. Yes, I too know the old scrolls. The city itself must agree with the council. The people, those you are supposed to be representing, must mirror whatever foolish and decidedly treacherous sentiments you are hawking. They must be actively crying out for a change in rule. Correct me if I am wrong, Malvus, but I do not hear such an outcry.'

Farden smiled. Durnus had shut the upstart down. He flicked his eyes aside to watch the disappointment fall like dusk on the council member's face, but instead it was the mage who felt the disappointment. Malvus was smiling calmly. He slowly lifted a hand and cupped it around his ear.

'Do you not?' he said.

Durnus cocked his head, face falling. There was a faint whisper on the breeze. A murmur in the air. The great hall was silent save for furtive breaths as every ear strained to listen. Malvus had paid good coin for this moment. His tongue had been worked raw for it. He waited, a little anxiously, for his final card to fall to the table.

A chant. Drifting up from the city below. Audible even from that height. Tyrfing led Durnus quickly around the back of their thrones. Modren followed. Farden told Jeasin to stay where she was and followed too. He pushed through a small ornate door in the wall and darted up the steps, through the tower, and out onto the Nest. Ilios was there, wide awake, surrounded by three figures; two men and that thin woman with greenish hair. One of them was Loki. They were listening to the words wafting up on the crisp morning breezes. Words of misinformed, misplaced, and misunderstood discontent.

Tyrfing marched to the edge of the Nest so he could look down onto the granite patchwork of streets far below. Crowds were clumped together in the streets, marching and shouting in unison. Tyrfing pinched his eyes and read the disgruntled words from their hand-painted signs. There were preachers on every corner, doing their best to rouse the mobs even further. Soldiers and mages were gathering in the main thoroughfares, unsure as of yet what to do. The protests were loud but peaceful, for the moment. Tyrfing set his jaw and closed his eyes. Beside him, Durnus' keen ears listened to their shouts and songs.

Farden stood behind them, between the railing and the gathered gods and wondered what he had just witnessed. 'What in the name of Emaneska is going on?' he asked.

'Treachery,' said the tall, muscular man behind him, the one with golden eyes. Heimdall, he guessed. 'That is what it sounds like.'

'Now! Of all times!' Durnus let out a grunt and sent his fist flying through the railing. Stone crunched under his fingers. White light shivered around his knuckles, matching the pale marble dust that now clung to them. 'All this work, only to be undermined by that bastard. Do they not understand?!'

'It's not over yet,' said Farden, not entirely sure if it actually was not.

'Damn right it isn't,' hissed Modren. He turned to Heimdall. 'What are my men saying? Can you tell me that?'

Heimdall held his hand up for silence. He was given it. 'I cannot hear all of them, but for the most part they are loyal. I hear them speaking of crazy people in the streets. They are still yours. Not this Malvus'.'

'You should have seen this coming,' commented Verix, receiving a number of dark glances. Heimdall shook his head at her. Now was not the time for her truths.

'Ironically, we were too busy trying to protect their sorry hides,' spat Modren.

'You gullible little ingrates!' Tyrfing shouted to the crowds far below. They couldn't hear him. He doubted if it would have made a difference anyway. Their minds seemed to be made up. The hammer had finally fallen on their careers. 'This is the Marble Copse's work. Bunch of power-hungry purists. We've always suspected Malvus was at their head, well here's your proof.'

'It will not take much for this to turn ugly, if we are not careful,' said Durnus, breathing hard, trying to calm himself.

Loki shrugged. 'Seems to me that's exactly what this man wants.'

'Can't we just kill him?' Farden shrugged.

Durnus shook his head. 'There are plenty waiting to take his place. The Copse's influence runs deep. The city would be incited to riot, tear itself apart until we were either dead or locked away. They would be defenceless.'

'What a shame.'

'What do we do?'

'We bide our time. Malvus has played his hand. We hold ours back. We bargain for time, say that we need to discuss our abdication.'

'What about the wedding?' asked Modren, fuming.

Durnus looked up at the sky, searching for the faint glow of the sun in his darkness. 'It goes ahead. Who knows, if she comes tomorrow, these people won't be crying out for our abdication; they will be crying out for us to save them. Malvus' plan will ultimately fail. He may be dastardly clever, but his ploy is ill-timed.'

'Be careful,' warned Verix, in a quiet voice. She half turned away, as if making to leave. 'The seeds have been sown. There is nothing like a storm to make seeds sprout.'

The others digested her words like sour fruit. Muddle-headed, Farden took a moment to make sense of them. While the others stayed silent, he scratched his chin. 'Not two days back, and already things are falling apart,' he said. *And for once it's nothing to do with me*. That last thought was a guilty one, but he was glad for it.

chapter 21

"A dragon may forge two bonds in its life. The first, an essential, is the tearbook. A dragon's mind is a complex thing. Without the bond of a tearbook, a dragon's vast memories unravel like fraying thread. Fall away like sand in an hourglass. The tearbook holds these memories, transferred in the tears of the dragon during the initial bonding. Incidentally, this marks the transition from juvenile wyrm to adult dragon."

From 'Secrets of a Siren World' - written by the exiled rider Doorna in 651

'Another,' grunted a voice, a tired voice.

'Make that two,' said another.

'I thought you said you had a headache?'

'I do.'

A pause.

'Fair enough. Another two, Fash.'

Fash, the ample-bellied barkeep, nodded, and immediately went about pouring another two foaming ales from a spout set into the bar. Ingenious contraption.

As two overflowing glasses clanked onto the brass bar-top and Modren flicked a few coins into a nearby wooden bowl. Fash didn't like to touch coin. Coin was the dirtiest thing a man had in his pockets, he always said. Perhaps he was right, and in more ways than one. The barkeep thanked the two men and went to serve the others scattered around the long winding bar.

Farden sipped his ale, letting it cool his tongue. The tavern, the *Insatiable Madam* as it was branded, was quiet for so late at night and for a day as busy as it had been. It had a sober air, for a tavern. Never a good thing, especially when it was an Undermage's last night as an unmarried man. The soldiers and mages had come as invited, but the day's work of quashing would-be riots had numbed the mood. The plan had originally been one of celebration, but after their original venue had turned a little hostile, they had switched taverns in an effort to keep the peace, and the idea of high spirits was now a little bruised. The men sat around on brass-topped tables in groups of twos and threes and talked in low tones. Every now and again they would raise their empty glasses to the Undermage sat hunched at the bar and rouse a cheer. It was the best they could do. It had been a day of questions, and the answers bothered them like black flies around a dying goat.

Krauslung had found its own knife-edge to balance on.

'You're telling me you can't feel anything?' Modren asked again, resting his chin on the rim of his glass.

Farden looked over his shoulder and counted the mages in the room. Then he counted the Written. A trio of them sat near the fireplace. One, a woman he couldn't remember, caught his eye and he turned away. 'Not a thing,' he replied.

'Not even a shiver?'

'No.'

'Well, you're missing out,' sighed Modren.

Farden looked confused. 'Tyrfing said that.'

'Well he's right,' Modren sipped his ale. It was a pale colour, wonderfully cool and suitably strong. Perfect for numbing the day. Glancing sideways at his comrade, Farden could see there was something bothering him. It could have been a myriad of things, and Farden had never been known for his empathy, but the crux of it was that his friend should have been happier on the eve of his wedding.

Modren wore an informal suit of mail and dark leather. He had a frown to match. Every wisp of a half-dead memory he had of Modren had been him with a grin on his face and a glint in his eye. A different Modren sat in front of him tonight. Perhaps it was the weight of Malvus' little plot and the day rounding up trouble-makers. Perhaps he was nervous about the wedding. Perhaps he was just upset that Farden had come back only half the man he had been. Farden was clueless. He decided to get him talking.

'Nevermar's made me numb to it,' he admitted.

Modren turned slightly on his stool. 'When did you start taking that red poison? After the Battle, I mean, not the years before.'

'Elessi's been telling stories, I see,' said Farden. He rubbed his bearded chin as he tried to drag the memories from the fog. 'Maybe a year after Krauslung.'

'By Evernia, that's a long time.'

'Hence why I can't feel whatever it is you want me to feel.'

'Haven't you heard the stories? The rumours? Seen the markets?'

'I've seen the markets…' Farden shrugged.

'Something has happened to the magick in this world. As if it's sprung a leak somewhere. It's why the magick markets have exploded, and why we're hearing more and more rumours of strange goings-on. Strange creatures appearing in the mountains and in the forests. Beasts talking, more than usual that is. People waking up and speaking spells they've never heard before, burning houses to the ground with a song. In the meantime, every single mage and Written has felt themselves grow stronger, almost like their abilities and their Books are just waking up. Do you know how many School recruits we've had to initiate over the last year?'

Farden shook his head.

'Ten thousand. Peasants and foreigners are turning up at the gates in droves, showing magickal skills that they shouldn't possess.

We've had no choice but to take them in.'

'So that's what Malvus meant.'

'But Malvus doesn't know the half of it. We need them Farden, every single useless one of them.'

'Why?'

Modren gave him a strange look. 'To fight her.'

Farden sipped his ale.

The Undermage sipped too. A full minute went by as the two men stared at the rows of painted bottles standing like soldiers behind the bar. Amber liquids showed their faces where the paint and script had flaked. Some were as dark as varnish, and probably as strong. 'You going to help us?'

Farden laughed. 'And how exactly am I supposed to help?' he asked. He didn't mean to sound so callous, but it was the truth. He was about as much use as a paper sail. 'Even if my magick still lives, I don't know if I want it back.'

Modren pointed at Farden with the lip of his mug. He looked crestfallen. 'It hurts to hear you, of all mages, say that.'

There was a clatter of feet outside a nearby window, and a trail of fire flew across the mottled pea-green glass. Torches, followed by the clank of mail and steel. A distant shout rang out. Something about Arkmage swine. Farden sighed and gulped half of his tankard down. The ale was disloyally exacerbating his headache and his aches, but he was nothing if not stubborn. It would numb him eventually. 'You would say the same if your Book was to blame for *her*, for Vice, for all of that,' Farden waved his hand at the window.

Modren rapped his knuckle on the brass bar-top and signalled Fash for another brace of ales. 'Maybe I would. Maybe I wouldn't. You're you, I'm me,' he said, stamping an end on that trail of conversation. He could remember how his old friend worked.

Farden grunted. 'Well said.'

'As long as you can still wield a sword, I'll be happy.'

Farden didn't feel like he could wield a quill, never mind a blade, but he nodded nonetheless. He had to give his friend something. 'What do these scars say?' he said, jabbing a finger at his cheeks.

'That you need to duck more?'

Farden grinned at that.

'Durnus and Tyrfing told me you don't want to talk about Albion, and whatever it is you did these last years. Though, knowing you and your tendencies, I can imagine.'

'I bet you can. There's only one thing we Written were bred for. And there's plenty of that work in the Duchies.'

'Well, all I can say is it made you even uglier. I didn't think that possible,' chuckled Modren, finding solace in a little humour. Farden was glad of it.

'It's like looking into a polished helmet, isn't it?' he countered, and the two banged their mugs together. 'So,' Farden said. 'Marriage.'

'That's right,' coughed Modren.

'Never took you for the type. I never thought the Arkmages would let such a thing happen, if I'm honest.' Farden sipped his ale.

'The laws say not to breed. Don't say anything about marriage.'

'And Elessi is happy with that?'

Modren nodded matter-of-factly. 'She is.' There was a moment. Modren posed a question. 'You know she had feelings for you, once?' He had to add the "once."

Farden let his lips hover in the foam of his beer for a while before shaking his head.

'Well, she did.'

Farden cleared his throat. 'If it bothers…'

Modren interrupted him with a hand. 'It doesn't. Never has. She's got nothing but anger for you now, old friend.'

'Hatred would probably be more accurate. And that explains a lot,' Farden sighed. 'Rather a lot, actually…'

'Looks like she got what she wanted in the end, though.'

'What's that?'

'A mage.' Modren grinned. Farden chuckled. He could see a little of the unease sliding off his friend. He decided to change the subject, to keep the words flowing. 'So where are the dragonriders? Or Eyrum? And where's Lerel for that matter? Are they not invited?'

Modren tapped the side of his nose. 'Lerel is, well, Lerel is just late. I'll explain later. You won't know what to make of it. As for the Sirens, we haven't heard a peep from them in months. We send hawk after hawk and not a single reply in return. They must be busy battling with the ice. Last we heard it'd swallowed up another breeding ground. Let's hope this spring helps.'

'Undermage?' ventured a voice standing behind them, a young voice by its tone.

Modren turned and saw a young mage standing at attention. He had a face spattered with orange freckles, a mop of curly hair, and eyes so bright they had probably never seen the darkness of a battle. He quickly threw up a salute. 'I'm off duty, lad,' said Modren.

' 'pologies, Modren, sir, I just wanted to wish you the best of luck for tomorrow,' he said. His eyes kept flicking to Farden.

Modren raised his tankard to the young man. 'Why thank you, lad. What's your name?'

'It's Bringlin, sir.' His eyes were still stuck on Farden. Modren nudged his friend, and Farden turned to look the young man up and down. He was a keen-looking mage. Fresh out of the School. The young man stuck out a hand. 'And may I say, sir, it's an honour to meet you. We've heard a great many stories.'

'I'm sure you have,' grunted Farden, trying to be polite. He took the mage's hand in his and shook it once. The man beamed.

'A cheer for the Undermage and Farden!' he announced. He raised his tankard and the whole of the tavern joined him. Modren and

Farden nodded their thanks, though Farden felt himself pawing for his hood. Too much attention for a recovering hermit.

Before the young mage went back to his table, he leant close to Modren and lowered his voice to a murmur. 'I'm part of the assignment for tomorrow. The Winter Regiment. There's a lot of talk going 'round sir. May I ask…'

'That's quite enough, thank you Bringlin,' Modren cut him off. He reached into his pocket and brought out a coin, flicking it towards the mage. 'Why don't you get your table some ales on me, hmm?' Modren turned back to the bar, leaving Bringlin to retreat, sheepish, and Farden to wonder.

'What was that about?'

'Nothing,' Modren shook his head.

'I'm not that drunk, Modren.'

'Told you, it was nothing. Just loose lips in the barracks. You remember.'

'Modren, what's tomorrow aside from your wedding?'

The unease slid right back on. Modren put his tankard to his lips and drained the thing. He slammed it back on the bar, wiped his lips, and stepped from his stool. 'Come. I've had enough of this place.'

Farden scowled, but did as he was told. He gulped down his ale and followed Modren to the door. The whole tavern got to its feet in salute, but the two men barely spared them so much as a wave. Out into the night they went, slamming the door behind them.

Outside, the air was tinged with a spring frost. The two men paused on the tavern's steps to take in the night around them, staring up at the sky between the curving rooftops above. The moon was a bright coin rolling lazily across the south. A seagull had missed its bedtime. From a chimney pot, it cried to the frayed lengths of silver cloud splayed across the star-speckled sky.

'What aren't you telling me?' asked Farden.

Modren rubbed his eyes, restoring a little of the clarity the half-dozen ales had stolen from him. 'Nothing you need to know,' he sighed. Farden stepped out onto the cobbles so he could face the Undermage. He stumbled into a passer-by as he did so, a young girl with a fountain of black hair and a pale face. Farden mumbled a quick apology to her as she hurried past, nursing a shoulder.

'Sorry,' he managed.

'Don't you worry,' she whispered in a soft voice, without turning.

Farden watched her until she vanished down a nearby alleyway. When he turned back to confront Modren, he found him marching across the cobbles, towards the Arkathedral. 'Look,' he said, 'I've already had my fill of secrets from those bastard gods and the others. I don't wish for any more. Why would you need a regiment of mages at the wedding? What's going on?'

Modren stayed silent.

Farden pressed him. Questions and answers rattled back and forth like heels on the cobbles. 'What are you worried about?'

'It's just a precaution.'

'Against what? Her?'

'No.'

'Then what?'

'Nothing.'

'Don't play the halfwit. It is her you're worried about. You think she's going to attack?'

'Perhaps.'

'How do you know?'

'We don't. We're just being cautious.'

'And how does Elessi feel about an army at her wedding?'

'They won't be... She... It doesn't matter.'

Farden hiccuped, and said no more. Modren put a hesitant hand around his bony shoulder as they rounded a corner and came face to face with the Arkathedral. The giant fortress was painted orange and milky silver by the innumerable torches and the moon. 'How do you feel about her?'

'Who, Elessi, or my… her?'

'Your daughter.'

There was a pregnant pause as Farden pondered. After the ale, it was like shouting a question into a wall of fog and waiting for an echo. 'I don't know,' came his answer, as the forest of guards stationed at the Arkathedral's huge gates parted to let them enter.

Modren took his arm from Farden's shoulders. 'What kind of answer is that?'

'A truthful one. I don't know her. I've never even met her.'

'Don't you realise what she's been doing, Farden?' Modren sounded angry.

Farden stopped dead in his tracks, halfway cross the cavernous atrium. 'No, apparently I don't.'

Modren kept his voice low, but it was tight and seething. 'She's killing mages, Farden. Written mages. Skinning the very Books from their backs and then disappearing without so much as an explanation.'

Farden kept walking, feeling the bite of anger in his stomach. 'How do you know it's her?'

'Stories. Witnesses. We've followed her trail. Besides, who, or what, could kill so many of our Written with such ease? Where's your ambivalence now, hmm?' Modren challenged him. Farden didn't reply. He scuffed his boots against the marble floor. 'I thought so. Your girl's a murderer, Farden. Pure and simple.'

Farden's knuckles popped as he clenched his fists. 'How many?'

'Left or killed?'

'Left.'

Modren looked wistfully at the ceiling. 'There's only twenty-eight of us left now, old friend. All safe and sound behind the city walls, waiting for their revenge. Gods have mercy if she tries anything here.'

The coin dropped for Farden. 'Bait,' he said, making Modren flinch. 'You're using the wedding to draw her out, aren't you?' It was Farden's turn to sound angry. It was an all-out play. A gamble. Power for power. Draw her in when they were ready, and see what she was made of. Who cares that it was a wedding.

'Don't know what you're talking about…'

'Does Elessi know?'

The Undermage began to walk away. Farden raised his voice. He didn't care about the people around them; guards, servants, mages, residents of the Arkathedral, milling around the atrium like rich folk on market day. 'Does Elessi know?' he shouted after Modren, his hoarse voice echoing damningly.

Modren swivelled on his toe and came marching back. He grabbed Farden by the shoulder and wrenched him close, so close they could share the smell of ale on their breath. 'You shut your mouth!' he snapped. He looked around. People were staring.

'Does she know?'

Modren stared at the floor. 'She might suspect…'

Farden spoke slowly, his tone dangerous. 'Your own wife-to-be, Modren. Your own wedding. Bait for a war. Just a worm on a hook. How fucking noble of you,' he growled. With a snarl, he shrugged himself free of the tight grip and stormed up the stairs, boots squeaking against the polished marble. Modren had to jog to keep up with him.

'Farden, stop!'

'How dare you use her like this,' Farden was ranting, looking around for more stairs.

'Stop!'

'You three have gone too far with this. It's despicable. It's ridiculous. It's dangerous and stupid. It's...' Farden ran out of adjectives. 'Where is she?' he demanded, swaying ever so slightly. He couldn't deny the wave of nausea that swept through him. The alcoholic numbness he had been so eagerly waiting for had finally began to seep into his bones, but it was making him feel worse, not better. *Not now*, he told it.

A strong hand grabbed his arm. 'If you calm down, I'll take you to her,' Modren hissed in his ear.

'You're damn right you will.'

Modren pointed in the general direction of up. 'She's in our room.'

Farden waved a hand up the stairs. 'After you,' he said.

Modren muttered something dark to himself and took the stairs two at a time. He led Farden across a short landing, and then up another winding waterfall of marble steps. Up, they strode, further and further into the Arkathedral. The torches and lamps were being snuffed by the servants. The corridors and hallways grew dark as Modren steered Farden towards his wife-to-be. They said nothing. Farden silently fumed and collected his words, while Modren just let the clattering plod of their booted steps form a decision in his mind.

At long last they came to a lone door at the end of a corridor, deep into the Arkathedral. Farden looked around. A single torch had been left alive at the mouth of the hallway. It threw long shadows across their feet. Modren turned around and crossed his arms. 'Well,' he nodded to the door. 'If you must.'

'Somebody must.'

'She won't listen to you. In fact, she'll probably rip you in two with that tongue of hers.'

'If that's what it takes, so be it.'

'Last chance, Farden.'

'Keep it for somebody else.'

'Stubborn bastard,' Modren sighed. He put his hand on the

doorknob and twisted it. The door opened with a gentle creak and revealed a room even darker than the hallway, full of shadow and dark shapes. Farden pushed past Modren and into the room.

'Elessi?' he called.

Click.

The mage was plunged into utter darkness. There was a creak as a spell spread across the door and sealed it tight. Farden hammered at it with his fists, but it felt like he was clobbering a stone wall, not wood. 'Modren!' he yelled. 'MODREN!'

Farden felt his way around in the darkness for something solid. A flimsy crate, a bundle of cloth, a pole… a pole! Farden snatched at it. It felt sturdy enough, solid wood. He felt his way back to the door and began to jab at it as viciously as he could. It was hopeless. The pole lasted for three hits before the spell snapped it in two. Farden tossed the splintered halves into the darkness and began to hammer the door with his fists again. He was about as useful as the pole.

Something in Modren's spell punched him, spun him around, and tossed him to the floor. There was a flash of light as his head hit the cold marble. Pain populated the darkness before his rolling eyes, filling it with faces and swirling teeth. Farden gasped, desperately dizzy. He could feel the ale swimming in his blood. His head pounded through its numbness. His stomach tightened. His body had given up.

'Fine,' he spat, bile rising, head wet with blood. 'You win.'

Farden had just enough time to vomit before the unconsciousness swallowed him.

❦

Modren rubbed his eyes with his fingers and trudged back up the hallway. The ale was creeping into him too, making his steps and eyelids heavy. He sighed, but it was a sigh of resentful satisfaction.

The right thing had been done. No woman, especially Elessi, deserved to be told that their wedding was a sham, even if it was the truth. Elessi would have her wedding. He would make her his wife. Modren would make sure of that. He put his hands in his pockets and let out a low, troubled whistle.

Somebody whistled back at him. Modren turned to see a woman leaning up against a window, framed against the orange of the city. She was wrapped in a blanket and borrowed clothes, sandy-haired, the sort of figure a man's eyes can't help but wander over, no matter if his wedding was in the morning or not. It was the woman Farden had brought back with him. He had seen her earlier at the dreaded council meeting.

'Shouldn't you be in your chambers?'

'Shouldn't you?'

Modren approached her, holding out a hand. 'Modren,' he offered.

She didn't take it at first. She just stared at him, or past him, Modren couldn't tell in the dark. Damn this shortage of torches, he thought.

It was only when she reached out her own hand that he remembered she was blind. 'Jeasin,' she said. It was hard not to notice the familiar tinge of Albion in her accent. 'I like how quiet it is here,' she said.

Modren nodded, gazing out at the city. 'Let's hope it stays that way,' he said.

'After what I 'eard today, in your council, chances are slim.'

'Aren't they just?'

Jeasin ran a hand through her hair. Modren squinted. He swore he recognised her from somewhere. 'You seen Farden?' she asked.

Modren looked back down the corridor. 'Not a whisker,' he lied.

The woman sniffed. 'Figures. Still managed to 'bandon me, even though he promised.'

'Shall I walk you back to your room?'

'Probably for the best, seein' as I don't know the way.'

She held out an arm, and stiffly let Modren guide her away. 'You a mage like Farden?' she asked, feeling the armour around his wrists.

Modren smiled. 'Yes, but nobody's like Farden,' he muttered, and she nodded, as if that made the most perfect sense in the world.

chapter 22

"Krauslung was founded with blood and sea-water, and it will end in the same manner."

Words from the scholar Lasti, who was scribe to the Arkmage Los

A hesitant morning. Mists rose from the sewer-grates and punch-holes in the gutters. Steam lingered around the maws of drainpipes. Windows had steamed in the dawn. People were yawning and stretching in their beds. The night had been long for some, shorter for others. Groups were still being carted off to the prisons for their riotous persuasions. Malvus' allies, it seemed, were many, and already the preachers were dusting off their boxes and robes for another day ahead.

Beneath all of this, lost in the winding, forgotten tunnels of the sewer system, in the kingdom of sludge and rats, crouched a figure in the dark. Dead rat eyes swivelled. A sliver of grey tongue spoke, yet it did not move. Claws clutched and clasped with no muscles behind them.

'Sssssssswe feel it…' said the voice of many, hissing from the chest of the dead rat. 'The day is finally here.'

A nod from the figure, not a sound for concentration. A hot storm brewed in that sewer, in the heart of the girl. The steam rising from around her, rising up into the city above, was its proof. Its herald. She could barely contain her power.

'Are you ready?' wheezed the rat.

Silence but for the dripping.

'Are you ready?'

A tight smile this time. 'More than I'll ever be.'

'Then let the dead stars fall.'

❦

Somebody else was smiling. Actually, *beaming* was probably more accurate. Elessi's cheeks ached as she stared out from her window on the southern flank of the dew-clad Arkathedral.

The chambermaids pulled the last string tight on the corset and stood back to admire their work. Elessi glimpsed at the mirror. 'How does it look?' she asked, as though she didn't trust her reflection.

'Wonderful, miss,' chorused the girls, an inch away from an eruption of giggling. Elessi turned to face the mirror and smoothed down the ruffles in the dress with her hands. It was a gold dress, as tradition stated, with white panels in the skirts for dancing. Beside her lay the long box in which it had been delivered. Underneath the wreckage of a torn paper ribbon was a note, written in green ink:

FOR ELESSI, ON YOUR WEDDING DAY,

DURNUS AND TYRFING.

Elessi smiled at herself once again. She had never imagined this day, and this dress, would ever come. Many a thousand long nights of wistful staring out of windows had led to this, and a thousand miles of travel too. She didn't care that the bastard Farden had returned. She didn't care for the riots, the turmoil below. They all paled. This was her wedding day. She would have it, if even for a few moments. She would have her mage.

There came a knock at the door, and one of the maids went to answer it. As soon as she opened it, she flinched and tried to shut it again, but an arm had already wedged itself between it and the frame. 'It's bad luck!' cried the maid.

Elessi turned and saw the arm, wrapped in polished, mirror-like armour. 'Modren! Don't you dare! Go away,' she cried, quickly retreating behind the door.

'I don't want to see you,' he said, abruptly realising how bad that sounded. 'I mean… I have a little gift that I thought you might want.' Another hand came through the crack in the door, this time holding a tiny blue flower shaped like a bell in its fingers. 'Springknell,' he said, in as deep a voice as possible, a voice that wasn't used to wrapping around the names of flowers. 'Thought it might go well with your dress.'

Elessi rolled her eyes and blushed at her maids. 'What are the guards going to think when they see their fearsome Undermage deliverin' pretty little flowers to his wife-to-be?'

'They're none the wiser. I hid it under my cloak,' laughed the voice behind the door.

'Away with you!' she ordered, smiling as one of her maids passed the flower to her. It fit neatly into the hem of her dress.

'Until later,' he said, and the door was swiftly shut.

Elessi went eagerly back to the mirror. The maids brought her a chair and then began to arrange and tame her curly locks. Elessi folded her hands on her lap. She would have her wedding.

❦

Modren checked his armour one last time. Today he was a soldier made of mirrors and polished plates. Tyrfing had truly outdone himself with this suit. It had all the beauty and grace of ceremonial armour, but beneath its engraved curves and polish it had all the impenetrable strength of a granite cliff face. It veritably hummed with power and shield spells. Part of him silently prayed that today would only demand its ceremonial side.

Modren began his walk to Manesmark. There was a window open somewhere on that level, and it had let a breeze loose in the corridors. It was a brisk thing, and it felt good on his hands and neck and face. It ruffled his combed hair and toyed with his green-black cloak as he walked.

As he passed a brace of guards, they clacked their spears on the marble flagstones and saluted. 'Undermage! Best of luck.'

Funny, how men offered luck, whilst women offered congratulations. Modren smiled and saluted them with a twirl of his hands. 'I'll need it,' he chuckled, drily. *We'll all need it.*

There was a checklist in his head, and his thoughts were a quill, mentally scratching a dark line of ink through each task and chore. His armour was on. The flower had been delivered. Elessi was getting ready. The Winter Regiment was in place. The Evernia guard had been moved. The Arkathedral guard were busy locking down the fortress. The newly-formed Halfangar Regiments were in disguise and should be ready. The bellringers were stationed by their bells. The Written were arranging themselves around Krauslung's gate and Manesmark. Tyrfing and Durnus were heading to the Spire. *Done, done, done…* the orders rattled off in his mind like slingstones in a cave.

As Modren descended some steps, he came across a long corridor peeling off to his right. The single torch still stubbornly burnt near its mouth, sooting the pale ceiling with its funeral flames. Modren took a step forward and angled his ear. Silence. Only the torch dared its noise. The Undermage eyed the lone door at the corridor's end. It was still stuck fast and solid. The way he had cast it, the spell would hold for several days. The wedding would be over by then.

Farden would be livid, but so be it. Modren shrugged. There were many things more important than Farden's feelings. They could do without him.

Modren walked on, a small spark of anticipation growing in his stomach. Was it excitement? Was he nervous? Was it worry, mutating into fear? He knew little of any of those, but it was something. He quickened his pace, steel-clad boots making music on the stone.

❦

Wretched. The early sunlight showed it well in the mirror's face. Farden couldn't help but stare at himself. Part of him hoped it would get up and walk away, leaving him there sprawled on the floor, like a sad corpse. Then it wouldn't be him, and he could be content in simply feeling like death rather than looking like it as well.

At the end of a meandering trail of sweat, broken glass, and vomit, lay the mage. His arms and legs were dead weights. His throat was raw like a hunter's fresh kill. His skin was clammy and cold, sweat-rimed.

The only mercy was that his headache had died with the morning light.

The old mirror had warped with its years in storage. It made his face bulge in odd proportions, as though his dark-rimmed eyes were trying very hard to escape their sockets. Farden reached a hand up and pushed it away. 'What a state we are,' Farden whispered to it. He had to get up, he knew it.

With a wrench and grunt, he pulled himself up from his stupor. It took him almost five minutes to get to his feet, and when he did, he tottered around the room, feeling the world spin. When it finally settled to its normal kilter, Farden began to take in the room that he had only seen in darkness. It was a storage room, as he had guessed, packed with objects covered in dust sheets. Another mirror lay on the floor, smeared with vomit. It was smashed and broken and its old wooden frame was snapped in two. Farden didn't remember doing that.

The morning light was pouring through a high and narrow window in the far wall. Far too high to reach and far too thin to offer any escape. Farden looked back at the door, the door that snake Modren had sealed shut. Farden picked up a sliver of glass and hurled it at the door. It smashed without so much as a wooden thud, just a hard-edged clink that only stone or steel could offer. So the spell held fast…

Farden gingerly began to poke around under the dust sheets and behind corners. It was all just furniture; old, battered furniture that nobody had a need for. Farden had hoped for some sort of metal curtain rod or stout table leg, but neither was to be found. Farden put his hands to his filthy face and began to realise he would be stuck in here for a good while. He would miss the wedding. Exactly as Modren had wanted. He would miss the fight, if there was one. The stupid fools.

Farden sighed. Well that simply would not do.

❦

As the dawn rose, Krauslung slowly came to life. To to the north, a line of servants and well-dressed guests began to flow and trickle up the long hill to the juvenile Spire, the former laden with crates and boxes and plates and packages of food. Carts pulled by bears and cows followed them with barrels of wine and ale, ready for the merrymaking. Soldiers stood along the path, staring intently at the passers-by. Conversation buzzed like flies in the warming air. Everybody had something on their lips.

Word had it the Arkmages were to abdicate.

The riots had called for it, after all!

Malvus had finally brought them to task, confronted them!

But why was the army here?

Would the wedding still go ahead?

The Arkmages have already been thrown down by the righteous Malvus, tossed into prison!

That's preposterous! They had been sighted at the Spire already.

Quiet down near the soldiers!

The rumours raged on, a blaze of opinion.

As the trickle of guests grew into a river, two figures emerged from a skinny door in the shadow of a ramshackle inn. Both wore hoods and stolen finery. One was old. One was young. The older one put a hand behind the younger one's back and was rewarded with an insolent shrug.

'Calm yourself!' came a hiss.

'Then leave me be. I need to concentrate!' came the reply.

'You need to move quicker. We'll look suspicious if we dawdle.'

'Shut it, Lilith.'

Lilith went to backhand the girl, but the glance of sheer power and venom in Samara's eyes almost caused her to choke. She slowly lowered her hand, and nodded.

'Hobble or something. Make it look like I'm escorting my old aunt.'

Lilith gently cradled her frail hand in the bend of Samara's arm and put on a limp. Together they joined the line of guests that were walking to the wedding. A rainbow-coloured line of the city's finest, bedecked in jewels and trinkets and their wedding best. Political turmoil or not, the Arka's upper echelons wouldn't be seen dead missing a social occasion.

Samara and Lilith tucked themselves behind a pair of plump

old men and listened to them waffle on about Hâlorn trade taxes. Behind them, a woman was shepherding a gang of uncomfortable yet incredibly well-dressed children onwards. Samara glanced around, and met the eyes of a guard scanning the crowd. He caught her gaze, looked her up and down, and didn't bat an eyelash. Samara allowed herself a little smile. Nobody had any idea that a monster walked in their midst.

❦

Snap!

The dagger-blade fractured, sending Farden crashing into the wall. Marble met cheek, and he slid to the floor. He lifted a hand to nurse a tooth and a bitten lip. A shard of dagger had narrowly missed his neck. It lay in a pile of slivers on the floor, broken, embarrassed. Farden kicked it away and quickly began to claw at where the hinge had been fastened to the marble. He had already chipped away a little of the stone. He managed to prise one of its edges up with his fingers, but that was as far as he got. The door was stuck fast in the frame.

Farden grit his teeth as the spell bit his fingers again. It was like being clouted with a bat. The pain leapt up his arm and reverberated down his side. Farden pummelled the door some more, exacting some futile revenge. The echoes of his fists hitting the solid door were nothing short of mocking.

'Gods damn you, Modren!' Farden shouted to the room. He kicked out at a nearby crate and marched in a furious circle. He had to get out of that room before it was too late. Their plan was utterly ridiculous. Trying to coax his daughter out of hiding was like waving a red flag in front of a minotaur. If she was what they thought she was, then could they stop her? Ridiculous. *And how dare they use Elessi's own wedding?* Farden demanded. Surely, if the decades had taught them all anything, it was the value of rash decisions.

Such was life.

Farden clenched his fists until they shook. He stared at the door with every inch of his being. A dusty fragment of a memory came floating through his head then, an old echo from his days at the School, of his classes with Jasfell Sund. The Locksmith they had called him. He knew the inside and out of every lock spell that had ever been dreamt up. He could hear his monotone voice drifting through the stark classroom.

What is the easiest way to open a door? A key! they had chorused. *Of course, young ones. Every door has a lock, every lock its key, and every key its teeth. It is the same with our spells, young ladies and gentlemen, you just have to get the teeth in the right place.*

The mage held his breath until his chest burnt. He kicked out at the nearby crate one more time. No. He couldn't just let it burst back into his life again, as dangerous and accursed as his magick was. It had ruined his life, and others' in the process.

Farden winced, abruptly torn. How much was Elessi's life worth? How desperate was he to get out of that godsforsaken room? Was he truly that stubborn?

Farden swallowed the tough lump that was lodged in his throat. He gently tugged his sleeve up to his elbow, unfastened his vambrace, and looked down at the black key symbol tattooed into his wrist. It was like staring at the stark outline of a frozen body in the dirty snow. Dead to the world. Long gone. Farden sighed.

If anyone knew about resurrection, it was him.

The ash tree had taught him that.

'Fuck it!' he cursed, and then marched to the door. He knelt to the stone and spread his fingers over the door. It was cold, rough, immovable. Farden scrunched up his eyes and pushed until the tired muscles in his arms stood like knotted ropes under his skin. Nothing happened. The door refused to budge. Farden strained and strained, like a grave-robber caught by the dawn, he frantically tried to dig up whatever he could remember of his magick. Would it kill him? Possibly. He filed that thought away and pushed harder. He didn't have a choice.

For an age, nothing happened. Farden began to sweat. He got cramp in his arm. The nausea began to rise…

Something flickered at the base of his spine. He winced as the pain of it darted into his skull, firing up his headache once again. Had he cracked open his eyes he would have seen a faint glow flash across his tattoo. Then it happened again. Another flicker. Another pulse. Farden held on tight as the magick came, inch by painful inch.

The door began to rattle viciously. Modren's spell began to fight back. *Gods, this spell was strong.* He couldn't remember feeling a spell like this before. He pushed and pushed with everything he could grasp at.

Farden held on for dear life as his magick burst forth in one debilitating strike. It burst from him like a tidal wave, cracking the doorhandle in two and turning half the wood into powder. Farden flew backwards under the pressure, crying out as he was tossed into the stiff embrace of a gilded wardrobe. The impact drove the breath from his lungs. He lay in a mass of splinters, wheezing like a fish that had suddenly found itself on a mountainside.

It took more than a minute for Farden to move. His fingers twitched, then his arms, then his legs, and then finally his eyes fluttered open. He rolled out of the wreckage and slid onto the glass-strewn floor. He looked at the door and then, ludicrously, he began to laugh. Had anyone stumbled across the corridor at that precise moment, it would have been a sight beyond odd. A filthy mage lying on his face, bleeding from several angles, surrounded by broken things, covered in stale vomit, giggling to himself. Farden put his forehead to the cold floor. His body was on fire. His head pounded, but he had done it. He had done it.

With his muscles shaking and glass digging into his ribs, he pushed himself up, stepped through what was left of the door, and began to run as fast as his body would bloody well let him.

❦

'She's here,' said the breathless runner, skidding to a halt.

'Who?' asked Modren, hand flying to his sword hilt.

The boy pointed in the general direction of the city. 'Your wife, sir. I mean, your… er,' he stammered.

'I understand,' Modren said, waving the boy back out of the tent. He waited until he was gone before he exhaled. The Undermage adjusted his armour for the hundredth time. Modren was a man who had once beaten a minotaur to death with a rock, a man who'd drank a Huskar chieftain *and* his bear under a table, a man who had climbed the slopes of Lokki just for a training exercise. He was the Undermage of the Arka. A Written. Magick elite. A scarred veteran, and yet here he was, terrified of meeting his wife-to-be at the scales of marriage.

Modren peered through the crack in the tent flap and looked at the veritable sea of guests that had arrived. It wasn't them that scared him; it was the little pulpit and the set of golden scales standing at the end of the long carpet that split the crowd in two. Modren scanned the crowd. The blind woman, Jeasin, was near the front, looking bewildered in borrowed clothes. Durnus was sitting in front of her, surrounded by guards. Verix and Loki sat apart, silent and watchful of the skies. A few council members could be spotted too, probably there at the behest of Malvus. He hadn't dared to show his face. He had been polite enough to stall his coup for a day. If Modren looked closely, he could also see some of his Written hidden in the crowd, ready and waiting.

A hand snaked around the flap and a wizened old man with an unfortunately massive mole on his nose ducked into the tent. Modren stepped aside, momentarily stunned by this stranger's boldness. He was about to demand who in Emaneska he was when the man ran his hands through his sparse white hair and turned it dark and bushy. 'Can't stand all that gossiping and staring. It's incessant,' the man muttered, in Tyrfing's voice. The Arkmage wiped his armoured hands across his cheeks and chin, producing a beard and a familiar face. He stood straight and his bones straightened and clicked back into place one by one. Shapeshifting at its best. Tyrfing cleared his throat with a wince. 'How are you feeling?' he asked, hoarsely.

'Odd.'

'Marriage,' snorted Tyrfing. 'Some men choose war instead.'

Modren chuckled and ran a hand through his white-blonde hair. Despite the cool air, there was a hint of sweat on his brow. 'Have the guards seen anything?'

'You need to focus on your wedding, Modren, and nothing else,' Tyrfing replied, pouring himself a glass of turquoise wine from a table nearby. He sniffed it, sipped it, and then gulped half of it down. 'Not a sign. Not a hint. We're seeing more trouble from the rioters than we are from her.'

'Maybe she won't come. Maybe we were wrong…'

'I won't consider that for a second. We stick to the plan,' said the Arkmage. Tyrfing finished his glass. 'I'm sorry, Modren, that this is your wedding day…' he would have carried on, but he winced as another cough fought its way out.

Modren held up a hand. 'I'm not. As much as I don't like it, it's better we have it now, than on a tomorrow that may not exist.'

Tyrfing nodded. There was sense in that, be it bitter. He held out a hand and Modren clasped it. They felt their keys pulse, and then Tyrfing stepped out into the sunshine. 'She's here, you know.'

'I do,' Modren said. In that moment, the skalds began to play their ljots and pipes, and an elegant tune filled the morning air. There was a murmuring sigh as the huge crowd got to their feet. Modren adjusted his armour one last time, and, as Tyrfing held the tent-flap aside for him, the Undermage stepped out onto the dew-touched grass and strode confidently towards the golden scales, all eyes upon him.

❦

'For the tenth time, Bringlin, take them aside and let the others pass,' ordered Lieutenant Rossar, his forehead resting between finger and thumb, a sign of exasperation.

'Sorry, Lieutenant. Please, miss, stand aside,' Bringlin ordered the woman and her child.

'What is the meaning of this, soldier? We shall be late to the wedding!'

'It will only take a moment ma'am. It's for your own safety.'

The mages were spread out like a safety net across the road, just shy of halfway to Manesmark. The sun beat down on their silver and bronze armour, brand new and branded by the forge-mark of the Arkmage himself. It was the kind of armour that straightened the back, lifted the chin, and puffed the chest. It didn't need any spell for that.

Further up the hill, another hundred or so stood in two wings, either side of the road, ready to pounce. The Winter Regiment's orders were simple: *Keep the preachers and rioters in the city, Stop and question any and all girls between the ages of eight and eighteen. And if you see Farden, stop him.*

Bringlin began to run through the questions, trying not to smile and instead keep an air of toughness about him. The poor girl standing before him looked no less than terrified. She was a sliver above eight maybe, all golden curls and gawping blue eyes. The mother, on the other hand, was a fearsome-looking woman, perhaps half bear. The size of a small shed, she was huffing and puffing so much that her head looked set to blow. She had her hands set firmly on her ample hips and was in the process of boring a hole in Bringlin's forehead with her narrowed eyes. Bringlin tried his level best to ignore her and stared at the girl. She shivered in her finest pink dress. Bringlin stared into her little blue eyes, letting his magick do its interrogating while he went through the routine questions. 'What is your name, miss?'

'Kinl, sir.'

'Where are you from?'

'Krauslung?' chirped the girl.

'Where exactly?'

'The big white house on Haverff Alley?' Every answer was another question.

'Who's wedding are you going to?'

'A maid's?'

The woman huffed some more. A few of the other guests pointed and tittered as they passed by on the road, and she turned a shade of red. 'Really, mage, these questions are pointless. We're already very late. Whoever it is you're looking for, it's obvious my little Kinl isn't her.'

Wary of the lieutenant's eyes on his back, Bringlin withdrew his magick. He was satisfied; the little girl was about as magickal as a pebble. 'Fine,' he said, waving them back to the road. 'Enjoy the wedding.'

'Hmph,' was all the large woman could say as she dragged her little girl up the hill. Bringlin crossed his arms and turned back to the crowds. He heard a faint whisper of music on the breeze. *So the ceremony had begun then*, thought the young mage, as he stared up at the powder-blue sky and the black smudge of the Spire against it. Bringlin sniffed the air and caught the scent of hot food, wine, farska, cakes, and ale. He sighed, stretching, and wondered if they would have a chance to sample any of it. It's not every day there's a wedding…

'Look lively, lads. Bringlin, wake up! Another one for you,' came the muttered order from a nearby sergeant, a gruff man with a scar across his lip like a makeshift moustache. Bringlin turned around and spotted another young girl amongst the line of passers-by. She had her hooded head down and was busy helping an old, frail woman navigate the pebbles lodged in the dusty road. Bringlin stepped forward with his hand outstretched.

'Ladies, if I might have a moment of your precious time,' he announced, making them halt in their tracks.

The old woman looked up first. She too wore a hood. She seemed to be nursing her arm, as though it had been recently broken. They didn't look like beggars; their clothes were well-stitched, all silk and wool, reasonably fine for the crowd they travelled with.

'What's the problem, mage?' asked the woman, with a yellow smile.

'A few questions, if you don't mind,' Bringlin gestured to the side of the road. He could feel a few of the mages moving behind him. Cautionary procedure.

'Questions?' asked the girl. She lifted her head and Bringlin assessed her face. She was young indeed, but older than the last few. Fifteen maybe, and strikingly beautiful for her age. She had pitch-black hair that flowed like oil down her neck and chest. Her eyes were a swirled mix of blue-green that never seemed to settle on one hue. Bringlin found himself staring. 'Surely that's not necessary. We're just going to the wedding,' she said, quietly. The mages edged closer. She certainly fit the description.

'Why don't you just let us pass, hmm?' added the woman by her side.

'It will only take a moment, then you can be on your way,' Bringlin shook his head. 'We can't be too careful.' As he spoke, he let his magick begin to creep outwards, probing the girl and the old woman for any sign or hint of power. He opened his mouth to ask his first question, but instead he flinched, and gasped. His magick hit a brick wall. He couldn't help but recoil from it, flinching as though he'd been slapped. He blinked at the girl, who stared straight back at him. He went to reach for his sword, but it felt as though his arm were made of ice.

'Sh… she…!' Bringlin choked, jabbing a finger at them. The other mages began to shout. Spells flickered. It was then that a familiar-looking man, utterly dishevelled and covered in what appeared to be a mixture of broken glass and vomit, barrelled through the line of people on the road, and flew straight into the girl and the old woman.

❦

If a soldier had covered their eyes against the sun, and squinted as hard as humanly possible, he might have just been able to make out Heimdall, standing like a guardian over the city. He was a speck on the white canvas of the Arkathedral, framed against the powder-blue sky. Beside him stood a slightly larger speck; a speck with feathers, wind-ruffled wings, and a beak that glinted like iron in the sun. Ilios was leaning out over the railing, claws grating on the marble, the sort of sound that makes a spine shiver. He whistled questioningly.

'Not a sign,' he replied, surveying the lines of people drawn out over the Manesmark hill. 'Not yet.'

Another whistle.

'If she is here, her magick is shrouded from my sight.' He closed his tawny eyes for a moment and pulled a face of concentration, of strain. A world of whispers flooded his ears, thoughts mumbled to an empty room. Asides and mutterings. An ocean of tongues.

Where is my brooch? I could have sworn I left it beside the box…

How dare she wear gold to a wedding! Estice should know better after last year.

If I get sat next to one of these screaming children, I'm going to have to plug my ears with that wig of yours.

Be my guest.

You don't want any of that wedding slop they dole out. It's watered down I tell you. That's why I always bring my own mörd to these sorts of things.

She's a maid, I hear, a simple maid.

Yes, but he's the Undermage.

And a handsome one at that.

Dangerous, I hear.

They all are. Malvus was right.

And how much did he pay Gondty for you to say that, Helsin?

Enough.

The god winced as he delved too deep. He was almost deafened. He opened his eyes and took in the sky. There was a smattering of clouds swimming in the high atmosphere. Heimdall put his hands on the railing and took a slow breath. Weakness was starting to seep into him, like spilt oil into the cracks of a flagstone. He had been at this too long. 'There are too many whispers in that crowd, not enough shouts.'

Heimdall turned to face the glittering sea. It was a blue blanket strewn with white jewels. A ring of fishing ships toiled on it. Heimdall let the sounds of the waves drown out the city for a moment.

And for a moment he almost missed it.

A shout.

It's her! The girl is here!

Let her go, Bringlin!

Now, Samara!

Stay down, Lilith.

Heimdall swung his gaze north to the hill. Colours were

popping and exploding from the grass, colours no human could ever see nor understand. They whirled and fountained from the dirt. The god narrowed his eyes at the hill and saw people fleeing, no, *flying* in all directions. Guards where lying on their backs with their armour ripped open. A thunderclap echoed over the city. Heimdall slapped his hand on the marble. He uttered one word to the gryphon, and one word only. 'Go.'

And go the gryphon did. Ilios leapt from the railing before the word had even left the god's lips. He swooped down, plummeting like a stone until his wings flared and he was skimming the rooftops with inches to spare. He flew north with the speed of a lightning bolt, leaving Heimdall to stare and watch as something hellish unveiled itself on the hill. As the twin bells began to ring, he couldn't help but wonder what the strange, tight feeling was in his chest.

❦

The mage was iron-clad, running through a trough of jellyfish. That's what it felt like. Every movement was a conscious battle. Every step rewarded him with a sting, but he kept on running. He was running out of time, and he knew it. Somehow, deep in his bones, he knew. He felt as though a giant thumb was pressing down on the back of his neck, harder and harder with every passing moment.

The road was clogged with people, the sun hot, and the guards numerous. Farden's hood was yanked low over his face. Exactly how he had made it through the main gates unchallenged, he would never know, but he was on borrowed luck. It wouldn't be long until they stopped him. Every step brought him more guards and more soldiers, more finery for him to clash with. He stole a quick glance down at his wretched clothes. He looked as though a sewer had spat him out.

Farden wove in and out of the crowds as fast as his legs would let him. His body was drained. Using the magick had set his muscles and organs aflame. Every fraction of his being wanted to simply fall into the grass and watch the sun fly overhead, to let Elessi have her day and leave them to their chances. But no. He couldn't. Farden looked at every face he raced past, trying to imagine what she would look like. She was here. He was positive. How? He didn't know. Perhaps it was the blood-tie between them. Perhaps he knew the same thirst for blood, that if it were him they were hunting, how he wouldn't resist a chance like this, army or no army.

A soldier stood in the centre of the road, arms crossed and eyes keen. Farden ducked down and tried to go around, but he had already seen him. Something about him must have caught the man's attention, maybe his pace, his hood, maybe his cloak spattered with vomit, who knows. Whatever it was, he stamped his foot and cupped a hand around his mouth. 'You there! Halt!' he yelled. Unfortunately, his words had the complete opposite effect. Farden doubled his pace, much to his body's outrage. He darted away from the soldier, breaking away from the road and ploughing through the long grass.

'Stop that man!' came the cries.

If people are good at anything, it is getting in the way. The chase was quickly noted by the line of people sauntering up the hill. As more soldiers peeled out from the crowd and gave chase to this sweating, filthy vagabond, up ahead a selection of try-hard, silk-clad heroes stepped out from the crowd with their hands held forward and bravery on their face. Their spouses and daughters and mothers looked on, glowing with pride for just a tantalising sliver of a moment, right up until Farden's fists decided to introduce themselves to a few jaws and ribs. The men were sent reeling, crumpling to the grass. More shouts and screams followed. Wincing with every step, lungs aflame, Farden sprinted on.

'Stop him!' yelled the people on the road, in one giant voice. Soldiers stepped into his path, spears low and hands on swords. Farden dodged them by running back across the road and leaping up a little knoll. For a moment at its paltry summit he was free. Between his pounding feet and head, he could hear the faint hint of music in the air. He looked to the north and caught sight of the splash of white at the base of the Spire. So close, but still so far away. Ranks of mages had formed a line across the road. Farden's heart fell. Between his pounding feet and head, he could hear a faint hint of music in the air. So close… He had to try.

As the mages caught sight of him, Farden dashed back onto the road and ploughed his way through a flock of young women. It was a bad choice. Faced with a grizzled rogue sweating and panting and pawing at them, they screamed like there was no tomorrow. The noise brought the attention of almost every mage for a mile around crashing down on him. All except one: a young man questioning two women by the side of the road, just up ahead. Farden saw the gap and charged for it. He might have made it had it not been for the spine of a rock hiding in the grass. He clipped it with his toe and it sent him him flying. Not to the grass, no, that would have been too easy. He bowled straight into the backs of the women.

Farden's head exploded with colours even before he felt the kiss of the soft, dewy grass. Somehow, gods only knew, he managed to roll and tumble onto his knees. *Run!* screamed his thoughts. But he didn't move. It wasn't because his legs had given up, nor was it the fact that a score of mages were seconds away from seizing him in their steel grips and wrestling him to the floor, it was a reason intangible. A tingling in his gut. Something that made his skin prickle in ways he couldn't describe.

Farden turned, inch by gentle inch, until he was looking straight into a pair of blue-green eyes, eyes that had stepped out of a mirror and found a fairer body. Eyes that glared right back, scraping at the back of his skull.

Time limped past as they stared at each other. Even when a dozen hands pushed him to the ground, Farden still kept his eyes fixed on his daughter. She was strikingly beautiful. Painfully so. She had the face of her mother but the colouring of her father, right down to her jet-black hair. She was a perfect blend. A perfect storm.

'Farden,' she whispered, like ice sliding across ice.

He ventured a smile, and then remembered who and what she was. She spared no such smile for him. This was no teary reunion. He could feel the heat of her in his veins as she knelt in the grass. A frail woman thrashing by her side, staring at him with wild eyes. Shouts filled the air.

'It's her! The girl is here!' somebody was shouting. A mage leapt forward from the crowd, the young man from the tavern. Farden's tongue scrabbled for his name. He had to stop him.

The young man barged the old woman aside and grabbed the girl's arm with all the bravest intentions in the world. *Poor fool.* Farden didn't need his magick to realise he'd just sealed his fate. He could see the grass around her flatten as though a fist pressed it down. The air grew hot around. 'Let her go, Bringlin!' he bellowed hoarsely, the name bubbling up from somewhere.

'Now, Samara!' yelled the thin old crone in the grass, the one clutching an arm to her chest. *Samara.* That was all Farden could think of. *That was her name.*

Silence reigned for her answer, as if her spell had snatched the wind from the air and the voices from the throats of everybody nearby. She turned to the old woman. 'Stay down, Lilith,' she ordered, calm as could be. Then she stood straight, and thunder clapped for her.

The spell ripped outwards through the gathered crowds. There were no screams, only the sound of clothes ripping and ribs popping. Farden felt at least one of his break as he sailed high over the grass, together with a dazed clump of men in silver armour. Bringlin flew over them all, bearing the very brunt of the spell. A body had never looked so dead, so *twisted.*

Farden crashed to the ground with a cry. Only the thick grass spared him the full pain of the fall, but even so, he fell crushed and beaten. His rib sent sparks flying through his eyes. Shaking, he managed to lift his head from the dirt. He narrowed his eyes at his daughter. Samara was now a good distance away, standing in a wide circle of bruised grass and broken people, arms raised to the sky.

It was then that the screams began.

chapter 23

"In many ways, the gift of belief that the gods gave to the humans was a double-edged blade. In one way, we are free beings, capable of a great many feats. Yet on the other hand, we can choose not to believe, and in that respect, we shape the world in a way that may not be its best direction, and shun the gods who made us."

From the writings of the infamous, and anonymous, critic Áwacran

Bunting crackled overhead. Birds tweeted in the spring sun. Children played in the shadow of the Spire. The world was none the wiser. Innocent, yet about to be soiled.

Modren dared a surreptitious glance down the carpeted aisle. She was only halfway down the aisle now. He was quickly rewarded with a sharp nudge from Tyrfing. The Arkmage rolled his eyes. But Modren couldn't help it. Elessi was nearly by his side.

His wife-to-be walked sedately up the narrow aisle, her maids and the skalds at her back to carry her train and keep the music flowing. The crowd clapped gently as she took each slow step up the seemingly endless carpet. Despite how serene she was attempting to look, Elessi couldn't help but beam with happiness. She looked from side to side as she walked, nodding to the people she recognised and smiling at the ones she didn't. Who cared if she didn't know them. They knew who she was.

Elessi did look for one person in particular as she walked. A gaunt face from a past long-forgotten. She found Durnus instead. He sat alone with his guards, smiling in her direction. Tyrfing stood at the scales with Modren, back turned. The blind Albion woman sat by herself, alone, yet surrounded, fidgeting. Farden was nowhere to be seen. *Good*, she thought. It was another broken promise, but she was glad for it.

Eventually, she reached Modren's side, and they slowly turned to face one another. As the crowd began to take its seats, they stared and smiled, taking in the dress, the armour, every inch of the other. Elessi looked beyond beautiful with her brown curls and glinting eyes. Modren looked like a polished war hero, proud. He leant forward to whisper in her ear.

'It's not too late,' Modren said.

Elessi shook her head, curls catching the wind. 'You're not escaping now, Undermage,' she replied. There was a firmness in her quiet voice he knew better than to argue with.

Modren looked up and over the crowd, to where the city lingered in the distance and smiled.

Tyrfing took a stand behind the golden scales. They were a big and ornate affair, full of curves and twists. He looked a little proud as he rested his hands on their bulbous head. After all, he had made them himself for this very occasion.

The Arkmage cleared his throat with a grimace and began his speech. 'We have gathered on this hill today to celebrate the union of two Arka. They have come before you to be wed in the tradition of our people, and in the sight of the gods,' he paused, unintentionally, as he caught the eyes of Verix sitting in the crowd. He had never expected that line to be so literal. Modren smiled as he too felt the strangeness of it. Tyrfing coughed and continued. 'It is a public commitment that they make, and you as Krauslung's people are witnesses to the vow they make here today, to each other, and to themselves, as the scales dictate.

'The scales. The symbol of the goddess Evernia is one with many faces, and today it represents a balancing of two people, and the effort they must make together to keep the scales steady, today, and for the rest of their marriage. It represents the end of a life walked alone, and the beginning of a life walked together. It represents equality. It represents the difficulties, the problems, that marriage and life will present, and the act of balancing each and every one as they come.' Tyrfing reached behind him, where a small lectern had been placed, and took the two polished weights from its wooden top. They were small things, made of white metal and each inscribed with one name. The one in his left hand said *Elessi*, and the one in his right, unsurprisingly, said *Modren*. Tyrfing held them out for the crowd to see, and then handed them to their owners. 'Now is the time to make your own promises to each other, in the sight of the gods, and of your witnesses,' he announced. He glanced at Durnus, and found his old friend trying not to smile. Only he knew how long Tyrfing had spent practising these lines.

Taking the sun-warmed weights in their cupped hands, Modren and Elessi turned to face each other. Modren spoke first. He too had spent nights practising his lines. He took a deep breath, and tried to ignore the crowd. 'Elessi, my only wish is that I had met you earlier. You came out of nowhere, and then you stayed. Now I can't imagine having a day without you, nor spending a night without you beside me. This is my promise to you, that I will always be by your side, to protect and love you, until the gods see fit to take me to the other side,' he said. The crowd clapped as he placed his weight on the scales. They tipped with a creak. Tyrfing frowned. He thought he had oiled them.

Elessi took a while to compose herself. Little tears were trying to escape from the corner of her eyes. 'Modren,' she began, her voice cracking at the edges. The crowd settled down and fell deathly silent to hear her speak. 'Modren, you are the finest man I have ever known, and I too wish I had met you sooner…' She took a moment to take a breath, managing to laugh at herself as she fanned away another set of tears. Modren couldn't help but smile. Nor could half the crowd. They may have been a haughty bunch, but they still had hearts that pumped crimson. Elessi waved her hand across the crowd and towards the city. 'I may not be the prettiest girl in Krauslung, nor Emaneska, but you make me feel like it. I may not be the smartest mind, but you make me feel like an Arfell scribe. I may not be the strongest, but you lend me your strength. And I may not be the richest woman here, but now…' she paused as she placed her weight in the scales. Modren's side slowly raised to meet hers, and after a little wobble, they settled, perfectly level. Elessi continued. '…now I am. Because I have you. I love you, Modren.' The last four words were whispered just for him, but the crowd saw it on her lips, and rose to its feet clapping. Confetti began to rain down on the hill, thrown from the balconies of the Spire. As the cheers rose to the clear blue sky, Modren and Elessi kissed. They were finally wed.

Tyrfing clapped as hard as any. He grinned like a mad man, happy for the couple, happy for the crowd, happy for the day, and happy that he had delivered his lines. He looked across the clapping, cheering crowd of Krauslung elite and met every eye he could. Then he looked down at Durnus, and found him sat rigid as a flagpole, not a single iota of emotion save for a cold dread on his pale face. In that moment, hands frozen mid-clap, Tyrfing knew what Durnus had heard. Behind the roar and noise of the crowd, the pealing of bells could be heard. Two bells, in fact, high in the towers of the Arkathedral. Bells whose peals might as well have been the sound of axes falling on bare necks.

Durnus got to his feet. There was an edge to his jaw that worried Tyrfing. 'Modren,' he said. But Modren was too busy holding his bride and waving to the crowd. 'Modren!' he barked, startling the Undermage.

'What?' Modren asked, and then followed Tyrfing's eyes down to Durnus. The Arkmage spread his hands wide and felt the air.

'Do you feel it?' he asked.

Modren clenched his fist. Elessi put a hand on his steel chest. 'What's wrong? What's going on? Is it... ? No...' she said, her mouth falling open. Her cheeks, so red mere moments ago, ran white. 'No, not today! She can't!' she cried.

Modren kissed her one more time and then gently pushed her away. 'Get in the Spire, now! Take as many as you can!'

'Modren...?' she whimpered, scared. She stood alone at the scales, hands clutching her golden dress. The crowd was still clapping.

Modren's eyes were wild, juggling so many emotions. Fear, guilt, dread, anger, they were all there. 'Go, Elessi! Get to safety!' he ordered. She grabbed him by his steel collar and dragged him close, eyes almost even wilder than his.

'I didn't wait all this time to marry a corpse, you hear me? You better come back to me. You understand me, husband? You come back alive on our wedding day.'

Modren nodded, as sure as anything. 'You're not escaping now, Elessi, don't you worry.'

Elessi leant to kiss him again, but Modren was already marching down the carpet, Durnus and Tyrfing in tow. Modren wrenched his sword from its scabbard and lifted it high into the air. 'Written! With me!' he yelled, and a dozen figures barged their way out of the crowd, swords held high in unison and crackling with fire and sparks. The fight was on.

❦

Farden tasted grit in his mouth. Sour, crunchy grit between his teeth. He spat and rolled onto his side. His arms were numb from the shock of the spell. They could barely lift themselves, never mind his body. He floundered like a fish in the grass.

His hand encountered something sharp, jagged, and wet. Farden shifted his head and found the body of a young mage lying behind him, broken and awkward. Bringlin. His red eyes stared up at the sky, blood running from their corners. His armour was ripped open at the chest and painted a muddy red. Steel, bent backwards and feathered like paper.

Farden shivered as a breeze sprang up around him. He swivelled around to try to unfasten the mage's sword. His daughter was still standing motionless in the grass. That old woman was crawling away from her as fast as her knobbled knees could move, heading for safety. For some reason she kept looking back at him, hissing something venomous, shouting to Samara. She was far too busy to listen.

Eyes heavy, body screaming, inches from falling unconscious, Farden fiddled with the buckle of the mage's scabbard. His fingers were slippery with Bringlin's blood, but somehow he managed to get it undone. He yanked it from the man's belt, and held it tight to his chest. Now all he had to do was get up.

Farden looked around. He could see other bodies moving. Some crawling to safety, others trying to staunch their frantic bleeding, wailing at broken faces and shattered bone. A scattering of mages were trying to get to their feet. They were having the same trouble as Farden. Their limbs were as dead as Bringlin.

The breeze swiftly turned into a wind. Farden could feel the ground trembling beneath him. He stared up at the sky. It was a blue so pure and close that it felt as though he could reach up and smudge it with his thumb. He lay back and let the wind fan his face. He felt his eyes grow heavy…

Elessi. The name slapped him. The wedding was barely a mile away. Farden could hear bells tolling, or was that just a ringing in his ears? He prayed it was the bells. At least they would have warning of this cataclysm. Elessi would be safe.

A blur of white and brown flashed past his eyes. A sharp keening wail made him flinch. A hunter's cry, piercing and terrifying. Farden lifted his head to watch the gryphon swoop down, claws outstretched and beak wide. Any normal person would have soiled themselves with fear. Samara broke her concentration just long enough to move her hand and meet the plummeting Ilios with a bolt of glimmering white light. Farden's head snapped back as the spell ricocheted, sending another round of stars to burst in his eyes. When he'd recovered, he scrambled onto his elbows, blinking frantically.

Ilios was nowhere to be seen. Only a few long feathers pirouetted in the building wind. Samara had raised her hands to the sky again, eyes closed, deep in concentration. 'Ilios!' he yelled, as loud as his raw throat and bruised lungs would allow. He thumped the grass with his fist. Gods, this girl was a monster. Farden grimaced as he stared at her. A beautiful monster, so terrifyingly, tormentingly close.

The nearby mages were beginning to make a stand. Surely this was what the Arkmages had prepared for? Catch her away from the city. Pen her in with fire and flame. Strength in pure overwhelming numbers. But where were the reinforcements? The swarm of new recruits? The rest of the Winter Regiment? The army? The Written? Samara stood unchallenged, save for a handful of tottering mages and one paralysed Farden.

It was as though Krauslung had heard him. Like a swarm of bees, figures broke from the city gates and began to form up in ranks. Soldiers and guards peeled from the screaming crowds and began to march. Boots trampled the grass. Spears levelled. Hundreds upon hundreds, ready to fight this one, single assailant. It was surreal, yet nobody spared a moment to scribble its poetry down, or to do justice to it with paint. There was work to be done.

Farden ached to join them. Whether it was necessity, anger, or the fact it was *his* daughter, his duty, his selfish right to be the one who killed her, he ached for it. If only his legs would do him the courtesy of answering his pleas. As he struggled, he watched the soldiers split into two pincers. They were at least half an hour away, but running fast. The nearest were a glittering sea of fresh armour, a mixture of grim faces and fearful ones. Strength in numbers always called for new recruits.

Farden tried to stall her, to give them some precious time. 'Samara! Stop!' he bellowed over the wind. It got fiercer with every passing moment. His daughter's name still felt foreign coming from his mouth. 'SAMARA!' he tried again.

She barely spared him a flick of her eyes. She was deep in concentration. Farden squinted in the wind as it whipped his face. He could see the veins popping out from her skin, even at that distance. Sweat was trying to run down her face. A whirlwind of dirt, stones, and uprooted grass spun around her feet. A few feathers too, the bitch. Her knees bent as the spell forced her down and down, as her clawing fingers reached up and up. Farden looked up at the sky, wondering what she was reaching for.

It hit him like a brick. *One to which the stars succumb.*

It was now or never. His legs be damned. Farden began to crawl towards her, sword in both hands, bellowing her name into gaps in the wind. Behind him, the mages had formed up. Spells began to fly overhead. Fire, lightning, water, and ice, they darted overhead with whip-cracks and hisses, only to dive uselessly into the dirt a few yards from Samara's feet, forced down by her own spell. This time his daughter did spare a glance, and she caught Farden's eye as he frantically shimmied through the grass, sword outstretched. She opened her mouth to speak and Farden heard her words in his mind.

'You can't stop me, *murderer*!' she said, the word spat out as an insult.

'I have to!' he cried. The gale stole his words but somehow

she managed to hear him. 'You have no idea what you're doing!'

'I know exactly what I'm doing!' she snarled.

'Killing a lot of innocent people, that's what you're doing! You've been brain-washed, Samara!' Still the name tasted strange.

'None of these people are innocent. You've stolen the world for yourselves, forgotten the true gods. Lived like kings!' Lies by rote, spilling from her mouth. Practised and embedded. It made Farden's heart sink. He had hoped...

Farden managed to get to his knees. 'The daemons? They enslaved our kind! How can you spout such mindless...?'

'My kind? I'm nothing like you!' she sneered, as her hair lashed her face. 'You knew my father, you know what he was. My mother too. I'm nothing like you scum!'

Farden was speechless. *I knew her father...* his mind echoed. He just knelt there, confused. Samara was bearing her teeth at him.

'I'll see you dead before the day is out, murderer!' she was shouting.

Farden hit his chest with the flat of the sword and held up his hands. 'If you want to take revenge on me, then take it. Don't involve these others!' More firebolts flew past him, fire skimming his fingers.

'They are as guilty as you are!'

'Guilty of what?!'

Samara wrinkled her lip. It was a foul expression, made filthier by the pure and simple fact that she was his blood, even if she didn't know it. 'Existing,' she said deep in his mind, somehow managing to echo, as if she had stolen all his thoughts and left a bare hall.

So be it. A monster, and a mindless one at that. Farden grit his teeth and pushed his knees through the grass. He held his sword out in front. Arrows zipped past him now, but they too were forced into the grass before they could touch her. The wind snapped them and tossed them into the air. Farden quickly glanced behind him and found another formation sprinting down the hill to join the fray. Archers, soldiers, and mages. Farden spied some Written in their ranks. It didn't take long for their spells to come flying in. The difference was palpable.

Farden fell to the grass as four giant fireballs flew over his head, singeing his hair. But even they failed to reach her. The ground burst into fountains of charred soil as they buried themselves at her feet. Samara pressed on with her spell.

Farden shut his eyes and tucked his head under his hands as the mages began to cast everything they had. He cowered and prayed for some smidgeon of accuracy. Fire scorched his hands and neck. Lightning flicked him as it passed him. Arrows whined. In that place, caught in his daughter's hurricane and in the wake of spells, time seemed to slow. He vaguely remembered this sensation. He watched yet another fire spell pass over him, sliding sedately past his shoulder, a crystalline globule of orange ridges and white crests. It fell to the earth like all the others. The ground was churned into dust as each and every attempt was rebuffed, a crescent of destruction that refused to reach his daughter. Farden soon lost sight of her behind the wall of dirt and flame.

The wind was reaching its crescendo now. He suddenly felt a lurch as the ground beneath him dropped an inch. The world began to shake. The spells paused for just a moment. Farden could have sworn he heard Modren bellowing over the roar of the wind. Farden buried his face in the grass as the spells began to fly again, faster and harder this time. There was a dull boom as the ground sagged again. The mage caught a brief glimpse of his daughter through the wind-chased chaos. She had dropped to one knee, as if bearing some terrible weight. There was a desperate look of pain and effort on her face. Her body was twisting and contorting in the most unimaginable ways. The ground at her feet was cracking and splintering. One of her feet was slowly sinking into the earth. Stones cracked and crunched. Wind screeched. Still she reached for the sky. Samara's spell was taking its final breath.

'Samara!' Farden yelled again over the roar.

Kadooom!

The thunderclap threw everyone to the grass. Soldier, archer, mage, onlooker, every single person within a mile of Samara felt the ground fly out from under them. Spells flew high into the air like fireworks as their casters tumbled onto their arses.

It was then that they all saw them. Three stark pinpricks of light, stuck high in the blue ceiling of sky, teetering in the unreachable rafters. Stars bold enough to face the day's sun.

'Stars…' Farden mouthed.

❦

Only Durnus stayed standing. Legs stuck fast in the grass, arms outstretched to steady himself against the shockwave, he stared with smoky eyes at the whirlwind that was the girl's spell. Eyes weren't needed here. He could see every inch of Samara and her power. She glowed like a brand in the night. Her spell was like a pillar of white glass reaching high into the darkness. Durnus followed the pillar up, and saw three white specks at its distant tip. Cold. Calm. Waiting for Samara to drag them down into the kingdom of men. Durnus could almost feel their stares.

The Arkmage clapped his hands together and a shivering ball of lightning blossomed between them. Durnus let it grow and grow, until he held it above his head. As the men around him pointed and yelled to each other about the lights in the sky, Durnus raised his spell high, straining, and then threw it with all his might.

By the skin of the spell's teeth, it made it through her whirling maelstrom, just close enough to knock one of her legs out from under her. Samara faltered, momentarily losing her concentration. If Durnus were closer, he might have seen an expression of utter horror on her face, as if it was the first time she had ever felt the sting of magick. Horror was quickly usurped by hatred, however, and now, knocked to her knees, she pulled all the harder.

Durnus spat. He turned to a nearby Written and yelled in his face, over the roar. 'Get the people away from here, now!'

'Right away, your Mage!' replied the man, sprinting away.

'Are they what I think they are?' asked a voice from behind him. It was Modren. Durnus nodded. 'Then may the gods help us.'

'Modren, my good friend, the gods are right here with us, and as helpless as the next man,' Durnus looked behind him, where two faint shimmers of light told him that the gods were standing high up on the hill, watching the chaos. Modren followed the Arkmage's gaze. They were two solitary specks, standing still amongst a crowd of panicking, running people. Their chins were high, as were their eyes, glued to the sky.

'Ready the men,' ordered Durnus.

Modren narrowed his eyes. 'For a fight they've never had before, it seems.' And with that, he turned on his heel and began to bark order after order to his men and mages. They moved to his bidding with alacrity, following every word like trained dogs of war. Only Durnus stayed behind. With a grunt, he raised another spell, and hurled it down the hill once again.

❦

'*Three?!*' a shrill shout punctured the roar. Samara flinched as another spark spell sprayed dirt in her face. The strain was almost unbearable. One of her shoulders had been wrenched from its socket already. The other was soon to follow.

'Three?' Lilith yelled again. 'That's it?! Where are the others?'

'Too...' Samara held strong as yet another huge ball of lightning struck the ground around her feet. The earth groaned underneath her. She was almost done. Just a little more. '...difficult,' she managed.

Something twitched, like a ljot string snapping. Not in her arm, but elsewhere, in the air about her. The spell began to weaken, and Samara dropped her arms to the applause of thunder. She rolled to the broken earth as yet another spell came flying in. She barely deflected it. Lilith darted forward and grabbed Samara by the scruff of her collar, dragging her to the little outcrop of rocks she had been hiding behind. 'Where are the others?' she cried.

'It was too hard!' Samara snapped. The whirlwind still spun around them, masking their little escape.

Lilith was purple with either rage, or disappointment, or both. Samara was too exhausted to care. 'I knew it! I knew you should have bloody waited! Come on, we need to leave!' she yelled.

Samara shrugged her off and stumbled to her feet. 'I'm staying!'

'To do what?!'

The girl looked up into the sky, where the white stars were growing bigger and brighter as each chaotic second ticked by. 'To watch,' she said, 'and to finish Far...' But she said no more, and instead, promptly toppled over. Her eyes rolled back into her skull. The girl was out cold. The spell had drained her like a drunk with a wineskin.

'Move yourself, you foolish girl! We need to leave!' Lilith began to haul her away from the chaos and the exploding spells. With the dust and the smoke and the fire, nobody saw them leave. Besides, they were all too busy watching the stars falling.

In the higher places of the sky, where the blue groped at the cold, black edges of the emptiness, where the air couldn't reach, where the lungs would shrivel in a moment's work, the falling stars made no noise. No fire seeped from their flanks. No roar followed them down. Their tails were dust and diamonds. It was almost serene, peaceful, in a strange way, to see three stars falling in arrowhead unison, silent as could be.

Then, with a solid, resounding boom that made the mountains shake for miles around, they punched their way deeper into the sky. Fire licked at them. Smoke belched from their tails. Dust hissed as it burnt away in the furnace of falling. The grey-green land rose up to greet them in a firm embrace. The world beneath was full of running, panicking shapes, small as any ant. The stars, just for a moment, seemed to clench themselves together. Had anyone dared to face them, in the seconds before they plummeted into the earth, they might have seen a smile in their rocky faces.

One. Two. Three.

They hit the ground in quick ear-splitting succession. They spread themselves wide across the gap between Manesmark and the gates of Krauslung. Much to the horror of hundreds, one ploughed straight into one of the wedding tents, reducing it to a gaping hole of ash. It was like watching boulders being thrown into a millpond. Wave after smoking wave of rock and dirt exploded from the stars' graves. Soldiers flew aside like broken dolls. Mages screamed their shield spells and prayed for safety as they huddled behind them. The wedding guests simply cowered behind anything that resembled shelter and beat the flames from their clothes. It was carnage, chaos, mayhem.

And that was just the opening act.

Aghast, Farden stared as one of the stars collided with the top of the distant hill. Even from there he could see the chairs and charred bunting flying in all directions, specks of white in a fountain of rock.

He was so horrified he barely flinched when the second and third stars crashed behind him. One fell so close it showered him with dirt and pebbles, forcing his face into the ground with its shockwave. Farden winced as a pebble clacked off his skull. There would be a lump later, if there ever was a later.

Without the spell forcing him down, Farden summoned an energy he didn't know he had and got to his feet. One foot shakily plodded in front of the other. One, then the other, and so forth, until he was striding up the ruined hill as fast he could, wading through a pile of screaming people and fallen soldiers. His sword was lost. All he had was his fists and his armour. He almost laughed at the thought of facing the fallen stars so empty handed. One, then the other, his feet stumbled on towards the Spire.

❦

Somebody grabbed his arm as he marched through the jumbled ranks of bewildered recruits. 'Farden!' came a cry. It was Tyrfing. His face was smudged with dirt. The robe he had been wearing had been half-torn away, betraying the Scalussen plate-mail hiding underneath, greener than a springtime emerald. 'What are you doing here?' he demanded.

'Wasting time talking to you,' came the grunted answer, as Farden shrugged himself away. Tyfing barked a few orders to the men, rallying them into some semblance of order, and darted after him.

'You shouldn't be here, not in your state!'

'Where's Elessi?' yelled Farden, as he broke into a stiff jog. 'And Modren?'

'Modren is heading towards the Spire as we speak. Elessi is hopefully locked safely inside.'

'Hopefully?' Farden grit his teeth to keep from cursing at his uncle. Their feet pounded the torn grass, pushing through anyone that got in their way. The people trapped on the road had no idea which direction to run, so they ran in all of them, like headless fowl. 'Just remember, you wanted this!'

Tyrfing didn't have an answer for that.

'We need to go faster,' said Farden, wincing as he stumbled on a rock.

'Hold on to your legs then,' Tyrfing warned him, as he clamped his hand onto his nephew's shoulder. To Farden's utter surprise, his legs began to fly beneath him, just numb bits of meat, flailing at the grass. They moved faster than he had ever imagined a pair of legs could move. Tyrfing's did the same, and together they sprinted at the pace of sabre-cats up the hill, towards the Spire.

It was a field of fire that welcomed them. Ash had replaced confetti. A gaping, smoke hole had been bored into the hillside, only a few dozen yards from the scaffolding of the Spire. What had been white was now either black, or various shades of dirt. Bitter-tasting air had replaced the sweet smell of wedding bouquets and waiting food. What was left of the feast had been thrown into the dirt.

Modren was there, barking orders as if his throat was possessed. With the help of the scattered Written, he was frantically trying to rally the soldiers together while at the same time getting the people into the Spire or simply out of the way. Tyrfing began to shout his own orders, marshalling a nearby squad of bewildered soldiers. The air was touched with sulphur. It eked from the hole like pus from a wound.

As Tyrfing left him, Farden's legs returned to their aching selves, and he stumbled forward to stare at the hole. Soldiers were quickly lining up around it, spears and swords glinting in the midday sun. Mages and archers formed second and tertiary lines, nocking arrows to their bows and winding up their finest spells. They would need it for what was about to come.

Farden winced as the heat from the star's scar seared his skin. The sulphurous smoke caught in his throat, and he quickly backed away. Modren caught sight of him.

'Farden!' he yelled over the masses. Farden looked up and caught the Undermage's gaze as he marched through the ranks. 'How?' he shouted, once he was near enough, mouth agape and arms wide. 'How the fuck did you escape?'

Farden shrugged. 'Must have been magick,' he said, and then, 'is she safe?'

Modren nodded. 'In the Spire, locked in with the rest.'

Farden looked to the infant Spire, a bristling mass of scaffolding and stout brick. Its lower levels might hold. He hoped it had a cellar. 'And is it done?'

'What?'

'You and her.'

'Yes.'

'Well, what a lovely day it must be for you.'

Modren glared. His mirror-steel armour was covered in dirt and garnished with bits of singed grass. 'Well you better have some of it left, because your bitch of a daughter has brought some uninvited guests,' he snapped. There was no trace of humour in his voice. He was doing it for the men. They stared at Farden with narrowed gazes. The word "daughter" rustled through their ranks.

Farden scowled. 'What...' he began, but a shiver in the ground interrupted him.

'You're about to see,' muttered Modren, as he dragged Farden away from the hole and back through the ranks. Durnus was there, and Tyrfing, and a handful of Written clad in Scalussen armour. One of them silently handed Farden a sword, nodded, and said no more. There was still work to be done. Talking could wait.

At least they didn't have to wait long.

If was safe to say that when a black tail snaked out of the

smoking pit, every soldier but the bravest took a little step backward. When the clawed hand, brandishing talons curved like yellow scythes, reached up and cracked a rock in half, they took two.

'Steady now!' ordered Tyrfing. He glanced behind him, down the hill, and saw movement in the other two craters. He cursed under his breath. *Let the men hold*, he begged whomever was listening.

There was an almighty roar as the creature sprang from its pit, letting the rocks and earth tumble down behind it. Suddenly there it stood, brazen in the daylight for all to gaze at. And gaze they did, with every fearful eye the Arka had.

It was the face of it that drew the most eyes. A twisted snout and a cluster of orange eyes. An itchy jaw that refused to stop gnawing on the air. Black lips hiding jagged teeth and a throat like a blast furnace. Two notched ears, bitten by gods knew what, and a patch of hair growing between two horns, twisted and furled like a goat's. No wings, just spines.

Tasting the stares, the daemon postured as though standing for a portrait, letting the ranks take in the rest of its monstrous appearance. He must have nudged twenty feet tall at a slouch. The sunlight seemed to make his grey skin pucker and fester, crystallising until he wore a carapace of rocky armour. Trails of white and yellow smoke leaked from its cracks. His tail swished back and forth behind his knobbly spine like a frayed whip. The smell of him was hard to bear, especially at such a close distance. He stank of sulphur and year-old meat, of forest fires and grave-soil. The stench made the nearest men gag and falter.

There were a few moments of dry-mouthed silence between the daemons and the Arka. From the windows and doors of the Spire to the firmly bolted and stuck-fast gate of the city itself, silence reigned like a cold king. The grotesque trio of daemons surveyed their welcome parties with sneers. The soldiers and mages assessed their uninvited guests with wide eyes. Claws clenched. Spears caught the sunlight.

And then they spoke.

'Kiss the dirt you rose from, insects, and show us your respect!' the daemons boomed in perfect unison, sharing the same voice between all three. Sulphur leaked from their maws as they raised their heads and hands, like preachers to a congregation.

Tyrfing and Durnus looked at each other. They could feel the tension, the pressure in the air, pushing down on the knees of their armoured men and women, as if the air itself had doubled in weight. Durnus nodded, somehow knowing Tyrfing was looking straight at him, and together they raised their spells. By their side, Modren saw their fire. He clanged his sword against his breastplate. The daemon looked right at him, chest heaving.

'At the ready!' Modren bellowed, staring straight back. His sergeants and captains carried the order all the way to the gates. A thousand balls of fire sprang into being across the Manesmark hill and below. The grass was whipped into a hissing frenzy. The sound of bowstrings stretching sounded like a forest leaning to one side. Swords and spears bristled from the ranks like spines of a horde of quillhogs.

At the forefront of it all, Farden was stuck staring at the daemon, his exhausted mind still trying to make sense of what his eyes were telling it. He dumbly raised his sword with the others, unsure if he would be a help or a hindrance. All he could think about was Samara, nothing else. How could she bring such a trio of creatures down on the world? Physically, mentally, morally? He had harboured a secret wish for them all to be wrong, but now, the truth ached. It stank, like the very creature in front of him. Farden looked up at the daemon and felt the fear it leaked. The ground beneath the mage's boots thudded as the creature took a step back, not from fear, but from readiness. Its tail cracked, swishing back and forth.

'You dare to challenge us?' the daemons hissed. With metallic screeching, their claws slid further from their fingers, and glinted dully in the sun. Nobody gave them the satisfaction of a reply.

'And you, cousin?' grunted the daemon by the Spire. This time his voice was alone, and this time he stared straight at Durnus. The Arkmage could feel the prickly heat of his many eyes on his skin. 'Yes, I smell your blood. The blood of our race, tainted by theirs. You would stand with these creatures, instead of us?'

Durnus didn't reply. He barely moved. He knew he had to remain silent. It was answer enough for the daemon.

'So be it,' the daemon said, snorting smoke. With a snarl, he unhinged his jaw and screeched at a pitch that would have made a banshee weep. Half the soldiers in the front row clapped their hands to their ears, dropping their weapons. They were swept aside with screams as the daemon took a swipe at them with his hooked claws. Those who wore Tyrfing's armour held strong, but the others were not so lucky. Blood sprayed the ranks behind.

'Let fly!' Tyrfing and Modren bellowed as one. A hundred firebolts surged into the daemon's face, and he stumbled backwards, clapping his claws to his face. But he wasn't shielding himself, much to the abhorrent dismay of the mages and soldiers; he was cupping his hands together, and inhaling the fire.

'Shields!' yelled Modren, as the daemon puffed out his chest. Fire spewed from his lips. It bubbled and flowed like liquid, wrapping around shields and licking at visors. A dozen fell, while another dozen ran in circles like human torches. The water mages did their best to save them.

'Ice spells, as you please!' came the next order, and this the daemon did seem to fear. Shard upon shard of white ice burst from the ranks alongside a volley of arrows and deadly short spears. The daemon had nowhere to go. He turned to catch the volley on his rocky hide, but he whined as they dug deep and caught the flesh underneath.

'Curse you to the void, you blasphemous creatures!' he

screeched, swiping arrows from his clustered eyes. One had been pierced, and it dribbled fiery blood along his cheek. The monster could bleed after all, and the army saw it. Fear began to melt like a glacier in the sun, and they reformed their ranks.

'Again! Written, forward!' Modren bellowed. He held out his hands and threw a barrage of lightning at their grotesque foe. Around him, Written emerged out of the ranks, shimmering with power and polish like diamonds emerging from sifted granite. As they cleared the ranks, they paired up, clasping each other with one hand and firing spell after spell with the other. Ice, lightning, light, fire, force, wind, and sheer will flew at the daemon, wave after wave. Farden found himself marching forward with them, sword raised but useless.

As the daemon took another step back, the Written seized their chance to press forward. It was an onslaught the daemon had never expected, and caught off-guard, he had no retaliation but to screech and to lash out wildly as the magick pressed in on all sides.

Of all the things to slay a daemon, it was a simple wine barrel that did it in the end. It may not have delivered the killing blow, but it helped, nonetheless.

As the daemon stepped back once more, his foot caught the rounded edge of the barrel and he slipped, like a drunkard on a cobble. The creature toppled backwards and the mages surged forward once again. Furnace-mouth wide and bellowing, the daemon crashed headlong into the Spire.

It was then that the Written saw the error of their eagerness. As the daemon tumbled into the weak scaffolding, he lashed out with every limb. Stones flew aside as though they had been hurled by catapults. Men and mages ducked and braced their spells as the huge blocks cart-wheeled through the ranks. With a deep boom, the weakened wall of the Spire gave way, and caved inwards.

'Elessi!' bellowed Modren, suddenly sprinting toward the door. He threw up a shield spell as he ran, but he was not quick enough. A shower of bricks rained down on him. Tyrfing's armour did its work, but the bricks bludgeoned him into the ground. Blood tricked down the mage's forehead. His legs were pinned. Modren desperately clawed at the dirt. 'Elessi!' he yelled again. A hand grabbed his wrist and pulled weakly. Modren looked up to find Farden standing there, eyes clenched, sword fending off the stone chips and dust, heaving with all his feeble might. 'Come on!' he was yelling.

Modren pushed himself up so he could see his legs. Half a boulder had pinned him. The armour had barely kept it from crushing him.

'You aren't Undermage for nothing!' Farden was still pulling. Modren slapped his free hand on the grass and the boulder crumbled into pulverised rubble. Farden yanked him onto his feet, but was rewarded by a savage thump in the chest.

'Get out of my way!' Modren spat as he ran for the door. Farden ignored him and followed, ducking and weaving as best as his tired legs could. Behind them, there was a massive crash as Durnus threw a spear of ice deep into the daemon's side. Tyrfing followed it with another.

'Let me help, you fool!' Farden shouted, as the Undermage grappled with the door. The huge frame had sagged under the impact of the daemon, and the door was stuck fast. It was like wrestling the root of a mountain.

'You've done enough!' Modren spread his hands over the door and strained. Farden couldn't help but join him, even though he felt as useless and as blunt as the bricks that rained down around them. He snarled and began to hack at the door-frame with his sword while Modren pushed with every ounce of his Book. His magick made Farden's head pound.

Above them, the daemon thrashed and whirled, burying himself deeper and deeper into the Spire with every twitch and every spell that wracked his hide. Over the racket of the dying monster, screams could be heard.

Modren began to attack the door with his fists. Farden was out of breath already, but he dared not stop hacking. Even the Undermage's words were vicious strikes upon the immovable wood. 'Come! On! You! BASTARD!' he thundered. Suddenly the door gave way, and the two mages flew into the dusty darkness.

People. Clamouring to get out. They had been blocking the door from behind. They surged out into the sunlight, nearly trampling the fallen mages, and scattered in every direction, screaming and yelling. Modren dragged himself and an elderly woman to her feet and thrust her towards safety. Leaving Farden to marvel at the splinters protruding from bloody holes in his upper arms, Modren ran towards a growing slope of rubble, underneath where the roof was caving in. Farden turned and stared at the horrifying sight: legs and arms and dusty faces straining to free themselves, pinned by wood and stone. Women, children, men, guests and guards, council members and servants, there must have been almost fifty of them in varying stages of burial. Farden fought to his feet and dashed to help. He might have been a cold soul, but he still had a thread of humanity in him. These people were here because of him, after all.

With both hands, he dug into the rubble and hoisted a child free. Next came a woman, then a man with a broken leg, and so on. Modren was furiously digging at the other side with the help of two guards. They were shouting and pointing furiously at something deeper in the pile. Farden abruptly felt as though he had swallowed a brick.

'Modren?!'

'Just keep digging!' came the reply, frantic now. Muffled shouts were coming from somewhere. Farden cast his aches aside and did what Modren told him. He dug and he dug with all his might. The stones flew past his shoulders and like ghosts of dust people slowly crawled and limped from the holes he had made. The deeper he went, the more injured they were. Modren was doing the same, only faster, stronger, and more frenzied.

It was then that the Undermage uncovered two familiar figures, as dusty as could be but incredibly unhurt. They rolled from the rubble, bewildered, oddly silent. Modren grabbed Loki and Verix in each hand and pulled them close to his face. 'Where is she?' he cried above the sound of the dying daemon. Loki could do nothing but stare upwards at the rocky hide convulsing above them, sending showers of splinters and stone down upon them.

'In there!' Verix pointed to the rubble. The truth was useful for once. Modren dropped them as quickly as he had grabbed them.

'Farden!' he cried. The mage ran to his side. 'She's under... *this*,' Modren mumbled and cursed as he hauled brick after obsidian brick out of the pile. It was all he could say. The dust took the rest of his words and laid them to rest. His gauntlets clanged off each brick, as if they were the teeth of a vice. Farden was there with him, his Scalussen armour glittering in the light of the fire and lightning above.

Farden licked his lips, making cement of his tongue. 'I'm sure she's...' he began, but his words failed when they caught sight of a golden patch of cloth trapped between the grip of two rafters.

'Elessi!' Modren shouted, as he dragged the huge beam clear. His magick and desperation lent him strength, and somehow, limbs shaking, he did it. Farden dug until he found a face. The breath stuck in his dirt-lined throat. There was not a lot of blood, but any would have been a travesty on Elessi's face. A smear of it led a straight trail from her nose to her ear. Her eyes were fluttering, but she was alive. She gasped as she saw Modren and Farden above her. 'Is it dead?'

Farden looked up. 'Not yet,' he said. 'We need to move!'

'Help me, Farden,' Modren yelled, as yet another beam came crashing down beside them. The daemon was in his final throes now.

'My leg!' Elessi cried, as Modren dragged her free. It was broken. Two places at least. That was obvious from the angle it hung at. They did not waste any time fixing it now. The infant Spire was caving in, and the daemon with it. As Farden yelled to the stragglers, Modren ran to the door and burst into the sunlight. Farden was hot on his heels with Verix, Loki, and a handful of others. They barely made it out before the door-frame collapsed, spraying them with a shower of dust and splinters. A cheer went up from the army as the daemon disappeared into the rubble.

'That building is cursed,' Farden muttered, eyes roaming over the crushed and broken walls, the arrows in the splintered scaffolding, the severed and smoking tail of something dead and ghastly lying in the bricks. Tyrfing and Durnus were running over, he could see their Scalussen armour glinting through the dust cloud. He raised his sword to salute them, and as he did, the sky was blackened with smoke.

There came an enormous whooshing sound, like the noise of the wind folding in on itself. Everyone was thrown to the ground again, much to the screaming of Elessi. In the space of a blink, a daemon stood between them and the approaching crowd, wreathed in the smoke of whatever spell he had just cast. He turned to stare down at the five figures sprawled on the grass, and his black lip curled at the sight of the gods.

'The prayer must be strong to bring such solid apparitions to this earth,' the daemon growled. This one had just two eyes, grey, tinged with red, and curled horns.

'Strong indeed,' said Verix, getting to her feet. Farden caught sight of her shadow and saw it had sprouted faint wings.

The daemon laughed. 'Strong enough to stop me?'

'No, but these humans are.' Verix pointed to the smoking wreck of the Spire, and the black corpse that lay draped across it. By her side, Loki wore a smug look.

The daemon snarled. Cinders flew from his black-sand tongue. 'I think it is time for you to return to where you belong, cursed ones!' Verix stood her ground proudly as the creature lifted a hand, brandishing five wickedly hooked claws. Before Modren or Farden could even flinch, the daemon swiped, and Verix was cloven in two. She melted like a pillar of smoke, vanishing into the breeze.

The daemon paused to admire his work, and then raised another hand to finish Loki and the rest. His claws dripped with the blood of men from further down the hill. He bled orange from several cuts, but still he couldn't help but grin as he flexed his arm. Elessi felt for Modren's hand as the Undermage summoned a spell with the other. Farden thought of a vulture-headed boat and clenched his teeth.

Two huge spells ploughed into the daemon's back and sent him reeling. Modren's spell was already in full swing as the daemon cart-wheeled over them, his curled claws flailing, He ducked, feeling their wind kiss his neck, and then chased them with his spell, burying a shard of ice in the creature's rib. The daemon fell to his knees, snarling and whining.

In a moment of utter fury, all patience dissolved, Farden stood up to face it. He ripped the cloak from his back and raised his empty, glittering fists. He didn't care for his lack of magick. He didn't care about his lost sword. He didn't care that the daemon, even on his knees, still towered over him. He didn't care that his heart was trying to beat its way out of his chest, this was his problem, and he would see it finished, even if it took his bare hands. *They deserve better...*

To his surprise, the daemon hesitated. His claws raked the ground, but he didn't move. He licked his black lips and clicked his jaw, staring intently at the glittering gold and red armour on the mage's fists, forearms, and legs. He spat fire at them.

'What are you waiting for?!' Farden challenged him. 'Let's finish this farce!'

Still the daemon didn't move. He snuffled and hissed as Farden boldly took a step forward. 'Godblood,' he whispered, backing away. Tyrfing and Durnus were suddenly at the mage's side, clutching spells between their charred fingers, ready to pounce.

They didn't need to. Before the daemon disappeared, he pointed a claw at Farden and bared his black teeth. But it was all he did. With a blast of wind and a puff of charcoal smoke he was suddenly gone, whisked into the ether. Tyrfing ran to the lip of the hill and looked down at the city. There was no sign of the other daemon either. They had both vanished. 'It's over!' he shouted. The roars and cheers began to rise into the air.

'For now,' said Durnus, over the noise. He looked to the mage by his side. 'It would appear that something about you scared him off, Farden.'

Farden looked down at his forearms, gleaming in the sun. Dust never did manage to cling to Scalussen metal. 'It would indeed,' he murmured. Durnus sighed, patting Farden's wrist.

'Secrets,' he said. 'Even metal keeps them now.' He made a simple gesture of touching Farden on the shoulder before he turned to walk away. Farden was left staring into space, knuckling his red-gold fists into his tired and dusty eyes. The stench of sulphur made him want to vomit. He resisted, for now.

All was silent again on the hill of Manesmark. Graveyard silent. Even the soldiers refrained from muttering. They stared at each other, conveying their confusion and relief in wide-eyed gazes and deep frowns. They had been witnesses to chaos. A chaos that had fallen from the sky. Dazed and confused, they milled about like bloody drunkards.

All was silent until a wretched scream tore open the sky. It was Modren, kneeling beside Elessi. Farden and the others rushed to his side, but he shoved them away. 'Leave her be! Give her room!' he shouted. She was lying twisted in the charred grass, eyes staring blankly at the sky. Modren gently lifted aside the curls that had fallen across her face, and revealed a long gash across her neck and chest, ripping into her golden dress; a gash that had already turned ugly and purple, a gash raked by a daemon-claw.

'Is she alive?' Farden burbled.

'I don't know!' panicked Modren, gently rubbing Elessi's cheek. Her head was limp like a doll's.

'Here, move out of the way!' Tyrfing muscled Farden aside. He rubbed his vambrace on a patch of cloth and held it up to Elessi's lips, which by now had gone a faint blue. Whatever poison had invaded her blood, it had acted like lightning. She was even cold to the touch.

Every single onlooker held their breath as Tyrfing brought his eye level with Elessi's lips. He stared at his vambrace, waiting for a sign, praying for something, anything. Not today, they all prayed. Not today.

Suddenly there it was: the faintest mist imaginable, but a mist nonetheless. She was alive and breathing, but dangling by a poisonous thread. 'Quickly! Get me a healer!'

'Out of my way!' shouted Modren, as he gently picked Elessi up from the torn, blackened grass. Farden walked by his side, sword dragging through the dirt. 'And where do you think you going?' hissed Modren, without taking his hard eyes off his bride.

Farden narrowed his eyes at Elessi's curls, dangling over Modren's arm. Her gold dress was stone-ripped and dusty. The way her hands hung, so limp, so grey and lifeless, filled him with a hot rage. He tested his next words in his mouth before he let them loose. They felt right. In fact, he had never been so sure of anything in his life. 'I'm going to find my daughter and I'm going to do what I couldn't do before,' he said. Modren looked up, a deep frown on his forehead. Farden picked up a fallen sword, eyed the blood along its edge, and then slammed it down the grass. He left it to wobble. 'I'm going to kill her,' he spat.

Loki alone stayed behind while the army trickled away. He stood in the broken circles of mud, dust, and the pinpricks of blood. He watched the bewildered soldiers leave without him, and looked on with a confused face. Dazed, shocked, they had left a man in the rubble. His whimpers were quiet now, and getting quieter by the moment. Loki went to stand over him.

His back was broken, that much was clear from the way he was slumped in between the two black stones. His skull was open to the air, seeping blood. His face caved in on one side. Not much hope for this one. His chest shuddered with every breath.

Loki bent over him, one foot on the stone by his head, and watched. He had never seen a man die before. It didn't take long. The man blinked at him, once, maybe twice, before his crushed lungs failed him. He shuddered one last time, and then sagged, in ways only a corpse can. Loki watched his eyes fall unfocused, distant. Already heading to the other side.

Loki flinched, and backed away. He couldn't help but shiver. Not with the cold, for the wind was strangely warm. Not with fear. He had felt none at the dying man. Not with guilt, nor sorrow. Such things were for human bodies, not his. No. He trembled with power, the power of a soul passing through him.

'How very interesting,' he said aloud, to the dead man, the stones, and the gathering crows.

to be continued...

1568 years ago

'knights!'

The nine turned as one. In the weak candlelight and dressed in their long white robes, they resembled ghosts loitering in the shadows.

The man standing between the door frame was a Pen, a Scalussen scholar. They and the Smiths had made Frostsoar their own, and in a way, they ruled the land around it. Powered by the wealth the armour of the Scalussen Smiths brought, and armed with their intelligence, they had created an independent land. Not lawless, no, but autonomous, whatever that word meant. Some had told Korrin it meant free. That was a precious thing in the Scattered Kingdoms, when all under the sun scrabbled for land and power.

The Pen was a rotund man, as scholars often were. He wore a silk gown and the traditional silk gloves of his office, made from the weavings of the rockworms that lived in the gaps between the ice sheets and the dark, dank earth beneath it. The nine knew this man well, though not by name; he was always hovering around their training yard, watching, noting, lingering. He had been there the day that the thousands had come to be tested. He had a neatly combed patch of silvery grey hair atop his head. His face was round like his belly, flushed pink in the cheeks. He had the look of a man who intensely enjoyed the mastery and use of long sentences. As he spoke, he tasted every word, twirling it around on his tongue before wrapping his lips around it.

'Esteemed warriors, Gäel, Demsin, Chast, Estina, Balimuel, Lopia, Gaspid, Rosiff, and Korrin, I and High Smith Aurien thank you deeply for your ubiquitous patience. I am Master Wellen, and I know

you have been anticipating this moment for many a day now.'

'Many a day? Try a year,' muttered Estina. 'Nobody's told us anything apart from eat, sleep, train.'

Gaspid, who had become the unofficial leader of the nine, elbowed her. 'Quiet down.'

Wellen seemed well aware of Estina's fiery tongue, and also utterly immune to it. He looked at her as if studying an interesting specimen. 'All of you, despite some of our initial doubts at having chosen the right candidates,' a tiny glance in Korrin's direction, 'have excelled in every aspect. We now feel it is time for you to move to the next stage of our ambitious exploit.'

'And what is that?'

Master Wellen smiled. 'Come,' he waved. 'I will show you.'

Swivelling on his heel, the Master led them deeper into the corridors, until the air grew hot and smoky around them. Like moles they tread deeper and deeper into the earth, passing through tunnels intricately carved and forged from iron and black marble.

Soon, they came to a wide balcony where the tunnels unfolded into a huge cavern, thick with steam and heat and smoke. A hundred forges burnt orange beneath them. Countless workers and Smiths scuttled to and fro like ants, tending their fires and anvils and benches. The cavern rattled with conversation, ringing out with the sounds of hammers and chisels.

'Welcome to the Forges, Knights. They run as deep as the tower reaches high.'

The nine stared at the bustle below. The heat was welcome on their cold cheeks.

'This way,' Master Wellen ushered them on, around a corner and down a spiralling set of iron steps to a secluded section of the Forges. Those they passed seemed nervous and excited. Eager smiles met their gazes wherever they turned.

'And here we are,' Wellen finally said, as they reached a

hollow in the rock, lined with candles and torches. A few men and women stood by, clad in sooty Smith's robes. They held tools in their hands. They looked exhausted. One man, dressed in a robe of brown and red, stood apart from the rest. He was a tall man, and broad too. His hair was of flaxen gold and his eyes were tawny, flecked with bronze. He stared at the nine with an expression as blank and yet as deep as a column of unused parchment. The nine nodded to him, but he did not move. He too looked exhausted.

But it was the armour that held their eyes. And how wide those eyes became, as they roved over the nine flawless suits of armour standing against the wall of the hollow.

Polished, *thought Korrin. No. He instantly shook his head. The word failed miserably. It failed just as all the others did.* Intricate. Masterful. Gleaming... *The words paled in comparison and sounded ill-fitting on his lips. The armour was simply beyond description. Crimson red and summer gold, it shimmered in the candlelight. It seemed almost liquid in the way that its scales warped and bent. It seemed to shiver and glow as if it were still molten. It stole his tongue away, and he and the rest of the nine could do nothing but simply stare in numb silence at the wall of metal before them.*

Each breastplate had been engraved in painful detail with an animal of some sort. Korrin's eyes roved over them, naming each one: an eagle, a bear, a dragon, a wolf, a snake, a bastion, a sabre-cat, a hawk, and a coelo. Their eyes and tusks and teeth glittered with jewels. Korrin found himself longing for the wolf, naturally. It looked exactly like the wolves of the star-lit ice, the ones he watched in the quiet hours, the brief hours when he was alone and thoughtful.

After a while, Lopia, the southern man the others had taken to calling Lop, rubbed his stubbled chin and took a deep breath. 'Well,' was all he could say. The others nodded, agreeing with the sentiment.

'This is your armour, Knights, the Nine. The finest armour the Smiths of Scalussen have ever made, the finest armour that Emaneska

and the gods,' here Wellen glanced at the tawny-eyed man. 'have ever seen.'

'What are we, Wellen? You call us Knights, but Knights of what?' Balimuel rumbled. 'What is all this for?' The others looked expectantly at the Master. The question had burnt inside them all for so long now.

Wellen smiled. If his hands hadn't been clasped behind him, they would have seen them shaking. 'You are to be Knights of Scalussen. Guardians, if you will. Protectors, as the name Scalussen means.'

'Protectors of what?' asked Estina.

'Why, of Emaneska, of course.'

'All of it?'

'All of it.'

'Just the nine of us?'

'The nine, indeed.'

They all blew great, heavy sighs, heavy with awe and disbelief. Korrin's eyes were wide. 'So this is what we've been training for?'

'Correct, master Korrin.'

'And you didn't think to tell us this beforehand? Estina asked.

'Why? Would you change your mind now that you know?'

'I...' Estina faltered. Her scarlet lips pouted. 'No. Of course not. It's all just a bit sudden.'

'You have all the time in the world, Knights.'

'Some of us don't, Wellen,' said Demsin, the oldest of the group, a grey-haired woman from the island of Albion. Even though she was quicker than a lightning flash, and as agile as a dragonfly, she had sixty years under her belt. She was an old warrior, beginning to feel the ache in her bones.'

Wellen smiled again, wider this time. 'You need not worry about age any more, Demsin. Nor do any of you. This armour will take care of that.'

'Of what? Of...' the words sounded silly in his mouth, Korrin thought, but he'd already begun. '...Age?'

'Indeed,' said the tawny man. That one deep, rumbling word was like a boulder crashing to the floor.

The nine swapped glances. It was a long while before any of them spoke. Balimuel was the first to step forward, his big boots clomping on the stone. He scratched his beard with a blue fingernail. 'So,' he began. 'Which one is mine?'

Did you like Dead Stars Part One?

Then help Ben out by showing your support.

For today's indie authors, every bit of exposure helps. If you liked **Dead Stars** and **The Emaneska Series** then why not tell a friend? By sharing and recommending, you support the author and help them to keep doing what they do best - writing books.

You can now follow and support Ben Galley on Facebook and Twitter:

Go to: Facebook.com/BenGalleyAuthor

Or say hello @BenGalley

Thank you for your support!

Lightning Source UK Ltd.
Milton Keynes UK
UKOW042005210613

212647UK00002B/30/P

9 780956 770066